continued . . .

A Texan's Luck

"This is an absolutely delightful story from the Old West. A definite winner."

—Rendezvous

When a Texan Gambles

"Beauty and the Beast meets the Old West . . . Thomas's second Texas title is even better than the first, which is terrific."

—Booklist (starred review)

The Texan's Wager

"An exciting Western romance filled with engaging characters . . . fans will know they won by reading *The Texan's Wager*."

—Midwest Book Review

The Texan's Dream

"Packs a powerful emotional punch . . . [Thomas's] latest Western historical romance highlights the author's talent for creating genuinely real characters . . . Exceptional."

—Booklist

Twilight in Texas

"A powerful Lone Star romance that brings to life the decade after the Civil War . . . filled with action . . . loaded with tender passion . . . another exciting tale."

—Midwest Book Review

To Wed in Texas

"Thrilling . . . a story that readers will want to read again and again."

—Rendezvous

To Kiss a Texan

"Compelling . . . fans will appreciate Thomas's subtle humor and her deft handling of sensitive topics."

—Booklist

THE TEXAN'S TOUCH

"Delightful and memorable characters and a roller-coaster pace . . . Another wonderful read from a true shining star." —*Romantic Times*

TWO TEXAS HEARTS

"Jodi Thomas is at her remarkable best in *Two Texas Hearts*."
—*Debbie Macomber*

TEXAS LOVE SONG

"A warm and touching read full of intrigue and suspense that will keep the reader on the edge of her seat." —*Rendezvous*

FOREVER IN TEXAS

"A great Western romance filled with suspense and plenty of action."
—*Affaire de Coeur*

TO TAME A TEXAN'S HEART
Winner of the Romance Writers of America
Best Historical Series Romance Award

"Earthy, vibrant, funny, and poignant . . . a wonderful, colorful love story." —*Romantic Times*

THE TEXAN AND THE LADY

"Jodi Thomas shows us hard-living men with grit and guts, and the determined young women who soften their hearts."
—Pamela Morsi, *USA Today*
bestselling author of *Suburban Renewal*

PRAIRIE SONG

"Thoroughly entertaining romance." —*Gothic Journal*

THE TENDER TEXAN
Winner of the Romance Writers of America
Best Historical Series Romance Award

"[A] marvelous, sensitive, emotional romance . . . spellbinding."
—*Romantic Times*

TEXAS RAIN

JODI THOMAS

BERKLEY BOOKS, NEW YORK

THE BERKLEY PUBLISHING GROUP
Published by the Penguin Group
Penguin Group (USA) Inc.
375 Hudson Street, New York, New York 10014, USA
Penguin Group (Canada), 90 Eglinton Avenue East, Suite 700, Toronto, Ontario
M4P 2Y3, Canada (a division of Pearson Penguin Canada Inc.)
Penguin Books Ltd., 80 Strand, London WC2R 0RL, England
Penguin Group Ireland, 25 St. Stephen's Green, Dublin 2, Ireland
(a division of Penguin Books Ltd.)
Penguin Group (Australia), 250 Camberwell Road, Camberwell, Victoria 3124,
Australia (a division of Pearson Australia Group Pty. Ltd.)
Penguin Books India Pvt. Ltd., 11 Community Centre, Panchsheel Park,
New Delhi—110 017, India
Penguin Group (NZ), Cnr. Airborne and Rosedale Roads, Albany, Auckland 1310,
New Zealand (a division of Pearson New Zealand Ltd.)
Penguin Books (South Africa) (Pty.) Ltd., 24 Sturdee Avenue, Rosebank,
Johannesburg 2196, South Africa

Penguin Books Ltd., Registered Offices: 80 Strand, London WC2R 0RL, England

This is a work of fiction. Names, characters, places, and incidents either are the
product of the author's imagination or are used fictitiously, and any resemblance to
actual persons, living or dead, business establishments, events, or locales is entirely
coincidental.

TEXAS RAIN

A Berkley Book / published by arrangement with the author

ISBN: 978-0-7394-7626-0

BERKLEY®
Berkley Books are published by The Berkley Publishing Group,
a division of Penguin Group (USA) Inc.,
375 Hudson Street, New York, New York 10014.
BERKLEY is a registered trademark of Penguin Group (USA) Inc.
The "B" design is a trademark belonging to Penguin Group (USA) Inc.

PRINTED IN THE UNITED STATES OF AMERICA

CHAPTER 1

∞

Texas Hill Country
1854

TRAVIS MCMURRAY WATCHED STORM CLOUDS ROLL IN FROM THE north as he pushed his horse into a gallop and headed toward the Guadalupe River and his family's land just beyond. The sky darkened around him from dusty blue to gray, mirroring his mood. Here, in these rolling hills, lay the only place he had ever felt he belonged. Here also lay memories he would spend a lifetime trying to forget.

His powerful mount danced at the edge of the muddy riverbank while Travis looked for the exact place to cross. He ignored his tired muscles, tugged his hat low, and rushed into the water that separated Whispering Mountain Ranch from the world.

He could smell it now, feel it on his skin and in his heart. Home.

A faint flicker of sunlight blinked off the hills, welcoming him back. The river swirled. He leaned low over the horse's neck, calming the animal with words as they fought the current toward the far shore. A stand of brush hid the only place where a horse could climb the steep bank beyond. His father had planted the bushy trees almost thirty years ago. Now, only Travis and his two brothers, Teagen and Tobin, knew the secret entrance to the ranch.

Travis smiled. One of a hundred secrets, he thought. His father had planned well. Whispering Mountain stood like a fortress in the middle of a wide-open Texas.

He reached the far bank and slipped behind the cedar that grew almost as tall as live oaks. If enemies followed him, they'd think they'd blinked and he'd simply disappeared, horse and all. Travis moved along the shadowy cavelike path, half green with cedar, half black with rock. He slid from his mount and led the horse as they climbed. When he saw sky a few minutes later, Travis inhaled deeply. He'd made it back in one piece, and those wanting him dead would have to wait another day.

After almost two years he was finally home. He swung onto the saddle and raced toward the ranch house, suddenly hungry to see his family.

He'd fought one too many battles across the rapidly changing landscape of a newborn nation. He needed to be home where nothing changed. He wanted to sleep without having to listen for trouble approaching. He longed to relax and remember who he'd been before he wore a badge. Travis had heard one too many outlaws promise revenge lately. Maybe if he took some time off, their threats would stop echoing in his mind.

His sister, Sage, watched from the back porch as he neared. He spotted her a moment before she recognized him. The McMurray boys all had their father's wide shoulders and height, but Sage was small, even as a woman. If she'd been a colt, he would have named her Wildfire. The fact that all her brothers were older and bigger never frightened her for a moment. When she was younger, she'd often stood before the three of them and threatened to take them all on in a fight.

Now she jumped over the railing and ran toward him, her long braid flying behind her. Though dressed in trousers and shirt, no one would mistake her for a boy.

As she ran at full speed to him, Travis lowered from his horse in time to catch her and swing her around as he'd always done. They were both laughing when they hugged.

Travis had been ten when she was born. They'd lost their father the March before. Four months later their mother died. Neighbors said their mother, Autumn McMurray, never recovered from the birth of Sage, but the boys saw the light go out of her eyes when she learned of her husband's death. Autumn stayed alive long enough to give Sage life, and then she joined her husband, Andrew, in death.

As he always did, Travis looked for a hint of his mother in Sage's face. But she had blue eyes, not brown, and hair streaked with sunshine, not dark and earthy. Their mother's Apache blood reflected in him alone, not Sage or his brothers. "You filled out." He sat her down. "In several places."

"It was bound to happen." Sage laughed. "You've been gone so long I could have had a batch of kids by now."

He shook his head. "No. With those clothes, I'm guessing you're still an old maid."

"Eighteen is hardly an old maid, and what else would I be comfortable in? I had to wear my brothers' hand-me-downs most of my life." She looped her arm in his and they moved toward the house. "Besides, I plan on changing the 'old maid' part soon."

"Got the unfortunate prey in sight?" He tugged at her braid thinking it didn't matter how old she thought she was, she'd always be his kid sister. "Maybe I could wing him for you so he couldn't run so fast."

When she made a face, he added, "Just a flesh wound, nothing serious. Some men think better after they've lost a little blood."

Travis wasn't surprised when she tried to trip him.

"I don't know who yet," she admitted. "But the annual spring dance is tomorrow night at Elmo Anderson's barn. Teagen and Tobin don't even listen when I talk about it, but now you're here, you can take me. It'll give me a chance to look at the quality of the pickings." She hugged his arm. "I'm so glad you're here. I was down to begging Martha to escort me."

Travis laughed. The old housekeeper wouldn't budge from this place if a herd of buffalo crossed McMurray land.

"Now, you're elected," Sage said simply, as if he'd solved a problem.

Travis groaned. He had no doubt Sage would have her pick of the single men once she set her mind to marriage, but the thought of going to a barn dance made him wish he'd checked the dates before asking for a month's leave from the Texas Rangers. One annual barn dance shouldn't have been hard to miss; after all, Sage had mentioned it in her last two letters. He mumbled an oath at his lack of planning.

Sage slapped at his arm. "Stop that. One of my brothers has to take me off this property, or I'll never marry. I'll end up like the three of you, single forever. Tobin won't even consider going with me. He might have to talk to someone not related to him. And Teagen gave his standard answer that he didn't have time for such nonsense."

As always, Travis felt her pain, even now when most of it was worry over nothing. "All right, if I can get the smell of the trail off me by tomorrow, I'll take you, but don't expect me to dance." Except for a few people, he'd never found the townsfolk particularly friendly.

"You're not going to believe how the town around Elmo's trading post has grown up. We've got a lean-to that a traveling blacksmith uses, a barn and corral for folks passing through, and there's talk of framing out a church this summer. A stage line may come through before long, and when that happens we'll need a hotel and some place for folks to eat. We'll have a regular town."

Travis shook his head. "I'm not interested in being part of any town. I'll go to the dance and just hang out in the shadows and make sure you're all right until it's time to leave."

"Oh, wonderful." Sage stepped on the porch. "Then everyone will say, there's poor Spinster McMurray and one of her skulking brothers." From the second step of the porch she stood eye level with him and pointed at his nose. "One dance, so I won't have to worry about being a wildflower."

"It's wallflower, kid, and that you'll never be." He grinned. "We should have never taught you to talk. I *told* Teagen it would be a mistake." He started to step on the porch, but her hand on his chest stopped him.

"You're not coming into Martha's house until you strip. She'll make me help with spring cleaning all over again if I let you track in half the mud in Texas. You swam the Guadalupe instead of taking the bridge, didn't you?"

"It's faster," Travis answered as he tried to pass her.

She didn't move.

He raised an eyebrow. "You can't mean I'm to strip out here? Don't you think I'm a little old for that?"

"We've both seen you, and all your old parts, a thousand times." Sage moved to the door. "I'll tell Martha to have food ready by the time you're finished. You'll find soap on the washstand. I'll bring out a towel and a clean set of your clothes."

Travis swore as he moved to the side of the house. He'd stripped off all but his pants when she reappeared with a towel and clothes smelling of the cedar chest he'd left them in almost two years before.

Sage studied him. "These should still fit. You don't look a pound fatter. You've got a new scar on your shoulder."

"Took a bullet in a battle on the border last year. It went right through, so didn't see any need in worrying the family."

Sage nodded as if he made sense. "You're tanned so dark, if one of the cowhands rides by, he might shoot you for an Apache."

He didn't smile. "I am Apache."

"Half," Sage said. "Just like all of us."

Travis pulled water from the well. Though Sage tried, her words never made him feel better. His high cheekbones and dark eyes marked him as mixed blood while his siblings could have been as Irish as their last name. "Lucky me," he mumbled as he splashed water over his head. "Maybe they'll shoot the half that's Apache. Problem is, which half would that be?"

When he shook the water from his hair, Sage had gone. He grabbed the lye soap and began to scrub away a month's worth of trail dust.

Martha came out once to ask if he wanted a steak or ham. The chubby little woman didn't even smile at him, which didn't surprise Travis. Martha hadn't liked any of the McMurray boys since the day she arrived from New Orleans in answer to an ad. Teagen told Travis once that Martha had just gotten out of prison when she'd traveled to Texas for the job, but the boys had to hire her because she'd been the only one who applied after their mother died. She'd loved baby Sage dearly, but made the brothers sleep in the barn most of that first summer until they decided to act "house-broke" as she called it.

To Travis's knowledge, Martha had never left the grounds around the house, but she stood before Teagen each month and took her pay in cash. She would quote Travis her list of supplies before he went to town and insisted on paying for any items for her personal use. In the eighteen years since his parents died, food had been on the table every meal. Good, hot, solid food. That, Travis decided, said more than a smile.

"You going to the Spring Dance?" Travis yelled as Martha turned to go back inside.

"No," she answered simply. "Sage is waiting to cut your hair. Best show some sense and get out of the rain before God mistakes you for a tree and strikes you with lightning."

Travis was so wet he hardly noticed it had started to rain. "I know," he said, remembering what followed all her warnings. "If I get dead, it'll mean more work for you."

"Right," she mumbled into the thunder.

He grabbed his clothes and made it to the porch just as a downpour hit. The log home his father built stood solid against the storm as Travis dressed on the wide porch. Ten years ago they'd finished out the second floor for the men, but everyone called the main part of the house Martha's. From the moment she arrived, she'd treated the place like her own. That first year "Don't get mud on my clean floors" had been a constant echo around the place. A few years later, when Teagen and Travis had been almost men, she'd added, "No smoking or drinking in my house." They'd challenged her only once and watched their supper fed to the hogs.

Travis smiled when he entered the house. Nothing had changed. His father's tartan carried from Ireland still hung on the north wall. The beads his mother wore at her wedding were looped across the McMurray Clan colors. An Apache girl and an Irish boy had fallen in love and stood against the world.

He crossed to the kitchen and wasn't surprised Martha had cooked a table full of food. While the storm raged, Travis ate and talked of his life as a Ranger. Martha stood by the stove acting as if she wasn't listening. Sage sat across the table taking in every word. If she'd been born a boy, she'd be riding with him by now, for Andrew McMurray taught his children to love Texas—he'd even died for its freedom.

After dinner Travis watched the sun set over the newly washed earth as he smoked one of Teagen's thin cigars on the porch. He was full and cleaned up to a point that he almost looked like a gentleman. Almost, he thought, for there was no amount of scrubbing that could take the wildness out of him. Part of him had to roam, had to live on the edge, had to be alone. He knew, without a doubt, that the west section nearest the hills would never have a house built on it even though the brothers called it Travis's. His place would remain pasture land forever.

Sage moved up beside him. "Teagen and Tobin probably won't make it in tonight, what with the storm. They'd come if they knew you were here."

Travis smiled down at his little sister. "They're staying away because they fear you'll badger them about going to the dance."

She shrugged. "Maybe. Maybe they finally decided to climb Whispering Mountain and sleep on the summit."

Travis looked west to where the hills were almost mountain

height. One stood out, purple in the night. "Maybe none of us will ever climb the mountain." He and his siblings had all grown up on the legend. The Apache believed that when a man slept on the summit of Whispering Mountain, he'd dream his future.

"Father did," Sage reminded Travis. "Right after he brought mother here, he climbed the mountain one night."

"He dreamed his death," Travis whispered into the evening shadows, wondering what it must have been like for his father, newly married and not yet eighteen, to have dreamed that he would die before he turned thirty and leave his family behind.

Sage slipped her arm through her brother's and stared at the mountain. "The dream saved us," she said, as if she'd been old enough to remember. "If he hadn't dreamed, he wouldn't have prepared. If he hadn't left Teagen all the detailed plans, the three of you wouldn't have been able to save the ranch."

Travis closed his eyes, wondering how long he'd have to live before the memories would fade. His father had gone to fight for Texas Independence. He'd left them alone as he headed for a mission called Goliad. Andrew McMurray had lined his sons up on the porch and hugged each one. Travis remembered thinking his father might crush his ribs with his hold. Then he told them to look in his desk for instructions if something happened to him. "Don't forget," he'd said as he rode off to join the fight for Texas.

Three months later they got word that he'd been killed with hundreds of other Texans at a little mission. That night, the boys had gathered round their father's desk and opened the bottom drawer. His letter began, "If you are reading this, I'm not coming back." The writing was bold, direct, just as their father had always been. "Take care of your mother, and no matter what, hold the ranch."

The letter explained how Autumn, being Apache and a woman, could never claim the land as hers. But if the boys could keep everyone away until Teagen turned eighteen, then he could claim the ranch.

The last words written to Teagen, eleven, Travis, ten, and Tobin, just barely six, were simple: "Today, my sons, you have to become men."

Sage pulled Travis back to the present. "I wish I'd been there to help," she whispered as she rubbed her cheek against his shoulder.

"No, you don't. It was bad. He'd taught us to shoot and to ride. He'd built his ranch so that no one could come near the center. But there was nothing he could have done to prepare us for the men who came to take our land by force. As soon as word circulated that he was dead, there were those who thought they could step on the land and take all we owned."

Travis finished his cigar and said good night. He knew he wouldn't sleep, but he needed to be alone. The memories of those early days were too thick in his head to allow him to be good company. Sage seemed to understand.

Tomorrow he'd take her to the dance and try to make the best of it, but tonight he'd walk the boundary of Whispering Mountain Ranch with a rifle in his hand. He'd long since grown taller than his weapon, but memories would keep him company tonight. A part of the little boy who'd had to grow up at ten years old still haunted the man.

CHAPTER 2

TRAVIS SPENT THE NEXT MORNING TRYING TO AVOID SAGE. KID SISTERS were no fun when they turned into women. She pestered Martha, and then him, with worries over her hair, the length of her dress, and what ribbon to wear at her throat. Martha didn't seem to mind the talk, but Travis escaped to the little study where the family kept their library of books. He pretended to be lost in a book every time she passed. He would have ridden the ranch, but a fine mist started before dawn and, according to Sage, hung around just to frustrate her.

Travis found refuge in the library. He loved the book-lined room almost as much as he loved campfires and night skies. Here, among the many volumes, he felt near his parents. Andrew McMurray had cherished books. When he came west, half the weight of his luggage had been reading material. He met their mother, Autumn, at a mission where he'd gone to teach reading. Both were seventeen—too young to care about their differences but old enough to recognize true love. According to Autumn, she'd fallen for Andrew the moment their fingers touched beneath a book they both held. After they married and settled Whispering Mountain, Andrew made the journey to the Austin Colony twice a year to pick up supplies shipped from New Orleans. He'd trade a horse for a wagonload of goods and always packed within the necessities would be the latest books from back East.

Travis ran his hand over the leather-bound copies on every subject from law to ranching. He also noticed the stack of new novels piled on the desk and wondered if his brothers ever had time to read them. When Sage was in school, her teacher, a widow named Mrs. Dickerson, always sent home lists of books the boys should buy each year. She might not have taught them, but she made sure they were well read.

He pulled a book called *The House of the Seven Gables* from the stack and dropped into the nearest chair. Anything would be better than listening to Sage plan her husband-hunting trip to the dance.

Hours passed. He was lost in the book when Sage tapped on his shoulder.

"You'd better get dressed. We need to leave before it starts raining again."

Travis stood, reluctant to pull away from the fiction. "All right. Hitch the wagon while I change into the clothes Martha ironed for me this morning." He might as well stop dreading the evening and start getting it over with.

Sage folded her arms. "I can't. I'm all cleaned and pressed."

He looked at her. True. She wasn't just clean, she was spit and polished. For a moment he wondered where his sister was beneath all the ribbons and ruffles. The brothers had tried not to make her into a boy, but they may have gone too far. She looked as if she were wearing a bushel of lace.

"Hurry up." She pushed his leg off the arm of the chair. "I don't want to be late to the year's only dance."

There she was, he thought, bossy as ever. He remembered when she'd been five and Teagen had ordered her a china tea set for Christmas. She'd made them all sit down and have tea every night for a month. The conversation was always the same. They drank lukewarm tea, and she threatened to kill the first one who broke a piece of her set.

Travis took the stairs three at a time wishing either Teagen or Tobin had shown up to take his place. He'd made it to twenty-eight without ever having attended a barn dance and dreaded this one more than any gunfight he'd ever experienced. The folks around, even the upstanding ones, had never been too friendly toward him, and he guessed nothing would change just because they set the meeting to music. But Sage seemed to have her heart set on going.

Thirty minutes later he waited beside the buckboard while Sage stood on the porch and tied a scarf around her hair as if it were the most important thing she'd done all day. "I don't see why we can't ride horseback," he mumbled. "We could make it in half the time."

She didn't answer.

He studied the sky while he waited. Rain still lingered far off along the horizon. He'd lived outside for so many years, he could feel the weather as if it were a part of him. When he noticed Sage still standing on the porch, he got the hint and tromped through the mud to carry her to the wagon.

"Don't drive too fast," Sage said as she settled on the bench. "I don't want to lose all the curl I burned into my hair." She pulled her skirts around her knees. "And don't get those muddy boots within a foot of me."

"You're welcome," he said after he circled and climbed up on the other side.

"I'm sorry." She touched his arm. "I'm just excited. You don't know what this means to me. I've been planning it since Christmas."

He smiled, for the first time understanding how important this must be to her. The brothers had each other when their parents died, but Sage had only been a baby. "Well, then, I'd better get the prettiest girl in Texas to Old Elmo Anderson's annual party in one piece." He held the reins to a pair of matched bays that could have pulled ten times the wagonload at twice the pace. The McMurrays raised horses, and these were fine examples of their stock.

Twenty minutes later the wagon rolled across the only bridge that connected their ranch with the rest of the world. Travis sometimes told people he lived on an island, for it seemed that way. The river bordered the ranch from the north and east, the hills from the south and west. A lone man on horseback, if he knew the exact path, could make it through the cliffs between their land and the settlement in a few hours. The boys, when they traveled that way, never left any sign.

The bridge, two miles north of the ranch house, made access to the ranch easy but almost doubled the time it took to reach the settlement. Travis remembered, down to the smell, what it had been like the day he and his brothers burned the old bridge. Their father had been specific: If they were to survive, they had to totally isolate themselves from the world. The bridge that had taken Andrew McMurray a month to build burned within an hour.

It wasn't rebuilt for seven years. Until then, Travis or Teagen had packed everything they needed into the ranch using the hidden path between the hills. Their mother's father and a few braves had come for a short time a year after Andrew and Autumn died. He'd taught them how to mark a trail that they could follow but that no one else would see. He'd also shown them secrets about raising horses that not even their father knew. Then one night he and his men had left as silently as they'd come.

Travis watched the land as he drove the wagon looking for any sign that his grandfather might still be watching over the ranch. Once in a while he swore he saw one of his grandfather's markings on a branch or in dried mud, and he wondered if the old man were still around.

Twilight cooled the air by the time they reached Elmo Anderson's barn. Bedrolls spread out beneath buckboards revealed that some of the families must have arrived the day before. Several covered wagons, loaded for travel, stood circled to the south of the barn. New folks moving in or passing through, he thought. People were coming to Texas by the thousands—Germans, English, French—as well as a steady flow from the other states. Some wanting to get rich quick, but most only wanting a fresh start.

Travis noticed horses tied to a line thirty yards from the road. Saddles and gear had been stacked a few feet away. Hired hands, he thought, and from the looks of the mounts, some must have ridden long and hard to get here. Not counting those married, men still outnumbered women twenty to one out here. Sage would have her pick of single men, and Travis would make sure her pick measured up.

Sage had been wiggling in the seat for an hour. She was starting to look more like she thought she might be shot before anyone asked her to dance. "Promise me you'll stay close, Travis. There will be people here I don't know."

"You'll recognize most." He winked. "The others will want to know you."

She nodded but didn't look like she believed him. The Mc-Murrays hated strangers with good reason.

"I won't let you out of my sight." He knew few in town and remembered only one young woman near his age. Madeline Ward. She'd been a few years younger than he, but he'd seen her in the settlement on trading days. Her father started blacksmithing at the post about the time Travis joined the Rangers. She'd be twenty-five by now and probably had half a dozen kids, so Travis saw no problem in fulfilling his one duty of keeping an eye on Sage.

His sister had a death grip on his arm as they walked into the barn. "Take it easy," Travis whispered. He thought of adding that it was just a dance, but he guessed she might get violent. Apparently, this was her grand crusade.

Suddenly she smiled and let go of his arm. He watched as she ran to a circle of young people about her age who'd gathered near the fiddler's stand. They all hugged and squealed, welcoming her into their group.

Unlike her brothers, Sage had attended the little school in Mrs. Dickerson's kitchen after Teagen turned eighteen and it was safe for the McMurrays to leave their ranch. School ran three days a week every fall and spring. If the weather turned bad, the girls spent the night in the widow's parlor, and the boys took the loft in her barn. Ten families were each responsible for a month of provisions and wood for the widow, in exchange for the schooling and occasional lodging of the students. Tobin had been thirteen when they'd rebuilt the bridge. He could have gone to school a few years, but either he thought he was too old or he feared people too much to bother. Travis and Teagen saw no point in trying to make their little brother leave the ranch, so only Sage attended.

Travis couldn't help but laugh as Sage hugged all her friends. He didn't call one person in this part of Texas friend, but his kid sister had more than she could talk to.

Moving into the shadows, he watched her. He couldn't help but wonder what would have happened if his father and mother had lived and the McMurray boys had been allowed to grow up a little at a time. Maybe Teagen wouldn't be so angry. Maybe Tobin would talk to people. Maybe *he* wouldn't feel the need to look behind himself so often.

Travis took a step backward, hoping to go unnoticed, and slammed into something soft and alive.

"Beg your . . ." he started as he turned to find a woman, no taller than his shoulder, standing behind him.

Fiery green eyes glared up at him. "Almost killed me, ye did!" She swore, using words he'd never heard come out of a woman's mouth. "If ye'd hit me any harder, I'd be dead on the spot." She rubbed her hands across her body as if checking for broken bones. "Ye make a habit of backing about in the dark?"

He couldn't hide his grin as Ireland flavored her every word. He wasn't surprised when the hood of her navy cape slipped slightly to reveal red curls.

"I'm sorry. I didn't expect anyone to be standing so close behind me." He removed his hat and tried to focus enough in the darkness to see her face.

She was small, maybe an inch or two shorter than Sage, and except for a colorful scarf at her throat, covered in dark blue wool. He couldn't help thinking that she would blend almost perfectly with a midnight sky. Still, how could she have gotten so close without him hearing her?

"I wasn't standing behind ye." She smoothed her hands down her coat and tugged up the hood, almost disappearing into the shadows. "I was hiding, and I'll thank ye to turn around and go about yer business so I can get back to mine. As far as I'm concerned, ye're a tree growing here in this barn, and I've nothing to say to ye."

Travis didn't budge. "'Tis sorry, I am." He echoed her accent. "When did hiding become a business?"

Silently she stared at him as if she thought him slow-witted.

"Mind telling me why you feel the need for such an occupation?" he asked. Most of her face might be in shadow, but he found himself dying to see what she looked like.

She rolled her beautiful green eyes. "Now, sir, if I was hiding, it should be logical that I'd be doing it so I won't have to talk. Turn around before I have to get rough with ye."

Travis slowly followed orders deciding that this dance might not be as boring as he'd thought. Sage was obviously having a great time talking to friends, and he had someone of interest to watch.

When he glanced back, she'd vanished as quickly as she'd appeared. He was surprised how disappointed he felt. He watched the crowd, seeing a few faces he recognized, but none with green eyes.

The Widow Dickerson came over after half an hour of dancing with every old man she could talk into taking her around the floor. She was actively looking for husband number three. Since she had a drink in her hand and he was half her age, Travis thought he would be safe talking to her without having to dance.

"Evening, Mrs. Dickerson."

"Evening, Travis. It's good to see you home." She had a way of moving her head back and forth like a clock's pendulum when she talked. A habit that must drive her pupils crazy. "I saw your brothers at the trading post a few months ago, and they said you were overdue for a visit."

"Yes," he nodded, not surprised she asked about him, for Mrs. Dickerson tried her best to keep up with everyone.

She smiled and waited.

That was it, he thought, the entire scope of his conversation skills.

"Nice dance," she said, as if coaching him.

"Yes," he answered, trying to think of another word to say. "Lots of new folks."

She nodded. "True, but several are with the wagons heading north in the morning. They only stayed this long because of the dance. Won't be much fun where they are headed."

"Oh." He frowned trying to think of more than one-word answers.

Mrs. Dickerson didn't seem to notice. "Last I heard, Elmo is looking for someone to take them farther upriver, but everyone knows it's not safe much past Fort Graham."

Travis nodded. He tried to listen, but he'd caught a glimpse of color, no more than a scarf, slip through the side door. The woman he'd stepped on was leaving. He felt a pull to follow her. One touch, one look. He hadn't even seen her whole face, yet he almost ran for the door.

"If you had time, you could take them." Mrs. Dickerson nodded as if she'd solved the homesteaders' problem. "Sage tells me you've been all over Texas."

Travis forced himself to pay attention to the old teacher. He didn't want to spend the first break he'd had in two years taking farmers north as she suggested. They always seemed to buy land just beyond where the forts could protect them. The warring tribes in the top half of the state weren't like those in the south. He'd seen enough burned homesteads already. Texas had plenty of outlaws and rustlers in the south to keep him busy. He didn't need to go north.

He glanced once more at the door, wondering what the little lady he'd stepped on would do if he followed her.

Mrs. Dickerson spotted Homer Carter and patted Travis's arm. Once more Travis forced himself to stop daydreaming.

He stared in the direction the teacher was looking and noticed Homer. The man had cleaned up since the last time Travis saw him, but his face still looked like leather.

The schoolteacher handed Travis her mug and waved goodbye as she hurried to trap her next dance partner.

He sat the mug down and glanced in Sage's direction. She looked like she was saying yes to a dance with a lean cowhand. He appeared more boy than man, but Travis didn't miss that he still wore his gun belt even though Elmo had asked everyone to check guns at the door. Most men removed belt and all, but this kid wanted everyone at the dance to know he wore a weapon.

Travis shook his head. He didn't like the fellow already. In fact, if he were guessing, he'd say Sage's new dance partner would never be man enough to marry his sister no matter how many weapons he showed off. Travis debated pulling him aside and filling him in on that fact when he finished dancing. After all, if his faults were so obvious from half a barn away, Travis would be doing him a favor by letting him know he didn't have a chance.

It's just a dance, Travis reminded himself. He couldn't find fault with all his sister's dance partners, even if it did appear easy to do so.

As the music started, he took a deep breath and moved to the side door. Maybe he'd better get some air. Being a big brother was hard work. He told himself his action had nothing to do with green eyes.

Once outside, he looked around for the woman who'd stood behind him. He'd seen her leave, but not return. So, unless she'd turned in, she must be somewhere outside hiding as she'd done all night.

There were enough campfires around that he should at least be able to spot her shadow if she were moving about. He told himself he wasn't really interested in talking to her, but he might ask about her health. After all, he could have hurt her when he'd stepped on her. Travis vaguely remembered the feel of her foot beneath his boot heel when he'd moved backward. And something soft had brushed his arm as he'd twisted around. He closed his eyes. He shouldn't be thinking about what part of her body had felt so soft.

Travis circled the yard. A few mothers were putting their children to bed in bedrolls beneath the wagons. Their lullabies blended with the music from the barn. An old woman rocked in a chair on the porch of one of the new little houses that had been built beside the trading post. Her head was back, her eyes closed. He couldn't tell if she was listening to the music or sleeping. In the tall grass by the barn door, two young girls sat catching fireflies and giggling.

Travis moved into the shadows, watching and hoping he wouldn't step on the little woman again. Coming to a dance, then trying to hide, seemed a little peculiar. He smiled realizing that was pretty much what he'd been doing.

When he reached the line of horses tied to a long rope, he spotted someone moving among them. Most of the folks who'd ridden in had taken time to unsaddle their mounts, but a few hadn't bothered. Travis shook his head. He could almost hear his little brother Tobin complaining. Tobin loved horses more than any man alive. He wouldn't have understood why they hadn't taken time to remove their saddles.

Travis recognized the shadow in blue creeping down the line. He moved closer, making sure she couldn't see him following.

He passed the first mount and noticed the reins had come loose from the rope. Knotting them firmly, he moved to the next. Untied. He looped the leather back to the rope and followed the shadow. She might be just playing a joke . . . making tired cowhands chase their horses after they'd danced all night.

Or she might be playing an old trick that was no joke. First untie, then spook a group of horses. When they scattered in different directions, it wouldn't be hard to guide one away and be gone before the cowhands realized they hadn't rounded up every mount. A dance like this would be an easy place to steal a mount.

If that was her game, the little lady was about to break the law, and his time off was over.

He slipped the Texas Ranger badge from his pocket and pinned it to his shirt. Time to go to work. As he pulled his jacket over the badge, he hoped he wouldn't have to arrest anyone tonight. Especially not someone with green eyes. He'd already seen them angry; he didn't want to see hate in them as well.

As he tied the last few horses back in place, he watched her run toward the barn. She didn't look back, but made a wide circle around a group of men heading out of the dance. Her cape flew around her like wings, making him smile. His father used to tell stories of Ireland and how fairies lived in the woods.

Travis had asked him once if he'd brought a fairy with him to Texas, and his father had frowned. "No, son," he'd said. "There's no room for fairies in Texas."

Travis watched the little woman disappear near the barn. Maybe his father had been wrong.

CHAPTER 3

∞

RAINEY ADAMS MUMBLED AN OATH AS SHE WATCHED THE GROUP OF young cowhands head out of the dance. They joked with one another as they ambled toward the stack of saddles and gear they'd left piled several feet from the horse line. She'd seen the behavior before. Men in groups left a party for one of two things. Smoking or drinking. These boys were probably building up their courage to ask a girl to dance. By the end of the evening, several would have failed in their quest and would turn their efforts toward fighting to reestablish their manhood.

Men were such strange creatures, Rainey decided as she pulled her hood over her red curls and hoped they wouldn't notice her in the shadows. She didn't care what the cowhands did, but the direction they were headed worried her.

They walked toward the horses!

One was sure to notice the mounts had been untied, and from there it wouldn't take many brains to figure out what she'd planned. Even if they hadn't seen her leave the barn, she was still a stranger. She'd learned the hard way that the newcomer usually gets blamed if something goes wrong.

Rainey slipped into the blackness behind the barn door and watched, telling herself she'd been careful tonight. There was no way anyone would guess that she'd been involved if trouble came. Only one man had even noticed her moving about, and he'd almost crippled her with his big feet. He'd been tall, solid as an oak, when he'd slammed into her. She might have yelled at him, but he didn't look like he wanted to be there any more than she did.

"Only, I've a mission tonight," she reasoned in a mumble to no one. "I have to have a horse by tomorrow morning or I'll be left behind to starve. The big man is not stopping me, and neither will these boys sneaking out for a drink." With no money left, the choices were few. "I'll borrow one horse, that's all, and be on my way in the safety of the group of wagons heading north. As soon as I get to the fort, I'll turn the horse loose to come home none the worse for wear."

Closing her eyes, she wondered if the fort would be any better place than Galveston. She'd sworn to disappear to where no one would find her, but Rainey had feared the coast of Texas might not be far enough. . . . Fort Graham might be too far.

She shoved aside her worries and watched the group of men circle their saddles. One pulled a bottle from his gear, and they began passing it around. As whiskey poured from the bottle, the men's voices rose. She waited, hoping they wouldn't notice the horse line . . . praying they wouldn't make so much noise that they frightened the horses themselves. She pressed her back against the rough barn wall, trying to melt into the night as she lingered. If they'd just finish their drinking and go back inside, she could go about her business of horse borrowing with no one the wiser. She only had one more leg of her journey.

Past the group of men, she saw something move. She stared, frozen, watching the form of a man take shape from the darkness. He shifted again so slightly she wouldn't have noticed if she hadn't been focusing. Rainey recognized him. The tall-as-an-oak stranger. He stood alone near the horses, his hat low, not even allowing moonlight to touch his face. She tried to remember what he'd looked like when he'd apologized for tripping over her, but she couldn't envision his features. Only solid muscle.

One of the cowboys saw him, too. "Hey, you. What you doing over by our horses?"

Another youth turned toward the stranger. "Yeah, you didn't ride in with us. I been here over a year and know most men who work in these parts. Where're you from?"

A stout cowhand, who sounded like he'd had more than his share of whiskey, walked toward the tall man. "I don't believe I've seen you before, either. You're not from around here. Who invited you?"

The tall stranger appeared to be deaf. He made no attempt to answer their questions or explain why he came to the dance.

The thought crossed Rainey's mind that if the cowhands found the horses untied, they might think the stranger did it.

She took a step toward the men. She might be a horse borrower, but she couldn't stand by while another took the blame for something she'd done. It wasn't her way and never would be, no matter how much she wanted to stay invisible.

The cowhands seemed to read her mind. They all turned to the stranger asking questions so fast he couldn't have answered them. Strangers in this part of Texas were not uncommon and oftentimes meant trouble. Since the Battle of the Alamo, every outlaw in the States and Mexico seemed to have found his way to Texas, blending in with the just plain folks already living here. She wasn't surprised the cowhands didn't give the stranger a chance.

But he wasn't helping matters, remaining silent as a post. Rainey didn't miss the way his hand slid down his leg as if feeling for an invisible gun. He must know he was in trouble. Ten to one were poor odds, even for a man built of oak. In seconds they'd find the untied horses, and the stranger would be blamed.

Without further thought, Rainey headed for the drunken group. She had to stop this before the silent man was beaten to a pulp.

Running past the cowhands with their angry shouts, she flew right toward the stranger.

She closed her eyes and braced for the impact, but at the last moment he caught her and lifted her off the ground. He swung her around once, then eased her to earth as if he'd done so a thousand times.

Rainey laughed at the sheer joy of feeling like she'd taken flight. Then, before he could say a word, she circled his neck with her arms and, standing on tiptoes, touched her mouth to his. When she pulled away, she laughed. "Sorry I'm late, darling."

On impulse she touched her lips to his again and felt him smile as he held her to him for a moment. The warmth of his mouth against hers surprised her. His big hands circled her waist, and in this stranger's embrace she felt safe for the first time in months. She was almost sorry when he straightened and ended their play-like kiss.

The cowhands backed away. Questioning a stranger was one thing. Interrupting lovers was quite another.

Rainey barely noticed them walking back to the barn. Suddenly she became very much aware that she was plastered against this silent man who hadn't done a thing to save himself. She lowered off her toes, her body moving down his. Through their layers of clothes she felt the lean strength of him.

Her fingers crossed his chest as she wondered if a heart beat beneath the wall of muscle.

"Want to tell me what's going on?" he whispered against her ear as his hands gentled to almost a caress at her waist.

Rainey looked up, trying to see his face. His voice was rich, but not all that friendly considering they'd just kissed. If she could call pressing her lips against his kissing. She had a feeling there was more to the act, or couples would have given it up ages ago.

"I had to do something to save ye, lad. Those men were about to find out . . ." She hesitated, realizing she couldn't very well tell him what they were about to discover or she'd be admitting her own involvement in the crime. She didn't have the time to tell this stranger how desperately she needed a horse so she could travel with the wagons tomorrow to the fort a few days away. He probably wouldn't understand, or care.

She didn't have time to explain, but she seemed to have the time to continue leaning against him as if he were the first lifeline she'd encountered in this sea of wilderness. How could the feel of a man silently comfort her?

"Before they found out what?" His low words brushed across her cheek. His question came slow, almost forced from him as if he would have been content to simply stand beside her but knew he had to talk.

He stood so still waiting for her to finish her sentence that she feared he didn't breathe. Her hand reached just inside his coat and touched his chest once more, spreading across his heart. She'd never been so bold and surprised herself by realizing she felt a need to touch him.

The tip of her fingers brushed metal, and without seeing it, she knew he wore a badge. Her fingers traced the outline of the cold steel. A circle star. She'd heard of the men who pinned on such a brand. They were called Rangers. Hard men who saw no bend in the law.

Rainey pushed away, missing the nearness of him while the heat of his body still warmed her skin but knowing he wouldn't understand. Closing her eyes, she pledged to be more careful. "Oh, and what does it matter anyway? If ye're too dumb to try and save yourself, I may just be wasting me time fretting over ya. Maybe I should let them beat you senseless?" Frustrated, she turned away. This was not the time to find herself attracted to a man. She had far greater problems.

She took one step before he caught her wrist in a firm grip. "I was in no danger." His voice came low again. Velvet in the night.

She tugged at his hold, but he didn't release her. She slowly pivoted to face him, looking up into the shadows of his face. "Ye may not have thought ye were in danger facing ten men, but if you don't turn loose of me, you'll be meeting your Maker by midnight."

He released her hand. "I'm sorry to have detained you," he said, touching his hat in polite salute. "I thank you for saving me."

He removed his hat, and she noticed dark hair a bit longer than most, a straight nose, high cheekbones, and brown eyes that stared with a coldness she found frightening. Maybe this man *had* been in no danger.

"I'm Travis McMurray." He offered the hand that had just been restraining her a moment before.

Rainey tried to remember the name she'd been using of late. "Molly," she blurted. "Molly . . ." She tried to think. It was something Irish, but what?

"Give it time." Laughter flavored his words. "It'll come to you, kinda like that accent of yours tends to."

She straightened her back, trying to look taller—trying to control her anger. He'd noticed. She couldn't help but wonder what else the man had noticed about her and her business. If there was one thing she hated above all else it was people not minding their own business. No matter how good he felt, she could do without his prying.

Taking a step toward the barn, she glanced back and said without any accent at all, "And to think, I wasted a good kiss saving your life. I should have let the men bash your head in, for they'd surely find no brain to inhibit their progress."

He had the nerve to fall into step with her as if he'd been in-vited. The man truly had no sense of danger. They were almost to the barn before he spoke in a voice so calm it surprised her. "Will you dance with me, Molly, or did you just come to steal a horse?"

Suddenly too many people were near. She couldn't risk arguing with him. So she lifted her head and took his hand. "I did no such thing," she lied as he pulled her close. "I came to dance."

He winked at her. "Sure you did, Molly," he whispered near her ear as he pulled her into the crowd of dancers.

This time the warmth of his touch felt familiar, and she allowed herself a moment to enjoy it knowing that when the dance was over she'd be forcing it deep into her memory. His hand spread solid and strong across her back, warming her skin through layers of fabric. When he turned to face her, she fought the urge to rise to her tiptoes and kiss him.

Rainey laughed at herself. Even being near him was like juggling fire. Yet she realized that if this were another time, another place, Travis could be a man she'd find worth knowing. But for the moment she could pretend she didn't have to disappear in a few hours and she had the time to dance.

A few minutes later she decided that if Travis McMurray had ever had a dance lesson, he should demand his money back, as he apologized for stepping on her foot. Either his feet were too big, or her arms too short, because they didn't seem to go together at all. When he wasn't bumping into her, they were trying to go opposite directions, looking as if they were in some kind of strange tug-of-war set to music. She decided watching his boots was her only defense as the music played on.

He was busy apologizing for the third time when the torture finally ended and she looked up. To her surprise, the man of oak was smiling.

"Where'd you learn to dance?" she asked before thinking.

"I didn't," he answered, "but it didn't look all that hard."

His words were so honest, so true, she had to laugh. His eyes turned warm, and she knew without a doubt that she'd discovered one of very few things in this world that Travis McMurray couldn't do.

A pretty girl appeared at the oak's side. "If you're going to dance, Brother, you'll have to dance with me next."

Rainey felt his grip on her hand tighten as though he didn't want to let her go.

His sister insisted.

Travis's fingers squeezed Rainey's hand once more before stepping away.

She looked up and saw a promise in his brown eyes. A promise she knew he'd never be able to keep.

Rainey watched as the young woman in lace and ribbons pulled him away. Though he argued, he gave in. While they tried to dance, Rainey Adams slipped away. She hadn't come here to dance, or for that matter, to kiss a stranger. She had a mission. It was time to get to work.

He might suspect her if she took a horse from the line, but Travis McMurray would never know if she borrowed one from the wagons.

CHAPTER 4

Travis handed Sage the blanket from beneath the buckboard seat and climbed up beside her for the ride home. Thin wisps of clouds floated in the night sky, but any threat of rain had vanished.

She cuddled into the wool and asked, "Now, explain to me how you could possibly give away one of Tobin's matched bays to a total stranger?"

"It's not important." Travis stared at the pale lines of dirt marking the wagon tracks and hoped the night stayed clear enough to see them until he reached the bridge. From there, he could drive home in total blackness; he knew his ranchland well even after being gone most of ten years.

Sage would not drop the question. "I'm glad you see it that way, because I promise you, Tobin won't. He raised the two from colts, training them together from the beginning. You know a matched set like that is worth five times what just two horses would be. And, if I know Tobin, he's got buyers waiting for them."

"Tobin has trained a hundred others exactly like them over the years." Travis tried to make light of the fact that when he went to get the wagon, one horse had vanished. "You ever figure maybe Little Brother spends too much time with the horses?"

Sage refused to be distracted. "But how, without saying a word to me about it, could you give away one of the McMurray horses? I could understand if you lost it in a bet, or sold the set. After all, we are in the business of raising and selling horses."

Travis didn't want to talk about it. How could he explain that the first girl, besides his sister, he'd ever danced with had stolen the bay? Or at least he thought it was the green-eyed girl who'd kissed him.

He didn't know for a fact that she did it. Maybe someone else decided the best horse at the annual barn dance to take would be the one that belonged to a Texas Ranger. It had to be her, whatever her name was; no one else would have been so brave. Most of the people around here knew the horses belonged to the McMurrays, and no one would ever be fool enough to try and steal anything from a McMurray again.

As they moved through the night, Travis remembered what it had been like those first weeks after his father died. His mother took to her bed, pregnant and heartbroken. Teagen and Travis must have read their father's letter a hundred times. Every night they prepared, reloading guns, setting traps. Every morning they rode the land looking for any sign that someone had stepped foot on McMurray property. Tobin had only been six and was wounded in an ambush the first day. He'd looked so tiny propped into a chair on the front porch with a rifle on either side of him. Of the three brothers, he'd been the best shot even then, but his job in those weeks was simple . . . to fire a warning if anyone rode toward the ranch house.

He'd handled his pain and his mission like a man, leaving his brothers one less thing to worry about while they rode guard and tried to keep their father's stock alive. The only time Tobin fired was the day their mother gave birth to Sage. Autumn McMurray had been inside the house and hadn't made a sound during the delivery, then she called Tobin's name softly and told him to come get the baby.

Tobin tried to wrap Sage in a blanket, but with his bandaged arm and her wiggling it wasn't easy. He carried her to the porch and fired one shot in the air. By the time Teagen and Travis rode in, Sage was yelling up a storm and their mother had bled out from childbirth. They kept Sage alive and fat on goat's milk until Martha arrived. Three weeks after Sage was born, a marshal left word at the trading post, where they picked up supplies, that a housekeeper had arrived and was waiting at the stage station fifty miles south. Travis collected his supplies from the post and hurried home as always. He then rode alone to the south and collected Martha. She went with him without question, as if having a half-grown kid, fully armed, slip into her room before sunup was nothing unusual in her life. Two days later, when they made it back to the ranch, she'd been shocked at how healthy Sage looked considering three little boys were taking care of her. Martha bonded with the baby at first sight.

Tobin healed slowly during those early weeks, with a scar that seemed to run straight across his heart. For months he talked little, somehow blaming himself for his mother's death since he'd been the one with her. Finally he began to work with the horses his father bred so carefully with stock from Kentucky. As the colts were born, so was his mission. Travis couldn't count the times he'd found Tobin asleep in the barn near a horse about to foal. The funny thing was, the horses seemed to understand Tobin and welcome him among them.

"He's going to thump you a good one." Sage pulled Travis back to the present as she repeated one of Martha's sayings. "Tobin will never understand."

Travis nodded, realizing he'd better think of a better story. In theory a fourth of the horses belonged to him. But he'd never taken more than a fresh mount now and then when he returned home. More often than not, Tobin had one already picked out. He'd say, "This one's got the heart of a Ranger. He'll keep up with you."

Sage leaned her head against his arm, and Travis hummed softly as she fell asleep. She might be all grown up now, but she hadn't changed. The only time she wasn't talking was when she slept. He thought of asking if she enjoyed the dance, but he already knew. He'd seen it in her eyes. She hadn't met the man who'd win her heart. From the unshed tears he'd seen sparkling in her eyes as they said their good nights to the neighbors, no man had even come close to being right.

A few hours later Travis carried Sage into the house. His brothers stood, nodding their greetings as he crossed to his little sister's room and put her to bed as he'd done all her life. He tugged off her shoes and covered her with a blanket before returning to the fire where Teagen and Tobin waited.

They toasted his homecoming and the two oldest settled in to talk, but Tobin stood. "I'll put up the horses," he said, "and be right back, so don't start telling all of your adventures without me."

Travis nodded once, then added, "I loaned out one of the bays. I'll get him back tomorrow."

Tobin left without asking more.

Travis knew the explanation was sketchy, but it was all he could think to say and still be telling the truth.

When Tobin left, Teagen offered his brother a cigar, and they lit up with a shared smile. Even though they were in their twenties, they still listened for Martha's steps. The woman could smell cigar smoke from three rooms away.

"How was the dance?" Teagen asked in his straightforward way.

"Not bad," Travis answered. "Saw Mrs. Dickerson. I think she's hoping to get married again and give up teaching."

Teagen nodded.

"Elmo Anderson told me to tell you that new saddle you ordered should be in by tomorrow or the next day."

The older brother nodded again. "You coming home to stay this time?" He'd asked the same question for almost ten years. For Teagen there would never be anything but the ranch. For Tobin it was horses. Neither seemed to understand that for Travis it would always be the open land, the roaming. He loved them all, but Travis knew he was born to travel. If it hadn't been the Rangers, it would have been the army, or something else. He needed the sky for a roof and the horizon for walls.

"What did I miss?" Tobin said from the doorway.

The brothers pulled their chairs in a circle by the fire, and Travis told them of his adventures while they related everything that had happened at the ranch. Finally, long after midnight, the talk turned to Sage and how much they'd all miss her if she married.

Teagen suddenly laughed. "We sound like a bunch of old maids."

Tobin shrugged. "We are. Sage is our only hope of having a next generation. There's not a woman in Texas who'd marry any one of us."

Teagen leaned back in his chair. "True," he said matter-of-factly. "Martha says piss and vinegar must run in our blood to make us so mean. I'm the oldest, I'm already hard-boiled, but Tobin, you're still young. You could marry."

"I'm almost twenty-four. An old man, so stop talking about me like I'm still growing."

Travis looked at Teagen but pointed to Tobin. "He'd have to talk to a girl if he married her. Unless we can find one who looks like a horse, I don't think there's much chance of that."

Tobin almost knocked Travis out of his chair with a playful blow.

They were still laughing when they climbed the stairs to the men's quarters. Three rooms, all exactly alike. Travis waved good night as he closed his door and fell into bed. He thought he'd fall to sleep in a few breaths, but the pretty face of a redhead filled his mind. He'd almost told his brothers that he'd danced tonight and a girl had kissed him. But he didn't want to sound like a pup. If he told them details, he'd probably end up telling them about how, likely as not, she stole his horse.

Travis rolled over. Tomorrow he'd ride to the trading post. She had to be traveling with the group of wagons heading north. He'd get his horse back and lecture her on the law. She could get shot for taking a horse. If he were playing by the rules, he should arrest her and let some judge decide what to do with her. But it was hard to think about cuffing someone he'd kissed.

Well, could be he didn't kiss her, but she definitely kissed him.

He thought about why she must have taken the horse. Maybe she had a good reason and he should hear her out before he started his planned lecture. Maybe her sick ma and pa were in a wagon. Maybe she was a widow trying to make it alone. She looked to be in her twenties, so it could be possible. She might have spent her last few dollars burying her man and now she had to make it back to a little farm alone. Or she could have been on the run from a father who beat her regularly.

Travis spent an hour thinking about her and finally decided two things. One, he'd take an extra horse with him, an animal that wasn't part of a matched set, in case any of her stories sounded good. And, two, when he saw the woman who called herself Molly, if he got the chance, he'd return her kiss.

He drifted off a few hours before dawn calling himself a fool. No matter how hard he tried, he couldn't push the feel of her against him from his thoughts. She'd somehow branded him with her touch. The softness of her body pressed close to his was something he wouldn't be forgetting any time soon. She fit him, he decided and wished mating could have been so simple. No verbal sparring, no courting, just one man and one woman bumping together to see if they fit.

By the time the smell of bacon woke him, the sun was up. Travis stretched, thinking how good a bed felt. Even when his travels took him into towns, he usually chose to camp out a mile or so away from people. He said it was because the smell of civilization bothered him, but in truth, the filth of hotels never appealed to him. He knew the sheets were changed once a month if the room had been rented every night, but most places rented half the bed. So a stranger might wander in and claim his half during the night.

He'd seen signs asking all boarders to wash their feet before going to sleep, but Travis felt they should have washed the rest of their bodies as well. Even on slow nights when he could get an almost clean room alone, the odors of former guests kept him awake.

Travis stripped to his underwear and went down the back stairs to the washroom. He wasn't surprised to find hot water and soap waiting. By the time he washed and returned to his room, clean clothes were on his bed.

"Thank you, Martha!" he yelled as he dressed while moving down the front stairs.

A few minutes later when she plopped a platter of food in front of him, she answered, "You are welcome."

As he shoved eggs into his mouth, she added, "Everyone else has been up and working for hours."

He didn't answer. Martha seemed to have the idea that being a Texas Ranger was some kind of long game he played and one day he'd grow up and come back home to do real work. None of the boys had ever asked her about her past, or doubted the rumor that prison had been a part of it. For all he knew, Martha had a hatred of lawmen based on personal experience.

He stared at the eggs hoping she hadn't gone to prison for poisoning someone. Taking another mouthful, he smiled. If she didn't kill him for all the wild things he did growing up, she wasn't going to poison him for sleeping late today.

Travis stood shoveling in the last bite of bacon. "I have to go into town. Do you want me to pick up any supplies?"

Martha shook her head. "I get my supplies on the first of the month, and anything I forget we can just do without until the first rolls around again."

"I'll be back before supper, I hope. If not, I'll leave word with Anderson. I have a feeling Teagen will by riding over tomorrow morning to see if his saddle came in, so tell him if he doesn't see me tonight, there will be a note waiting."

She didn't even look up as he left.

He caught two horses in the corral and saddled one, then headed for the back trail through the hills. It was faster than the bridge road. Travis pushed hard, thinking that he should have been at the trading post before dawn. By now the wagons would be a few miles north. He'd catch them easily on horseback, but he could have saved time if he'd reached the post before his green-eyed thief left with his horse.

When he stopped to talk to the owner of the trading post, old Elmo Anderson claimed there was no woman named Molly with the travelers. He'd supplied every wagon himself and could not remember any woman fitting Travis's description. Elmo also swore that if a McMurray bay had been among the horses, he would have noticed it. Most of the wagons had been pulled by oxen, a few by mules, and the few riders between the wagons were on nags. Anderson couldn't remember even a cart pulled with one horse.

Travis took the time to talk with a peddler who'd traveled from south of the post. He said he hadn't seen a soul all morning, so she couldn't have gone south. Any other direction would be open country and far too dangerous for a woman to travel alone. His little thief seemed to have vanished.

Travis rode on to the wagons hoping that she'd joined up with the rest somewhere along the north road. If she were on the bay, she would have been wise not to let anyone near the post see her ride away. The cowhands might not recognize Travis, but they'd know a McMurray horse.

Two hours later, when he caught up to the settlers snailing their way across a shallow river, he saw that Anderson had been right. No horse. No woman who'd called herself Molly was among them.

She'd disappeared.

The travelers were newly arrived from Germany and few spoke English. He'd seen them at the dance, keeping mostly to themselves. Travis had assumed Molly was with them even though she'd tried to act like she was Irish. Since Anderson hadn't known her, she wouldn't have been a daughter of a local family. How could a woman walk alone into a dance and no one notice? Or, for that matter, walk away with a horse without a soul seeing her go?

Molly with the green eyes was growing more interesting by the minute.

He told himself he knew how she'd done it. Like him, everyone thought she belonged with someone else. No one at the dance knew everyone, so pretending to be with first one group and then another would have been easy for her.

Grinning, he realized that at one point she'd pretended to be with him and no one had questioned her.

William Ackland, the oldest and self-appointed leader of the group of Germans, offered to share their noon meal after Travis made sure all the wagons made it across the river. Ackland spoke a passable English and didn't mind acting as interpreter. The women, shyly at first, asked questions about what lay north—the people, the weather, the settlements past Fort Graham. The men asked about the land, and then what danger they might encounter.

When Travis finished answering their questions, he asked a few of his own. Not one remembered a redheaded woman at the dance. He was beginning to think she'd been a dream. Only a dream wouldn't have kissed him or stolen a horse. A dream wouldn't have spread her fingers over his chest as if needing to know he was real as dearly as he had wanted to hold her when he'd danced with her.

One woman said she met a young woman named Sally who might have had red hair beneath her scarf, but she seemed too afraid to even join the women in conversation. The German woman thought she must have been a local.

Travis doubted that would be his fearless Molly who'd run past a dozen men when she thought she was saving his life. But it made sense that she'd play more than one part; after all, she'd played two with him.

When the leader asked him to travel with them for a while and scout, Travis couldn't decline. Most of the men looked like farmers, and no one, as far as he could see, carried a gun handy. The new settlers had no idea how treacherous Texas could be. They thought their eight wagons would protect them.

"I'll go as far as the next trading post," he said to William Ackland. "From there maybe you can find a supply wagon heading for the fort. You all will be far safer traveling with men who know this part of the country."

As Travis swung back into the saddle, he decided heading north to find the redhead was as good a direction as any. If he didn't find her, he'd need the ride home to think of a reason he'd lost the bay.

CHAPTER 5

∞

Rainey Adams crawled out from under the sagebrush where she'd curled up to sleep and stared at the trading post a quarter mile away. Even the late sleepers from the night before had long ago left the area around the barn where the dance had been held. But to her surprise horses were gathered at the entrance to the mercantile. Too many, she thought. Something, besides everyday trade, must be going on.

Rainey pushed back through the brush and into the shadows of live oaks growing near the creek. This had been her refuge since she arrived almost a week ago, and the clearing was starting to feel like home. The branches, newly green, formed a roof and the rocks were her furniture. The few belongings she had were safely hidden away in her traveling bag behind a fallen log.

She'd paid for passage on a freight wagon, but asked to be let off before they reached the trading post. She wanted time to study the place before going into the little settlement. A woman alone needed to be careful. She'd watched those coming and going, waiting for the right people to travel on with before announcing herself. She had one more leg to her journey, or at least she hoped there would be only one more stop. When she'd reached Galveston, she'd thought to settle there, but the town was wild, and the only boardinghouse for women that she'd found had been loud and dirty. Though her money was getting dangerously low, she didn't bother to look for work in Galveston.

Rainey also knew that if her father followed her, the coastal town would be his first stop. She would be safer to journey inland. She'd met several families on the ship from New Orleans, and most of them were moving north, traveling with the freighters or spacing their wagons between them for safety.

One older driver, with hands crippled up from years of holding the reins on a mule team, offered her a ride as far as the Anderson Trading Post if she'd do all the cooking when they camped and pay for half of the food. She kept her bargain. He ate most of the food as they traveled north dropping off families at farms and settlements along the way. By the time they reached the Anderson Trading Post, she'd been his last company to leave.

The old freighter insisted she take a blanket and half the remaining food. He also offered her a pistol, but Rainey refused.

She'd waved goodbye to him, then disappeared into the trees at the last bend in the road before the trading post. By the time she'd worked her way through the brush to where she could see the post clearly, the freighter had unloaded and was heading back south. She'd almost waved him down and asked for a ride back to the nearest town, but he'd told her the fort lay three or four days further and he'd heard one of the officer's wives was sickly and had been asking for a nurse. He'd made her promise to wait until a group of wagons was heading that direction because he claimed one wagon alone wouldn't be safe from this point on.

Rainey agreed. And thanked him for the help. She knew nothing of nursing, but she had taught school since she was thirteen and figured it was time to give nursing a try. That is, if she could get to the fort and if the poor woman were still alive and in need of a nurse.

Frowning, Rainey sat on a rock a few feet from the stream. The *ifs* in her life were starting to outnumber the *maybes*, and that was never good news.

Last night, at the dance, she'd had a clear plan. She picked out a good horse, borrowed it without anyone seeing, and hid it near the stream. After dawn, she hoped to blend in with the eight wagons heading north. The German farmers would be miles away before they noticed they had a stranger among them. If she was lucky, they might even think someone in their party had invited her. She'd played that game to get on the boat from New Orleans and had been surprised at how well it worked.

But this morning nothing worked as she planned. She'd overslept. The horse wandered off and was nowhere in sight. The Germans must have left before dawn. Bad luck followed her like a hungry mouse running toward the smell of ripe cheese. Maybe she should develop a new strategy and plan to fail; surely then she'd succeed at something besides making a mess of her life.

She'd waited days for the German wagons. Who knew how long it would be before more settlers passed the post heading north. She couldn't live out here in the woods forever without someone in the small settlement noticing. She'd been lucky to find this small bend, but several times she'd heard folks watering their horses less than thirty feet away.

Six months ago, when she'd decided to run away from her father's matchmaking scheme, she thought marrying some nitwit fish merchant twice her age whom she didn't love would be a fate worse than death. Since she arrived in Texas, she'd reconsidered.

Rainey pulled off the red wig she'd slept in and scratched her head. The hairpiece she'd borrowed from an aging actress on the boat from New Orleans not only hurt her head, she was sure it had fleas. Hurrying to the edge of the stream, she tried her best not to swear at the latest turn of events. As if oversleeping and losing the horse wasn't enough, now she sensed trouble at the trading post. This was not turning out to be a good day. Not that she would recognize one if it came along.

She might be an "old maid," as her father called her constantly, but she was not without resources. From the time her parents started running an exclusive girls' school near Washington, D.C., she'd read. Surely she'd learned something in all those years of books that would help her now.

At thirteen Rainey had taken a teaching position at her father's school, not because of any great love of teaching, but so she could stay at school and practically live, as she always had, in the library. She'd seen enough of the way her father treated her mother to know she never wanted marriage. She thought he would pay her a rightful wage when she reached sixteen, the legal age to teach. She would save her money before heading out on her own. After all, her aunt May had left home and made it in New Orleans alone. Her letters to Rainey's mother told of grand adventures and fascinating people. Rainey planned to do the same.

Her father, however, made other plans. On her sixteenth birthday he said she'd have to wait another year to draw a wage, but he did increase her responsibilities. At seventeen he made her head of one of the dorms but again refused her a salary, claiming that she was still a minor and therefore everything she made legally belonged to him. At eighteen her mother died and her father refused to talk to her for months. She allowed him his time. At nineteen the school made enough money for her father to build a grand house for his second wife, but he said she must stay in the dorm because it wouldn't be proper for her to live with him and his new wife. When she turned twenty, he said she was ungrateful for all he'd done for her.

At twenty-one, when she threatened to quit if he didn't pay her, he called her a worthless old maid. A week later he handed his plain little bookworm of a daughter over to the middle-aged widower with six children who owned the fish market. The widower didn't seem to mind, her father had said, that she was worthless and money hungry. They'd both agreed that with a stern hand she would make a passable wife.

Rainey refused to marry and her father refused to listen. He simply said she had no other choice.

Two days before the wedding Rainey took wages for a year of work from her father's safe and boarded a train to New Orleans.

She fought back tears as memories came back raw as ever. Her father had said she'd never had the spine to disobey him and if she ever tried he'd crush her like a bug. She felt like she'd been waiting for the blow to come since she boarded the train almost two months ago.

Moving along the edge of the water, she tested its depth with a stick as she forced her thoughts back to today's crisis. Somewhere in her reading she'd learned that the best way to get from one place to another without leaving a trail was to wade along a stream. Problem was, without the horse, no one would bother to look for her, and even a stream in this wild country might be over her head. No one would care, or probably even notice, if she and the fleas drowned.

Except for that tall man she'd kissed last night. He might spend a minute wondering what happened to her.

She'd been hiding in the brush last night when Travis Mc-Murray looked for his horse. It had been so dark she could only make out his shadow, but she knew who he was with one glance. The look of his outline against the night sky seemed familiar, as if it had always been in her mind. Her own private ideal formed from a hundred heroes inside a hundred stories.

He might be a hero, but Rainey knew she'd never be his lady.

Of all the horses tied up around the dance, why'd she have to take the bay that belonged to him? His eyes had been so cold when he'd stared at her that first glance. She had no doubt that he'd snap her in two if he knew she took his property.

Not that he had any proof. She frowned at the rope lying on the ground a few feet away. Tying knots had never been her talent. There was no telling where the bay had wandered. Still, should that tall, dark Texan suspect her, she'd be double dead if he caught her. He'd probably shoot her on sight and then dance with her just to torture her dead body.

She'd almost be willing to risk it to be near him again. Never in all her life had she touched a man the way she'd touched Travis McMurray.

Rainey pulled off the clothes she'd slept in and slipped into the cool water wearing nothing but skin and the tiny rope necklace that held her only treasure. She washed her hair with the last bit of soap she'd bought in Galveston. It was poorly made and smelled too strongly of lye, but at least she'd die clean.

Frowning, Rainey thought of her mother. The doctor had said she died of a fever, but Rainey always thought it had been more from unhappiness. For as long as she could remember, her mother had looked sad, the kind of bone-deep sadness that made her age twice as fast as most folks.

Rainey closed her eyes and remembered the last time she'd seen her mother. Her father had made Rainey pack her things and leave home to live in the dorm that housed the youngest girls. He told her he was giving her extra responsibility, but she knew it was just extra work.

Her mother had cried when she'd seen her only child leaving, but as always she hadn't dared question her husband. But, as Rainey slipped through the door, her mother had grabbed her hand and shoved a ring into her palm. "It was my mother's. Your father doesn't know I kept it. I want you to have it now."

For the first time in Rainey's life it seemed her mother had stepped from behind her father and shown her love. The action hadn't been to hold Rainey, but to say goodbye.

She touched the tiny bag that held the ring. As long as she had it, there was still a chance, a possibility that she'd find what her mother, who married at fourteen, must have never known. Freedom.

As Rainey dried, her hair haloed around her head in blond curls. She stretched in the slender beam of sun slicing through the trees and felt more like a wild animal running free in nature than a proper schoolteacher escaping a horrible fate.

She was changing day by day, molding into someone her parents would no longer recognize. Rainey smiled. Elisabeth Rainey Adams was coming into her own. She was no longer a product of her parents, but a woman making it alone. She'd taken her middle name—her mother's maiden name—as her own, and now she would build a life to fit the new name. She would make her way and answer to no man. Smiling, she daydreamed of sleeping in a huge bedroom with a fireplace warming the room and a featherbed beside a light left burning all night.

She would have it all . . . if she could come up with a new plan. So far she felt like a frog who kept jumping into muddier water. The bedroom with the fire and light looked farther away every day.

Now she had no choice but to wait for the next wagons going north, and she had no idea how long that would be.

She combed through her short curls. Cutting her hair had been a brilliant idea, along with getting away as fast as possible once she built up enough courage to run. She'd thought she could dress as a boy and slip onto a train just like heroines do in novels. After all, at her height, people often thought her years younger than she was, and her slim body looked more like a boy than a girl anyway. She'd read the schedules carefully every time she took students back and forth to the station and knew them by heart. Finally, just before her wedding, the dorm was clear for the break, her father was busy planning a party he'd forgotten to invite her to, and the safe had been left open for a few minutes while he checked the mail. She recognized her chance.

She took the money, praying he would leave early to prepare for the party. The moment he did, she packed one bag, cut her hair, dressed as a boy, and ran to the train station in time to catch the last train. With luck he wouldn't notice she was gone for a day, maybe two, and she'd be halfway to New Orleans by then.

The disguise worked, too. No one noticed she was a woman. Once she got on the train, she wrapped her cape around her like a blanket and pretended to be asleep. In the days that followed, she traveled south, and then west to New Orleans, living on apples and a box of sweets one of her students had given her for Christmas.

Once in New Orleans, she changed into her only dress and searched for her aunt's house. There had been no letters from Aunt May since a year before her mother died, and when Rainey reached her aunt's last address, she found out why. Her aunt had died six months before her mother. Mrs. Haller, who ran the boardinghouse where her aunt had lived, felt sorry for Rainey and insisted on taking her in for the night. When she learned why Rainey had left home, she helped Rainey book passage from New Orleans to Texas.

"I've known girls like you before," Mrs. Haller admitted, "on the run from bad marriages or bad home life. If you think there's a chance your pa will come after you, change your name, your look, even the color of your hair. Then he can ask all he wants, and no one will remember you passing this way."

"I think he'll come," Rainey admitted. "Not because of me, but because of the money."

Mrs. Haller nodded. "Some folks are like that, I guess. If he finds you, will he hurt you?"

Rainey remembered the bruises on her mother's cheeks. She nodded. This was the first time she'd ever dared cross him because a piece of her had always known that if she did he'd be angry enough to kill her. She'd not only stolen from him, she'd disgraced him, and her father would never forgive that. "He'll kill me," Rainey whispered.

"Then you got to go all the way to the end of the earth, child. Go where he'll never find you, and when you get there don't have nothing to do with the law. He's probably already filed charges on you for taking that money that was rightfully yours."

The memory of Mrs. Haller's words stayed with her.

"The end of the earth," Rainey mumbled as she tugged on the trousers and shirt she'd worn for the train ride. Though she had washed them, they still looked dirty. She'd used them a few times to slip into the settlement on busy days. When several families were milling around, everyone thought she was someone else's kid.

The Ranger might be looking for her, but no one would give a boy a second glance. There were always youths coming and going at the trading post. She'd be able to move about without many questions. She'd lost so much weight in the past few weeks, her disguise hung on her frame.

As she dressed, she studied her small stash of supplies.

In a cotton napkin lay food she'd lifted from the table last night. She took inventory. A half loaf of bread and several meat pies almost as large as her palm. Two apples and a handful of nuts. Not much. Not enough if she had to wait days for the next wagons.

When she'd traveled with the old freighter, she'd felt like she was going somewhere. She was disappearing like Mrs. Haller told her to do. When she reached the trading post, she wasn't sure that she was at the end of the earth, but she felt like she should be able to at least see it from here.

Since it appeared she'd overslept and missed her chance of traveling with the Germans, her only choice was to survive a little longer on her own. And to do that, she needed to know what was going on at the trading post.

She circled around to the back of Elmo's place, staying in the shade as much as possible so that anyone passing wouldn't get a good look at her.

By this time of day there were usually several wagons and horses pulled up to the loading porch. Folks stopping by to talk more than shop. Travelers looked to be pausing for a noon meal in the shade of a tree that grew between the trading post and where the Germans' wagons had been last night. Maybe she'd pick up some news. If it looked busy enough, she might even brave going into the post. She had enough money to buy a pickle, then stand near the back and eat it while she watched folks come and go.

A few men sat in chairs near the corner of the porch where Mr. Anderson kept a jug of whiskey on a barrel. They were regulars. She'd seen them before, though she'd never walked close enough to them that they'd noticed her.

Pulling her hat low, she headed for the corner of the building.

Someone jumped from the porch of the trading post and walked, in long strides, toward his horse. Like a man taking stock of his surroundings, he glanced first at her, then at the men by the barrel. He was almost as tall as Travis McMurray, but his hair was brown and his eyes blue.

Rainey froze, staring from him to the bay tied to his saddle with a lead rope. The same bay she'd borrowed, then lost, last night.

As he untied the reins to his horse, Elmo Anderson yelled at him from inside. "Teagen! Wait a minute."

The man didn't slow down.

"Wait I said!" Mr. Anderson appeared on the porch, his dirty apron flapping in the wind like an old flag, his wrinkled face set in anger. "We'll get men together and be ready to go by morning. There's no need for you to go alone and get yourself killed. All the talk right now is rumors, nothing more."

"Yeah, McMurray," interjected one of the men who'd been at the far corner of the porch. He stood beside the store owner. "You can't go this one alone. Not on something one cowhand said he saw three days ago. He could have been drunk or lying to his boss to explain why he was late." His words already sounded slurred with drink. "Maybe he just rode through here an hour ago and told us his tale to stir things up and get everyone frightened."

"And if he's not lying?" the man near the horses said. "If he did see a raiding party camped between here and the fort just waiting for the next settlers who come by?"

The man Elmo had called Teagen looked like he had a hair trigger on his anger.

The drunk wasn't smart enough to notice. "Those Germans are farmers, they'll be easy pickings. My guess is they would also be little help to your brother against a raiding party, so he's probably already dead. If you wait, we'll help you catch whoever did it."

Teagen swung into the saddle. "My brother's not dead and I've no time to argue. If those wagons are going to be attacked, Travis may need backup now, not tomorrow. He's already got half a day's start on me."

"But we heard there may be twenty or more of them, outlaws and Apache raiding together." Mr. Anderson shook his head. "Twenty to one. Those are tough odds even if Travis is a Ranger."

"Twenty to two." Teagen pulled his horse around so fast he almost knocked Rainey down.

The two powerful animals danced around her, making her feel like a squirrel in a stampede. She finally managed to jump on the porch.

"Sorry, kid!" Teagen yelled.

"How can I help!" she shouted back, thinking of how she'd watched the German children play all week. If they were in trouble, there must be something she could do. "Please, mister, there has to be something I can do."

Teagen shoved his hat back a few inches but looked at Elmo. "You know this kid, Anderson?"

"Yeah," Elmo said, without really looking at Rainey. "He's from one of the homesteads around here, I guess. He's fond of my pickles."

Teagen nodded once as if willing to take a chance. He tossed her the lead rope to the bay. "Can you take this horse back to my place, boy? I'll make faster time without him."

She nodded, grabbing the rope.

"Tell my brother, Tobin McMurray, that I've gone to help Travis. Elmo got word this morning that there are raiders on the north trail. I'll be back as soon as I can."

The powerful man glanced at Anderson. "Saddle the bay for . . ." He looked at Rainey. "Got a name, son?"

"Sam." Rainey said the first name that came to mind.

"See you when I get back, Sam." Teagen kicked his horse and was out of sight before she could think of anything to answer.

The drunk mumbled under his breath about the wild McMurrays and how they were a law unto themselves. "They ain't never taken any help from anyone, and I guess they don't plan to now," he added as he stumbled back to his chair. "Bunch of rattlesnakes, if you ask me. Living out there on their land as if they owned their own piece of the world."

While Rainey watched, Mr. Anderson tossed a fine saddle on the bay and said, "If you can read, boy, I'll give you directions to the bridge. It's almost due west. Once you get there, you're on McMurray land, and my guess is they'll find you fast enough. I swear, they can smell it when a stranger walks on their property."

Elmo pulled a paper from his pocket, and as he scribbled a map, he added, "You tell the youngest McMurray that Travis followed a wagon train north. Tell him Teagen lit out of here when he heard Travis might be in trouble."

The drunk leaned his chair back against the porch railing and added, "I don't know anyone, except the men who work for them, who's ever been on their land. You'd be safer riding off to fight them outlaws and Apache with Teagen, boy."

Rainey swallowed and tried not to look scared. She couldn't believe Teagen had entrusted his valuable horse to her. He must have been so worried about his brother that the horse lost importance. No matter what the drunk said about them, there was honor in Teagen's action.

A few minutes later she realized she had a horse, and a saddle, and no one watching which way she went. She wasn't about to go north, but she could go south and be halfway to Austin before anyone noticed. The freighter had shown her the road when they'd traveled to the trading post.

Once she was in the capital, she could sell the saddle, if necessary. After all, McMurray had almost given it to her. Then she'd have enough money to start a life.

Rainey used one of the words she'd heard a sailor say and made the bay turn west. If she vanished, she'd have two McMurrays on her trail. One was frightening enough.

Mrs. Haller's words drifted through her mind. "Change your name, your look, even the color of your hair, and stay away from the law."

She'd take the horse to their ranch and think up another plan. Her dressing like a boy wouldn't fool anyone for long and Travis was the law. So far she was doing a lousy job of following the rules for staying alive and on the run.

Things had to work out her way some time. They could turn no worse.

CHAPTER 6

∞

TRAVIS RODE A MILE AHEAD OF THE FARMERS' WAGONS AND WATCHED morning spread across the rolling green hills of Texas. A love for this wild land ran in his blood. He never tired of seeing it even on days like today, when he'd rather be home watching the sun rise over Whispering Mountain.

He'd scouted for settlers several times over his ten years with the Rangers. Most of the assignment was boring routine he could have done in his sleep. But his nerves stayed on edge. One percent of the time something went wrong, and, when it did, there was usually little time to think about what to do. So, in the calmness of daily routine, he prepared for trouble and watched.

His hand slid over his Colt, wishing the wagons would move faster. They were halfway between Anderson Trading Post and Patterson's Crossing. If trouble planned to greet them, it would come today when they were too far from civilization to ride for cover in either direction. That's why he'd had the wagons moving at first light and would push them hard all day. He wanted to be out of this no-man's land as quickly as possible.

As he watched the sun rise, his mind drifted back to two nights ago when the strange woman had kissed him. He probably didn't know her real name, but it would be a long time before he forgot the way her lips felt against his. He frowned, remembering how their bodies molded together. For a second, before she pulled away, she'd felt like she was melting into him.

He couldn't help but wonder what that feeling might have been like if they'd had no clothes between them.

Travis decided he must be brainless for dwelling on such a thing. He tried to concentrate on watching for any sign of danger. The woman was probably halfway to Austin by now without giving him a thought. For all he knew, she might kiss a different man each night and he was just one of an endless line.

He'd learned a long time ago that most folks admired him for his skills as a Ranger, but because of his mixed blood, they'd rather not have him too close to their sisters. The first girl he ever looked at had been a blacksmith's daughter. She'd smiled at him one afternoon while he waited on the porch of Anderson's place for his brother to collect Martha's monthly supplies.

The girl had the bluest eyes he'd ever seen and ribbons in her wheat-colored hair. She walked right up to him and told him her name was Madeline Ward in a voice that sounded like music. He remembered how awkward he'd felt trying to talk to her, like she was a whole other kind of creature he'd never encountered.

When her father came out, he'd looked like he wanted to murder Travis and might have tried if Teagen hadn't followed Harley Ward from the trading post. The muscle-bound Ward yelled for Teagen to keep the half-breed away from his daughter or there would be hell to pay. The next thing Travis knew, he was pulling his older brother away from a fight with a man twice his width. The McMurray boys were tall, but lean and not out of their teens. The blacksmith probably could have taken them both in a fistfight.

Travis heard later that the father beat Madeline so badly that she couldn't attend church for a month. He wished he'd stayed and let the blacksmith pound on him for a while. Maybe he would have released all the anger before he turned to his daughter.

Partly out of duty and partly out of dread of running into Madeline again, Travis decided a week later to join the Rangers. By the time he'd turned twenty, he'd honed his skills to the point that no man would call him a half-breed to his face.

Travis turned his horse back to the wagons and swore to

himself for wasting time worrying about something that should have been forgotten long ago. In truth, the blacksmith might have done him a favor. He loved being a Ranger. It was the only kind of life for someone like him . . . a man who belonged nowhere. His brothers and sister would fit into the community, but Travis knew there would always be those who saw him more Indian and less McMurray.

As always, when he thought of Madeline Ward, he silently wished her well, hoping she'd escaped her father's wrath and was living happily somewhere safe. He'd asked about her once, but no one knew where she'd moved.

A thin line of smoke rose to the north, pulling Travis back to full alert. Most wouldn't have noticed the puff that climbed toward passing clouds, but he recognized the sign. Someone a mile away had just put out a small campfire.

A lone buzzard circled in the same area. The bird was probably waiting for the remains of whatever animal had been killed for breakfast, telling Travis that whoever camped to the north was living off the land and not packing hardtack and beans.

Travis turned his horse and headed back to the wagons. The signs could mean nothing, another traveler ahead of them, a brave soul homesteading alone, or they could be warning of an ambush. If so, the outlaws were sloppy, but then, they hadn't expected a Ranger to be riding along with the Germans.

He kicked his horse into full gallop, glancing back only once to notice the smoke had vanished.

"Circle the wagons!" Travis shouted to William Ackland, the leader of the small band of farmers, when he got close to the wagons.

Ackland started to question but reconsidered. He waved with his hand and the wagons began to pull together. The German was smart, he'd learn fast—if he stayed alive long enough.

Travis swung from his horse and helped unhitch the horses and oxen so the wagons could be used to build a corral around the stock. He explained to Ackland as they worked, "We've got company up ahead. It may be nothing, but I'd like to check."

"Other travelers?" the German asked hopefully.

"Maybe," Travis answered. "But no one's passed by the post in several days heading north, or Anderson would have made sure you folks traveled with them." He thought of adding that anyone coming from the north would know better than to be so sloppy with their fire in open country. "If it's Indians, they may want to trade."

The little German looked frightened. "We've heard stories."

Travis closed his eyes and guessed what they'd heard. Stories of killings and captures. He'd heard them, too. Hell, he'd even seen some of them. Horrors committed by different tribes against each other and the invading settlers, horrors repaid in kind. He forced his face to remain stone. He wanted to yell at the man, asking hadn't he known that this was a wild country when he signed on for the journey? But, instead, he said calmly, "All we can do is prepare, Mr. Ackland. By circling we'll protect our stock. If it's traders, we'll meet them outside the circle of the wagons. If it's a war party, we'll have cover. I'll ride out and report back."

William Ackland nodded and straightened. "We will be ready. Every man has a rifle."

Travis wished every man had three, but he only added, "If I come back riding hell-bent for leather, have the guns ready to fire. If it's a raiding party, as soon as they know we're aware of them, they'll attack."

Grabbing his horse, Travis glanced around the circle. Women and children, he thought. Too many women and children. If raiders were coming, the men would be dead before they could reload, and the women and children would think they were in hell. He had to make sure that didn't happen.

He glanced back at Ackland. "Tell everyone to stay put until I return. Even if you hear gunfire, don't go outside the circle."

The German nodded.

Travis jumped over a wagon tongue and rode north. He didn't need to check his weapons, he knew they were ready. His life had depended on it many times.

Just out of sight of the wagons, he turned west. If whoever put out the fire was heading toward the settlers, he didn't plan to be in their path before he got a chance to size them up. He climbed on higher ground and eased his horse silently through tall grass.

The morning was still cool, calm, but he smelled their camp before he saw it. He slipped from his horse and moved closer, invisible in the grass.

Travis swore as he recognized their kind. A raiding party

made up of outlaws—men too mean to live in any civilized world. He also saw two Indians, probably acting as scouts, and a child, tied to a rope like a dog. The kid was on the far side of the camp, and Travis couldn't tell if the child was a boy or girl, only that the youth was so thin he, or she, seemed almost bird-like. The child's movements were slow and stiff as if bones had been broken once and hadn't healed right. Shivering into his coat, Travis noticed the child was almost nude.

Travis had heard reports of a bad gang raiding near the mouth of the Colorado River. It was said they'd steal anything they could use in trade and kill anyone who got in their way. They must have drifted north.

The men moving about the campsite didn't seem in any hurry. They were saddling up, but leaving their gear behind. Preparing to ride hard and fast. Most had double weapons strapped both to their bodies and their mounts. None looked nervous or excited. They apparently saw the Germans as easy pickings. They planned to kill the men and take everything, wagons and all. The women and children would probably be tied up in one of the wagons and sold somewhere in Mexico within a few weeks. Or traded to tribes farther north, where the captives would later be bartered for supplies at one of the forts. By the time the women and children were traded off, they'd be near dead from starvation.

Travis knew he was looking at the rock bottom of humanity. Men who would do anything for money. Men who put no value on life.

They began to saddle up and he should have moved away, but one of the Indians caught his attention. Apache. He didn't usually see them this far south. Though his mind knew evil could have any skin color, his heart didn't like the idea that someone from his mother's tribe could be one of the raiders.

Travis focused. The Apache wasn't young, maybe forty. He favored his left side as he walked and a deep scar crossed his forehead. Travis couldn't help but wonder what had happened in his life that had made him leave his people and band with the outlaws.

He watched closer. The Apache's face was hard, his brown eyes cold, dead inside.

His eyes!

Travis felt the realization like a physical slap. If he were staring at the Apache's eyes, the Apache had spotted him.

Travis didn't bother to crawl away. He stood and ran.

A shot rang out as he reached his horse, another followed. A fiery bullet sliced into his leg like a knife made of lava.

He kicked the horse into full speed and shot out of range. Within seconds he heard the thunder of horses behind him. It crossed his mind to lead the outlaws away from the wagons, but he knew they'd just double back and attack. If they got there before he could, he wouldn't be able to help the Germans fight. There was a good chance some of the men weren't fully armed, for he'd noticed several cleaning guns a moment before he ran. The Germans would have a better chance if he forced the battle now.

Travis hit the circle of wagons at full speed. His horse thundered inside as the Germans pulled the opening closed. They'd spent the hour he'd been gone building a blockade with trunks and boxes. Before he could rein in his horse, the children disappeared into wagons and the men raised their weapons. There was no problem with language; they all seemed to understand the danger.

Pulling his rifle, Travis slid from his horse, surprised when his left leg wouldn't hold his weight. Hopping, he made it to the barrels of water stacked almost shoulder high. A cloud of dust rode directly toward him.

Lifting his weapon, he waited for the outlaws to come into range. With his rifles he could take down two. There would be no time to reload. He'd have to pull his Colts.

He counted twelve men riding toward them, guns ready. The Apache weren't just scouts; they were part of the gang. Travis held his weapon steady. For the first time in his life he'd be firing at his mother's people.

If he were lucky, he'd get four before the band hit the wagons. Then it would be hand-to-hand fighting. The Germans weren't fighters. They'd waste most of their shots, firing too early, taking too much time to aim. He glanced around. In truth none of them looked like they'd stand a chance against a seasoned fighter. Most would be cut down without ever striking a blow.

If he could get four, maybe five before they broke the blockade, he'd fight the rest, he hoped one at a time. He touched his throbbing leg. Pain volted through him in lightning strikes the width of a heartbeat apart. Warm blood filled his hand and he swore.

Travis straightened in resolution. He'd kill as many as he could before he lost too much blood to fight.

Then, almost like a dream, he saw two men running from among the horses. Both were tall, powerful and fully armed. His brothers.

They moved in and set up on either side of him, placing rifles and pistols within easy reach. His younger brother pulled out powder and bullets, lining everything up to reload fast.

There was no time for questions. Travis smiled and raised his weapon. The odds had just gotten a great deal better.

Their first volley took down three outlaws. Teagen passed Travis another rifle and they aimed in unison. The second round of fire took down another man.

"You missed, little brother." Teagen smiled as he tossed his rifle to Tobin for reloading.

Travis grinned. "More likely the fellow has two bullets in him." He raised his last loaded rifle and fired again. Another outlaw tumbled from his horse. Those left circled, unsure what to do.

The McMurray brothers moved back while German men took their place. Travis leaned heavily on Teagen. "If they break through," Travis said between clenched teeth, "take my Colt and knife. I've lost too much blood to be of any help in the fight."

Teagen was already tying a bandanna around Travis's blood-soaked leg. "They won't break through!" he yelled above the gunfire. "The farmers will see to it."

Travis tried to focus. His brother was right. The Germans were holding the outlaws off. They kept up constant firing with three shifts. "You . . ." He couldn't get the words past the pain.

His brothers spread out a bedroll and lay him down. While Tobin cut away the leg of his pants, Teagen said calmly, "We got here right after you left. I decided to help these folks turn their wagons into a fort, then we talked about how to fire against intruders." He shrugged. "I figured you'd bring back more than a dozen."

Travis fought the pain. "There's a kid tied up at the outlaw camp. Tell Ackland to send someone to get him. It's due north."

"I'll do that." Teagen glanced at the Germans. "Doesn't look like there will be enough outlaws left to return to camp."

Tobin stood, his face lined with panic, his hands red. "There's so much blood. I can hardly find the wound. I'll get water." He passed Teagen the soaked bandanna. "Press this where his blood is pumping out."

Teagen pressed the leg wound with one hand and gripped Travis by the shoulder with his other. "Don't worry, Travis. We'll get you home alive."

Travis closed his eyes and sank into the blackness. Relax, he thought. He was safe; his brothers would keep their word.

CHAPTER 7

Rainey watched from the porch of the McMurray bunkhouse as two men on horseback moved toward the main house. They were both tall and lean with a way of handling their mounts more with their legs than the reins, informing Rainey they'd been born to ride. One led a third horse. As they neared, she could tell the extra animal pulled something behind him on long poles that scarred the ground.

Slowly she crossed into the shadow of the barn for a closer view. She'd managed to stay on the ranch the past three days by being invisible most of the time. When she returned the horse she'd tried to steal at the dance, Rainey explained to Tobin Mc-Murray that his brother Teagen had told her to bring the animal to the ranch. Before she could finish explaining, Tobin ran for the nearest horse. She danced around him, repeating all she'd heard at the trading post as he saddled up. A few minutes later the housekeeper tossed him a pouch of supplies when he rode past the house.

"Take charge, Sage!" the brother called Tobin had yelled at a girl on the porch.

Rainey stared at the young woman she'd seen with Travis at the barn dance. She and Sage were around the same height and age except the girl looked far more like a woman in her trousers and shirt than Rainey did. Sage also had an air about her, a pride in the way she stood—like she belonged to this time, this place.

Rainey feared any pride she might have felt had long ago been beaten out of her by life. And she'd learned the hard way that she belonged nowhere.

When Sage's brother had ridden out of sight, she turned her questioning blue gaze to Rainey. "Who are you?" she asked, suspicion in her tone.

"Sam, ma'am." Rainey kept her voice and her hat low. "Mr. McMurray told me to bring the horse and wait for him here."

Sage didn't look like she believed Rainey. "Which Mr. McMurray?"

"The big one," Rainey said before realizing that every man named McMurray she'd met had seemed a mountain. "I think I heard Old Elmo call him Teagen."

From that time on, Sage McMurray seemed to stop worrying about Rainey. "Martha," the girl yelled, "find this kid something to do. I'm going to have my hands full until Teagen and Tobin get back."

Sage grabbed her hat and headed toward the barn, yelling at a few of the hands who'd stopped to see what was happening.

To Rainey's surprise the men followed Sage's order.

An old housekeeper stepped on the porch. She took one long look at Rainey and then met her eyes. Rainey had no doubt that Martha knew her secret, but to her surprise, the housekeeper didn't say a word about it. She assigned Rainey to the bunkhouse cook and said simply, "You can sleep in the corner of the kitchen so you can be the first up to light the cook fires. There's too much snoring in the bunkhouse for the likes of you."

Rainey thanked her and had a feeling her lie would be safe with Martha for a few days. She'd have somewhere to sleep and regular meals.

But now that was about to end because the McMurray men were almost home. At least two of them were. There was no mistaking the riders now.

Rainey strained her eyes trying to make out which of the McMurrays headed toward her. If one was Teagen, he might pay her a few dollars for bringing the horse back to the ranch. Tobin, the one she'd barely met, probably wouldn't remember her. But if Travis returned, he would know her even dressed like a boy. Unless he was a lot dumber than she thought, he'd already figured out she stole the horse the night of the dance. Bad luck and bad news were two companions who'd followed her since the moment she'd stepped on the train to New Orleans.

A shudder passed through her even though the day was warm. She couldn't face Ranger Travis McMurray. She'd seen laughter in his dark eyes, and something more when they'd touched. She didn't want to see the coldness again. No matter how he'd touched her, he'd still do his duty when they met again.

Glancing around, she thought of running. With two men riding toward her, the odds were not good. Running didn't seem much of an option. If she stole a horse from the ranch in daylight, someone was bound to notice and the only way out would be past the two men riding in.

Sage stepped from the shadows and shielded her eyes as she also spotted the riders nearing. "Martha!" Sage yelled. "Martha. Someone's hurt."

The housekeeper hurried onto the porch as the men grew close enough for them all to see that the riderless horse pulled a litter with someone covered in blankets.

Sage broke into a run toward the men, but Martha only straightened like an old soldier hearing a battle call. As she swung around, her gaze caught Rainey hiding in the shadows. "Boy!" she yelled, one eyebrow raised to claim her lie. "Get in here and help me!"

Rainey had no choice but to follow. The housekeeper issued orders in rapid fire as they moved through the house. "We'll need water. Build the fire in the stove and haul in extra buckets." She swung a large pot from beneath a cutting board table. "Fill this half full and get it to boiling as fast as you can. Once it boils, move it to the back of the stove and start another one. After that keep one boiling and one ready until I tell you to stop." She faced Rainey. "If I need your help, can you handle the blood or even the sight of death if it comes to that?"

Rainey nodded. Following orders seemed far better than just standing around panicking. She'd nursed sick students and cleaned up after them. Blood could be no worse. She'd also bathed her mother's body and dressed her for the funeral. If she could do that alone, she felt sure she could do anything Martha asked of her.

While Rainey scrambled to do everything at once, Martha piled medical supplies and cotton for bandages on a tray. Rainey couldn't help but think that this ranch was well stocked and guessed there was no doctor near enough to send for or Martha would have already issued that order as well.

When Rainey ran to the well for water, she saw the horses pull up a few feet from the back door. Teagen and Tobin, covered in a layer of dust, swung down. Tobin grabbed Sage and

held her tightly as she cried while Teagen removed the blankets
from the body lying on the litter.

Rainey dropped an empty bucket as she recognized the
Ranger's black hair.

Travis lay beneath dusty wool, his clothes looking as
though they'd been soaked in blood.

She moved a step closer, unable to resist. Travis was so still,
she didn't know if he was alive or dead. The smell of sweat and
blood blended in the air, thick with death's promise.

Teagen's big hand moved the hair back from his brother's
forehead. "We got him here as fast as we could, but I'm afraid a
fever's already set in. He's burning up one minute and shaking
with chills the next."

Sage shoved tears from her cheek and knelt in the dirt beside her brother. She took his hand in hers. "You're home now,
Travis. Everything is going to be all right."

No one looked like they believed her words.

The brothers lifted Travis and carried him into the house.

Rainey followed.

"Put him in the library. I've already spread a blanket on the
desk," Martha ordered. "The afternoon light is best there for
doing what I have to do. We'll get him patched up and then decide if we take him upstairs, or bring down a bed."

No one argued.

As they moved into the study, Rainey ran to get more water.
She could do nothing for Travis, not with everyone around, but
that didn't mean she couldn't help. With her hat pulled low, she
stayed in the kitchen and kept busy. Each time Martha returned
for water, or more bandages, Rainey had them ready. She even
made coffee and set out mugs before Martha thought to ask.
When Sage appeared with clothes soaked in blood, Rainey
silently took them from her and put them in cold water to soak
on the porch. The day wore on as dread seeped through the
work like a heavy cloud settling to earth.

"How is he?" Rainey whispered to Sage, who stood in the
middle of the room staring at her bloody hands.

"He's bad," she finally managed to answer as tears streaked
her face. "He's real bad."

Rainey took a clean towel and soaked it in warm water, then
wiped the blood off of Sage's hands. "He's alive," she whispered. "That's something."

Sage looked at her as if she didn't understand Rainey's

words. "He's a Ranger with a busted leg right at his hip. Even if he lives, Martha says he'll limp. He may never ride. What kind of Ranger can he be?" She looked at Rainey as if daring her to find the lie in her words. "What can he do?" Sage swallowed hard. "He'll wish he was dead when he finds out how bad it is."

Rainey stared at the floor. Part of her wanted to tell the girl that there was more to life than being a Ranger, but she wasn't sure, for Travis, there could be. "I'm sorry," she finally whispered.

Sage patted Rainey's arm as she wiped her eyes. "You're a good boy. Thanks for your help."

Rainey watched as the youngest McMurray straightened. She'd aged in the past few hours. Sage was less a girl and more a woman now. She would do what had to be done.

Long after dark, Rainey sat alone at the opening to the kitchen. Down the hall, she could hear the family talking about how long it had been since Travis moved. Martha turned in, saying she'd take the first shift of watching him in the morning. Teagen and Tobin looked dead on their feet, but still they waited. Sage, after pacing for hours, dozed in a chair by the door to the study.

Rainey knew she should go. The bunkhouse cook would be yelling at her to help before dawn. But she decided to stay. Just a few more minutes. Just until there was some change in the Ranger.

Travis's brothers finally said good night to Sage and climbed the stairs. They'd slept in the saddle for two nights and were ready to find a bed.

"Call us, Sage, if he wakes," they both said several times.

Sage nodded as she stretched and moved to the ladder-back chair in the small library. "I will," she mumbled. "I'll be fine here. You both get some rest."

An hour later Rainey handed Sage a cup of tea. "If you want"—Rainey forced her voice low—"I could sit with him a spell, and you could rest in that chair." She pointed to where Sage had been sleeping earlier. "I'll let you know if he so much as moves a finger."

Sage hesitated, then nodded and stood, too exhausted to argue. "Promise you'll wake me if he seems in pain?"

"Promise," Rainey answered as she took the girl's place beside the makeshift bed they'd made for Travis on the library desk.

Before Rainey finished her own cup of tea, Sage was asleep just beyond the study door. The girl had spent her day crying until all her energy had flowed away. Rainey had held her own tears back. For her the work kept her going and her thoughts away from how near death Travis must be.

Without taking her attention from Travis, Rainey removed her hat and scratched her scalp. She didn't have to worry about falling asleep; she felt like she had fleas dancing in her hair to keep her fully awake. The damp curls tangled around her fingers as she wished for the hundredth time since she'd arrived that there was somewhere on this ranch where she could take a bath in peace. By pretending to be a boy, she couldn't make use of the main house's back porch every morning like the women did, and she wasn't about to join the men in the bunkhouse kitchen on Saturday night.

Rainey swore at herself for thinking about her own little problems while a man lay near death a foot away. Carefully she reached over and brushed his hair from his forehead. His hair was as straight as hers was curly. His forehead warm, too warm. She wet a rag and pressed it against his skin.

Travis McMurray was one good-looking man. Dark tanned skin, high cheekbones, delicious mouth. He looked nothing like the few pale, thin men she'd known who taught at the school or the weathered and tattooed men onboard the ship between New Orleans and Galveston. Travis was handsome, strong . . . born of the wind and open sky, she thought.

Rainey rolled her eyes. Maybe she should go back to thinking about fleas and bathing. What kind of woman was she to size up a dying man as if he were a hero in one of the novels she loved?

Only months ago she'd been a very proper lady. A teacher at a fine girls' school in Washington, D.C. She'd worn her hair in a tight bun, made sure her English was impeccable, always kept her gloves white. She'd once been afraid of what would happen if she made her father frown.

She smiled, betting he hadn't stopped frowning since he'd yelled for her to come down to work on Monday morning. Knowing him, he had yelled several times before he stormed up the stairs to her room and found her gone.

He'd almost broken her spirit when he decided there was only one thing to do with an old maid daughter who thought she should be paid. Marry her off so she could work the rest of her life for no pay. He was so sure she would follow his order, as she had all her life, that he hadn't even mentioned the match to her before putting the engagement announcement in the paper.

But I surprised him, Rainey thought. I ran from the hell of marrying an older man to the hell of trying to keep from starving in Texas. She looked down at her nails, broken and dirty. "I showed Papa," she mumbled, thinking of how her father had never even noticed how she hated fish—she fought back tears— or how heartbroken she'd been seeing her value in his eyes.

He'd called her plain all her life. Once, she'd heard him tell a neighbor that she would have been the runt of the litter if his wife had seen fit to give him more children. As it was, he was stuck with a mouse. Oh, he'd tried to make her brave. He'd made her live a life to the ticking of a clock. He'd forced her to be alone for hours when he thought her not listening. He'd taken the candle from her room when she'd been three so she'd learn to be brave in the dark. All she'd ever learned was to curl into a ball and wait for dawn.

In the end, after she'd been a good daughter for over twenty years, all he'd seen her as was a liability to be taken care of . . . a problem to be passed along to someone else. A tear drifted down her cheek, but Rainey refused to wipe it away.

A tanned hand crossed into her blurred vision and touched the tear. Rainey looked up into brown eyes. Travis!

"You're awake," she whispered. He looked weak and in pain, but very much alive.

"I knew your hair wasn't red," he answered. "It didn't fit, somehow."

Rainey reached for her hat, realizing she'd given herself away to the one person on the ranch who knew her to be a horse borrower. And he was a Ranger! He'd probably have her hanged at sunrise.

His strong fingers closed around her wrist. Even in his weakened condition, they might as well have been shackles. She'd never be able to break the hold.

Slowly, almost gently, he tugged her down beside him. She curled against his side, careful not to touch his bandaged leg. He released one of her wrists and circled his arm around her, pulling her close. She spread her fingers over his bare chest and felt as she had before for his heart. Somehow the feel of it pounding warmed her as if it were the only music her soul longed to hear.

He covered her hand with his own and took a deep breath. "I knew you were near, even before I opened my eyes."

She knew little of this man so close to her now, yet more surprising than the way she felt about him was how he seemed to feel about her.

"Your name's not Molly, is it?" The corner of his mouth twitched in a smile for only a moment.

She thought of lying, but her tired brain couldn't think fast enough. Panic made her jerk slightly. What good would it serve to tell him her name, he'd never see her again.

His hand moved along her side as though calming her fear. "Don't run," he said as he closed his eyes. "I need to talk to you. I need you close."

"But running is what I do best," she answered, trying to figure out how she could get away from him. Touching him might feel wonderful, but she had to be reasonable. She had to protect herself and follow Mrs. Haller's advice to disappear, to change, to stay away from the law. One mistake might mean her father would find her, and if he did she knew he'd make her wish for death if he didn't kill her outright. "I have to run," she whispered to herself more than Travis.

"I'll find you, I swear. If you disappear again, I'll find you," he mumbled as his fingers loosened and he slipped back into a place where the pain wasn't so overwhelming.

Rainey leaned closer, listening to his breathing. She trailed her fingers along his jaw line and touched her lips one last time to his mouth. As she leaned back, she whispered, "I wish I could stay. I have a feeling you'd be a man worth the knowing, Travis McMurray."

He would live, she decided, but he'd never find her. No matter how strong an attraction she felt toward this man, she couldn't stay and help him. She had to save herself. He had his family. He didn't need her. But she had no one and nothing but a will to survive. He might think of holding her now, but when he healed, he'd remember he was a Ranger and then he'd arrest her.

Brushing her fingers over Travis's hand, she almost wished he'd wake and hold her again. But he needed rest. And she needed to run.

Rainey woke Sage as she passed to the kitchen and collected a few supplies. From there she moved like a midnight breeze into the corral. By the time she saw a light come on up-

stairs, she was riding for the bridge and out of Travis McMurray's life.

As she rode, the tiny bag holding her grandmother's ring
thumped against her throat, reminding her of the one thing she
must never lose again. Freedom.

CHAPTER 8

As the days passed, Travis lost track of time. He drifted with the fever, eating and sleeping in no order. His family talked around him, and about him, as if he were a piece of furniture and couldn't understand. They took care of all his needs even before he thought to ask and whispered encouragement in short prayers near his ear.

From his bed in the study he paid little notice as summer dried the earth with endless days without rain. During the brief spells he thought of something besides the pain, he searched for her, the woman who'd told him that what she did best was run. Her lips had been cool when they'd touched his, but he'd felt her kiss through the pain that first night in the study.

He was a man who never let anyone close, and she'd managed to kiss him twice without ever giving him a chance to kiss her back.

Sometimes he lay with his eyes closed, listening to the conversations around him, listening for her voice . . . a voice he'd recognize whether it was flavored with an accent or not. But it never came. Once, in the middle of the night, he thought he felt her touch him, but when he'd opened his eyes, no one was there.

He tried to put a name with her face, but none fit. He never wanted to forget how her lips had felt on his, but with each day the memory faded. Only at night, when he drifted in and out of sleep, did he remember exactly how she felt against him. In the silence of midnight, when the entire house was still, he almost believed they were dancing again. Her hand in his. Her body brushing against him. Her foot beneath his boot. Her laughter close to his ear.

There was a kind of magic in her laughter, almost as if they shared a secret. Travis had a feeling she'd laughed very little in her life . . . but she'd laughed at his dancing.

He smiled, remembering, he almost whispered that he was sorry for trampling on her toes before realizing he only danced with a dream.

"I'll find you," he'd mumbled, loving the challenge. "I swear, be you fairy or real, I'll find you again."

It took almost two weeks before he felt his mind fully return, another week before he was able to sit up. The bullet had struck at the point between his hip and leg making almost any position uncomfortable. Sage treated him like a child, praising his slight progress from day to day. Teagen and Tobin were back at work, but usually one stopped by at noon for a meal with him. They must have known that between Martha's bullying and Sage's smothering he would have gone mad without them.

Teagen, as always, talked of the ranch, filling Travis in on details that he really didn't care to know. Tobin talked of horses, when he talked. At night they'd all eat in the study around Travis as if all the McMurrays had to be together to overcome his injury.

Travis asked only once about how the bay had gotten back to the ranch. When he realized everyone thought the fairy/woman was a boy, he saw no need for other questions. It didn't surprise him one afternoon when Tobin mentioned that one of the corral horses used by the cowhands was missing. Travis guessed who rode the animal over the bridge.

He slept the days away and spent hours plotting what he'd say to the girl when he found her. Maybe he'd just walk up like they were old friends and question her as if they'd only been apart for a few days. Or maybe he'd demand to know why she'd walked out on him . . . not once, but twice.

He even played with the idea of returning her kiss without saying a word to her. When his mind drifted in that direction, he reminded himself that he was still a Ranger and by right should arrest the woman for a horse thief.

In a strange way the little thief gave him a reason to push himself each day. She'd gotten to him as no other woman ever had.

Three weeks after the shooting, Travis tried to stand. His

right leg was weak from lack of exercise, but the left wouldn't hold any weight. Martha tried to tell him the bone might still heal, but he saw the doubt in her old gray eyes. Without asking Travis, she told one of the men to make him a crutch.

Travis hated even looking at the thing, but finally used it simply because he hated not being mobile more than he despised the crutch.

Once he could move about, he managed to make it to the kitchen for meals and to the porch to watch the weather. But no farther. He'd not step foot away from the house as a cripple. When he left home, it would be as a full man, or not at all.

When he advanced to a cane, he saw it as little progress even though the rest of his family celebrated. With each step he had to pause and regain his balance. Travis was a man who'd never known fear, but now, suddenly, he was afraid of falling. Or worse, not being able to get up once he fell. The few times he had tumbled, the pain had almost knocked him out.

Days shortened and fall settled in with cloudy mornings and evening breezes. The house grew more confining. On cool days Travis paced the porch without a coat, welcoming the discomfort like an old friend. His mood grew darker than any storm that might cross their land and the family left him to his brooding.

One question kept shifting through his mind, polluting any other thought or plan he might have. How does a Ranger do what has to be done if he can't ride? How can he stand and aim a rifle when he has to use one hand to hold a cane?

Finally, when Travis had yelled at everyone in the house, his siblings ganged up on him. When he refused to join them for Sunday lunch, they filled their plates and moved to the study.

Travis frowned as they filed in. He wasn't in the mood for company, and from their expressions his family looked more like a war party than dinner guests. He'd never been a man to drink, but if he could have, he would be passed out on the floor. It might not make anything better to drown his troubles, but at least he could forget them for a few hours.

Martha set a plate in front of him, but Travis wasn't hungry. He didn't want to eat, or read, or talk, or even look out the window. It had taken him some time, but he'd finally reached the bottom of the well. He felt he could sink no lower and still be breathing. All he'd ever loved to do in this life had been taken away from him. Since he'd been eighteen his career had defined him. He'd not only lost being a Ranger, he'd lost himself.

"Something wrong with the pot roast?" Martha asked with a poke to his shoulder.

Travis looked up from his plate. "It's fine," he growled. If she had her way, he'd not only be crippled, but fat. "I thought I'd wait for the jury's verdict before I eat." His brothers and Sage did look like they were about to pronounce sentence on him.

Martha huffed and left the room. She never wanted any part of what she called their "family business."

Travis waited for the door to close. He knew the others had been talking about him behind his back. Hell, he'd been so short-tempered, he wouldn't be surprised if they'd voted to send him to the bunkhouse. Leaning back in the chair, he crossed his arms and waited to hear what they had to say.

His older brother stood first and paced in front of him. "You're alive, Travis." Teagen stated the obvious. "Stop storming around here like you're in hell."

Travis swore and lifted his cane. "I can't seem to get rid of this. What kind of Ranger walks with a cane? I can't even get in a wagon without help, much less set a horse, so don't have me trying to dance about still being alive."

"There are other things you can do," Sage said calmly.

Travis turned his gaze to her. "Like what? There is nothing else I've ever wanted to do."

"You could stay here. Help us run the ranch," Tobin said from his seat on the windowsill.

Travis shook his head. "I can't even climb the stairs. If I stay here I'll be sleeping in the study the rest of my life."

Sage tried again. "You could work at the Ranger office."

Travis closed his eyes, feeling anger build inside him. Anger not at Sage, but at the world. "What would I do there? Watch everyone else go out on assignments? I'd hate that. Besides, what would I be—the cripple who sweeps up and makes the coffee? Or worse, I could limp around and remind every man what might happen to him one day."

"Stop it, Travis." Martha's voice cracked like a whip as she entered the room with a tray of mugs. "You've never been a whiner. Don't start now."

"I'm not whining." Travis answered. "I'm being a realist. I see no future for me. Not here. Not anywhere." He'd always thought that if he ever took a bullet, he'd recover or die, either way he wouldn't have to worry about not being a Ranger.

Sage stood and lifted the mugs off Martha's tray. None of her brothers seemed interested in coffee, but she needed something to do. "You'll find something."

He faced her. "What?"

Sage whirled suddenly. "Climb the mountain, Travis. Find the answer there."

Silence hung in the room, thick as the smell of coffee. All knew the story of how their father had climbed Whispering Mountain and dreamed his future.

Travis lifted his cane. "How can I do that?" He smiled at his sister almost as if she'd said something funny.

To his surprise it was Teagen who answered. "We'll carry you."

"What? Are you mad?"

Teagen met his stare. "Tobin and I can carry you. It's not that much of a climb. We made it several times when we were boys, remember."

Tobin stood and set his cup down. "I'll get one of the narrow bunks from the bunkhouse. We can use it as a litter. Then you'll have something to sit on so you can stand once you're at the summit." Tobin's gaze told Travis that his little brother had seen him trying to stand and knew it was painful for him even from a sitting position. It would be impossible from a bedroll on the ground. "Travis and I could carry you up before dark and leave you to dream."

"I'll get blankets and pack a few supplies," Martha said. "I'll not have you starving up there."

"Wait!" Travis shouted, but only Sage turned to listen. "We need to think about this. I haven't decided to go."

"Yes, you have," she answered. "You've no other option. You said so yourself and waiting will serve no purpose. I don't think I can stand another day of you yelling at everyone. So you're going if I have to help carry you."

Travis set his jaw and didn't say another word. He'd never been a coward and he didn't plan to start being one now. They were right, finding out what his future held, no matter how dark, had to be better than staying here thinking he had none.

What if he dreamed about his death as his father had? What did it matter? He felt like he was already living in hell. And maybe, once he got out of their sight, he might not sleep at all. Then he could say he'd tried it and nothing happened.

As he waited for his brothers to return with a bed and wagon, he smiled for the first time in weeks. He'd be sleeping under the stars tonight. Alone! All this family around had been like living in a beehive. If Tobin wasn't dropping in to tell him a story about one of the horses, Sage was asking his advice, or Teagen thought he had to go over the accounts with him. Even when Travis managed to persuade his brothers and sister into leaving him alone, Martha was always about, cleaning the room or trying to feed him.

"Ready?" Teagen asked as he walked in the study with Travis's coat folded over his arm. His gaze met his brother's. "This was Sage's idea, and I think it's a good one, but if you're against it . . ."

Travis nodded once, knowing, crippled or not, no one could make him sleep on the summit of Whispering Mountain if he didn't want to. "I might as well get it over with. At this point I don't really care what my future holds, just as long as I have one."

Teagen handed him the coat. "We can get to the mountain with a wagon, but we'll have to climb the rest on foot." He hesitated. "We'll have to strap you on the bunk, Travis."

"I know." Travis fought down the pain as he stood and buckled on his gun belt for the first time since he'd been shot. He pulled the leather strip over the Colt to hold the weapons in their holsters. "I'll take a rifle as well."

Teagen nodded as he pulled one from the rack by the door. "We'll build a good fire that should keep any trouble away."

Travis grinned without humor. "Wouldn't want to take a bedroll and keep me company?"

"No," Teagen answered in his no-nonsense way.

"How about you, little brother?" Travis asked as Tobin walked into the room. "Camp out on the summit with me tonight."

His quiet brother shook his head and looked away. But Travis had seen fear flicker in his eyes. A fear they all shared. Once, when they'd been kids, they'd all sworn they'd never climb the mountain to dream. They'd told one another that they didn't believe the legend. They decided it had only been a coincidence that their young father had dreamed his death the night he'd slept on the mountain.

But today Travis saw the truth in them all. If a tiny part of each of them didn't believe in the legend, they wouldn't be climbing the mountain.

Travis insisted on walking to the wagon now loaded down with the bed from the bunkhouse. He swore as Teagen and Tobin lifted him into the back. Neither brother took offense. They seemed to understand.

The day was crisp with fall, the sky clear. Travis wouldn't have cared if it had been pouring rain. Now that he'd set his course, he wouldn't turn back. Because he could see no future for him beyond the walls of his study, he'd lost his fear of what any dream might reveal.

Within an hour they reached the base of the hill everyone called Whispering Mountain. On the north side they could have ridden horses halfway up. On the south the slope was steeper, but faster on foot. No one had said anything about taking Travis up halfway by horseback. He would have had to lie over the saddle like a corpse, and he guessed his brothers had rather walk than see him like that.

As they unloaded the gear, Travis noticed Tobin wore high-topped moccasins strapped almost to his knees, but Teagen had on boots. Travis preferred boots, also, but knew Tobin would be far more sure-footed for the climb.

They lifted Travis out of the wagon and strapped him into the bunk, leaving his arms free. As Tobin pulled the ropes tight across his waist, Travis fought the pain.

Tobin didn't loosen the knot. "You know, if you're going to cuss at us every time we try to help, it'll get mighty boring listening to you all afternoon."

Travis grumbled to himself. He knew they were only trying to help.

"Yeah!" Teagen yelled from the other side of the wagon where he was coiling rope so that it would fit on his shoulder.

Travis wanted to suggest they forget the whole thing, but the fresh air and open sky had already lifted his spirits. "All right. No swearing unless you drop me."

His brothers moved to the bunk. "No promises," Teagen said as he lifted a supply bag on his back and tied the ends across his chest.

"I could hold that." Travis pointed at the bag.

Teagen shook his head. "No chance. If we drop you off a cliff, we'd hate to lose the supper Martha packed as well."

Travis leaned back, trying to relax as they shouldered the bunk and began to climb. The path might be too windy for a horse, but with the bunk braced on their powerful shoulders, they managed it. After an hour rocks made the climbing too steep to carry the bunk. Tobin took the lead and climbed to a spot big enough for the bunk, then he lowered ropes. This part of the climb went easier because Travis could help pull himself up as Teagen moved beside him.

Three hours into the journey they stopped to rest. Teagen took a long drink from one of the canteens and said, "I don't remember this being so steep when we were kids."

Travis laughed, remembering. "We were mountain goats then."

"Going down will be lots faster," Tobin suggested.

Travis nodded. "You two should make it in less then an hour without me."

Tobin frowned. "I just thought of something, Teagen. We've got to come back and get him tomorrow."

Travis had already been thinking it. "How about waiting until Tuesday? If I know Martha, she packed twice what I'll need to eat. I'm armed, and if you pile up enough wood, I could keep a fire going both nights."

It wasn't a question. Travis hadn't asked permission. He needed to be alone. He waited for their argument, daring them to try and make him less of an adult.

Teagen retied the canteen to the bed, showing no sign that he'd even heard the comment.

Tobin shook his head, then grinned. "Sage is going to have a cat. She's been mothering you for weeks."

"If I get in any trouble, I'll fire off a couple of rounds."

Teagen and Tobin lifted the bunk and moved over easy ground for the last bit of the journey to the summit. Travis leaned back and watched the sky, feeling more like a man than he'd felt since he'd been shot.

CHAPTER 9

TRAVIS'S BROTHERS STAYED WITH HIM UNTIL AN HOUR BEFORE SUNSET. They piled up enough wood for a week and checked several times to make sure everything he needed lay nearby. The bunk was close enough to the fire for warmth, and all Travis had to do to reach extra wood was to lean behind him.

For a while after they left, he listened to them moving down the mountain. Then all was silent as he watched the sun set. He stood by the fire for a while, but the uneven ground made it dangerous for him to move around. The muscles in his left leg were unsteady, holding his weight one moment and unable to do so the next.

He sat on the bunk and watched the fire as the sky darkened around him. Sleep was the last thing on his mind. He'd missed the outdoors as if it were his home. He'd forgotten how good a campfire smelled in the dusky air and how alive the growing darkness seemed around him.

Travis felt no fear. The only varmint who'd ever worried him had been human, and he'd see none of those here. The fire would keep any wild animals away unless they were mad, then they usually made plenty of noise, allowing him time to aim. He thought of how strange it was that man seemed the only creature who didn't show signs of madness before inflicting needless pain.

He tossed another log on the fire, enjoying the warm display of colors dancing in the flames. Even if he never dreamed, the trip had been well worth it. He felt his spirit healing.

When the stars came out, Travis lay back on the bunk and stretched his leg straight feeling the pain ease. He watched the shadowy smoke drift to heaven and thought of the green-eyed girl he'd danced with weeks ago.

"Where are you?" he mumbled aloud, knowing no one would hear him. "I said I'd find you, and I will."

He could almost feel her body pressed beside him. He couldn't remember what her kiss had tasted like, but the feel of it came back almost as strong as it had that first night. Her mouth had been soft and her bottom lip had trembled slightly.

Travis grumbled. He should have told her not to be afraid. He was so used to people fearing him, he hadn't even thought of saying something. She'd been such a slip of a girl, barely reaching his shoulder. She probably thought he'd snap her in two. In truth, he wasn't sure he'd know how to be gentle with her if she came into his arms. Maybe he would hold her too tightly if he saw her again?

"When," he corrected. When they embraced he'd remember to be careful. He'd touch her so lightly she'd think his hand no more than a breeze against her skin. He wanted to know every part of her. He'd take the time to memorize the feel of her.

Travis turned away from the fire. He needed to stop thinking about her. He was acting like a half-grown pup, mooning over a girl. He'd held plenty of girls in his arms . . . hundreds. Travis reconsidered. If honest, he'd held very few. A widow crying when he'd had to tell her that her husband died. A few saloon girls who wanted him to feel their wares. A handful of hugs from women who were happy to see a Ranger arrive. Add them all up and he couldn't think of a dozen.

That was it, he thought. How could he have gotten so old with so little time spent around women? Sage didn't count. Neither did Martha.

Maybe the only reason he was thinking about the woman with green eyes was that he had so few others to think about. In his life there had always been a crisis, a Ranger needed somewhere. His job left little time for anything else. Could he be thinking of her now simply because he had the time?

No, that couldn't be right. No woman had ever made him feel the way she did—made him consider things. He'd spent an hour watching the stars and thinking of what he'd say to the fairy woman when he saw her. He might not know much about women, but he knew one thing, she was different.

Since she appeared to be one of the few women in the world who hadn't been too afraid to talk to him, maybe he should go easy on the little horse thief.

Maybe she didn't have good sense. That would explain it.

No, he argued with himself, she had sense enough to steal a horse out from under his nose . . . twice.

He fell asleep without giving any thought to dreaming. The fresh air, the smell of the fire, the stars above made it seem like he was already dreaming. He could forget about his leg and everything he couldn't do and pretend it was just a normal night sleeping in his favorite place.

Open space would always be his home.

Travis slept soundly with no dream disturbing his rest. Finally, an hour before dawn, the cold woke him. The fire was almost out. He tossed logs on it and watched until a spark caught them, then he pulled the blankets around him and fell back asleep.

The dream settled over him silently almost like a forgotten memory drifts into thought. He was sitting by a fireplace burning bright into the shadows of a room lined with books. He'd propped his left leg up on a stool, and the smell of tea brewing spiced the air. He was aware of everything around him, but it was the book in his lap that fascinated him. He noticed light blinking through the curtains, first pale dawn, then full bright, but he didn't stop reading. An excitement pumped through his blood as if he were in the middle of an outlaw capture or about to find a vital clue to solve a mystery. He didn't look up from the book, not even to watch the sun rise.

Travis shifted and opened one eye. The morning sun blinked bright in his face. He rolled to his side and pushed himself to a sitting position. He could never remember sleeping past dawn in his life. Usually at first light he'd already downed a half pot of coffee.

Staring at the campfire, he wished his brothers had lugged up a pot and coffee. The memory of the odor of tea in his dream came back to him so strong he swore he could almost smell it. Tea. He hated tea. One winter when he still lived at the ranch, they ran out of coffee and Martha tried to make them all drink her tea. The stuff tasted like hot water sweetened with elm bark. He promised himself he'd die of thirst before he ever forced down another cup of the stuff.

Travis rummaged in the bag of food and pulled out a biscuit. Even cold, Martha's biscuits were great, soft and fluffy. He washed it down with water and leaned back to think about his dream.

As near as he could tell it told him nothing about the future, except maybe one day he'd find a book that would keep him up all night. That wasn't all that unusual. Often when he was home he would read all night.

The smell of tea could have been coming from the mixture of green wood he'd burned last night, and the fire in his dream sprang from the campfire a few feet from the bunk.

No magic. Nothing special about the dream. No great message. But it did feel good to think about how his father may have slept on this very spot and thought of the future. Travis was more than ten years older than his father had been when he'd climbed the mountain to dream. He realized how young his father must have been when he died. Only two years older than he was now. He remembered his father as being tall and quiet, almost like Tobin. Andrew McMurray hadn't wanted to leave his family when the war with Mexico started. Trouble had seemed a world away from their ranch. But he'd gone because it was his duty. Andrew had lined his three sons up and hugged each before he left. Maybe he didn't believe his dream would come true, but he must have worried about it or he never would have left the letter telling them what to do.

Travis couldn't shake the dark mood that followed him all day. He used his cane and forced himself to walk around, staying clear of the fire. If he fell he could always crawl back to the bunk and pull up, provided he didn't fall into the fire. But he didn't dream he died burning. He didn't even dream he could walk again, or ride, or go back to his life as a Ranger. He dreamed he was reading.

All his life he'd been a man of action, and now, when he supposedly had one look into his future, he dreamed of a study, which shouldn't surprise him, since he'd spent the past few months sleeping in one.

He'd been a fool to even test the legend. It was just that—a legend, nothing more.

By midafternoon the sky grew cloudy, but Travis didn't smell rain. He wondered if his brothers were worried about him. Sage had probably driven them nuts by now, but he knew Teagen and Tobin wouldn't come unless he fired rounds. They would give him the time he'd asked for.

Before dark, he ate the last of Martha's bread and cheese. He checked his guns out of habit, enjoying the weight of the Colt in his hand. It felt familiar, like the night around him and the fire. He could almost believe for a time that he was whole and the world was right once more.

He leaned back waiting to fall asleep. If he were to glimpse the future, it better come tonight. As he drifted, he thought of how the wind always chilled his face when he rode hard.

When the dream came, it was almost the same, only this time he was standing. He held a book in one hand. Big, heavy, black—like a family Bible.

Fear cut off his breathing. His mind kept racing, saying over and over again, "One chance, one chance." He tried to look around the room, needing to see someone. Needing it so badly he felt like he would have given his life for one view.

One chance, he thought. One chance. His heart pounded in his ears as need and longing mixed with fear.

He could hear movement, like rats circling in a dark cellar. He tried to see, but smoke whispered through his dream, blocking his view. He had the sense that time was running out.

Forcing air from his lungs, he took action. In one swift move he opened the Bible, reached for the gun inside, and fired. The blast echoed off the walls as the Bible hit the floor.

Travis woke with a jerk. For a moment he didn't know where he was. The dream seemed so real. The room of smoke, the Bible, the gun in his hand.

He closed his eyes and tried to shove it all from his mind. A nightmare. Nothing more, he told himself.

But the dream still haunted him as his brothers carried him down the mountain a few hours later. He'd told them of his first dream, but couldn't bring himself to mention the second.

He'd forget it, he decided. In the legend a man only gets one dream. The second one didn't count. He'd shove the nightmare from his mind and never think of it again.

Only when he was back in the study and night came, he fought sleep, not wanting to see any part of his vision again. He never wanted to feel as if he were trapped, as if his entire life balanced on one shot from a gun hidden inside a Bible.

Finally peace settled in, and when he dreamed back in his bed at the ranch house, he dreamed of dancing with a woman with green eyes.

CHAPTER 10

∞

Rainey Adams thought long and hard about selling the horse she borrowed from the McMurray ranch, but when life comes down to whether to eat or not, rationalizing is often served as a side dish. She reasoned that if she starved, she'd never be able to pay Travis and his brothers back for the horse, and if she didn't sell the animal, it would have nothing to eat and would die, providing no help at all to anyone.

So, three days after she reached Austin, Rainey walked down the dusty streets to a livery and sold the horse for what she hoped would be enough for a month's room and board and clothes suitable for job hunting.

Rainey had circled the town for two days and found Austin busy and overrun with visitors. Traders, soldiers, families moving in, all crowded the walks and cafés. Most looked as if they'd gone longer than Rainey had without a bath. She moved among them as invisible as the occasional rat she noticed darting from alleyway to alleyway.

Though this town was rough and smelled of campfires and unwashed bodies, it had a liveliness she'd never noticed in Washington. Here the people seemed more real, as if layers had been washed away. There were no family names. No assumed respect given because of a man's dress or even occupation. If Austin were a painting, the artist would have used only primary colors, no subtle shades. The very town seemed so alive she swore she could hear a heartbeat pounding beneath the muddy streets. Building seemed to be going on everywhere with wagon loads of lumber log piling at almost every intersection.

After Rainey collected the money for the horse and saddle, she went to a small mercantile she'd noticed the day before. Though off the main path on a side street, the place had a sunny look, as if whoever owned the store cared about first impressions.

Her choices were few here, but the clothes seemed well made, and, most important to Rainey, the place had few customers. No one would question or notice why a ragged boy bought a dress. She'd thought of changing into her one dress. Though it hadn't been washed properly or mended in weeks, it would pass if she wore her blue cap over it. But she felt somehow safer, more invisible, in the trousers and baggy shirt.

Plus, something about her wanted to be presentable when she did switch into her real clothes. Many books commented that a women not properly careful of her dress must be not only an embarrassment to her family, but mentally impaired. So Rainey walked into the store in her boy's rags thinking she'd change all at once back into a proper lady.

The woman who ran the place had warm honey-colored skin and apple cheeks. Her kind eyes were framed with laugh lines. She seemed a bit overwhelmed as she tried to watch the store and take care of a child just learning to walk. She barely glanced up when Rainey entered.

"Let me know if I can help you!" she yelled from near the back.

"Thanks," Rainey answered. "I'll manage."

Rainey made sure she was the only customer in the store, then bought a rose-colored dress, shoes, and a proper bonnet. At the last minute she added undergarments, a nightgown, and a small handbag. They were the first things she'd bought new for herself in years. At the school, without an allowance or wages, she'd always made do with hand-me-downs from graduating students.

The blue wool cape with its wide hood was an exception. Her mother made it for her last year, telling Rainey that her father had noticed her shivering and ordered the cape made so she wouldn't become ill and neglect her duties. Rainey loved the cape. Though it looked serviceable and nothing special, her mother had put extra care into it. Double stitching on the border and two small hidden pockets inside the lining.

Her one dress and the cape were now packed into her traveling bag she'd left by the mercantile door.

As Rainey paid for her things, the woman smiled. "You'll want to wash before you put these on, dear?"

Rainey panicked for a moment, realizing her disguise hadn't fooled the store owner any more than it had fooled Martha at the ranch.

She glanced up into a face that looked almost too old to have a toddler.

The woman winked. "Don't worry; I thought you were a boy until I saw how you touched the fabric. Boys don't feel cloth the way women do." She laughed, enjoying talking to someone. "My ma used to say that I was a watcher in a world full of the blind. I seem to always see things that are right there for the seeing, but no one else notices."

Rainey didn't know what to say. Though she'd tried not to get close to anyone, she'd been careful when she'd had to, knowing her safety depended on her being able to play a part, and now she'd shown herself up so easily. A mother wrestling a baby hadn't been fooled.

"I'm Pearl Langland," the owner said. "My husband is delivering supplies to a farm halfway to San Antonio today. He won't be back until late. If you like, you could wash up in our room in the back. There's even a hip tub if you want to haul water from the well for a bath. I don't mind at all, dear. It'll be nice to have the company."

"Thank you." Rainey couldn't believe the woman's kindness. "I'd be eternally grateful."

"You're from up north, I'm guessing." Pearl led her to the back room. Their quarters couldn't have been more than ten feet wide and maybe fifteen feet long, but in one room the Langlands had made a home.

Rainey frowned again. She'd worked on erasing any hint of her accent. The lack of food lately must be making her mind turn to mush.

When Pearl glanced back, she laughed a deep laugh that filled the small room. "I told you I was good at guessing. It's a game I've played all my life. Most folks listen for clues, but I watch. It's the little things that give secrets away. You wouldn't believe what I've guessed about some of the people in this town. I swear they wear their lies like ribbons on their chests for anyone who has a mind to look."

"What gave me away?" Rainey asked, feeling safer with this woman than she had since she'd boarded the train just outside of Washington.

Pearl shrugged as if her talent were nothing. "It was the way you counted out the money. Most men, even boys, just hand you a handful and don't bother to count out the amount to the penny. Women usually are more accurate."

Rainey wanted to hear more, but Pearl pulled the tub from the wall behind the back door and suddenly Rainey had other priorities. The mercantile owner also produced a clean bath sheet and tiny samples of soap that peddlers must have left at the store.

"Take your time." Pearl picked up her toddler and moved back toward the store. "I'll be out front if you need anything. I'll stand guard and no one will bother you, I promise."

For a moment Rainey couldn't believe Pearl had left her alone in her home, trusting that she wouldn't steal something. Then Rainey looked around. There was nothing worth the taking—a few old clothes on pegs. Several bowls of peaches on the table. A toy horse with a broken leg.

She relaxed, glad that she'd given Pearl her business and thankful to have a priceless bit of privacy. Rainey followed the woman's advice and did take her time. While the water heated, she laid out her new belongings as if they were priceless and on display. She soaked until the water became cold and scrubbed her hair twice. Then she climbed out, dried off, and put on her new under things. The soft cotton felt wonderful against her skin. It had been weeks since she'd felt truly clean.

Wearing only her undergarments, she washed her old clothes in the bathwater and scrubbed them as best she could. She left them in a bucket while she scrubbed the rags piled in one corner that Pearl must use for the baby. They were smelly and stained. Finally, she cleaned up her mess and slipped into the first new dress she'd worn in years.

After hanging the clothes to dry on the back porch railing, Rainey smiled up into the sun, feeling better than she had in months. Her short hair dried naturally into curls, and for once she couldn't feel fleas.

Pearl tapped on the door just as Rainey pulled her new comb through her hair.

"Mind if I interrupt? Jason's hungry."

"No. Please come in. I'm all dressed." Rainey turned as

Pearl walked in and caught the surprise in the older woman's glance.

"My, my. I knew you were a woman, but I never dreamed there was such a pretty one beneath all that dirt."

Rainey blushed. "Thank you kindly, but I've never been anything but plain. I came to terms with it years ago." She did feel pretty, though, in a dress that had never belonged to anyone else.

She remembered when she'd been little and attended the school her father ran. As the schoolmaster's daughter, she never had fine dresses like all her classmates. Her father thought brown or black would be proper for his daughter. Even if she had talked her parents into allowing her to have a new dress for parties, Rainey was smart enough to realize that she'd still be the last one asked to dance. No young man had ever called on her. Not even one. When she'd moved from student to teacher, it had been a blessing, for she felt like she no longer had to compete with the others. Her dresses became plainer, dulling into grays, until she sometimes felt as though she'd faded into the very walls of the school.

"I like that rose color." Pearl tugged Rainey back from the past.

"Me, too," she said, thinking that as soon as she got a job, she'd buy the green one she'd seen in the store. She swore she'd never wear gray again.

Pearl pulled a meat pie from the cool box. "And you are pretty in it," she said. "But I warn you that a girl thinking herself plain can sometimes make it so." She winked at Rainey. "So take my compliment. Carry it in that imaginary pocket in your mind. Pull it out now and then and remember that at least one person noticed how pretty you are. Couldn't hurt."

Laughing, Rainey promised. She didn't know if she'd be able to think herself pretty, but she could see kindness in this tall woman and she would remember that.

Rainey must have been staring at the pie, for Pearl added, "I'd be honored to have you join me for lunch."

Rainey shook her head without taking her gaze off the pie. "I couldn't. You've been so kind already."

"Of course you can, dear. I hate eating alone, and the pie will be spoiled soon if we don't have it all. While we eat you can tell me how you happened to end up in these parts. I've no one but boring men to talk to most of the time, so it will be nice to have a visit."

Rainey began talking as she helped clear the peaches from the table. Pearl sat down with the baby in her lap and listened. By the time they'd finished the pie, Rainey had told Pearl all about her travels. Even including her short life as a horse borrower. It felt grand to tell the truth to someone. As she ended her tale, Rainey smiled, thinking that for the first time she had something to talk about besides what she'd read in books. She had lived an adventure.

Pearl leaned forward and covered Rainey's hand with hers. "You had good reason to leave home," she said. "Don't ever look back. It may have been the first time you chose a path for yourself, but you done right. You'll be safe here in Austin, I can feel it."

Staring at Pearl's hand, Rainey understood. She hadn't said much about her father, only that he tried to make her marry a man she didn't know, but Pearl had picked up on how it had been for her.

They spent the afternoon talking. Rainey held the baby while Pearl waited on customers and helped her stock while little Jason slept. Rainey insisted on making a peach pie to pay Pearl back in a small way for having eaten half her lunch. The smell of baking peaches filled the kitchen and drifted into the store. Pearl swore she sold three bags of peaches that afternoon because of the smell customers enjoyed while in the store.

"I wish we had the money to hire you," Pearl said as Rainey organized the spices. "The place looks better today than it has since the baby came. I don't seem to be able to do as much out here with him holding on to my skirts, but my Owen never complains." She laughed. "In fact, he told me yesterday that he wouldn't mind if our little Jason had a brother or sister." She blushed.

"I'll find something." Rainey tried to sound hopeful. "But first I'd better be off to find a place to board for the night. In this dress I could never go down to the creek to sleep tonight."

She'd just walked through the door when she noticed a tired man climb from his wagon and walk toward the store. He was stout, and balding, with a mustache that seemed to run from ear to ear. "Pearl!" he yelled as he neared the door. "Are you in there, or did you finally get an ounce of wisdom and leave me?"

Rainey heard Pearl's laughter. She rushed into his arms a moment later, and they hugged wildly, as if it had been days not hours since they'd seen each other. Rainey smiled as she walked away. She'd made a friend today. And to know her new friend was loved made Rainey feel good, even hopeful.

The good hotels all had Full signs swinging above their doors. A few places said they took men travelers only. She'd asked a man at one of the hotel desks, who looked like he might have been in Austin a while, if he knew of a place where respectable young women boarded. He said there was one fine women's boardinghouse and one not so grand on opposite ends of a street called Congress Avenue. One stranger asked if she might be the new schoolmarm, and Rainey realized she looked exactly like what she'd always been, an old maid schoolteacher. She'd been thirteen when students first called her Miss Adams, and she felt she'd aged a decade for each of the eight years she taught.

She didn't want to go back to teaching, but at present it seemed her best option. Jobs for women were few in this part of the world, and respectable jobs were almost nonexistent. She walked the busy streets reading posted notices in windows. A cook needed at one place, but offering less money than a boardinghouse would charge each week. Several notices were posted for house servants, promising room and board and a half-day off each week, but little pay. She found two ads for clerks, but one business wanted a man, and the other position had been filled before Rainey could find the address.

By dusk she decided to drop her bag off at the less expensive boardinghouse and make sure she had a bed for the night.

When she first saw the rooming house, she thought it looked respectable enough, only it was gray, the one color Rainey decided she hated. The old woman who ran the Askew House said she only had one room, a small third-floor space with a tiny window overlooking the alley.

"I'll take it," Rainey said and followed the rail of a woman up the carpeted stairs.

"I'm Mrs. Vivian. My husband and I came here with Mr. Stephen F.," the owner said.

"Stephen F.," Rainey repeated as she followed.

Mrs. Vivian stopped and turned around. "Stephen F. Austin." She raised her chin. "We were part of the original three hundred."

Rainey wasn't about to repeat anything else. Whatever Mrs. Vivian thought she was because she and her husband arrived first seemed to be very important. "Yes, ma'am," Rainey whispered.

"I run a respectable house." The landlord continued up the steps.

"I understand," Rainey said without having a clear idea what the woman meant but guessed if she asked for a list of what wasn't respectable, horse borrowing would probably be on it. So she followed up to the second flight of stairs.

When Mrs. Vivian learned Rainey was looking for work, she insisted on collecting the entire first week's rent in advance. It was twice what Rainey hoped it would be.

"Don't know if you'll find work." The old woman pulled her mouth into a bow of wrinkles. "Most places don't pay women enough to live on." She raised one rather bushy eyebrow. "I guess they figure any proper woman would find a husband to provide for her." The landlord looked her up and down. "You're not very big, but you should have no problem finding a man to marry you if that's what you came to Texas looking for."

"No." The last thing Rainey wanted was Mrs. Vivian trying to match her up with a man. "I came to work and make my own way."

The old woman raised her nose. "It's not easy. Leastwise if you plan to make an honest living, and I don't rent rooms to those of them that don't."

Rainey touched the top button of her blouse, making sure she looked totally respectable. "My parents died of fever on the boat from New Orleans," she lied. "We'd planned to start a girls' school in this area." It was the only thing she knew, she realized, and she'd never be able to start a school without a great deal of money.

Mrs. Vivian shook her head. "I wish you luck, but staying alive seems more important than reading and writing in this part of the world." She appeared to have lost interest in the conversation. "The room comes with supper at seven each night and breakfast the next morning also at seven. If you miss either serving, I don't keep a plate warm for you, and I don't refund any part of your board." She handed Rainey a key, pointed to the door, then headed back down the stairs mumbling rules she'd memorized years ago. "Male visitors are not allowed past the parlor, and there are no exceptions or refunds if I ask you to leave for breaking that rule. You'll use the bathroom on the second floor, but you'll have to carry your own water up from the pump in the kitchen. If you ask Mamie, my slave, to tote or wash clothes for you, I expect you to pay me a quarter a bundle.

The first outhouse in back is for my ladies, but after dark I rec-
ommend you use the chamber pot. My house backs up to Saloon Row. I won't be responsible for your safety after dark."

"I can take care of myself," Rainey said.

The landlord glanced back over her shoulder. "I hope you
carry a loaded pistol with you, 'cause someone your size
wouldn't have a chance against a man."

Rainey nodded, not wanting to admit she carried nothing
for protection.

Mrs. Vivian left without another word. Rainey unlocked the
only door on the third floor and looked around her new home.
The room reminded her of a cabin on a ship. It could not have
been a smaller space and been called a room. But on the bright
side, it was clean. She leaned across the bed and opened the
window. If she looked up, she could see the sky, but if she
looked down, she not only could see but smell the filth of the alley below. Heaven and Hell. She had her own little slice of each.

While unpacking her few belongings, she listened to bits of
conversation drift up from below her window. Two women on
the porch behind the saloon were complaining about their late
night as they smoked thin cigars. Parts of a song reached her
window from the kitchen below, and one man, already drunk
for the evening, talked to himself as he found his way to the
privy.

Rainey looked out and decided the buildings along the alley
must act as a chimney, for sound carried everything said, even
softly, to her window. She smiled, remembering a place in the
great hall of the school. One spot in the entire room where a
person could stand and hear everything said within those walls.
She used to love standing in that spot and feeling a part of all
around her.

She almost laughed. This window could work to her advantage. If she listened closely, she might be able to pick up the accents that seemed to have blended into a way of talking that
sounded slightly different from any dialect she'd ever heard.
Then, alone in her room, she could practice until she sounded
like a Texan. She'd be safest if she blended in here.

A few minutes later, when she walked into the dining room
at exactly seven o'clock, Rainey found the other seven residents
of the house.

A stout woman named Margaret Ann Mathis stood and introduced everyone.

One mother and her grown daughter from Germany spoke little English. Margaret Ann explained that they were waiting for the woman's husband to finish with the fall crop so he would have time to come and get them.

Three sisters had been in Austin two months waiting for their supplies to arrive so that they could open a dress shop. Though they smiled at Rainey, they were boredom in triplicate with dull eyes and hair in different stages of graying.

The last woman was in her late thirties and introduced herself as Mrs. Dottie Davis. She wore widow's black and nibbled at her food while the others were being introduced.

As soon as Margaret Ann finished her duty of introducing everyone, she sat down and, like the others, began eating. Rainey followed suit, noticing the food, though simple, was well prepared. Compared to the meals on the train and the ship, this looked like a feast.

After a few minutes Widow Davis broke the silence by asking if Rainey knew the history of the Askew House.

"No," Rainey answered. This entire town seemed far too new to have much history.

"Then I must tell you," the widow whispered.

"Not the murder of Lora again," Margaret Ann protested. "How can you keep telling that story when we don't know what really happened?"

Widow Davis pouted. "Lora was too young to be traveling alone, if you ask me. That was her first mistake"—she raised one eyebrow and stared at Rainey—"and maybe her last."

The closest of the three sisters agreed, then poked Rainey and added, "About your age. We heard the story from a woman who lived here the night it happened. Miss Lora was young with doe eyes and hair so blond it looked almost silver."

Widow Davis interrupted. "She came to marry a Frenchman back in forty-nine just before half the men in America went crazy over the gold rush. Poor child barely spoke English and didn't know enough to come in out of the rain. They say the man she was to have married still paces in front of the Askew House some nights as if hoping for an answer to exactly what happened to his bride even though it's been years."

Mrs. Vivian was busy serving dinner to her guests and showed no interest in the story. Maybe she'd heard it one too many times.

The widow talked on while she chewed. "A few of us remember like it was yesterday and not five years ago. Mrs. Vivian had just started the place and my Henry was still alive. We had a restaurant down a few blocks." The chubby woman lowered her voice as the landlord left the room. "Seems like I remember Mrs. Vivian's husband and only son went missing down near Galveston a few months before. She had to make a living somehow, so she opened the house to women only."

Rainey smiled at the phrase. "Did they ever come back from missing?"

Everyone who understood English at the table shook their head, but one of the three sisters answered, "Not yet. We heard the husband died. If you talk to Mrs. Vivian, her son is due back any minute. Some say he just went to California and will never came back."

The widow agreed. "My Henry used to say both Miss Vivian's husband and her grown son were meaner than skunks. Never worked at nothing but being no good."

"What happened to the French girl?" Rainey pulled the conversation back on track. "How was she murdered?"

Grace, the oldest of the sisters, answered, "I've asked around and no one seems to know. All they found was her ivory dressing gown, hanging neatly on the back porch."

"Then how do you know she was murdered?" If all the women hadn't looked so pale, she would have thought they were kidding her.

"Blood," the widow said. "There was blood trailing all along one side of the alley. Lots of blood, running from building to building, as if someone had dipped a wide paintbrush in a tub of crimson." Everyone except the two German women leaned closer as she continued. "They said all her things, her clothes, her shoes, even her brush and comb were still in her room looking as if she might have just stepped out for a moment. The only thing missing was a small chest of valuables she'd brought as a wedding gift from her parents."

The talkative sister picked up the story. "They never found so much as a lock of her hair. No one reported seeing or hearing anything that night, but that little bedroom on the third floor has been hard to rent ever since."

"My room," Rainey whispered, but no one seemed to hear.

The widow shook her head at one of the old maid sisters.

"How could she have been killed and no one hear? It gives me chills in the night, it does. People die in this town sometimes, but not like that. Not with their blood marking the alley."

They finished the meal and all said their good nights. Rainey climbed to her room and watched from her window. The three sisters made a trip to the privy together, with two standing guard while one went inside.

For them the alley was an evil place to be feared, but Rainey couldn't help but wonder how much of the story was true. A young woman going out back at night—maybe. Folding up her dressing gown and placing it on the porch while she crossed to the privy—very unlikely. Someone killing her and dragging her bloody body down the alley without anyone seeing or hearing anything—impossible. Judging from the noise, the alley was almost as busy as the street.

She leaned out the window. A drunk was settling down in the corner of the saloon's porch. Two girls with feathers in their hair were smoking and complaining. It was too dark to tell if they were the same two she'd seen earlier. A few houses down, a man with a wagon appeared to be unloading barrels. He swore each time he strained.

At nine she heard the doors to the boardinghouse being locked. Not wanting to waste the one candle, Rainey dressed for bed in her new nightgown and settled in, listening to the voices below. As she drifted into sleep, she thought of Travis McMurray and wondered how he was doing.

Sometimes, when she thought of him, she decided he seemed the only real thing in her make-believe world. He'd been so solid. For the short time she'd been with him, she felt as if she wasn't invisible.

She wished she'd stayed a little longer by his side that last time. His arm had felt so good around her shoulder. She wouldn't have bothered him, but she might have spread her hand out on his chest just to make sure he was breathing normally and not in too much pain.

Her last thought was that she must be crazy to dream of a man she barely knew. But she couldn't help wishing she'd touched him, or that he'd touched her.

At dawn Rainey began her search for employment. After wearing trousers for weeks, she found that her skirt seemed heavy and cumbersome. The heat of the day made her feel like she was melting inside all the layers of material. By midafternoon she decided to abandon her quest early and return to her small room on the third floor of the Askew House.

She found the three sisters in the drawing room planning their store. Mrs. Vivian sat in the office working on her books. When Rainey said hello, the landlord looked surprised that anyone would bother greeting her.

"Mrs. Vivian, I was wondering why you named this place the Askew House?" she asked just to make conversation.

Mrs. Vivian looked pleased. "My maiden name was Askew. When my husband returns, I plan to change the name." The thin woman straightened and held her head high. Loneliness surrounded her, and Rainey guessed that she knew her man would never return but chose to live the lie.

Rainey didn't dare ask how long he'd been gone. The son also seemed a topic no one addressed to Mrs. Vivian.

Once in her room, Rainey cried into her pillow, feeling as if she'd spent a lifetime alone. When she'd been a child her mother had never had time to talk to her, her father never bothered unless he was angry, and the other girls at school considered her beneath their station so never offered friendship. Now it seemed she'd made it all the way to Texas and found only lonely people populated the state.

She tried to see one good thing. At least on the third floor she couldn't hear the clock that chimed in the foyer every hour. If she had her way she'd never live by the sound of a clock again. For as long as she could remember, her father had insisted every detail follow a schedule.

Rainey let her mind drift back to her life before. The order to it all, the boredom. Now she couldn't believe she'd let it go on for so long without saying or doing something, but she'd been afraid of what might happen with change. Boredom had been bearable, change frightening.

Finally, exhausted, she drifted off to sleep and almost missed dinner. She ran down the stairs not realizing until she stepped into the dining room that she'd forgotten her shoes. She slowed, moving in small steps so that no one would notice.

Tonight, since she was no longer new, no one bothered to speak to her. The meal was eaten totally in silence except for the German mother and daughter, who whispered to each other with words no one else understood.

The widow, Dottie Davis, looked tired and Rainey couldn't help but wonder what they all did during the day.

Rainey almost ran back upstairs. Somehow the others made her feel even more alone. She told herself she simply needed sleep. But after dark she couldn't force herself to close the window. She found the conversations she could overhear far too interesting.

Slowly, hour after hour, she began to recognize the voices and give each one a name. This was her world, she reasoned. She was a watcher, a listener, but never a part of all that went on around her. It had been that way all her life. Most of the girls in her class in school never bothered to learn her name. She'd been a shadow as a student and as a teacher. Why should anything be different here?

The sadness of it might have smothered her, but in the corners of her mind Rainey remembered the Ranger who'd danced with her . . . who'd kissed her . . . who'd told her he'd find her.

She'd heard once that somewhere in the world everyone has someone thinking about them. If that were true she could only hope that someone would be Travis McMurray.

CHAPTER 11

Two days later Pearl Langland called on Rainey at nine in the morning.

Rainey had planned to dress and look for a job, but she'd fallen asleep after breakfast. The night's conversations in the alley seemed the only interesting part of her life, so Rainey lost the battle that morning with sleep.

"Wake up." Pearl pounded on her door. "Rainey, if you are in there, open the door, I can't hold little Jason much longer."

Rainey pulled on her cape as a dressing gown and let in her friend. She didn't try to pretend everything was fine. Her mother's words echoed in her ears—that no respectable woman remained in her nightclothes after dawn. She held her head high and waited for Pearl to say something.

The mercantile owner's wife looked at Rainey and nodded once as if she understood. After setting the baby on the floor she said, "I've thought of a way for you to make money enough to at least pay for your room and board. Are you interested?" She hadn't come to lecture, she'd come to help.

Rainey listened even though she wanted to scream that she'd tried every way to get a job. No one wanted to give a woman, a stranger among them, employment. She'd even considered dressing as a boy and working at the stables. That might be her only choice next week when she was asked to leave the Askew House. Mrs. Vivian had made it plain that no credit would be extended.

"My Owen takes in peaches in trade sometimes from the farmers who don't have cash to pay for supplies. He says he'll make you a good deal on the peaches or anything else he takes in."

Rainey remembered the bowls of peaches on Pearl's table. "What would I do with them?"

"Pies," Pearl answered. "He swears that pie you made was the best he'd ever tasted."

"You really think I could make money baking pies?"

"I put a pen to it, and I figure even buying the sugar and flour, you can double your money if you want to turn the fruit into pies. My Owen says there's not a café in town that has desserts worth eating. I'd loan you my kitchen if you'd help me watch Jason while you're cooking. Owen says if I could handle the store two or three days a week, he could sell double if he agrees to make deliveries."

Rainey smiled. "You'd let me use your kitchen?"

"I'd love the company. It would be hard work on your part. Lots of peaches are coming in right now. You'd have to can all you could. Once the season is over, we'll think of something else to cook." Pearl grinned. "I'd set up your books for free samples. Making pies is something I've never got the hang of, but figures, now that's another story. To my way of thinking it would be a good deal for everyone."

Rainey tried not to shout. Hard work, honest work, didn't frighten her. Starvation did. "When do we start?" The cooks at the school had taught her how to bake almost by the time she could walk. If Pearl thought she could make pies and sell them, Rainey would make all the market would bear.

"My Owen is loading the wagon now. He'll wait until I get back to the store before he leaves." She glanced around the tiny room. "You can work all day today making samples to pass out . . . unless you have something else to do."

Rainey didn't answer. There was no need. Pearl knew the truth.

She stood and dressed as fast as she could, then carried Jason for Pearl as they made their way back to the little store. Within an hour Rainey was pealing peaches with Jason playing at her feet.

About one Pearl closed the store for lunch and joined Rainey in the kitchen where five pies were cooling. "I love this smell," she said as she took a bite of the potato soup Rainey had made for lunch. "Where'd you learn to cook?"

"At the school where I taught. Most of the girls had parties and outings on the weekends. My parents were usually busy entertaining prospective students and their parents. I always felt like I was in the way, so I learned to keep busy in the kitchen. The school cooks could bake anything, and over the years they passed some of their talents along to me. After the girls returned from their parties, they'd follow their noses to the table and tell me of their adventures over soup or desserts."

"You were young. Didn't you ever go with them? There must have been so much to see and do in a big city like Washington. You could have met a young man." Pearl knew little of the kind of life Rainey talked about. For her, school had been a one-room house where she'd attended when the crops were in.

Rainey shook her head. "No. It wouldn't have been proper. My father wouldn't have allowed it." She shrugged. "Look what happened at the one dance I did go to. The man I danced with thinks I'm a horse thief."

Pearl raised an eyebrow at Rainey as she rocked her baby in her arms.

"All right." Rainey shrugged. "Maybe I did borrow his horse. But I care about Travis McMurray. I'd take the animal back if I could. I'd give anything to know how he's doing. When I left he'd lost so much blood. He might even be dead for all I know. You should have seen him, Pearl. His dark hair half covering his eyes with him so still he looked more like a statue, than a man."

Pearl gently laid the sleeping Jason in his crib. "You should write your Ranger and tell him you're sorry."

"He'd come after me with a rope."

Pearl laughed. "Well, at least you'll know he's still alive."

"Right, but then I'd be dead. You should have seen his dark eyes. He didn't look like the forgiving sort of fellow, and they say Rangers are the toughest lawmen alive. No matter how gently he touched me while we were dancing, he'd probably use me as target practice if he saw me again."

"Write the man," Pearl repeated, laughing. "Owen could mail it at one of the trading post when he heads down toward San Antonio. Your Ranger will never know where the letter comes from, and you can be honest or lie. He'll never know one way or the other."

"He's not my Ranger," Rainey whispered. "But as long as he can't track the letter, I guess it would be safe enough."

Pearl smiled as if reading Rainey's mind. "If he writes back, you'll no longer have to worry."

Rainey went back to work. She'd developed a pattern to the baking. As soon as two pies were cooked, the next two were ready to go in. When the last two went in the oven, she cleaned up her mess, put on a simple stew for Owen and Pearl's supper, and tidied up the room.

By six she'd given away all her pies to cafés along Congress and Colorado avenues and even brought one home to the Askew House. The owners of the restaurants had seemed pleased at having been given something, but most made no promises to buy any. Mrs. Vivian thanked her for the pie, but informed her that dessert was not usually a part of the evening meal on weekdays.

The other borders each thanked her, and Rainey noticed they all seemed friendlier at dinner. They talked of their favorite recipes for desserts, and Rainey borrowed a few sheets of paper from Widow Davis to write them down. When she finally climbed up to her third-floor room, Rainey thought she'd fall asleep immediately, but the idea of writing Travis stayed in her mind. She told herself if she could know he was alive, she'd be satisfied.

As she lay on her back trying to sleep, the words she'd write drifted through her mind. She couldn't tell him her real name. It wouldn't be proper to mention the kiss, but the dance might be all right to write about. She couldn't talk about the way he felt against her, yet she wondered if he thought about it as much as she did. She'd never thought of herself as soft until she pressed against him, her man of oak.

Her man . . . she smiled. Well . . . he was her man for a moment. She never planned to allow a man in her life, but she could have one to dream about. That seemed harmless enough.

Frustrated, she opened the window and listened to the slices of conversations that drifted up from the alley. Too bad she couldn't tell Travis of all the faceless babble she overheard. The barmaids who complained about everything, the boss who yelled at them and then took their place on the back porch so he could smoke, the drunk who grumbled that the Lord moved the privy every night just to confuse him. Tonight two gamblers were whispering secrets of how to win, then both wished they had enough money for another drink.

Rainey closed her eyes, remembering the Ranger's face and wishing she could hear his voice once more. Maybe she would write him one letter, just to know that he was alive. It could do no harm and it might make her feel better to know that somewhere he was walking around maybe thinking of her once in a while.

The next morning she walked up Congress Avenue collecting her pie plates. Four of the cafés ordered more pies. Since Owen was home to run the store, Pearl helped Rainey set up books and figure out, once she'd paid all expenses, how much money each pie would make. It wasn't much, but Pearl had been right, if Rainey could bake three days a week, she'd be able to pay for her room at Askew House.

On her next baking day the cafés doubled their orders when she delivered, and Rainey began a pattern of baking three days a week.

Owen wandered through the kitchen from time to time. At first he seemed like a stranger among them, but Rainey didn't miss the way he looked at his wife. Pearl was plain, seeming older than her years, but when Owen talked to her, or touched her shoulder, she beamed.

Rainey had never seen a married couple act so and found it fascinating. The few married couples she'd been around hardly talked to each other. Ninety percent of everything her father had said to her mother came in the form of an order. The other ten percent had been complaints. Rainey's father seemed to think that everything wrong had somehow been his wife's fault. He blamed her for their lack of money, their living conditions, and most of all their daughter.

But Owen and Pearl were a world within themselves. They seemed happy to have their little home and both cherished their son. Owen claimed Jason had his mother's beautiful eyes, and Pearl bragged that the boy would be as smart as his father. The couple didn't mean to, but they made Rainey even more aware of how alone she truly was, not only in Texas, but in the world. She'd known from the night she'd left home that there would be no turning back. The ring she carried tucked away in a tiny bag around her neck would be her only inheritance. Her father's second wife would give him the sons he'd always complained of not having, and from the looks of their house the new wife would also spend the money her father had so carefully hidden all Rainey's life.

Unless he found her, she knew she would have to make her

way without family. A good start might be to correct the wrong she'd done to the McMurrays.

That night, alone in her room, she wrote her first letter to Travis.

CHAPTER 12

When Travis returned from the summit of Whispering Mountain, everyone, including Martha, commented on how quiet he seemed. The angry sulking side of him had disappeared, but judging from his family's looks, the replacement was just as hard to watch.

He used his crutches and came to meals without being bullied, but the rest of the time he preferred being alone. If the family gathered around him, Travis found an excuse to move elsewhere. He asked few questions about the ranch and offered little in conversation to anyone, yet when they finally quit trying to make small talk, he felt no sense of relief. Out of boredom he began to read, glancing over every book in the library, but finding those on law the most interesting because he could relate to them. He settled into them as if they were old friends who came to visit. A part of the life he'd known for ten years linked him to every word. Before long law books were scattered all over the study and the porch.

Over the years an old judge in Austin had often handed him a book on law to carry in his saddlebags. Once after Travis had to put his horse down, he'd walked for miles carrying his saddle. He'd cussed the heavy book tucked into the bags, but he hadn't left it behind. There was something fascinating about how justice worked. Old Judge Gates was right about one thing: In order for it to work, it had to work the same for everyone.

While he read, he thought of his dream. The only place he'd ever stood with his hand on the Bible had been in a courtroom.

Did the dream mean that someday he'd drop the justice system and take the law into his own hands?

One rainy Sunday afternoon when he left the study for the solitude of the porch, he heard Sage complain. Teagen hushed her by saying that Travis had a right to his privacy.

As the days turned to winter, he pulled further and further into himself. Often as not, when he sat on the porch staring out across the land, he saw nothing, not even the weather he'd always loved watching. He spent many hours with his nose buried in a book and never read a word. With the loss of his job, he felt no sense of purpose. His wounds healed, but the pain remained, reminding him that he'd never be as strong. Much as he hated it, he needed the cane.

He was surprised one morning when Teagen barged into the study. His older brother still wore his coat, so he hadn't stopped by for an early lunch. Winter air followed him inside. Though Travis was out of bed and wearing trousers, he hadn't bothered to shave in days.

He looked up from the fire he'd been watching. "Morning, brother." He didn't bother to ask what Teagen wanted; he figured he'd find out soon enough.

Teagen grinned as he pulled off his gloves and moved closer to the fire. "I picked up supplies from Elmo's post this morning. He said one of the soldiers passing through on his way delivering supplies north dropped off a bag of mail. I waited around hoping the books we ordered last month arrived. No luck." He pulled out an envelope from the inside pocket of his coat. "But . . . this came for you."

Travis frowned. He didn't reach for the envelope. He'd heard from the Ranger station a few times when he had first been hurt, but they'd long ago gone on to other problems. "Who'd write me?" he said more to himself than anyone.

Teagen, as always, lost what little patience the Lord gave him. "How do I know? Why don't you open the envelope and find out?" He dropped the letter into Travis's lap and walked out.

Travis stared at it for a while, thinking of all the people he knew across the state. He'd seen little evidence that most of them even knew how to write, and the few who could weren't close enough friends to bother. He'd put enough outlaws in jail that one might write just to remind Travis that he still hated him. But outlaws usually yelled their death threats. Writing them seemed too civilized.

The ranch ordered supplies by mail sometimes. They received catalogs from as far away as New York. But letters were very rare.

Travis tapped the letter against the arm of his chair and wondered if Teagen was just outside the door waiting for him to open the letter. His older brother always liked a mystery.

He lifted the weathered and bent dispatch that had probably been stuffed from one mailbag to another. The front had his name in bold letters, then Whispering Mountain Ranch near Anderson Trading Post, northeast of Austin. Whoever wrote knew where they could find him.

Travis guessed few would know Whispering Mountain's location, but most men who hauled supplies north knew of Elmo's place. Trading posts and missions were landmarks along dusty roads holding settlements together.

On the back of the paper he saw the return address as Sam Irish, General Delivery, Eaton Erhard's Store, San Marcos Settlement.

Travis leaned back in his chair to think. He knew no Sam Irish. He hadn't been to Erhard's place at the headwaters of the San Marcos River in over a year. This had to be a mistake. Teagen occasionally got mail from Austin because the land was in his name. Tobin got inquiries about the horses he sold. No one wrote to Travis.

He opened the letter, prepared to be disappointed.

Dear Mr. McMurray,

You may not remember me, but I would like to inquire as to your health and tell you that I will pay for the horse I borrowed from your family as soon as I am able. I feel certain you would have loaned it to me if you had not been far too ill for me to explain why I needed it. True, you might have argued, but I must assume I would have persuaded you if I'd had the time and your attention.

Travis laughed, truly laughed for the first time since he'd been shot.

The fairy was back in his life.

She wrote on, telling him that though he knew Sam wasn't her name, she'd like to correspond as such and to please give his family her warm regards. She told of how worried she was about him and how she'd thought of him often. She also said that she sold the horse out of kindness because if she hadn't, it would have starved. She promised a dollar a week by post until her debt was paid.

The note was signed: *Warmest regards, R.*

He ran his thumb over the initial, guessing she'd just given the first hint as to her real name. The paper was rough, probably the cheapest sold, but the penmanship was flawless. Whoever this fairy woman was, one fact was certain: She'd been educated.

Travis read the letter a dozen times, then folded it into his shirt pocket, got dressed, left his crutches behind, and, using only his cane, went for a walk. When he returned, he asked Martha to pull the entire set of law books from the top shelf, and he began to search for rulings on theft. If Sam Irish made a habit of borrowing other people's belongings, his fairy might need a friend who knew the law.

Three hours later, when Martha brought him a tray for lunch, he was hard at work at the desk. That evening, at dinner, Travis came to the table shaved and smiling. Everyone waited for an explanation, but he only said that he'd found the law books very interesting and entertained them all with things he'd learned.

When Martha served dessert, he took his to the study, claiming he had more reading to do. Sage and his brothers stared at him, but no one said a word.

By midnight Travis had answered her letter and knew the hardest part would be waiting until someone in the family mentioned going to town so he could ask them to post it for him.

San Marcos was only thirty or so miles from Austin. If Elmo sent the mail with someone traveling south, his letter could reach the capital in three or four days. Then allowing two days for it to get on a stage heading south toward San Antonio, the driver might drop the mail at the halfway point—San Marcos—within another day.

Travis tapped his letter against his hand. In a week his fairy woman could be holding his answer in her hands. Smiling, he reasoned that on a fast horse he could be there in half the time and be holding her. The need to do just that surprised him. He'd only been with her for minutes, yet the memory of her in his arms lingered like smoke through his thoughts.

At dawn the next morning he found himself wide awake.

Grabbing his cane, he went for a walk. His thoughts were full of the fairy/woman. Over the weeks he'd sometimes feared he'd dreamed her up, but now he had the letter. He had proof. Now he could think about when he would find her.

Two days later Sage mentioned she needed sewing supplies and, since it was a clear day, thought she'd ride over to Elmo's place.

Travis didn't say a word at the breakfast table, but a half hour later, when Sage walked onto the porch, he handed her the letter.

As he watched his sister ride off, he thought it was a long shot that R. would even get his letter. The mail service was poor on good days and nonexistent in bad weather. The letter would probably sit at Elmo's place a week before someone picked it up. Then it would be days before it got from Austin to San Marcos. From there, it would wait in a general delivery slot with hundreds of letters never claimed. Even if she came in to check, there was a good chance she wouldn't find his letter to her.

By midafternoon he wished he'd never written. What if he frightened her by quoting the law? What if she thought he was angry or worse trying to lure her into a trap? And last . . . worst . . . what if she thought him a fool?

If he'd been able to ride, he would have gone after the letter. He'd have stormed into Elmo's store and demanded the thing back. But he couldn't ride. The letter would go out, and maybe, just maybe, if he were lucky, it would not reach her.

After several hours of sitting on the porch thinking about nothing important, he stormed back inside. Only he missed the rise in the doorframe and stumbled into the hallway, tripped over a rug, and fell headfirst. He spent the rest of that day and the next in bed, silently cussing himself and fanning away Sage and Martha every time they wanted to poke at the egg-sized knot on his forehead.

Martha said he probably had brain damage, but Travis knew it was too late.

He'd already mailed the letter.

CHAPTER 13

✺

Rainey was elbow deep in blueberry pies and laughing with Pearl when Owen returned from his deliveries to the south. He grinned and held a letter up so that she could see it, then slipped it into the pocket of her coat hanging by the door. "You got mail, Miss Rainey, all the way from a place called Whispering Mountain."

"Thanks, Owen." She fought the urge to wash up and run to the letter. But in the three weeks since she'd started making pies, the orders had doubled every week. "I've got a sample of that blackberry pie cooling, if you want to taste it and see if you think it will sell."

"Oh, it will sell, just like they all do." Owen smiled. "You'll fatten me up, but . . . I know you need someone to judge the product, so I'm afraid I have to sacrifice myself."

Rainey giggled. She'd learned to love Owen's sense of humor. He might not be the most handsome man in the world, but he was a hard worker and a good husband and father. She'd seen him work all day loading and unloading wagons, then come in and lift Jason off Pearl's lap so she could rest a while.

"You can read the letter." Pearl laughed. "I'll cut the pie."

Rainey shook her head. "I've waited over two weeks. I can wait a little longer. These pies are promised as soon as they cool."

Pearl sat little Jason on the floor and cut her husband a piece of the still-warm pie. "I was just talking to Rainey, dear. She says she's going to be late cleaning up tonight and would be happy to feed the baby and watch him if you've a mind to take your wife out to eat at one of the hotel restaurants."

Rainey turned back to her pies and grinned. She knew Pearl had been practicing just how to ask Owen to take her out and had managed it with such casualness it surprised Rainey. She glanced over her shoulder to watch this plain couple interact.

He winked and took Pearl's hand in his as she passed him the saucer of pie. "You mean a real evening out with my favorite girl? I've waited a long time for this."

Pearl looked younger. "We could walk along the main street after dinner like we had nothing to do but stroll. We might even walk over to where they're building the governor's mansion and get a few pointers for when we build our house someday."

Owen nodded as if her suggestion made perfect sense.

Rainey had seen how hard they both worked, all day in the store and then stocking well into the night. On days Owen traveled he often left before dawn, and she'd watched Pearl do laundry on the back porch after the baby was asleep. The baby's rags looked ghostlike blowing in the cold night breeze.

Owen glanced at Rainey. "You sure you don't mind staying?"

"I'd love to. After I deliver these pies, I'll come back and feed Jason, then catch up on my books. Take as long as you like."

It was settled, and two hours later, when Rainey returned to the store after finishing all her deliveries, the front was locked up for the night. Owen and Pearl were dressed in clothes Rainey felt sure they hadn't worn since their wedding.

While Owen pulled the wagon around, Pearl whispered, "This is our first time to step out. I was too afraid to at first, this being a strange town and all, then I was pregnant and didn't think it would be right."

"But what about before you married?"

Pearl's cheeks blushed. "I came as part of what Owen calls the Baptist Brides from North Carolina. Our little church had several old maids like myself, so our preacher wrote a preacher he knew here in Austin. The reverend here saw it as a way of increasing his congregation, so he agreed to welcome us. Seven of us want-to-be brides rolled into town in the worst storm you've ever seen and went to Sunday service with our hair wet and our skirts caked in mud. I swear the streets were rivers that morning, and I was asking myself just what had I gotten myself into. I was alone back in North Carolina, no family left, but starving back there looked better than drowning in mud here."

She peeked around to see if Owen was coming, then added, "After the service the preacher asked all single men to stay for coffee. I was almost a head taller than all the other women and most of the men who stayed. The others were spoken for almost immediately, and I was still standing there by the preacher."

Pearl lifted her chin, but Rainey could see in her eyes how frightened she must have been. "I was gripping the Bible my ma gave me the day I was washed-in-the-blood so hard, I broke the spine. I just knew I'd be walking back to the wagon alone and returning to North Carolina with my hope chest and no hope of ever marrying."

Rainey remembered how she'd felt at the fancy dances when all the other girls in their pretty dresses danced and she sat, in her serviceable gray, watching. She wanted to hug Pearl.

The tall woman smiled suddenly. "Owen pushed his way through the crowd of men. He walked right up to me. He was dripping wet and hadn't shaved in days. I found out later he'd ridden all the way from San Antonio in the storm to be there. He held out his hand all right and proper like. He says, 'I'm looking for a wife and would be honored if you'd consider pairing up with me for the rest of this life.' "

"And you said yes?" Rainey found the story unbelievable. "But how did you know?"

"I didn't. I straightened to my full height and looked him straight in the eye. I asked him right there in front of everyone why he was offering for me."

Rainey walked with her to the open door. "What did he say?"

Pearl lowered her voice. "He said because I was a true beauty, and if the others couldn't see it, that was their loss. I told him he was blind as a bat but that I had no objections to marrying a blind man." She blushed and smiled. "He wiggled his eyebrows and made me laugh. Then, like I'd done it all my life, I took his hand."

Rainey watched the tall gangly woman hurry out the door as the wagon pulled around the corner. Pearl was right, Owen must have been blind, but after weeks of knowing Pearl, Rainey also knew that Owen had found the true beauty that night.

He climbed down and helped her in the wagon as if she were a small dainty woman who might need his assistance.

Closing the door, Rainey looked at all she had to do in the next hour. Her pots and pans were stacked in the kitchen, and she had to record all of the sales before she forgot. Tonight, if she was lucky, her books would show a profit. She glanced at the corner shelf Owen had built her. She had twenty pounds of flour and sugar paid for as well as pans enough to make new pies before she had to pick up the used pans. In the past two weeks she'd bought all her supplies in advance and a toy for Jason with money left after she'd paid Mrs. Vivian.

Pearl told her the inventory was finally flush, and she'd see more money coming in from now on.

Her business had been good for Owen as well. She not only was a steady customer, catering her cooking around what fruit he took in trade, but a few people were coming in to buy her pies who normally didn't shop at his store. She made the money on the pies, and he made it on all else they bought. He'd started a shelf on the counter to display the pies. It had glass around all sides so she didn't have to worry about flies.

Halfway through her cleanup little Jason decided he had to be fed. He'd started eating soft foods, but most of it ended up on him or the floor. She couldn't help but laugh as she fed him. She'd never been around a baby, and he must have sensed her fear. For him mealtime was playtime, but she managed to get down half a cup of stew and crackers before he fell asleep still chewing.

She washed his face and hands and put him in the box that was his crib. Rainey didn't allow herself time to dwell on the fact that most women her age had babies of their own to care about. She had work to finish and no time to dream of a life she'd never have. After an hour she lit a small lamp in the corner of the one-room apartment and went to work on her books. The letter in her coat pocket kept calling to her, but she wanted to read it when she could give it all her attention. For now, knowing he'd written was enough pleasure.

She was almost asleep with the pen still in her hand when Pearl and Owen returned. They came in laughing softly and holding hands. Owen offered to walk her home, but Rainey could tell they wanted to be alone, so she grabbed her cape, put on her shoes, and hurried out saying she'd be fine.

Halfway home she reconsidered. She'd walked at dusk before, but never this late, not dressed as a woman. It crossed her mind that if she ever stayed so late again, she would be wise to change into her trousers for the journey home. No one would notice a boy running the streets, but a girl might not be so lucky.

Thank goodness her cape was so dark a blue. She'd blend into the shadows.

Rainey reminded herself she was no longer the frightened girl she'd been. She'd learned how to survive. Pulling the hood of her cape low so no one could see her face, she walked through the darkness. The urge to run pulsed in her veins, but she knew it would only draw attention.

Shoving her left hand into her pocket, she gripped the letter and somehow didn't feel so alone. She forced herself to think of what might be in it. The Ranger had written her back. No matter what the note held, it already proved one fact. He lived.

A drunk bumped into her, shoving her into a man sleeping in a chair. Both men mumbled oaths, but Rainey kept moving, pulling the wool tightly around her. She'd vanished into the shadows before either realized she was a woman.

When she reached the corner, she knew the quickest way to the Askew House was down the alley. Rainey paused. She swore she could feel the ghost of the Frenchwoman who'd disappeared years ago. What had they said—all they found was her dressing gown folded over the back steps and blood running along the side of the building.

Rainey closed her eyes and thought she smelled blood. She darted to the main walk and rushed around to the front of the house.

Mrs. Vivian was just locking up as she entered. "You almost got locked out, girl." Over the weeks the boardinghouse owner's temperament hadn't changed.

"I'm sorry. I worked late." Rainey wondered if the old woman would let her in after hours even if she knocked. She had a feeling the answer would be no. The Widow Davis had whispered once that Mrs. Vivian wore a wig, and after she took it off, she never stepped from her room.

"You missed supper and I don't give refunds."

"I understand." Rainey hurried up the stairs not wanting the bitter woman's mood to touch her tonight. "I'll see you in the morning, Mrs. Vivian."

"Seven sharp," the landlady snapped and turned to her room on the first floor.

Rainey opened her tiny bedroom door surprised to find a meat pie, an apple, and a small glass of milk on her nightstand. She stepped out in the hallway and looked down the stairs. The three old maid sisters smiled and waved, then giggling, disappeared into their room.

Rainey laughed. They must have had great fun sneaking the food out of the dining room. When they opened their dress shop, she'd be their first customer if she had the money.

She pulled off her coat and set the letter across from her on the nightstand. While she ate, she stared at the handwriting and felt, in a strange way, as if she had company for dinner. Then, in the candlelight, she carefully opened Travis McMurray's letter.

He must have never had a penmanship class in his life. His words were done with a bold stroke that looked to be more printing than script.

Dear R.,

I cannot address you as sir, for, unless I had a very vivid dream, you are not a male and I do not know your name. It is not, I'm certain, any more Sam than it was Molly at the dance. So I can only trust that your name, whatever it may be, starts with an R.

Rainey laughed. For a man who didn't talk much in person, he sure chattered across a page.

I am recovering as well as can be expected, though the confines of this study may very likely drive me mad before I heal enough to ride. I hope this letter finds you well and safe. As far as I can see, however, in your current occupation of "horse borrower," you may not rate safety as a factor in your life.

Are you aware you can be hanged for taking a horse?

Rainey frowned. The man as much as called her a thief. She read on.

I thank you for letting me know what happened to the animal. I'm glad to know neither he, nor you, are starving. I spent several hours looking at law books determining your crime, but finally saw it as a moot point since I have no intention of filing charges. In fact, I fear my brain may have suffered along with my leg for I often think of you as more a figment of a dream than real.

We did dance? he wrote, then marked out the line and signed his name.

Rainey fought back tears. She could almost hear him asking the last question and then growing angry with himself for being so foolish. She pulled out a piece of paper and pen. *We danced,* she began and then could think of nothing else to say without saying too much.

How could she feel so close to someone she'd only met a few times? She had read once that there are people in everyone's life that they spend a few hours actually with and the rest of their days remembering. Would Travis be that person to her? Would she spend the years wondering where he was, what he was doing, how he was aging?

After a while she blew out the candle and curled into bed with Travis's letter tucked under her pillow. As she did every night, Rainey opened the window a little to listen to the voices below. Somehow, the stranger's whispers were company.

After a few minutes Whiny and Snort, the two barmaids from across the alley, came out to smoke.

The one Rainey called Whiny complained about how she was turning black-and-blue from being patted on the bottom.

"It's part of the job," Snort said. "I heard a fellow call it a thorn in the job once. Ever' job has a few." Snort snorted a laugh. "You wouldn't do so much hurting if you'd eat enough to keep some fat on that backside. Men like a woman to waddle and wiggle just a little; you bounce like a loose fiddle string."

Whiny sighed. "I've tried eating, but that stuff Haskell sells isn't worth chewing. I got to get me a better way to make money so I can eat something that didn't die of old age."

"Oh, yeah, what do you want to do? Scrub floors over at the hotel? You'd be cleaning up mud and tobacco spit all day. Or maybe you wanta marry some farmer from around here who'll keep you working in the fields all summer so you can starve and freeze all winter while you're cleaning up *his* mud and tobacco spit."

"I almost married me a real man once. He said we was gonna be rich and I would never have to do nothing but keep him happy."

Snort laughed. "Well, what ever happened to that prince?"

"He got caught and sent to prison, but he swears when he gets out, he'll come for me."

"When will that be?"

Whiny whimpered, "Ninety-nine to life."

Snort made a sound, then swore about life being unfair.

"If I was a man," she whined, "I'd be a bank robber. I'd get me a gun and be rich in no time."

"You'd be *dead* in no time," Snort corrected. "The problem with a life lived by the gun is that folks tend to shoot at you from time to time. You think a pat on the bottom hurts, just wait until you get lead in your backside."

"Well, you think of something, then." As always, Whiny's voice deteriorated into a sob. "I don't know how much longer I can do this. The thorns are getting to me. If I'm going to do this the rest of my life, I'm going to drink all I can so maybe death will come a little faster, or at least it'll seem faster."

Rainey rose to her elbow and watched the two shadows below hug.

"I'll think of something, baby," Snort promised. "I swear. My pa said I was the smart one in his litter. I'll come up with the answer."

Rainey heard the back door open and close. She rolled away from the window and touched the letter.

She would never see Travis McMurray again, but it wouldn't hurt to write him one more letter. Maybe she'd tell him about some of the things she heard. She'd call her stories *Tales from the Alley*.

The only thing she missed about her home were the books. Not her mother, never her father, not even her room. Only the books. If she couldn't afford to buy anything to read, maybe she could write some interesting story that would make her Ranger laugh.

Or maybe she'd write the truth about the way she felt about him. After all, he'd never find her. He didn't know her name or her whereabouts.

Smiling, she wished she could see his face when he read her thoughts. Her true thoughts about him.

Rolling over, Rainey lit her candle. Beneath her first words to her Ranger she added, *The thing I remember most about our dance was the warmth of your hand on my back.*

Rainey smiled, wondering if she'd have the nerve to mail this letter. She tucked it under her pillow suddenly thinking of all the things she wished she could say to Travis McMurray.

After pulling the window closed, she snuggled beneath the covers. As always, she rolled into a ball, hugging her legs tightly, and wished for the dawn.

CHAPTER 14

∞

Travis knew it was too soon for the fairy woman to answer him back, but he still stood on the porch and waited for Teagen to return from the trading post. Because today was the first of the month, his brother had driven the wagon in for supplies. The hours since Teagen left passed slowly for Travis, yet he didn't go inside. He could feel himself growing stronger every day now. His leg no longer ached when he stood for more than a few minutes, and he trusted himself to walk around the house without the cane.

At breakfast Teagen had suggested that Travis ride along with him, and in truth, Travis felt he might have been able to. Relying on his cane, he walked to the barn and back several times a day and even managed the wagon for short periods when needed. But Travis wasn't sure he felt ready to let anyone but family see him limp. His left leg was still stiff and sometimes wouldn't hold his weight. The fear that he might fall walking into Elmo's place kept him home.

He rubbed the muscle of his left thigh, wondering if the ache he felt all the way to the bone would ever go away. And if it didn't, was he willing to stay here for the rest of his life? At some point he might have to decide whether to face the world with a limp or hide forever.

"Looking for another letter?" Sage asked as she wrapped a shawl around her shoulders and stepped onto the porch beside him. "You never did say who that letter was from."

She'd hinted before, but never asked so directly. He knew

he'd have to break down and lie. "Ranger, business," he said, then added, "about a horse thief who is north of Austin."

Travis smiled. He hadn't lied and Sage looked like she'd lost interest. Over the weeks he'd talked enough about the law to bore everyone in the house. They'd even suggested he go down to Austin and stand before a judge for questioning. They all believed he knew enough for any judge to make him a lawyer.

He moved the subject away from the letter. "If Teagen doesn't hurry, he'll be caught in the rain." The clouds were so low they seemed to be sitting on the top of Whispering Mountain. He realized he liked stormy days when thunder sounded so loud it shook the ground.

"There he is now." Sage pointed as a wagon pulled out of the fog near the river.

Travis studied his older brother as he neared. Teagen raced the storm as fast as he could with a loaded wagon. "Tell Tobin and Martha. Maybe we can get the supplies in before we all get wet."

Sage didn't move. "What's that in the buckboard? It looks like he's hauling a hog pin."

Travis leaned on the railing. It was too early for the spring hogs or chickens, but his sister was right. Teagen hauled something in a cage big enough to hold a calf.

The rain broke just as he pulled alongside the house. Tobin ran from the barn to help. Martha and Sage stood on the porch taking loads of supplies as Teagen and Tobin raced through the rain to empty the wagon.

Travis leaned on his cane and tried to see what was in the cage. Nothing, as near as he could tell, but a pile of rags at the bottom. The cage was old and roughly made. It made no sense that his brother would bring such a thing home.

"Help me get him off the wagon!" Teagen yelled at Tobin.

As his brothers lowered the cage, Travis saw something move among the rags. A thin hand gripped the bars with tiny, dirty fingers.

Without thought of the downpour, Travis grabbed his cane and limped into the rain. The ground shifted beneath him, but he didn't slow as he slung hair from his eyes and hurried forward.

He reached the wagon as they set the cage in the mud. A frightened face peeked out from beneath the layers of rags.

"Get him out!" Travis shouted as he recognized the child

he'd seen at the outlaws' camp the day he'd been shot. "Unlock the door!" The sight of the boy brought back the horror of the day. Seeing the camp. Knowing the farmers were about to be raided. Realizing he'd be their only hope of surviving.

Teagen pulled his hat off and let rain hit his face. "He came this way, Travis!" he yelled above the storm. "I didn't put him in there. The freighter who brought him to Elmo's said he bolts if you let him out."

Teagen's words were jumbled in the storm.

"Get him out!" Travis shouted as pale blue eyes stared up at him from behind the bars.

"I can't." Teagen sounded as frustrated as Travis. "The Germans you helped didn't know what to do with him, so they shipped him to you. He wouldn't let them touch him without fighting, and they're afraid if they let him out, he'll run out in the wilderness and starve. He's wild as a jackrabbit."

Travis closed his hand around the child's and forced himself to lower his voice. "Get him out." If possible the boy looked more frightened than he had that morning Travis had seen him tied up like a dog at the camp. His cheeks were so hollow, he looked more like a dying old man than a tiny boy. His hands were so thin, they were almost birdlike.

"I can't!" Teagen yelled again. "Somewhere in his journey to get to you, the key's been lost."

The rain washed down in sheets, pelting them all as Teagen continued. "We'll get him up on the porch and pick the lock." When Travis didn't look like he was listening, Teagen added, "If he runs in this rain, we'll never find him."

Before the brothers could lift the cage, Travis let his cane hit the mud. He patted the child's hand once, then moved to the next slat in the cage. With a sudden rage, he pulled, snapping the wooden bar. Before the child could react, Travis snapped another, then another.

In a flash the captive was out of his prison and jumping like a squirrel into Travis's arms.

The Ranger fought to hold him and remain standing. After a moment he realized he need not worry about the child falling, for thin arms had a death grip around his neck.

Tobin picked up the muddy cane and silently offered it to Travis. "Get him inside and warm. I'll take care of the horses." The remains of the cage were forgotten in the mud.

Limping, Travis made it to the porch. Without any thought of taking time to wipe his feet, he crossed into the house and headed straight for the fire in his study. Teagen walked behind him.

Travis's hand spread across the boy's back. He felt the bones of the child's rib cage as the boy shivered with fear and cold.

Carefully Travis lowered to the chair by the fire. He didn't know much about kids, but this one couldn't be more than three or four. The child began to shake violently but didn't make a sound.

Martha leaned over and placed a towel over the boy. "We need to get his clothes off before he catches cold." For once her voice sounded more worried than harsh.

Travis started to pull the boy away from him, but the child had a solid hold around his neck. If Travis pulled any harder, he might break the child's arms.

"I can't," Travis said. "Pull all the layers off you can and we'll keep him warm. He'll dry fast enough this close to the fire." He didn't want to think about how many times the boy must have been wet and cold with no one to worry about him.

Martha tugged at the rags and most of them shredded away. Then she tucked the towel around as best she could and went to get something hot for them all to drink.

Travis leaned his head back and closed his eyes. He could feel the boy's heart pounding as fast as a bird's against his chest. The child cried once, very softly, and turned his face into Travis's shoulder. The boy's cold cheek rested against his throat, and Travis thought he felt warm tears falling.

Muddy, wet, and feeling his leg cramping, Travis made no effort to move. He just held on tight and willed the tiny body to warm.

When he opened his eyes, his two brothers were staring at him. They were also muddy and wet but didn't seem to notice. The child was the center of all their thoughts and worries.

"The kid knows," Tobin whispered. "He knows you're the one who saved him."

"How could he?" Travis shifted slightly.

Tobin shrugged as Teagen tossed him one of the towels Sage brought in. "I don't know, but I can read him as clear as I do a horse. He's half wild and scared to death, but he knows he's safe now."

"He does smell like a horse," Teagen offered as Sage hit him with a towel.

"He knows," Sage interrupted, "because you're his hero. He

must have seen you that day before the battle. If one of the scouts spotted you, maybe the boy did, too. If you ask me, he wasn't trying to run away from anything, he's been trying to find you."

Travis frowned at her logic, but Tobin nodded. "Face it, Big Brother, you're his mother duck. The first thing he saw he could trust, and he's bonded with you for life."

"Surely he belongs somewhere," Travis reasoned.

"Maybe," Teagen offered, "but until we find out where, it looks like he belongs to you."

Travis wasn't sure he could take care of himself, much less a child. He thought of bringing up alternative plans like farming him out to some family who could do a better job than him of watching over the boy, but he didn't say a word. The grip around his neck told him plainly that the boy had no plans of going anywhere.

Tobin pulled off his muddy boots and asked, "What are we going to call him?"

Sage patted the child's damp hair. "Duck," she said.

The brother's nodded. They'd had no experience with names, and Duck sounded as good as any.

It took Travis an hour to get Duck to pull away enough to drink Martha's special warm milk with molasses blended in. Once the boy swallowed his first gulp, Travis had a battle on his hands to keep him from downing all of it at once. Half the cup spilled on him, mixing with the mud and rain already soaking his clothes.

Travis fought down an oath as the others laughed.

When the boy finally fell asleep, Travis lowered him to a thick bear rug on the floor and left him in Sage and Martha's care while he went to the back to clean up. When he returned, the boy was still asleep, but much cleaner and dressed in an old shirt of Sage's long enough to have been a dress on the kid.

Travis covered him and moved to the desk. He'd write the Rangers and ask if anyone knew of a child his age being kidnapped. Now that Duck was clean, Travis could tell he had sandy blond hair. He might have parents looking for him somewhere, but by his thin body and inability to speak, Travis feared he'd been captured very young, and if that was true, the chances were his parents were dead. They wouldn't have let him wander far at such a young age, or permitted him to leave them without a fight.

When Travis finished one letter, he started another to his fairy woman. He had no way of knowing if she ever got the first letter he mailed, but for some strange reason he wanted to write and tell her about Duck. Maybe he thought the woman would understand how the little one felt being all alone, or maybe he wanted to write because he had something to talk about besides his pain and her crime.

An hour later he moved to the chair by the fire and tucked Duck in, then relaxed. Everyone else in the house waited out the storm. He guessed Teagen was in the main room at his work desk. Tobin would be watching the storm from the porch. If it let up, he'd be heading toward the barn to calm the animals. Sage and Martha talked softly as they worked in the kitchen.

Travis felt a tiny hand touch his, then the child was back in his arms. Duck cuddled against his side and went back to sleep without even looking up to see if he were welcome.

Travis frowned. Duck must be one brave little boy, because Travis usually frightened children. Looking over as Martha entered, Travis pointed toward the child with his head and frowned, silently asking what to do.

Martha winked, but didn't offer to help. "That's just the way kids are—they climb on your heart and stay there. Nothing you can do about it." She collected the pile of towels and left without another word.

Travis thought about what the old housekeeper said long after she'd gone. She was right. Duck had climbed on his heart the minute Travis had seen him chained at the camp. He'd fought that day, almost lost his life, but even through the pain he'd worried about the child and hoped later that the Germans had found him still alive. With a shock he realized, if he had to, he'd walk that close to death again for this kid.

Travis cupped the boy's head with his hand. "It's all right, Duck," he whispered. "You're safe."

The boy relaxed in sleep, and Travis knew he'd feel the weight of the kid's heart against his for the rest of his life. What happened the day of the raid didn't matter; it was in the past. What counted was that they lived through it. They might be a little the worse for wear, but they were alive.

"You know, Duck," Travis whispered, "we're both going to be just fine."

Hours later, when the house was asleep, Travis returned to his desk and added a sentence to the letter he'd written about Duck.

In this midnight hour I think of you and how you vanished into the night. I found myself wondering what it would be like to sleep with your heart against mine. I know we are strangers, but you felt so right in my arms. I can't help but wonder if any woman will ever feel that way again.
You remain in my thoughts,
Travis

He sealed the letter before he could change his mind and scratch out the words he'd written. It felt good to be honest with her even if he'd told her something in the letter that he'd probably never had the nerve to say aloud.

CHAPTER 15

Rainey felt her blood chill as she leaned closer to the window so that she heard every word. The air held a frost tonight, and fog settled into the alley so thick she couldn't make out the women below, but she knew their voices. Snort and Whiny, the barmaids she'd listened to every night for over a month.

"We wouldn't have to kill him, would we?" the one Rainey called Whiny whimpered. "I don't know if I could do that. I ain't got a murdering bone in my body."

"It's our only way out of this place, don't you see, baby?" Snort answered, her tone soft as if she were talking to a child. "Otherwise, we'll be here until some customer, who thinks he didn't get his money's worth, kills us or Haskell kicks us out."

"He wouldn't do that," Whiny cried, her voice sounding barely old enough to be that of a woman.

"I seen him do it to a woman the day he hired me," the older woman answered. "I was in the back changing clothes. Haskell waited until she came in to work. He offered to buy her one on the house and she said, 'Just tell me the bad news.' I could hear him pouring her a drink anyway."

"Did you look out?" Whiny interrupted. "Was she old or scarred?"

"Both," Snort admitted. "She was eight, maybe ten, years older than me. Well on her way to being too wrinkled to attract anything but a blind drunk."

Snort made a sound half between a laugh and a cough. "Haskell shoved a drink toward her and told her it would be her last at his place. She cried and complained for a few minutes, but she knew him well enough not to stand within swinging distance. He yelled at her and she left without another word. I heard later she got run over by a stage pulling into town. The driver claimed she stepped right in front of his team."

Whiny whispered, "You think we're close to being offered our last drink?"

"I think I am. You, honey, are still new at the game, but I don't want to think about what'll happen to you when I'm gone. You need someone to look out for you."

"Then we do it," Whiny whispered. "We have to. I might as well take my chances of hanging for murder as die by horses stomping me into the ground. I can't spend my whole life waiting for my man to break out of jail."

"That's the spirit," Snort said. "Look on the bright side. Hanging is better than trampling."

"When do you think we should do it?"

"I heard Haskell tell that Old Lady Vivian across the alley that he expects to have a sum of money coming in soon. He asked her if she'd consider selling her slave." Snort snorted. "You know that Mrs. Vivian don't give up anything. I heard she even goes through the rooms the minute one of her ladies leaves. If they accidentally forget something, they never see it again."

Whiny had no interest in anyone but herself. "So we club Haskell when he's flush."

"That's right, baby, but we don't leave him in any shape to run catch us. We have to . . ."

Someone hollered for them and Rainey didn't catch the last words Snort whispered. Leaning back in her bed, Rainey lay perfectly still, pacing her way back through the barmaids' conversation.

They were going to kill someone, or at least hurt him. A man named Haskell? It sounded like their plan was to rob Haskell when he came into cash. Robbery or murder. Either way, Rainey wasn't sure she wanted to warn him if he was as evil as they talked about him being. He seemed like one of those people no one would miss. But if they were going to kill an innocent person, she had to do something—but what? If she went to the sheriff, it would be her word against the two barmaids. The sheriff might even laugh at her for reporting a conversation she'd heard. She couldn't even tell him what the two women looked like.

She could go down and tell the women, or even Haskell, that she'd heard the robbery plans. Maybe that would stop them. Or maybe the barmaids would simply continue their planning inside so they wouldn't have her listening.

It crossed her mind that the French girl might have overheard the plotting of a crime in the alley just as she had. Maybe she'd gone down to stop it and ended up with her blood painting a streak along the buildings.

If the girls were already thinking of killing one person, a short busybody with big ears might not seem like much to add to the crime. And if they did the killing, then discovered she'd overheard them talking, they'd have to kill her. Even to Rainey, the prospective victim, it seemed only logical.

Rainey decided she had to tell someone. But who? Margaret Ann, the self-appointed leader of the boarders, was packing to leave. Mrs. Vivian wouldn't talk about anything that might hurt the reputation of the house. The German mother and daughter would never understand her. Besides, they were busy packing and getting ready to leave, too. The three boring old maid sisters were already frightened of their shadows. They'd probably start taking shotguns to the privy if they knew. That left Dottie Davis, who loved a story. If Rainey told her, the widow would probably repeat the barmaids' conversation a dozen times within an hour, and by the time she finished she'd have them planning to murder all of Austin. Or the widow might just listen to Rainey and help her, if she were awake. From what Rainey could tell, Dottie Davis ate breakfast every morning, then returned to her room to sleep most of the day away.

Rainey shivered, but didn't close the window. She had to find someone she could trust not to overreact, but who would act if necessary. Travis McMurray. He'd know what to do. He knew the law.

After lighting her only candle, Rainey pulled out a sheet of the cheap paper she'd bought and began to tell Travis every detail she'd overheard. If he got the letter, and if he wrote her back, she'd follow his instructions. She just prayed his answer would come before the barmaids took action.

When she finished the letter, she blew out the candle and curled into bed. The night was too cold to leave the window open, but she didn't want to take the chance of missing something said in the alley.

As the hours passed, all she heard were a few drunken conversations about fate and two cowhands complaining that they lost all their money to a gambler with a gold tooth.

Rainey comforted herself with the fact that the women had talked about killing "him," so they were not planning to do in anyone in the boardinghouse. She fell asleep thinking of Travis and wishing she could dance with him again.

In her dream he held her against him and twirled around a dance floor made of polished oak. His hand felt warm against the small of her back, and he didn't step on her toes once.

Rainey had danced very little in her life, except when her father had made her take lessons with the rest of the girls in her class at school. It had been one of the few times she'd interacted with the rich young ladies. She'd had so much fun she'd almost believed she belonged.

Once she'd been old enough to go to the school parties, none of the young men asked her for a dance. They probably would have been laughed at if they'd asked the schoolmaster's homely daughter. She'd watched from the shadows, practicing the steps in her mind so she'd be ready.

Now she danced only in her dreams.

While she slept, her fingers searched for Travis's letter beneath her pillow. Somehow, holding the letter made her feel less alone.

A drunk stumbling down the alley woke her late in the night. Hungry, she slipped out of her bedroom and tiptoed down the back stairs. She knew Mrs. Vivian didn't want the boarders in the back of the house, but surely she wouldn't mind if Rainey had a small glass of milk and a slice of bread. After all, she'd brought pies several times over the weeks.

Even before she reached the last step, Rainey noticed a warm glow of light coming from the kitchen. She stepped as soundlessly as she could onto the floor, but found Widow Davis and the slave called Mamie staring at her. They were sitting at a small table in the corner, both leaning into their mugs of coffee. A deck of cards cluttered the space between them.

"Evening," the widow whispered. "We didn't expect company, but you're welcome to a cup of coffee."

Dottie Davis straightened, her eyes showing a bit of challenge in them. Everyone knew the law. Folks were not allowed to socialize with slaves. Several people had already been kicked out of Austin for preaching freedom to slaves or for teaching them to read.

Rainey smiled and nodded slightly, hoping Dottie under-stood that she found nothing wrong with the scene she'd walked in on.

Mamie stood, nervous. "The little miss only drinks tea. I'll get you some, child."

Rainey guessed the slave couldn't be much older than she, but maybe she thought she'd lived longer. "I'd love tea," she whispered. "And a bit of bread." Rainey pulled up a stool, mak-ing it plain she had no intention of taking Mamie's chair.

Smiling, Mamie silently accepted the kindness. "With honey spread on it?"

"Yes, please. But I can get it myself."

Mamie shooed her to the table. "I'll get it. You sit."

"Supper didn't agree with you?" Widow Davis asked as she gathered the cards from the table.

Rainey didn't want to complain. The meals for the most part were plain, but good. She couldn't bring herself to say something in front of the cook. "I guess I wasn't hungry."

Mamie set a thick slice of bread and tea before her. "Until now."

Rainey smiled her thank-you. "Until now."

The widow laughed. "Mamie and I were just talking about where Mrs. Vivian found that meat tonight. She claimed it was cow, but I swear it was deer."

Mamie nodded. "When she brought it in, I thought I was looking at leather, not dinner."

Rainey took a bit of the bread. "This is wonderful bread."

"I was teaching Mamie to play poker, but she doesn't take to the game. You wouldn't want to learn, would you?" She passed Rainey the honey.

"Thank you, Mrs. Davis," Rainey answered. "And I'd love to learn."

"Call me Dottie," the widow said. "I've lived here longer than any of the boarders, almost a year. Mamie and I have be-come friends over my late-night snacks. You don't have to worry about her telling, or Mrs. Vivian coming in. After she locks the doors she locks herself in her room and doesn't come out till morning. I think inside her room she can forget that her big house has renters."

"What happened to her husband?" Rainey asked as she sipped her tea.

"I heard once that he left in 'forty-nine. Went out looking

for gold. Though Mrs. Vivian claims he's just on a trip to Galveston. Everyone in Austin who knew him said he had quite a temper and was always looking to make fast money."

The slave nodded. "She acts like he's coming back any day. Ever month she makes me wash and press his clothes 'cause she says he likes them fresh. I swear, they'll all be nothing but rags from the washing if he don't show up soon."

Dottie shook her head. "He's not any more likely to come back than the French girl, if you ask me. She got dead and he got gone."

Mamie agreed.

"Only good thing he ever did was leave Vivian with this house. If he comes back, he'll take it from her," Dottie mumbled. "She better pray he stays gone."

Mamie shrugged. "She won't let me in her bedroom. Hands me the sheets at the door she does. But I've looked in a few times and seen his things setting around like he just left. She moved all her good furniture in there after he left so none of the boarders would wear it out before he gets back." She picked up her coffee cup and moved away. "She'll be the only one not surprised when he comes back."

"I'm sorry to be intruding," Rainey whispered to Dottie.

Dottie smiled. "We're glad of the company. You see, Mamie has to do laundry till late, and I've spent too many nights staying up into the wee hours to go to bed with the chickens. Mamie was just taking a break."

Rainey relaxed. Around the widow she never had to talk much. Dottie had a way of making one of her stories flow into the next. It was almost dawn when she finally climbed back to the third floor. Over several card games she'd made two friends.

She slept through breakfast the next morning and didn't mind a bit. She'd enjoyed her midnight company.

Because she didn't have to bake, she decided to finish Travis's letter. But the tiny room seemed to close in around her. She dressed and walked a block down to one of the cafés where she sold her pies.

The owner gave her a table in the corner, and Rainey wrote her letter, talking to Travis as if he were sitting across the table from her, listening. When she finished, she walked home feeling as if she'd spent the day with him.

At the end of her letter about the barmaids' planned crime, she added:

I enjoyed being with you today. You are as real in my thoughts as those around me. Sometimes I can almost feel your words on my cheek as you stand close to me and whisper as you did at the dance. I wish you had kissed the palm of my hand so I could close my fingers and save it always.

Then she signed the letter as she had before with an *R*.

She knew she was being very bold, but what did it matter? She'd never see her Ranger again.

CHAPTER 16

Travis took his third cup of morning coffee to the porch and studied the weather. Winter played with dried leaves, rushing them from one corner of the yard to another. He smiled, enjoying the crisp air and thinking of the letter he'd received last week. Just a note really and again signed with only R. She'd told him how she hated winter and the cold almost as much as she hated the darkness. She said she made a few friends, then, like it was important, she added that her hair had grown long enough to put up. She wore it with a ribbon around the curls so that it looked much like a bun.

Leaning against the porch railing to relieve the strain on his leg from standing, Travis tried to remember her hair and wondered if it stayed curly when it grew. He laughed. He'd spent so much time the past ten years trying to stay alive, he realized how a woman's hair grew had never crossed his mind. But it did now. Everything about his fairy woman drifted in his thoughts. If he had time today he'd write her that he'd like to feel her hair in his fingers. The moment the thought entered his head, he realized it wasn't a longing, but a need. With each day and each letter he needed to touch her a little more. The letters filled his thoughts, but he craved more. He longed to feel her in his arms. If he wrote how dearly he wanted her, she'd probably never write him again.

Martha clomped onto the porch. "Cold out here," she complained to no one. "My bones are getting so old that the only place I'm comfortable from November to May is by the stove."

Travis straightened. "Problem?" He knew she wouldn't be

out here pestering him unless she needed something. "The boy all right?"

Martha nodded. "Sage has him in the kitchen making cookies. He's eating more than he's making. She's singing to him and he loves it. If I were guessing, I'd say maybe he remembers his mother singing to him."

Travis relaxed, glad the kid they all called Duck wasn't in trouble. He didn't seem to know how to play, but he loved to explore. He could climb like a monkey. Twice they'd had to get the ladder and pull him down from the logs crossing at the ceiling in the main room. The first time Sage gave him a bath, he whimpered like a pup. The second time, he escaped. By the time they got him down, Sage decided to save bathing for another day.

Martha pulled her shawl around her and shivered. "I hate to ask, Travis, but . . ."

"What is it?" He knew she spoke the truth, she did hate to ask for any kind of help. He also knew he'd be doing what she requested if it were in his power.

"Teagen and most of the men are working a downed fence in the north corral," she said.

Travis already knew about the fence. The last storm had done major damage. The chances were slight any horse would leave Whispering Mountain land, but this time of year it was safer to keep the stock corralled. It would take several days of hard work, but the fence had to be rebuilt as fast as possible. They didn't just raise horses, they raised the best in Texas.

Martha continued. "Tobin is in the barn with two mares who were hurt when they got into the rocks during the rain. He said one could foal any day."

Travis also knew every detail of Tobin's problems. One of the mares might have to be put down if Tobin didn't watch the cuts and keep them clean.

"So." He turned to Martha. "You need my help." It appeared he was the only one left.

She nodded. "With Sage making cookies every day, I need supplies. I noticed you've been handling the wagon around the place and wondered if you're up to a run to town."

"I am." Travis knew he'd probably hurt like hell when he got home, but it would be good to see something other than the inside of the place and the view from the porch. His leg had finally grown strong enough to make it the few steps into Elmo's without a cane. "With one stipulation. I go alone."

Martha understood. Sage loved riding along, but if she went, Duck wouldn't stay with Martha, so he'd have to ride along, too. Travis left it up to Martha to talk Sage into staying.

Thirty minutes later, with Martha's list in his pocket, Travis pulled out of the yard and headed to the trading post. The morning was cold, but the sky clear. He'd have no problems with the weather, and with the two rifles beneath his seat, he'd ensured he would be prepared for any trouble that he might encounter. This part of the country had been safe the past few years, but now and again some "down on his luck" cowhand would try a robbery.

Travis made it to Anderson Trading Post with no trouble. Tobin had added a brace on the floor of the wagon a week ago so that Travis could rest his bad leg, and Sage made a pad out of deer hide for the bench. He still needed his cane to walk most of the time, but Travis no longer looked like a cripple.

However, he was thankful no one sat out on Elmo's porch when he pulled up. He could take his time climbing from the wagon, and inside he could buy the boy clothes while Elmo loaded the wagon. With luck, Elmo would go back inside before Travis had to lift himself up on the bench for the ride home.

The plan worked. He climbed back on the seat just as Elmo came out to load the last box.

"Good to see you up and about!" Elmo yelled from the back of the wagon. "How's the boy they brought in from up north last month? You McMurrays letting him out of the cage yet?"

Travis twisted as much as he could on the wagon seat. "He's doing great. The first week he wouldn't get two feet from me without throwing a fit, but Sage bribed him with cookies. Now he's running all over the place. He usually spends his mornings helping Tobin in the barn."

Elmo leaned on the wagon. "He talk?"

"Not a word. I'm not sure he even understands much English. If the boy ever knew it, he's forgotten. We're guessing he's almost four, so he must have been captured before he was two. From what I saw he was treated more like a dog than a boy while he was captured."

"Any hint as to where he might have come from?"

Travis shook his head. "Unless he can say something, we

may never know. He's not dumb, though. Seems to understand a few words in both Spanish and Apache. He likes to sit by the fire, but won't get too near a horse. Tobin's working with him, trying to get him to stand a few feet closer to the corral every day, but he seems happiest when all is silent and he's close to the fire."

Elmo laughed. "He aughta be right at home with you boys. Ain't one of you'll pass more than a few minutes talking."

Travis didn't answer or take offense. He figured Elmo was just stating a fact. The McMurrays had never had much to say to outsiders.

The trading post owner headed back toward the store, then turned. "I almost forgot. You got another letter from that Sam fellow in the San Marcos settlement. Must be a good friend. This is the third or fourth one in less than two months."

Years of watching his every move, every emotion, kept Travis from yelling or reaching too fast for the letter.

Elmo took his time handing it over, examining the envelope as if it held a clue. "What do you reckon a man would have on his mind to write so many letters?"

"I wouldn't know." Travis took the paper and shoved it into his pocket. "You pack the boy clothes?"

Elmo nodded, then waited, as if hoping for more information about the letter.

"I'd better be getting back." Travis circled the wagon and headed toward Whispering Mountain. He didn't look back. He knew the trading post owner was watching from his porch. He also knew he and the letter would be the topic of conversation around the stove for the next few days.

He thought of waiting until he got home to open the letter, but knew there would be the unloading of supplies, and by then Martha would have lunch ready. Sage would follow him around asking questions. She'd want to know who he saw and what he said. Sundays were her only day to go visiting, and she usually didn't leave the ranch without one of the brothers tagging along complaining about a need to get back before they even left the property.

Travis touched the letter in his pocket. He'd written her four times in the past month. Mostly, he talked of the boy. There were so many things he wanted to say. Questions he wanted to ask. Each letter he felt he'd be a little more honest. In a strange way they were getting to know each other on paper.

With a sudden jerk Travis stopped the wagon. He could wait no longer. Glancing around to make sure no one followed, he pulled the letter from his pocket. He told himself not to let the little woman he hardly knew matter to him, but it was too late. She did matter.

Travis swore. She'd lied to him about everything, including her name. She'd stolen two horses out from under his nose and run when he'd told her to stay. He laughed. "Sounds like the perfect woman for me," he mumbled as he opened the letter.

My dear Travis. She used his first name as if they were friends and the *dear* as if she cared for him. Travis smiled. He would do the same if he knew her name. Strange how he knew the feel of her and not her name. He read further.

At first her account of the two women plotting a murder appeared humorous. Women planning to kill some no-good man didn't seem like it would be all that unusual a conversation. He could almost picture his fairy woman curled up in her bed by the window as she listened.

Then it occurred to him that if the barmaids were serious, and R. had overheard them, she might be in real danger. He'd noticed over the years that once a person kills, it's not all that hard to kill again.

He reread the letter. She'd left no hint as to where she was, but he knew it could not be anywhere near San Marcos. Unless the settlement had experienced a grand growing spurt, there was no alley where saloons framed in one side and three-story homes were on the other side.

Travis folded the letter into his pocket and drove home. By the time he reached Whispering Mountain, he'd made up his mind about two things. One, Miss R. could be only one place close enough and big enough to fit her writing . . . Austin. And two, he planned to be on his way there by morning. The least he could do was find her and warn her.

He might not be able to handle a horse yet, but he could manage a wagon. The trip would take longer, but it made more sense than staying at the ranch spending his days worrying about his fairy.

All he had to do was come up with a reason to leave, and it had to be something besides mentioning the letters.

By dawn the next morning his plan had a few problems. He'd explained that night at supper that since he'd read all the books on law for the state and he'd been enforcing those laws for ten years, he planned to take one of the wagons to Austin and sit for the state bar exam. All he needed was for a district judge to call together a panel of practicing lawyers who would ask him questions. If he made it past the panel, he could serve a short internship and then begin his own practice. Judge Gates had been trying to talk him into doing just that for several years. Maybe it was time he listened to the old man. Or, Travis thought, used the bar as an excuse to go to Austin.

While his leg healed, he had to do something, and Travis explained that becoming a lawyer would be as good a way to spend his time as sitting on the porch watching the weather.

No one in the family thought his plan sound. They also didn't hesitate to say so. Sage thought he should wait until spring when the weather would be better. Tobin said if he waited a month then the two horses he had to deliver would be ready and he'd go along. Teagen saw no need for a lawyer in the family. In fact, he pointed out that most of the lawyers he met spent more time trying to break laws rather than uphold them. Travis would only be putting himself in rotten company by passing the bar.

When his siblings saw they were getting nowhere, Sage switched strategies. "If you think you have to go now, and you're taking a wagon anyway, I might as well go along, too. All of you have said I could go to Austin as soon as I grew up."

Teagen stood up from the table and tossed his napkin down. "Whatever for?"

Sage jumped and faced him as if they were the same height. "Because I'm tired of waiting around for the perfect man to ac-cidentally fall onto the property. I'm almost nineteen and haven't even met a man I'd consider marrying, much less one who likes me. Maybe if I go to the capital, I'll bump into one."

All three brothers ganged up on her. They shouted all the obvious holes in her plan. She was too young. Austin was a wild town with almost a thousand people. It could snow, or rain, and they'd be stuck by the side of the road. They could be robbed.

Sage faced them all. "I'm not too young. I'm almost an old maid. Teagen, you and Tobin can't leave the ranch right now, but I could ride along with Travis. If there's trouble, I could help." She dared one of them to argue.

Travis opened his mouth, but Duck caught his eye before he could say anything. The kid had been playing with a ball on the stairs, but he now stood facing Travis with a look of terror in his eyes.

Before Travis could say a word, the boy ran toward him. He'd somehow sensed Travis was talking about leaving.

As he did several times a day, Travis leaned and lifted Duck up. Though they'd fed him for weeks, he still weighed nothing. It had taken over a week for the boy to let Travis out of his sight, and now he held to Travis as he had that first night. His little bony arms circled Travis's neck as if they didn't plan to ever let go.

Tobin moved closer and whispered, "He's afraid you're going to leave him behind."

The argument about Sage going to Austin was forgotten as they all realized their yelling had frightened Duck.

"He'll be all right here at the ranch." Travis said the words, but he didn't believe them any more than the others did.

"He'll run," Tobin warned. "I can feel it. If you're not here, he'll run just like he did when the Germans tried to keep him."

Travis didn't have to close his eyes to see the cage. The memory of Duck's small hand gripping the bars would forever stain his mind. He wouldn't . . . couldn't . . . allow anyone to chain the boy up, not ever again. He wanted to go help his fairy woman. He wanted to make sure she was safe. But not if it meant seeing Duck locked up somewhere on the ranch. It might be weeks before he could get back, and the progress they'd made with the boy would be forgotten by then.

Teagen stepped closer and cupped the back of the boy's head. "He might be all right for a few hours without you. We managed to keep him busy while you drove into town, but come nightfall he'd start looking for you."

Sage agreed. "He's happy with me most of the time, but now and then I notice him looking around, nervous and on edge until he sees you."

Travis knew they were right. Duck was content to play around the house, even watching Sage and Martha cook while Travis read in the study. But every night he stayed close, refusing to go to his bed in front of the fireplace until Travis lowered himself into his bunk in the study. Only then would Duck climb beneath his covers and close his eyes.

He awoke to the sound of Travis reaching for his cane every morning. He might stay with Sage in the house for a while, but all of them had noticed the way he watched the door whenever Travis went for a walk.

"In time, he'll trust all of us," Tobin added. "But right now you're his mother duck. You're the one he needs to be near to feel safe."

Duck loosened his grip and raised his head. He stared at Travis as if trying to understand what was going on. The boy was smart. Picking up a hundred things a day it seemed. Travis knew he couldn't understand English, yet he'd sense something was happening and he'd been frightened. How scared would he be if he thought Travis abandoned him.

"If I go with you," Sage said, "I could watch out for him while you take the test if that's what you want. And we could check with all the authorities about finding his family. I'd also ride shotgun during the trip. I'm as good a shot as Tobin and a much better campfire cook."

Travis didn't like the idea of taking Sage off the ranch, but they couldn't make her a prisoner here any more than they could cage Duck. When he'd been her age, nothing would have stopped him from leaving. He glanced at his brothers. Though Teagen still frowned, Tobin nodded slightly in understanding.

"If you go," Travis began, "we leave before dawn and make the Wilson Trading Post by nightfall. They have a second-floor loft for their daughters. You can bunk in with them the first night."

"And the second?"

"By the afternoon of the second day we'll be into country where farmhouses are closer together. Any farmer will let us sleep in the barn. By the third night we'll be at Fort Croghan. From then on we can follow the stage trail into Austin. If we have to stop, we'll find lodging at the stations, but I can't promise anything clean."

Sage whirled around. "It doesn't matter."

Tobin laughed. "You say that now, but wait until you feel the bite of a bedbug or a roach crawling across the bridge of your nose while you sleep."

Sage made a face. "I don't care. I have to pack. I'll take a small bag for the trip and Father's old trunk to hold all the clothes I'll buy in Austin. Imagine, I'll get to eat at a café and walk Congress Avenue and shop in stores that carry more than three dresses. I might even find one of those ladies' shops where they make a dress just for me."

As she disappeared, Tobin leaned closer to Travis. "You're taking a monster, you know that, don't you? She's had her money building up from the profits of the ranch for the past eighteen years. She can buy half of Austin if she takes a mind to."

Travis nodded. "I have a feeling we'd never make it back on horseback. Lucky we'll have the wagon."

"Are you sure you're up to the journey?"

Travis wasn't about to let his brothers see his doubt. "It's time, and, much as I hate to admit it, Sage will be a lot of help. This leg will never get any stronger unless I start testing it."

The next morning with enough food to last a week and several buffalo hides to sleep on if needed, Sage, Travis, and the boy left for Austin. Teagen and Tobin rode with them as far as the bridge.

Travis knew he should be thinking about the half-baked plan he'd invented as a reason for the journey, but finding his fairy woman was all that weighed on his thoughts. He'd read the last lines of her letter so many times he could say the words with his eyes closed.

Once he was in Austin, he could always say he couldn't find a judge willing to test him or let him intern. Or he could even say he'd changed his mind. Or, maybe, he might try for it. At worst, being a lawyer might help him be a better Ranger once he healed enough to ride.

He smiled. It didn't matter what happened as long as he found his fairy. The need to see her had developed into an ache in the center of his chest. He told himself that if he saw her, faced her once more, he'd stop thinking about her. He'd discover there was nothing magical about her. She was just a woman, nothing more.

The only problem was, he knew he was lying.

CHAPTER 17

∞

"RAINEY, DEAR," DOTTIE DAVIS WHISPERED ACROSS THE DINING TABLE. "Will you help me move something after supper?"

"I'd be glad to," Rainey answered and went back to eating. She'd learned the rules of the boardinghouse well. No one, except the two German ladies, talked while Mrs. Vivian was in the room. Probably because the others had also discovered that anything they said in front of the boardinghouse owner would be twisted and handed back to them at a later date.

Rainey's first-day comment about not looking for a husband had been turned to "This young lady has no interest in men or in the respectable bond of marriage." Rainey was sure the Widow Davis's concern for her being out late the other night while baking had been twisted and repeated to Rainey as "The widow frets over you as if you had no sense at all."

Mrs. Vivian was a master at turning a phrase slightly to change the meaning entirely.

Because the three old maid sisters talked constantly about their shop, which was being built now that the materials had arrived, Mrs. Vivian referred to them as boastful-in-triplicate.

So all the women living at the Askew House ate in silence when Mrs. Vivian was in the room and whispered when she disappeared behind the swinging door that lead to the kitchen. In a strange way, it bonded them together. They whispered and stifled giggles when they talked like children playing games.

The stout little woman, Margaret Ann Mathis, who considered herself the leader of the boarders, had gone to San Antonio, leaving one place at the table empty. Mrs. Vivian had agreed to hold her room for a week at half the board fee, but no one seemed to know for sure if Margaret would be returning.

"Wear your coat," Dottie Davis whispered the next time she got a chance. "We're going out."

"But Mrs. Vivian locks the door at nine."

"Don't worry, I know another way out and in."

Rainey giggled. She felt like they were planning a prison break.

"Slip down to my room after nine. There is no sense going until she's in bed. The danger will be getting out and back into this house, so if you change your mind, I'd understand."

Rainey knew, as they all did, the rules of the house. If they were caught, they'd be kicked out. Though, with the three sisters leaving within the month for their apartment over their new store and the German coming after his family tomorrow, Mrs. Vivian might find her house empty if she did make Rainey and the widow leave.

"I'll be there." Rainey smiled at the widow. Over midnight tea and coffee the two had become friends. They often played poker with the kitchen's dried beans and laughed the next night when their winnings were served at dinner.

Mrs. Vivian came in to collect the serving plates, and they were silent for the remainder of the meal.

Rainey vanished up to her third-floor hideaway and read all three of her letters from Travis while she waited. He'd written about the law, about the boy, and finally about himself. She read her favorite line one more time.

> *Sometimes, when I think of you, it is more like I'm remembering a dream than something that truly happened. Then I think of how you felt against me. How soft you were. How warm. I know that you had to have been real, for not even imagination could create such perfection.*

Rainey laughed. She could never imagine her Ranger saying such things to her. But he'd written them . . . he'd written them to her. And that was enough.

Leaning back on her bed, she forced herself to return to the real world, knowing that he would always be a part of her daydreams.

She hadn't baked pies today. In fact she hadn't even gone to the mercantile. Though Pearl and Owen always welcomed her, Rainey knew they needed time alone. So, on days she didn't bake she tried to stay away, not even dropping by to do her books. Today had been cold and cloudy, forcing her inside with nothing to do. She'd sat in the drawing room for a while. The sisters were already taking orders for dresses, and some of the richest women in Austin were calling. Rainey enjoyed the chatter, but in the end she'd spent most of the day sleeping in her tiny room. There, all alone, she could pretend that someday she'd have a life with Travis. She knew he'd never marry someone he considered to be a thief, but there was no harm in pretending.

A little after nine o'clock, Rainey hurried down the stairs to the widow's room, ready for an adventure.

They didn't say a word as Dottie slipped on her black coat and motioned for Rainey to follow her to the back stairs. The kitchen was dark except for the warm glow of a banked fire. They moved silently across the floor to the washroom. Mrs. Vivian's slave did most of the cooking and all the laundry, so this was one room the owner of the house never went in.

The washroom smelled of lye soap. Several bags of laundry were stacked beside the door. "Mamie?" Dottie whispered. "Mamie, you still up?"

Mamie appeared and lit a candle. She looked about to drop with exhaustion most nights and tonight was no exception.

The widow turned to Rainey. "A few days ago I learned that Mamie has been taking in extra laundry at night. A whole bag for a dime. She does it after Mrs. Vivian goes to bed. She's hiding the money and planning to buy her freedom. Of course if Mrs. Vivian finds out, by right she can take the money."

Rainey didn't comment, she wanted to say she knew how Mamie felt, but in truth Mamie had it much worse. Though Rainey's father sometimes hit her mother, he'd never laid a hand on her. She'd seen Mrs. Vivian strike Mamie more than once in anger, and she often loaned her out to neighbors when she didn't think Mamie had all the work she could do.

"There's a free man who works for the blacksmith over on Sixth where Mamie takes a pot now and then to be repaired. He wants to marry her, but Mrs. Vivian says he'll have to buy her first."

Mamie held up her blistered, swollen hands. "I can't wash

as much as I could. Miss Dottie is plannin' to help me so I can be with my man." Her brown eyes filled with tears. "I told him I'd sneak out and lay with him, but he wants to jump the broom with me making it all right and proper."

Rainey looked from Mamie to Dottie. "What can I do to help?"

The widow nodded and moved further into the laundry room. "We'll be back in no time, Mamie. You make sure this window isn't locked when we return."

"Don't worry none. Mrs. Vivian don't ever come in here."

Dottie stepped up on a low stool below the window. She pulled her hood over her hair and slipped out the long narrow opening without a sound. She seemed to disappear into the night.

Mamie handed Rainey her navy cape. "I got this for you from the front hall. I figured you'd be needing it. Anybody within a mile could see that yellow hair of yours even if there's just one slice of moon left. You pull up that hood good, child."

Rainey circled the cape over her shoulders and head as she slipped out the window. To her surprise, her foot touched another stool on the outside of the window, making the escape easy.

It took her a few seconds in the dark alley to make out Dottie's form. Once she nodded, the widow began to move along the alley, staying close to the wall. They crossed a street and entered another alley, then another.

Rainey's senses came alive in the blackness. She heard the sound of music and laughter, and then shouts. Between the buildings came the noise of the night, the odd mixture of barking dogs, babies crying, and horses galloping. Bits of conversations drifted to her from open windows.

Dottie linked her arm in Rainey's, grounding her, and whispered, "When my husband died, his partner claimed he couldn't afford to give me half the worth of the saloon and restaurant they owned together, so he split the place and closed off the restaurant. He said it was mine, but I couldn't run it alone, and because my husband loved it so much, I couldn't sell it. What the partner didn't know was that I worked there some at night before my Henry had to take a partner. I knew what lay hidden in the cellar."

"You were a barmaid?" Rainey would never have guessed the widow to be anything but a proper lady.

Dottie shook her head. "I ran a gambling table in the back of the restaurant. Only a high-stakes game a few times a week."

Rainey thought of about a hundred questions she'd like to ask, but this was not the place, so she picked just one. "What's in the cellar?"

"Wine," the widow whispered. "Twenty-dollar-a-bottle wine. I can't very well pull up a cart and unload my half. The partner would never allow that. But if we can take a few bottles at a time, I know a man who'll buy them, and the money can go to Mamie. One bottle will be worth more laundry than she could do in a month. I wouldn't bother to collect it for me, but for Mamie's freedom, it's worth the risk."

In the third alley Dottie stopped at one of the cellar doors. "If it worries you that someone might think we're stealing this, I can do it by myself. All you have to do is be lookout so I don't come up from the cellar and stumble into a drunk. And with two bottles in my hands, I'll need some help with this heavy door."

"I'm with you." Rainey decided this was far more fun than borrowing a horse. She didn't want to consider the fact that she might be turning toward a life of crime.

Dottie pulled a key from her pocket. "I kind of forgot I had this after my husband died." She slipped the key into the lock and turned. "Lucky for me so did the partner. He hasn't bothered to change the lock."

The cellar door creaked as they lifted it only enough to slip inside. Dottie went first, then Rainey. The stairs were made of dirt with a few bricks shoved into places where rain had washed out what had been a rough step. As Rainey lowered the door closed, total blackness surrounded them.

Rainey was afraid to move. All her life she'd hated total darkness. When her father had taken away her candle at night, she'd cried for weeks and screamed for her mother. Her mother never came, and finally she'd learned to curl up into a ball and survive the night. But she never lost the feeling that something waited in the blackness only inches away. Something evil.

"Put your hand on my shoulder and follow me down," the widow whispered.

Rainey felt for Dottie's shoulder. At first there was nothing and she was a breath away from panic when her fingers finally connected with the widow's coat.

One step at a time they moved. The smell of dirt surrounded them, closing in as they lowered into the basement. Rainey felt like she was descending into a grave. A thin lace of spiderwebs brushed past her cheek, and she heard something far bigger than a spider scamper out of their path.

Dottie heard it, too. The widow was shaking so badly Rainey could feel it through her clothes. "There's as many rats down here as there are upstairs," she mumbled to herself.

When they reached the floor of the cellar, Rainey let out a breath and heard the sound echoed by Dottie.

"I know where the wine is hidden. It's only three steps away. If you'll stay exactly where you are, I'll get the first bottle and hand it back to you. If I only get two bottles, no one will notice. Then, to get out, all you'll have to do is turn around and go back up the steps."

Rainey nodded, then realized it was a waste of time. "I won't move until you return," she whispered. It took all her strength to let go of Dottie's shoulder.

"Hum," Dottie whispered. "So I won't lose my direction."

"Hmm, hmm." Rainey couldn't think of anything to hum. Not one song came to mind. "Hmm. Hmm." She sounded more like she was snoring. She giggled, then covered her mouth and tried to stop giggling long enough to hum. "Hmm. Hmm. Hmm," she tried, sounding flat and toneless.

Dottie's soft laughter came from a few feet away. "Stop laughing or I'll hit you with one of the bottles," she threatened through her own giggle. "If I ever find one. The stash is not nearly as big as it was when my husband lived."

Rainey closed her eyes and tried to pretend she wasn't standing in a cold damp cellar.

It didn't work.

She tried humming again but couldn't manage to carry a tune. After a few minutes she could stand the silence no longer. "Dottie," she whispered. "Dottie, are you all right?" Surely if the widow fell over something, Rainey would have heard the crash. "Dottie?"

Rainey considered running, but in the blackness it was hard to tell where the stairs were. Had they stepped one or two steps across the floor? If she moved and guessed wrong, she'd be lost down here with the rats until dawn. Or until someone came down from above, and she didn't even want to think about what the partner would do if he found thieves in his wine cellar.

"I got one," Dottie whispered. "Hold out your hand."

Rainey did, waving her hands slowly through the thick air.

A bottle tapped against her little finger a moment before she gripped it solid in her hand. "Got it."

Dottie's hand let go of the other end of the bottle.

Rainey waited again, hugging the wine against her.

"I've found another. Now, let's get out of here. I think I can make out a tiny bit of light where the cellar door didn't close completely." Dottie brushed against Rainey as she passed, and Rainey raised one hand to her friend's shoulder. As before, Dottie lead the way.

Within minutes they were back in the alley and retracing their steps. As before, they stayed well out of the light. Rainey counted her breaths until they were back at Askew House. Dottie passed the wine to Mamie and slipped through the window of the laundry room. Rainey handed over their treasure and followed. As soon as she was standing inside the laundry room, the two women hugged wildly, laughing and talking at the same time.

Mamie made tea and wanted to hear every detail of their adventure. They talked for an hour, then hid the bottles amid the stacks of dirty clothes and said good night.

As they climbed the back stairs, Dottie thanked Rainey. "I'll sell the bottles next week. If it's not enough to buy Mamie, are you willing to go with me again?"

"Yes," Rainey said without hesitation. "I've never had so much fun."

Dottie laughed. "I owe you one. Next time you want to commit a crime, just let me know and I'll go with you."

Rainey hugged the widow good night and climbed on to her room. Once she was in bed, she smiled, thinking that for the first time in her life, she had friends.

CHAPTER 18

∞

As he drove the wagon toward Austin, Travis tried to think of the test he would take when he reached the capital, but his thoughts were full of the fairy. He relived every word they'd said to each other a hundred times. He thought of the way she'd felt, the way she kissed him, the way she jumped into his arms that first meeting as if she were his.

He remembered her letters, realizing he no longer had to look at them because he knew every word. She'd talked of her dream of starting a school someday, and she'd talked of how she thought of him, but she never talked about herself.

He spent hours thinking of what he'd say to her when they met. Assuming she was there and hadn't moved on. For all he knew she'd borrowed someone else's horse and ridden farther south. Texas was big enough that she could disappear, and he'd never see her again.

No, he corrected, they would meet again. She'd been in Austin when she'd written the last letter, and if she was there, he'd find her. Austin couldn't have more than a thousand people. Over two hundred of those were slaves, then well over half of the others would be men. Eliminating children, that left only a few hundred women to sort through to find a woman whose name started with R. She would be there and he would find her even if he had to stand on the street corners and stare at every person who walked by. He'd seen her real hair only once, but he remembered the sunny color. Of course she could have that hidden behind a bonnet, or be dressed like a boy again. For all he knew she had other wigs in a rainbow of colors.

But if he could touch every woman, he felt sure he'd know the feel of her.

He laughed. If he tried that method of identification, he'd be arrested.

Travis groaned. If he didn't stop thinking about her, he'd need to stop off at the new asylum being built and check himself in. The woman who signed her letters with an R. was driving him crazy. If he'd heard one of the younger Rangers going on about a woman so, he'd be tempted to shoot first and apologize later.

Sage leaned from the back of the wagon, where she and Duck had been sleeping on one of the buffalo hides. "You want me to take the reins for a while? I don't mind. Is your leg bothering you greatly?"

"No," Travis answered the last question first. His leg ached, but that wasn't his real problem. He was an idiot, driving to Austin, when he should be home healing, to look for a woman when he didn't even know her name.

He smiled back at his sister. "I'll handle the team a while longer."

Sage settled back down beside Duck. The journey to Austin hadn't proven near as exciting for her as she'd hoped, but Sage, as she always did, made the best of it. She'd drawn in her sketch book and mapped out roads in detail. Travis wasn't sure she did the drawings because she was bored, or because she planned to someday make the journey alone. He thought maybe she just wanted to make sure she could find her way back home. He'd felt like that the first time he'd left Whispering Mountain.

For all of them, Whispering Mountain was the center of the world. No matter how far he roamed, he always knew how to get home.

They'd be in Austin before dark, and Travis knew an old couple who rented rooms to state legislators when the Congress was in session. It was more expensive than he would have paid if he'd been alone, but Sage needed a safe place, and he guessed Dr. Bailey and his wife could use the extra money in the off season. The doc had retired from public practice a few years ago, but the Rangers still called him in when they needed his help.

Also, Duck wouldn't have to be around so many people in a home. They'd learned fast that the boy didn't like crowds. He'd hold to Travis, or disappear into Sage's skirt folds as soon as he saw a stranger. They still planned to take him out in public for short trips, but both agreed that it would be better if he had a place to sleep and eat where it was quiet.

Sage leaned against the back of the bench. "As soon as I get to Austin, I'm going to have a dress made in just my size. I'm tired of cutting every dress down that I buy at Elmo's, and the dresses Martha has made me over the years have all had the same pattern."

Travis hadn't noticed. "You can ask Mrs. Bailey if she knows someone. My guess is if there is a good dressmaker in Austin, she'll know about it. Some of the congressmen who stay with her bring their wives and I've heard she loves being their unofficial tour guide."

"That's a good plan. Of course, I'll want to go in every shop myself to make sure."

"Of course." He smiled. "How about I make a deal with you? Every morning after breakfast Duck and I will go with you to whatever shops you want. Or if you want to shop alone, we'll stay home. Then we'll eat lunch at one of the hotels or little cafés along Congress Avenue."

"Sounds good," Sage agreed.

"But," Travis added, "in the afternoon you stay at the Baileys with Duck while I check in with the Rangers. I also plan to visit with a judge I know who'll give me some advice. I don't want to sit for this test on the law without even knowing what to study. Don't expect me to run all over town with you. I'll need to look over that box of law books we're hauling." When she looked disappointed, he added, "That doesn't mean you and the boy can't go for walks, or ride around in Mrs. Bailey's buggy. I've heard she loves to go for a drive down to the Colorado River in the afternoons and watch the sun set."

"All right," Sage agreed. "The mornings are mine. The afternoons are yours. Half a day is better than no time."

She crawled up beside him on the bench. "How much farther?"

"We'll be there before dark."

Fear floated in her eyes.

"Don't worry," he added. "You're going to love Dr. and Mrs. Bailey. They've got this big house right off the main street. She has a garden of herbs like none you've ever seen. I've heard folks say that every woman who stays there goes away with clippings enough to start her own garden. She's president of the women's quilting group, too, and has women over several times a month for tea then an afternoon of quilting." He tried to remember what else he'd heard. "Oh, and every Sunday she goes to church."

Sage smiled. "Sounds like great fun," she lied.

"I know." He understood. The McMurrays had never taken the time to make many friends. The only reason he knew about the Baileys' place was because he'd had to ride guard for one of the senators last year and he'd heard the man's wife talking about the place. "Maybe you'll meet some people your age."

"Maybe," she echoed, then forgot her worries as the outskirts of Austin came into view. By the time they'd gone another two miles, she could see farms packed so close together they could see one another's rooflines.

Travis watched her excitement, realizing he'd never seen the beauty of the place before. Even in winter Sage constantly pointed out things he hadn't noticed. She pulled out her sketchpad and drew outlines of homes, saying she wanted to show Martha how things looked.

When they turned onto Congress Avenue, she laughed at everything she saw.

They ate at a real café with Duck sitting between them, then they drove to the Baileys' just before dark. Mrs. Bailey seemed delighted to see Sage and told Travis they could have the left wing of the house all to themselves. It had a private entrance and a sitting room between the bedrooms that he could use as a study. Travis didn't bother to ask the price; he knew it would be expensive and he also knew he could afford it.

Sage's bedroom was all soft and frills while his across the little sitting room was clean and serviceable. The next morning a light breakfast waited for them when Travis entered the middle room. Sage was already dressed and ready.

He grinned. "I don't think the stores are open this early."

"Mrs. Bailey gave me a list of where I might find everything I need. She even told me of three women opening a new shop and said they might be able to help me with a dress that fits me. She said they haven't even opened yet and all the richest people in Austin are visiting them and doing fittings in their parlor."

Travis ate and tried to listen. An hour later they were on their way. Within three shops they'd developed a pattern. Travis would walk his sister into the shop to make sure all was safe, then he'd take Duck outside and they'd sit on benches usually

placed outside the shops. Duck liked to watch the horses and
wagons rolling by. Travis watched the people.

He had his share of enemies around the state and didn't
plan on running into any of them on this trip.

He and Duck stayed too long in one shop, and Sage insisted
he buy a new suit and coat for himself. Travis complained as he
tried on the suit, but drew the line at new shoes. He'd wear the
dark clothes he thought made him look like a preacher, but he'd
keep his boots.

When Sage had all Travis could carry, they had tea at one of
the hotels and walked back to the Baileys'. Duck curled up on
top of the buffalo hide in the sitting room and fell asleep.

Travis covered him with a quilt. "He didn't sleep well on the
cot in my room last night. I think I'll move it in here for me and
let him sleep right where he is now for tonight. He likes watching the fire, and I think he missed being close to it last night."

"I'll keep a close eye on him."

After moving the last of the boxes into her room, Travis
reached for his hat. "You'll be all right here alone?"

She yawned. "I'll be fine. I might take a nap. Shopping is
harder work than I thought it would be." She smiled at him.
"This morning shopping/afternoon resting plan might be a
good one. Duck and I will probably sleep the afternoon away."

He grinned, knowing the minute she knew he was gone
she'd be in her room opening every box he'd brought in and examining what she'd bought. "I should be back by dinner."

Sage forced herself up to walk him to the side door. "We'll
be here." She'd pulled the pins from her hair and was already
braiding it.

Travis grabbed his cane and left. He knew the streets of
Austin well and planned to cover as much ground as possible
before dark.

An hour later the pain in his leg forced him to stop. He
crossed into a saloon, took a chair by the window, and watched
people passing as he sipped on a beer. In truth, he didn't like al-
cohol of any kind. He'd seen it make cowards brave and fools
take their own advice, but he had to do something in the saloon
if he planned to occupy a chair.

One of the girls came over and asked him if he wanted company. When he said no, she drifted to the next table, where the
men seemed happy to have her join them.

When he'd sat as long as he thought he could without ordering another beer, or attracting attention, he moved on. The next time he stopped to rest, he picked a café and ordered pie and coffee. The coffee was weak, but the pie excellent.

He circled by Judge Gates's office and left a note with his secretary, then continued strolling the streets. All kinds of people passed him. Men in fancy suits who spoke with northern accents, laborers carrying supplies from one building location to another, drunks and gamblers.

At dusk he walked back to the Baileys', telling himself it would have been too much to hope for to find his fairy woman the first day. He and Sage had dinner with the doctor and his wife, then Sage turned in and Travis pulled out the books on law that he'd brought all the way from Whispering Mountain. About nine Mrs. Bailey's housekeeper brought him tea. Travis thanked her and left it warming by the fire.

The smell reminded him of the dream he'd had on the mountain. He closed his book and stared at the fire, thinking somewhere in this busy town his fairy woman might be thinking of him. She'd said in her letter that his nearness made her heart race. He smiled. The need to hold her was almost a physical ache deep in his muscles. He'd find her, and when he did, he promised himself he'd make her heart race once more.

The next day Sage announced she was dragging him to a boardinghouse where three sisters had agreed to see her about making her dresses. As they walked she explained that the sisters were supposed to be excellent and Mrs. Bailey said that in six months women ordering their dresses might have to wait a year to get them.

Travis was not impressed, but he managed to nod now and then.

When they got to a boardinghouse called the Askew House, Travis felt ill at ease. The place was obviously for women; even the drawing room chair didn't fit him. Sage had visited the afternoon before with Mrs. Bailey, so she now talked to the sisters and the landlord as an old friend and they catered to her like she was a princess.

He stretched his hand out to Duck, planning to wait for Sage on the porch, but Duck backed closer to Sage and the plate of cookies the sisters had offered them.

Travis knew he'd lost his porch partner. "I'll be waiting." He nodded toward the three homeliest old maids he'd ever seen and backed out of the room. He'd just walked into the dark foyer when he heard footsteps running down the stairs. Out of habit, he leaned into the shadows and waited for whoever seemed in such a hurry to pass.

A woman dressed in dark green ran down the stairs, paused long enough to slip on her shoes and grab her coat from a peg, then ran for the door.

Mrs. Vivian, the landlady, opened the door for the woman in such a hurry. "Running late today, Rainey?" she said in a clipped tone.

"Yes, Mrs. Vivian, but I'll be home before you lock the door. I may miss supper tonight, however."

The woman turned for an instant as she waved goodbye, and Travis caught a glimpse of blond curls. He gripped the handle of his cane. Every instinct told him to run after her, but he knew he'd never catch her on foot. He hadn't had time to see her face. He couldn't be sure it was even his fairy woman. Maybe he just wanted it to be. Finding her couldn't be so easy.

With measured calmness, he stepped into the foyer light as Mrs. Vivian closed the door.

"Oh, Ranger McMurray, I didn't see you standing there." The owner's face softened slightly. "Your sister was just telling me that you were wounded in a battle with outlaws."

He leaned on his cane. "That was months ago; I'm almost fully recovered." He reached for his hat, then turned back to the landlady as if just thinking of something. "I'm looking for a young woman of small build with blond hair who came to Austin about the time I was hurt."

Mrs. Vivian's gaze glanced to the door where Rainey had just gone. "Is she wanted for a crime? Did she have something to do with your being shot? Oh, don't tell me she's an outlaw."

He smiled and lied. "No. I was hoping she knows something about who the boy with my sister belongs to. He was rescued the same day I was wounded."

"Oh." Mrs. Vivian seemed disappointed. "Well, I have a young lady who fits that description. In fact, she just ran past you. Only she couldn't be the one. She came from Galveston. Her family moved from New Orleans, I think, and I'm sorry to say they all died onboard ship. She was left alone to make her way in Texas. She's a school teacher by occupation, I believe."

Travis smiled. Like most people talking to a Ranger, the

landlord gave out far too much information. "What did you say her name was?"

"Rainey Adams. But she's not the one you're looking for. She doesn't know anyone at all in Texas. In all the weeks she's been here, she's never once had a guest in the drawing room, and I hold it open and ready for just that purpose." Mrs. Vivian raised her eyebrows. "If she knew anyone, she wouldn't be staying here, I'm afraid. Money worries, you know. She rents my least expensive room on the third floor."

"Thank you, ma'am." He moved toward the door. "I'll be back for my sister in an hour."

Mrs. Vivian held the door open. "I'll tell her."

Travis walked slowly down the steps. "Rainey," he mumbled to himself. "I should have known it would be something unusual."

He moved around the house to the alley. There he saw the last bit of proof. A third-story window overlooking the alley lined on the opposite side by saloons.

He'd found his fairy woman.

By six that evening he was back at the Askew House. He thought of waiting for Rainey on the porch, but that might draw too much attention. The landlord seemed a nosy old woman, and he didn't want to do anything to cause suspicion. With his luck his little thieving fairy was doing something illegal, and the last thing she needed was people watching her too closely.

So he waited at the end of the street, where he had a clear view from two directions. His plan was that if he saw her coming, he'd fall into step with her. Maybe, if she grew frightened, he'd hold her arm until he had time to calm her. For if she ran he'd have no hope of catching her.

Like she'd told him, what she did best was run.

Travis moved to the corner where he could lean against the building and take some of the weight off his leg. He watched the sun set below a half-finished building that he'd been told would be a church. It was getting late and he guessed his fairy had missed her supper. Maybe he'd offer to take her to one of the cafés to eat. He'd like having time to look at her, talk to her. Then he'd walk her home and explain to Mrs. Vivian why she was out late. Surely Rainey would be in no trouble if she were with him.

Once they became friends, Travis decided it would be fun to continue to write her. He came to Austin enough so that they could see each other from time to time. He'd keep up with what she was doing and make sure she was staying out of trouble. She might not be the kind of woman who would ever invite him to her room, but he planned to make her heart race a few times as they strolled in the shadows.

Travis grinned. It wasn't as if he'd have to steal a kiss; she'd already given him a few without him even asking. He'd never taken much time to notice how it worked between men and women other than barmaids, but there must be something between buying a woman by the hour and marriage. Whatever it was, he planned to discover it with Rainey.

The evening turned dark with streetlights not close enough together to offer good light. Travis's eyes adjusted to the night. He missed little as he watched from the corner of the alley.

People moved faster now. There was no need to stroll. He noticed mostly men walking, a few delivery men running the last of their rounds, a few women of the evening talking loudly as they crossed from one end of town to the other.

If his sight hadn't been perfected by years of scouting, he might have missed the little woman in navy blue moving in the shadows. The hood of her cape was up, but a curl at her forehead caught the glint of the streetlight for a moment before she hurried farther into the shadows.

Travis didn't move. She was headed right toward him. For her to remain unseen, she'd have to pass within a few feet of him. He sensed she was frightened, for she was almost running.

Once he introduced himself, he'd scold her for being out so late. Didn't she know how dangerous the streets could be? This one looked calm enough with mostly shops and offices, but one street over the town turned ugly.

She moved closer, keeping out of the light. Her cape appeared old and not heavy enough for the evening air. She had her arms crossed over her with her hands tucked away. He knew without seeing that she wasn't wearing gloves.

There was no time to address her. She'd jump and scatter like a rabbit the moment she knew a man was near.

Without thought, Travis waited a heartbeat longer, then as she passed, swung out one powerful arm. He swept her off her feet and into the blackness of the alley before she had time to scream.

CHAPTER 19

※

Rainey ran as fast as her skirts and long cape would allow. She crossed to the last block before the Askew House. Thirty more feet and she'd be safe. She'd stayed too late again at Pearl and Owen's place, but the orders for pies were increasing every day. She'd burned her fingers several times trying to hurry, and now the cold made them ache.

She focused on the dim lantern that marked the boarding-house's front porch. With luck, she'd make it in before Mrs. Vivian locked the door; if not, she'd have to use the laundry window. The landlord truly didn't care if everyone was safely inside. She never bothered to check on anyone, either. Rainey could climb in the window, sneak up the back stairs, and claim she retired early. Mrs. Vivian would never know the difference.

But if she had to use the laundry room window, she'd have to walk alone down the alley after dark. It had been frightening enough when Dottie was with her. Rainey didn't know if her heart could take it if she had to walk into the alley alone.

"I'll make it before she locks the door. I have to," she almost said aloud as she forced herself to move faster.

Suddenly, from nowhere, something slammed into her just below the chest and swung her off her feet. For a moment she thought it was a tree branch, then she felt it curl around her, holding her in a solid vise.

She opened her mouth to scream. A gloved hand slapped across her face with efficient force to halt any sound. A second later her back hit the wall of a building so hard she thought she heard her teeth rattle.

Panicked, Rainey flew into action, fighting and kicking for her life. A man's body leaned into her, smothering her completely and making her efforts wasted. He was much taller than she, and solid. The smell of him seemed oddly familiar . . . a memory she couldn't get thought around as she fought for freedom. The only thing she owned worth stealing was in the tiny pouch around her neck, and she'd die before she gave her grandmother's ring up to a thief.

He leaned closer, pressing her against the building.

She froze, waiting for her chance to run or scream. One chance was all she needed, and she'd make him pay for the attack.

"Rainey," the man said, out of breath. "Rainey. It's me."

She knew no one in Austin who knew her name . . . no man called her Rainey except Owen, and he'd make little more than half the giant trapping her.

She clawed into her pocket looking for the knife Owen had insisted she carry when she walked alone. He'd told her twice to keep it in hand while she hurried home. "It will do you no good," he'd said, "if you can't get to it when needed. A murderer isn't going to stand around while you look for it."

The body eased off her just enough to let her breathe. "I didn't mean to frighten you, but you were moving so fast."

Her hand closed around the knife.

He freed her and stepped back.

Rainey saw her chance. She pulled the knife and raised it to his chest. If she were to die in this alley, it would not be without a fight. She thrust the blade forward with all her strength aiming for her attacker's heart.

He moved with an easy swiftness of one never off guard.

He grabbed her wrist an inch before the knife would have cut him. "Rainey . . ." He sounded less sure. "Is it you?" He released her hand. "Don't tell me I caught the wrong woman. There couldn't be two fairies your size roaming this part of Texas."

She looked up at the shadow before her. Big, frightening. Tall and strong as an oak. "Travis?" she whispered.

The shadow's head jerked up. "Thank God. I thought I'd just attacked the wrong woman."

Rainey moved toward the light. "You meant to attack me?"

He followed. "No. I only meant to stop you. The attack part sort of happened. Thank goodness it was you or I'd be explaining myself to the sheriff."

She heard his cane tap against the walk as they moved into the light of the street. There was no doubt Travis McMurray stood before her, all six feet four, two hundred pounds of him. He might be a little thinner than she remembered him, but no less powerful.

"You frightened a year off my life," she scolded. "I should turn you in myself. I don't believe I know you well enough, Mr. McMurray, to be attacked without complaint. My heart stopped in fear."

"Well, you almost stopped mine as well with that blade." He didn't sound like he believed his own defense.

As panic melted into anger, Rainey walked toward home. "What are you here for? To arrest me? Or did you plan to just scare me to death to save the cost of a noose?"

He tried to keep up with her. "No. I came to help you."

She stopped so suddenly, he almost tumbled over her. "I don't need your help. I don't need anyone's help. No matter what you or my father thinks I can make it on my own." Waving her hands as she left him, she added, "Why is it men think a woman can't make it alone?"

He couldn't hide his smile. She looked like a toy someone had wound up too tightly.

Grabbing her hand, he whirled her around and placed her fingers on his arm. "Slow down, Rainey. Walk with me."

She tried to pull away, but he locked her hand between his arm and his chest.

"Walk with me," he insisted.

She had no choice unless she planned to be arrested for brawling with a Texas Ranger on the streets of Austin. "It's not safe out after dark," she said as her steps matched his. "No one should be alone, so I'll keep you company if you are walking my way."

"I'm not worried," Travis answered. "After all, I'm traveling with someone who's armed with a butter knife."

"Paring knife," she corrected. "The blade is plenty long enough to reach your heart if you ever try attacking me again."

"I promise I'll do my best to remember that."

"You do that, Mr. McMurray."

"Have you had supper?" He asked in a voice that sounded more like he was interrogating her then asking her out.

"Don't change the subject. And no I haven't."

"Want to go over a few blocks and eat with me?"

"No."

Travis laughed. "I've got to be the worst man in the world at asking a woman to step out. First, I frighten you to death, then you try to kill me, and now you won't go out to eat with me even though we are both hungry. Somewhere along the line I need to work on my approach."

"You *are* the worst." Rainey fought down a smile. She had nothing to compare to, but he still seemed bad. "To start with right now and move backward, you are not supposed to hold a lady's hand captive while you walk beside her."

"But if I turn loose, you'll bolt."

"True." At this rate she'd never get to her long list of what he'd done wrong. "And don't argue with me. It's not considered polite," she said in her most teachery voice.

They reached the steps of the porch, and he took her hand in his. "Would it help if I said I'm sorry?"

He brushed his thumb across her fingers and felt the blisters. "Are you all right? Are you hurt?"

"I'm fine." Rainey pulled her hand away but didn't run. "I just burned my fingers a little. They'll be all right."

Travis studied her, but asked no more questions. He removed his hat and leaned against the railing. "I would like to talk to you about what you overhead from your window above the alley." He swallowed hard and she knew words did not come easy for this man. "I'd like to just talk to you before you decide to run again. I came all the way from Whispering Mountain to find you," he finally said in little more than a whisper.

Rainey took one step up the stairs so she could see his face more clearly. There was something so strong, so hard about this man. His jaw seemed already set to take any blow the world gave him.

"Is that all, just talk?" She studied his dark eyes in the dim light. The memory of his letters made her blush slightly. Thinking of him and standing in front of him were two completely different things.

"No," he answered. "I'd like to look at you, really look." He shifted as if knowing he wasn't saying what he needed to say correctly. "I won't frighten you again, I promise."

He straightened, widening his stance, this man of oak preparing for anything. When she didn't answer, he slowly turned to leave.

"I am hungry," she whispered, wondering if she was making a mistake. In her dreams he could be controlled, but in real life, she wasn't so sure. "Can you afford pie as well as dinner?"

He grinned and put back on his hat. He offered her his arm and didn't try to hold it prisoner. "I can."

They walked the two blocks to one of the cafés where Rainey sold her pies. The hostess smiled at Rainey and gave them a private table by the window.

"You've eaten here before?" Travis asked as he pulled out her chair.

"No," Rainey said. "But it always smells so good."

She watched the way he studied the room and the people. Within a minute she'd bet he knew where every exit was located and how many men in the room were armed. She told herself it was just part of his job, but she couldn't help but wonder if it were not also part of his nature.

They ordered. She asked about everyone at the ranch house and finally the boy named Duck.

"You got that letter." He looked back from where he'd glanced out the window. "I had no idea if you would or not."

"Four," she answered and stared down at her plate, not wanting him to see how much they'd meant to her. "And you?"

"Three, but I mailed five."

"So did I." She remembered how open she'd been in her letters, how close she'd felt to him. And now . . . it was like someone else sat across from her. She almost laughed when the thought crossed her mind to run home and write Travis about the strange man she'd met tonight whom she thought of as Mr. McMurray. Travis's letters were informative and funny. In them he'd asked honest questions and let her see a hint of his dreams when he'd talked of raising Duck. The stranger before her seemed distant, guarded.

Yes, she thought, she'd love to write the Travis she knew on paper about the hard man claiming his name. The man before her would never say the things written in the letters.

"What's so funny?" he asked without smiling. He pushed his half-eaten meal away.

She raised an eyebrow. "I was just thinking how I feel like I know you better by letter than I do the man sitting across from me."

"A paper man is a lot less threatening than a real one."

"Something like that," she admitted. "A paper one can't bruise my ribs."

He frowned. "I didn't mean to. You're about the size of Sage and I've never hurt her." He smiled. "She's here with me, you know. Jumps in every wagon leaving the ranch these days. Worse than a yard dog."

Rainey laughed. "You'd better not let her hear you say that."

He raised his hands. "Don't worry. I couldn't take another woman in my life mad at me."

Rainey smiled as the waitress delivered two slices of one of the pies she'd baked that morning. She found it interesting that Travis thought of her as one of the women in his life.

She took one bite of the pie, but after smelling it cooking all day, she'd lost her appetite.

He looked up as he finished his slice. "The pie is the best thing here."

Rainey pushed hers away. "I ate too much dinner."

He exchanged plates and ate her pie without commenting. Rainey guessed that anyone watching would presume they'd been together a long time.

She leaned back, thinking they'd talk when he finished eating, but as soon as he laid down his napkin, he asked for the bill and paid out. Without asking if she were ready, he stood and held her cape for her.

Without a word he led her out of the restaurant and across the street toward the capital. They crossed the grounds and took the first side street leading to a barn where the wealthy people stabled their animals. Travis opened a thin side door and stepped back for her to enter.

Rainey hesitated.

"It's all right," Travis said from just behind her. "They keep a lantern on in the barn."

She didn't have the nerve to tell him that she was afraid of far more than the light. But, she reasoned, if he were planning to kill her, he probably would not have bought her dinner first. She stepped inside.

Travis followed, his hand resting lightly at the small of her back. "Wait here," he whispered and vanished into one of the stalls where wagons were stored.

A moment later he returned with a bag. Rainey followed as he moved into the light and opened the bag that contained several little compartments. He tugged at one, pulling it free of the others.

"Open your hands," he ordered as he pulled the string on the bag wide.

Rainey did as he said, but stood ready to run.

Travis put his finger into the leather pouch and pulled out a milky salve. He took one of her hands and slowly moved his finger over the blisters. The cream cooled her burns like magic.

"What is that?" she asked as he rubbed the medicine gently over her fingers.

"It's a poultice Sage makes of slippery elm sap, beeswax, and aloe plant." His fingers moved over her skin. "I wish I'd remembered that she packed it earlier, but we left it in the wagon and didn't bother to bring it inside." His hand continued to gently touch hers. "Do your burns feel better?"

"Yes."

His fingers brushed over her palm where there were no burns. "Your hand is so small," he said to himself. "You should wear gloves."

She slowly pulled her hands away. "I'll remember that," she said. "Thank you for the salve."

He studied her in the shadowy glow of the lantern, then turned and helped her back through the side door. His hand rested on her shoulder in almost a caress.

As they walked out into the night, she said more to herself than him, "I guess you're finished looking at me."

He covered her hand that rested on his arm and walked across the street to the grounds of the state capital without saying a word. Lanterns glowed around the fine new building, but the windows inside were dark. "I'm almost finished," he finally said as he led her up one step and waited for her to turn to face him when he didn't follow. "Though I would like it if you removed your hood once more. I remember your hair blond and short that night after I'd been shot. I'd like to feel what it's like to the touch."

His request was so odd, she couldn't refuse. In the chilly air she removed her hood and shook her head slightly as blond curls tumbled down almost to her shoulders.

He was doing it again. Staring at her as if he were trying to remember how to describe her for a Wanted poster.

She ran her fingers through her hair self-consciously. "In another month it'll be long enough to put up in a proper bun.

When I used to teach, I always wore my hair up, even on Saturday."

To her surprise, his hand gently covered hers. When she lowered her fingers, his remained tangled in her curls.

Everything about him seemed so hard and cold, but when he touched her the gentleness surprised her. It was as if he hesitated, as if he feared he might break her.

"I don't think I've seen hair just this color before." He didn't smile as he studied the hair curling around his fingers. "It's like a clear morning sunrise. It doesn't fit your name."

She didn't know whether to say thank you or not. She could have moved away. One step and she'd no longer feel his hand in her hair. But, in truth, she liked the way he touched her, as if brushing something rare and priceless.

When his gaze shifted from her hair to her face, the warmth in his brown eyes surprised her. He lowered his hand to his side.

"Rainey," he said slowly. "I can think of ten reasons I came to Austin, but the true one is I'd like to give you back something you gave me."

Before she could ask any questions, he lowered his mouth to hers.

Rainey felt her body grow warm all the way to her toes. He wasn't holding her anywhere, but she couldn't have pulled away. His lips were warm and surprisingly soft against hers. They moved slightly as if asking for something she didn't know how to give.

She sighed and closed her eyes. His kiss was almost as good as it had been in her dreams.

He pulled a few inches away.

When she opened one eye, he was studying her.

"Again?" His voice was low, a breath away from her lips. "Would you mind if I continued?"

"Please," she whispered and his mouth returned.

She leaned into him, loving the way his warmth surrounded her. Finally the Ranger she'd felt before months ago was against her making every part of her feel alive.

His big hand circled her waist as his gentle kiss continued. Then, as if he were teasing her, his tongue brushed a thin line across her bottom lip.

Rainey opened her eyes, braced her hands on his shoulders and shoved a few inches away. "I don't think you are supposed to do that." Her teachery voice sounded again.

He smiled. "Didn't you like it?" His hands were easy now on the small of her waist. She could feel the warmth of them through the layers of clothing she wore. She could feel him caressing her gently even as he studied her.

Turning her head slightly, she answered. "I'm not sure. I think I like it. Do it again so I can tell." This might be the one and only time in the whole of her life that a man kissed her. She wanted to make sure they were doing it right.

His fingers tugged her against him as his mouth lowered once more. This time his lips didn't stay closed completely and when his tongue slid along her mouth, he parted her lips slightly.

She straightened again despite his groan. "Where'd you learn to kiss like that?"

Travis laughed. "How'd you get to be a full-grown woman without learning how to kiss, Rainey?"

She didn't want to tell him how few times she'd been around boys, or men, near her age, so she leaned forward and touched her lips to his.

He didn't respond.

She tried again.

He waited.

Frustrated, she opened her mouth slightly and touched his full bottom lip.

He reacted, pulling her close and continuing the lesson.

She'd done it, she thought. She'd finally kissed a man the way a woman kisses a lover. As he nibbled on the corners of her lip, she decided maybe she should be writing this down. She'd never remember all she was learning.

She pulled away. "How . . ."

He pulled her back. "Stop asking questions."

She meant to protest. How else would she learn if she didn't ask questions? But suddenly she was lost in the pleasure of it all. This was no boy kissing her in the shadows of the ballroom. This was a man probably unaware that he was her first. She could feel a hunger in his kiss. He tasted of excitement spiced with a pleasure she'd never known.

She wrapped her arms around his neck as his hands moved slowly up and down her back. The warmth of his touch melted all the way into her bones. She sighed, loving the feelings dancing in her veins.

He pulled back slightly. "You like kissing?"

"Very much." She leaned into him, letting the softness of her body press against him.

His hand moved along her back, molding her against him. "You feel so good against me."

She sighed again as he slid his fingers inside her cape so that not as many layers stood between them. He kissed her while his touch gently moved over her as if he needed to memorize the feel of her.

His mouth covered hers fully when his hand brushed along the bottom of her breasts. She jerked with the pleasure of it and might have fallen if he hadn't been holding her so tightly. When he repeated his action, she sighed softly and swayed with the wave of pleasure.

With the sigh, her mouth opened and he deepened the kiss, tasting her fully as though he'd been starving.

She didn't move, didn't protest as he molded her to him.

"This is what I've missed," he whispered against her lips, "since the last time I saw you."

His mouth moved from hers and trailed down her throat. She cried softly, missing the kiss.

He raised his head and stared down at her. She could see a fire in his eyes, a hunger and also uncertainty.

Placing her hands on either side of his face, she pulled his mouth back to hers. After a moment he understood and returned to kissing her.

She knew what he was doing would never be considered proper, but when he whispered her name, she held him closer.

His hand grew bolder, passing gently over her breast. Even through the layers of material she could feel the warmth in his touch.

Shaking with the wave of feelings flooding over her, Rainey cried out softly against his ear.

He held her tenderly, stroking her until she took his touch without fear. When he moved freely once more over her body, his caress seemed familiar, and she silently welcomed it as if it were something she hadn't known to miss all her life.

With his hand capturing her breast, he raised his head enough so that their eyes met. "You like this?"

"Yes," she whispered as he tightened his grip slightly and sent fire dancing through her veins.

"And this." He kissed her so gently she ached for more.

"Yes," she answered as she pressed against him, feeling his palm flatten against her soft flesh.

His words came low, whispered in her ear as almost a thought passing between them. "Then marry me, Rainey."

She pushed out of his arms and bolted several feet down the street before she heard him whisper her name once more.

The wind seemed suddenly bitter cold after being next to him, but she didn't turn around. She knew he followed but she wouldn't, couldn't face him.

Here she'd thought how nice the evening was after he finished scaring her half to death and bullying her. They'd had a pleasant meal, he'd doctored her hand as if he truly cared. They'd enjoyed great kisses and a touching that still made her shake with pleasure, then he proved himself insane by asking her to marry him.

All she thought she wanted was his letters. They were enough. Why did he have to show her more tonight? She liked the kissing, the touching, but that didn't mean she wanted marriage. She'd crossed half a country to be free, and she would not be giving that freedom up just because he made her heart race. She had more sense than that.

As she hurried along it crossed her thoughts that maybe Travis only wanted her for a night. Maybe he'd just offered marriage without ever planning to carry through. She didn't know whether to be insulted or relieved.

The dream of Travis McMurray was safe, but the reality was frightening. All these months she'd told herself that she would never give up her freedom and be ruled by some man. She'd fight to the death before she'd let her father catch her and force her to marry.

Then Travis appeared and tried to chain her with kisses.

She wasn't falling for it, no matter how much she liked the way he touched her.

CHAPTER 20

Travis followed Rainey through the streets seeing that she got home safely. He made no effort to catch up to her, even if he had been able. Except for a few very memorable parts, the evening had been a disaster. He'd had better days when he'd been outnumbered by outlaws. It appeared he took to stepping out with a woman with about the same skill as he showed when dancing.

If he hadn't frightened her to death pulling her into the alley, his proposal of marriage surely did the job. The only explanation he could come up with was that he must have suffered brain damage from being wounded. A minute before, the idea of marrying her had been the furtherest thing from his mind. He was simply enjoying holding her, touching her, teaching her how to kiss. Then suddenly it crossed his thoughts that she'd know how next time. And next time it would be someone else kissing her.

That was it, he decided. That was the moment all rational thought snapped in two and he asked her to marry him. Him! The man who never wanted to marry. Never wanted a family. Never wanted a wife at home worrying about him.

He followed her another block. He knew nothing about her that would even hint that she'd be a good wife. She was a thief. Definitely violent, she'd tried to stab him less than two hours ago. Maybe that should have given him a hint as to how the evening would turn out. No doubt about her being a liar: It had taken him three times to get her to settle on a name, and he wasn't sure she'd given him the right one yet.

So why had he asked her the one question he thought he'd never ask?

Travis swore, knowing the answer. This fairy woman brought the only sunshine to his colorless life. When he was with her, or even thinking about her, he felt more alive than he ever had. She felt so right in his arms, like a piece of his heart had always been missing and, somehow, she completed him. And touching her . . . he didn't even want to think about the way touching her made him feel.

Suddenly she stopped and looked back to see if he followed, and to his surprise she appeared relieved to see him. He walked to within stabbing distance of her, but kept his guard up knowing she probably had her little fingers curled around her knife.

"I hate to ask for a crazy man's help," she said, moving her fists to her hips. "But I have to get to the back of the boarding-house, and I don't think I'm brave enough to walk into that blackness alone. Would you consider accompanying me, Mr. McMurray?"

"Why don't you just knock on the front door?"

"Mrs. Vivian will not open it before seven a.m. It's one of her house rules. She locks the house up and takes the only key to her room."

He walked closer, relieved she didn't bring up the proposal. Maybe, if he were lucky, she'd just forget he said anything. After all, he'd only whispered it. "I'll see you safely home, be it the front or the back door."

She took his arm with one hand and lifted the hem of her cape with the other. They moved into the alley. Travis's eyes adjusted enough so that he led her around trash and mud holes. She was right to be worried: Behind the Askew House lay the dark side of Austin. As a Ranger he'd been called many times into the saloons to break up fights and drag away bodies. Rainey probably didn't know it, but she lived only a few feet away from a boiling pot of trouble.

When they reached the back steps of the Askew House, she tugged him to the side of the building.

"I can go in through the laundry window," she whispered. "Mrs. Vivian's slave will open it for me."

He followed her the few feet to a small window without asking how she knew about the special entrance.

She tapped twice, and within seconds the window slid open.

A young black woman poked her head out and smiled. "Welcome home, Miss Rainey. Me and the widow were about to give up on you. Miss Dottie says she feels like a little wine tonight and would like you to keep her company."

Rainey pointed with her head toward Travis. The woman closed her mouth and nodded once.

If Travis didn't know better—and he didn't—he'd think they were up to something they wanted kept a secret.

Leaning forward, Rainey tried to lift herself into the window. Frustrated, she turned back to Travis. "My friend usually leaves a stepstool here to help me make it in," she whispered. "It appears I'm too short to climb in without it."

"Maybe the window's too tall." He thought of asking why she didn't use the back door, but at this point Rainey's ways made as much sense as everything else in his life. "Will you accept my help?"

"Yes, please."

Slowly, so he wouldn't frighten her, he slipped one arm around her shoulders and slid the other beneath her knees. He lifted her into the window feet first, careful not to bump her head on the frame.

Once inside, she leaned out a few inches. "Thank you," she said and raised her hands to close the window.

"Rainey—" He moved closer, placing his hand on the open frame. "Would you step out with me some other night?" He thought of adding what he wouldn't do the next time, but the list was too long to bother with. "I plan to be in town several more days. I'd like it if we could have dinner again."

She straightened, all prim and proper now. "I don't think so, Mr. McMurray, but thank you for asking." The candlelight from the room beyond the laundry room silhouetted her in pale yellow, making her look like an angel.

He touched his finger to his hat in a salute. "Mind if I ask again?"

"Not at all, Mr. McMurray, if you don't mind if I'm unable to go."

She closed the window before he could think of anything else to say. Which was good, he decided, because with his luck he'd only hurt his chances of ever even getting her to speak to him again.

Maybe it wasn't her. Maybe she had just been there in the point in time when he realized that a woman in his life might not be the worst thing in the world. After spending months with nothing to do, his mind must have had too much time to think.

He walked out of the alley and circled round to the street lined with saloons. Maybe he should take the time to talk to a few other females and work the memory of Rainey out of his thoughts. What he needed was less thinking and more action.

An hour later he'd tried three saloons and found nothing but rotten beer and cheap women. Most of the females he saw were too big. One redhead was almost as tall as him and outweighed him by twice. A few were small, but bony, not rounded like Rainey. He didn't have to touch them to know that they wouldn't feel right in his arms. One woman only had the bottom set of her teeth and another smelled worse than the alley. All were willing to step close, but Travis couldn't bring himself to kiss any of them. One beauty in a smoky back room stuck her tongue out and circled her mouth as if she thought that might encourage Travis to join her.

He walked into the fourth saloon and relaxed when he recognized three of the Rangers he'd traveled with over the years. They were holding cards, but he guessed they were talking more than playing.

One was several years older than Travis and well seasoned. Everyone called him Dillon, and he pretty much ran the Austin headquarters. Travis had no idea if Dillon was his first or last name. Dillon had ridden out with Stephen F. Austin as a scout when the first settlers came to claim land grants passed out by Mexico. He knew the land and he knew his job.

The second, Roy Dumont, was younger, about the same age as Travis. He liked living by the gun, and Travis guessed that if he hadn't been a Ranger, he would have been an outlaw. He had a wife and kids on both sides of the border, so he traveled back and forth, being a Ranger unless the money was better for him to cross the Rio Grande and become an informant.

The third man, Michael Saddler, was young, still a pup. He wore the star for the excitement and what he thought was the glory. His folks had been killed a few years back in a raid near Parker's Fort, but unlike some, Mike bore no hatred for Indians.

Saddler stood when he saw Travis at the bar. "Look, men, we're seeing a walking ghost and he's all dressed up like a gentleman."

Travis forced himself not to lean on his cane as he moved toward them.

Out of respect all three stood and greeted him. He felt as if he'd stepped on solid ground for the first time since he'd been shot. He knew these men, understood them, thought like them.

When he pulled up a chair, Mike dealt him a hand, but no one paid much attention to their cards.

They asked about the raid on the Germans' small wagon train. They wanted details, unlike his family who only wanted to know that he was all right. In the next hour he relived everything that he could remember knowing that they'd relay his story exactly to others.

Dillon wanted descriptions of the outlaws and mentioned a few names that might fit those killed. When Travis finished his report, Dillon thanked him for eliminating one of the raiding parties that had bothered travelers for almost a year.

When they all ordered another round of drinks the talk turned to how to prevent small groups of settlers traveling without army guard from being attacked. All four men agreed that even if there were five times the Rangers signed on now, not all the roads could be protected. Every year the fort line pushed a little farther north and west. Every year folks living on the fringes died.

Finally Travis leaned back and asked each man what they were working on. As he had them, they gave him details.

Dillon had just finished enlisting Mike's help in searching out three brothers who had escaped from a prison north of Houston.

"You know them, McMurray," Dillon said. "You put two of them in jail a few years back. The Norman boys."

"Seth and Eldon?" Travis frowned remembering. "Weren't they raiding around Jefferson? Killed a whole family of Quakers."

Dillon nodded. "That's them. They had a little brother who went to jail about a year later. Everyone called him Fancy Frank because he always dressed up in black suits and polished boots. I'm the one who put him in for murdering a woman, and he swore to kill me if he ever got out."

Travis laughed. "If I rounded up every outlaw who made that promise to me, I could fill a church. I was one of the guards who took Seth and Eldon down to prison. Every morning Seth would start the day with a new way to kill me. Last one I remember was that he planned to cut my heart out."

Dillon shook his head. "I get the feeling these boys mean it.

If you're like me, you still watch your back. We posted a reward, but so far no takers."

He didn't know anything about the little brother, but he'd passed Seth and Eldon's pa at the courthouse once. The old man had a wild, crazy look about him that he must have passed down to his sons. "What about their pa?" Travis asked the other Rangers. "Any chance the boys are heading home?"

"Maybe." Dillon shrugged. "Old Man Norman lives south of here on a piece of dirt he doesn't even try to farm. I checked on him once. The neighbors say he killed his two wives, but if he did, it was years ago. Nowadays he runs just enough cattle to scratch out a living."

Travis couldn't get the Norman boys out of his mind as the conversation changed. They were bad news and he didn't like the idea that they were once more on the loose. It would only be a matter of time before someone paid.

He downed half of his beer in one gulp and turned to listen to Roy. Despite the fact the man had two wives, he liked the stout Ranger.

Roy Dumont said he'd just ridden in from the border and had as many questions as Travis about the Norman brothers. Neither was assigned to the case but both wanted to help, so the talk turned back to the brothers.

Travis smiled to himself. Rangers were like drunks, looking for adventure instead of the next drink. Funny thing was, the fights that always seemed the grandest were the ones you missed. He drew back into the circle and listened. Dillon had done his background work on this problem. If someone didn't find the brothers before they reached town, there was no telling the havoc they'd cause.

Austin was still struggling to remain the capital. If they got a bad reputation now, the folks in Houston would have the state papers moved and Austin would die. The two towns had been fighting over which should be the capital for years.

"The problem with the Normans escaping is that if they cause trouble here in Austin, no one in the state will feel safe." Roy spit at a spittoon three feet away, and none of the other men looked to see if he missed.

"You're right," Travis answered, glad to have his mind on work. "I'm not here officially. I'm still recovering, but I'll keep my ears open." He looked from Dillon to Mike. "If you need backup, you know where to find me. I'll be checking in at the office every few days to see if anything new has turned up. Since I know what Eldon and Seth look like, I'll keep a close eye out for them." He didn't mention that he would be sitting for a bar exam.

"Can you ride?" Dillon asked the question casually. The meaning had far more to do with Travis being ready to hit the trail at any minute than with his ability to sit a horse.

"No," Travis answered honestly. "I'm here with my sister and the kid I told you I found with the outlaws. We're hoping to connect him with any living family, but the chances are not good."

Dillon waited for more explanation about his condition. When Travis didn't say another word about his leg, they all knew the answer. None had missed the cane he carried.

"I understand. It wouldn't be fair to pull you back before you're healed." Dillon smiled. "In truth, if I need you, it will probably be right here." He looked around, then leaned in closer to the center of the table. "I heard the Normans kept a list of men they planned to get even with on their cell wall. Most were Rangers, a few judges and informants." He looked around the table. "With you in Austin, McMurray, that makes over half the list in town. It makes sense they'll come here."

"Any clue when?"

Dillon shook his head. "I heard a rumor that one of the barmaids here used to be sweet on Seth. Maybe he'll drop by for a visit."

Travis frowned. Dillon wouldn't have even brought the rumor up unless he believed it.

Dillon played a card from his hand, and the others did the same so anyone watching would think nothing more than a card game was going on. "Think about it. Old Man Norman may have been keeping an eye on the men on the hit list for his sons. All Rangers pass through here regularly as well as judges and lawyers they may think did them wrong."

Travis thought about it, then added, "There were four brothers. I killed one in a shoot-out when I captured Seth and Eldon."

All three of the other Rangers looked at him. Finally, after a full minute, Roy whispered, "Then I guess that makes you at the top of their list, McMurray."

No one nodded. No one needed to. Travis knew they were all thinking the same thing.

Roy finally broke the silence. "So, what's the plan tonight?

I hope there is no fighting or gunplay involved. I've been on the trail a month and was hoping to sleep in a bed tonight."

Dillon frowned. "One of us needs to get real friendly with a few of the ladies in here tonight and find out if they know anything. If Seth's been seen, I'd like to know it before I hear a bullet coming at my back."

The youngest Ranger glanced around. "Which girl you think Seth likes?"

Dillon nodded at a thin girl near the bar. "That's her. I've been watching her. She's about as smart as a cow chip, but she might know something."

Travis raised his eyes to study the woman at the bar. She was young, maybe not out of her teens, but she'd been playing this game for several years. She had that hardened look of one who no longer cared about anyone, including herself. He could read her story on her face. She'd probably started serving drinks at fourteen or fifteen, then began taking men to her room a short time later because it paid better. She'd been beat up several times by unhappy customers, and judging from the tobacco stains on her fingers she had more than one habit she was supporting by working here.

In his early years as a Ranger, Travis had stepped in a few times trying to help the barmaids out. More often than not they'd turned on him, claiming he was interfering with their business. Some were hard and cold, some were sweet and talky, but they were all in it for the money. He'd bet a month's pay that this one wouldn't help the Rangers unless she saw some benefit in it for her.

Mike scooted his chair back. "I'll go try to talk to her."

Roy put his hand on the boy's shoulder. "She'll eat you alive, kid. Let me try. I'm used to handling women. Both my wives say I have the magic touch."

Dillon shook his head. "You got enough woman trouble, Dumont. Last I heard the one you have on the other side of the border told her six brothers that she wanted to be a widow. She was tired of being half a wife." Dillon nodded once at Travis. "Let McMurray do it. He's all dressed up like a gentleman. They'll never suspect him to be a Ranger."

Travis wanted to scream "No!" The last thing he wanted to do tonight was talk with another female. But he knew what Dillon was trying to do. He was giving Travis a chance to be part of the team. If he had any hope of remaining a Ranger, he had to do his duty, but talking to this thin, homely woman seemed impossible.

He finished off his drink and stood. No use putting it off. There would be pride in trying, even if he failed. The failure would lie in not giving it his best shot.

He walked to the bar and ordered another drink.

"Evening," he said as he stood beside the woman and waited for the bartender to return.

Her smile seemed painted on. "Evening, fellow. You tired of talking to your friends and want to have a little fun?"

He glanced back to see the three Rangers leaving. They knew if he learned anything, he'd report in, and for now they'd be wasting their time watching. It looked better if they appeared to be calling it a night, leaving him behind. One man who'd been drinking might look like easy pickings to a girl wanting to make some money.

"What do you have in mind?" He forced himself to smile back at the barmaid who wore enough paint for a war party.

"Depends on how much silver's in your pocket. For the price of a drink, we can talk. A few bits more and I'll give you a taste of what might be for sale."

He placed a few coins on the bar. "A bottle, bartender, and two glasses. The lady and I are going to have a few drinks and get to know each other."

She tugged him to one of the back tables where the smoke hung in a gray cloud thick as soup. The bony woman ignored a chair and took a seat on his knee. He wanted nothing more than to toss her off, but instead, he shifted her to his good leg and told her he'd been wounded recently.

She asked no questions about his wound, but two drinks later she was whining about every injury she'd ever suffered. Her voice reminded him of a violin that was badly in need of tuning. She had a way of never ending a sentence. She just rolled on and on with breaks only when she needed a drink.

Her friend circled by and helped herself to Travis's drink. He knew he'd not touch the glass again. She laughed and asked him if he were man enough for two women.

When he said he was, but his pocketbook wasn't, she snorted, letting him know that at this hour of the night the price could be negotiated.

The girl on his knee began to whine about never having enough money to buy a new dress.

Travis stilled as if the air had suddenly grown frosty. Without a doubt in his mind he knew who he was talking to. Snort and Whiny, the two women Rainey had described in her letter. She said she heard them talking every night. Except for the night they'd whispered about murdering someone, Rainey commented that Whiny always complained and Snort tried to make her laugh.

He counted houses from the alley and guessed if he went out the back door of this bar he might be directly under the boardinghouse's third-floor window.

These women might not know anything about Seth Norman, but they were plotting a murder. The world seemed full of criminals tonight. He studied them carefully, trying to decide if they had been just passing time, or if one or both of them could truly be setting a plan into action.

"Have a seat," he said to Snort. "It looks like a slow night, and I've enough money to at least buy you a drink."

When the older woman plopped down, he filled both their glasses and said with a smile, "Now tell me ladies, do either of you know where I might find a way to make some fast money?" He forced a smile. "I'm not too particular about it being strictly on the up and up."

They giggled and eyed one another as only people who share a secret do.

"You have any ideas?" he pushed.

"Nothing," Snort said, obviously deciding not to take a chance on him. "We're just looking to have some fun." She leaned close and rubbed her mouth against his throat. She wasn't kissing him. Her action seemed more that of an animal smelling prey. She had considerably more meat on her bones than Whiny, but unfortunately most of it was flabby.

Travis fought down a shudder. No matter what else he learned tonight, he knew one thing. He hadn't been attracted to Rainey simply because she was a woman.

If a woman had been all he needed, there were two pressing up against him now who seemed more than willing. He stared at the bottle knowing he could never get drunk enough to want to sleep with either.

The one Rainey had called Whiny let the strap of her dress fall. Her pointy little breast slipped from the faded dress and drooped over the fabric. She looked up to make sure Travis watched. "See something you like?" she whispered in his ear. "I'll let you hold it for free, if you like."

Travis gripped the whiskey bottle so hard he was sure it would shatter in his hand. "No," he managed to say. "Maybe another time. I have to go."

He tossed a coin on the table. "Please, finish the bottle for me tonight, and I'll see you again when I'm more flush."

Whiny shrugged. He'd said the one thing to make her lose interest. He was broke.

Travis walked out the back of the bar and closed the door behind him. The cold night air hit him full in the face, sobering him completely. Like a deer, he wanted to push a hard breath out and get rid of the smells he'd just breathed in, but the alley was no place to draw more air in.

He looked up and could barely make out the third-story window. As he'd hoped, it was open. It seemed halfway to the moon.

"Rainey," he said as calmly as if she were standing right beside him. "Rainey, I know you're not asleep. Answer me."

After a moment she whispered, "What are you doing down there?"

"I met your two friends. We need to talk about them tomorrow. They may be in far more danger than you think they are."

The alley was silent for so long he feared she might not answer. Then her answer carried on the air. "Where?"

"The café where we had dinner. Noon."

"I'll try. But I'll not promise."

He smiled. Even if she did promise, he wouldn't believe her. "Rainey," Travis said as he started down the alley.

"Yes?" she asked.

"Good night, Sunshine."

"Good night," she echoed. "And don't call me Sunshine."

He walked all the way home with a grin on his face. Maybe she didn't hate him half as much as he thought. After all, she'd almost agreed to see him again. Maybe his brain would be clear enough in daylight to keep him from saying something crazy.

He crossed the grounds of the capital and entered the side door of the Bailey home. As always, the house smelled of beeswax and roses. He'd heard it said that Mrs. Bailey always kept fresh roses in every room during the summer when she could charge twice as much for a room, and there were plenty who would pay it to have their families close while they did their business.

When he opened the door to the sitting room he shared with his sister, he found Duck sitting on a short stool by the fire.

The minute the boy heard Travis, he jumped up and ran to him. As always, Travis swung him up and held him safe and sound.

The boy smiled.

Travis hugged him tightly and sat down in the chair beside the fireplace. "It's all right, Duck. It's all right. I'm not going to leave you. You will always be safe. If I go out, I promise I'll come back." Travis felt like he gave the same speech every time he left the room. Maybe it was not the words, but the sound of his voice that always seemed to settle the child down.

Sage appeared at her bedroom door with her arms crossed in anger. "He won't go to sleep without you here, Travis. And I can't go to sleep knowing he's sitting waiting." She walked farther into the room, her new blue dressing gown swishing against the polished floor. She leaned down to the little iron teapot that was delivered every night even though no one ordered it.

"He's fine with me while it's daylight, but as soon as the sun sets, he starts watching for you." She poured herself a cup. "Tonight he went from window to window waiting for you to come back."

Travis didn't know what to say. He wasn't sorry for being gone. He hadn't reported in at dark to anyone since his mother died, and he didn't plan on explaining his actions now. Not to his little sister, or to anyone else. If he told her he'd been working, she'd want to know details, and if he told her he'd stepped out with a woman, he'd never hear the end to the questions. So he said nothing.

Sage would calm down. She was like kindling. She fired up fast, but her temper never lasted long.

She brushed her hand over the boy's hair. "He's already asleep. All he needed was to know you were near."

Travis smiled down at Duck. "He'll grow out of it. He must feel pretty lost most of the time."

Sage walked back to her bedroom as he lifted Duck down onto the blankets in front of the fire. "Tomorrow," she started, "Mrs. Bailey and I are going to Sunday services at the chapel. They're having singing afterward that I think I'll really enjoy. You and Duck can have some time together."

"Will you be back by noon?" Travis looked forward to sleeping in and catching up on reading. He was glad she didn't ask him to go with her. He'd be fine here with Duck, and she'd be safe with the Baileys.

"No. There's a potluck lunch. I helped Mrs. Bailey make bread for it after supper. I should be back by three." She closed the door without expecting him to comment.

He opened his mouth to call her back, but what would he say? I've got a date to meet a horse thief to discuss a murder planned by two barmaids I saw a little too much of an hour ago?

A tiny hand touched his.

He looked down at blue eyes staring up from the blankets by the fire.

Travis growled.

The boy growled back, then climbed up in the chair with Travis. Duck put his head on Travis's shoulder and let out a deep breath as he went back to sleep.

Travis kissed the top of the boy's head. "I don't scare you one bit, do I, my brave little man."

He leaned back in the chair and thought of Rainey. "I probably don't frighten her, either, but if we're talking honest, son, she about scares me to death."

CHAPTER 21

∞

TRAVIS GOT TO THE CAFÉ EARLY SO THAT HE COULD HAVE DUCK SET-tled in a chair when Rainey arrived. For once, he hoped the boy wouldn't pick up on what the adults were talking about.

He'd enjoyed spending the morning with Duck. Because the Baileys and Sage had gone to church, Travis cooked a late breakfast of fried eggs over toasted raisin bread, then they'd taken off on a walk about the town. Duck grew braver each day, no longer holding on for dear life every time they passed a stranger. Sage had been right, the trip was good for him.

She'd bought him a new pair of trousers and a matching coat. The vest he now wore didn't make him seem so thin, and Travis hoped it would keep him warmer.

Dr. Bailey gave the boy a top, and Duck found it fascinating to wind the string around the brightly colored wood. Travis showed him several times how to spin it, but for Duck the fun seemed to lie in the winding, which made for a great toy at the café.

While Travis watched the door, Duck sat close to him winding and rewinding the top. The third time the waitress stopped to ask if they'd decided on one of the three choices on the menu board, Travis ordered for the boy. He wasn't sure Rainey planned to eat; after all, he'd only said they should met. This way Duck could eat while they talked. If she agreed to join him for lunch, Duck would sit quietly watching the people pass the window while they ate.

A few minutes later when the waitress delivered Duck's

plate of food, she smiled and asked, "Is Miss Adams joining you again?"

Travis had to think for a moment who she might be talking about, then he quickly said, "I believe so. That is, if she doesn't get tied up." He knew he was pushing it, but he added, "Do you know her well?"

The waitress laughed. "Not at all, she's usually in a hurry when she makes her deliveries here. I have had a few people offer me money if I'll tell them her secrets."

Travis frowned.

She tapped his shoulder. "Don't worry, even if I knew, I wouldn't tell. Pies that good should be magical, not just made from a recipe. I thought that was real cute of her to order one of her own creations last night." She winked at him. "And smart of you to eat both slices."

A customer called from another table and the waitress disappeared. Travis pieced the puzzle together, except for one part. Where did Rainey Adams make the pies? She obviously made enough to live on, so she had to bake a great many, but where? Not the Askew House or she wouldn't have been coming home so late last night. If she had a home, she would be living there and not at the boardinghouse.

One mystery about his fairy was solved. He now knew how she'd gotten those burns on her hands.

He smiled, deciding to keep his new knowledge to himself. Let her have her last little secret. He'd learned quite a lot this morning.

By the time Duck finished his meal, Travis had stopped watching the door. It was almost one o'clock. If she'd planned to meet him, she would have been there by now.

"Want to do some more walking about town?" Travis asked Duck as he dropped a few bills on the table.

The boy didn't answer, but when Travis stood, he gathered up his top and string and slipped his little hand in Travis's. The Ranger didn't miss the way Duck always walked on his right side so that he didn't interfere with the cane. Duck was smart; he'd talk in time.

They walked one block after another in no particular direction. He didn't bother to go past Askew House; she wouldn't be there. As far as he knew she had no friends, except the few ladies she'd met at the boardinghouse. Somewhere in this town she was probably baking, but he didn't even know who to ask.

When they walked past the Ranger station and jail, Travis decided to stop in and see if there were any news about the Norman brothers. He might as well report in on his failure to collect any new information from the barmaid. Maybe Dillon would assign someone else to give it a shot.

Mike Saddler was the only man in the office and he didn't look happy. Travis pulled a stool by the window and swung Duck up on it so he could watch folks passing and still feel safe.

"I'm glad you're here," the young Ranger said the moment Travis gave Mike his full attention. "I can't get the prisoners to quiet down. They keep yelling or asking for things I don't know if I'm supposed to give out. Dillon left for lunch and told me to be careful around them, but they scare me, if you want to know the truth."

"Ignore them," Travis suggested as he poured himself a cup of the strong coffee they all called Pecos mix because it was as thick as the river bottom mud in the Pecos River.

"I can't," Mike answered. "All my upbringing tells me that wouldn't be polite. I'm not trained for this."

"Throw a bucket of water on them. That usually settles drunks and fighters down," Travis mumbled as he broke off a hunk of hard bread and dunked it in his coffee to make the bread eatable and the coffee sweeter. It wasn't much of a meal, but he'd missed lunch waiting for Rainey.

Mike scrambled his hair as if his head hurt. "I can't throw water on ladies, but I'm not sure I should give one the brush she keeps asking for, and the other one has told me twice that it's past teatime."

"Ladies?" The young Ranger finally had Travis's attention.

"Yeah, one's a widow and the other is younger but just as pretty. Both of them look so proper you'd think they'd never steal a thing, but Dillon caught them last night red-handed."

Travis thought of a green-eyed girl he knew who looked to innocent to steal.

"One of them got blond hair and green eyes?" It was a long shot, but he had to ask.

"Yeap. She's the one who wants the brush."

"What did they steal?"

Mike continued scratching his head. "Wine. Can you believe that? Dillon said once they were caught they offered to pay for the bottles, but the saloon owner insisted we lock them up. It don't make no sense, but we've got to wait until tomorrow morning to get the judge to figure it out. The widow claims her husband used to own the cellar they were climbing out of and that she was only taking some of his wine. If that's true, it don't seem like we got much of a crime spree going."

Travis had already moved near the door leading to the cells. "Mind if I take a look at these women?"

"Go ahead, but if you poke your head in there, the young one will throw something at you. She hit Roy with her shoe this morning. Blacked his eye."

"It can't be her," Travis mumbled as he walked through the door leading to two cells reserved for short-term guests of the state.

He noticed a well-dressed woman in black standing by the window. She had her eyes closed and the sun was warming her face. She could have been a painting of the Madonna. He'd never seen a woman look less like a criminal.

Then he saw Rainey a few feet away. She was storming back and forth across the cell like a caged cat. Her skirt had mud all over it, and her hair was a mass of curls.

"Damn it, Rainey!" Travis yelled. "Why'd you stand me up for lunch?"

She turned and stared at him as if amazed such a nitwit could talk. "I'm sorry." She squared her shoulders and put her fists on her hips. "I seemed to have been detained."

Then both women laughed.

Mike ran in behind Travis. "You know this woman?" Suddenly his boring assignment became very interesting. "You know her, McMurray?"

"Know her?" Travis swore. "I plan to marry her when she gives up her life of crime."

One glance at Mike's face, and it was Travis's turn to laugh at how ridiculous he sounded. If Mike had any sense, he'd lock him up with them. But then, of course, he'd have to arrest Duck as well, for the boy would never leave his side.

Travis tried to explain. "I had scheduled a lunch with Miss Adams without knowing she planned a crime spree before meeting me."

The widow giggled. When Travis glanced at her, she was

smiling so mischievously, he couldn't help himself—he winked at her. He'd bet a month's pay that Rainey had told the widow all about him.

Rainey was not amused. "I never promised to have lunch with you in the first place, Travis, so don't go trying to add that to my list of crimes."

Mike looked torn. He admired Travis and didn't want to do anything to make him angry, but he had no authority to unlock a cell. He also had never seen McMurray laugh, not in three years of riding from here to the border with him.

"You telling me to let them out?" Mike asked, trying to guess what was going on.

"No," Travis answered. "Lock me in with them. I'll have a talk with these two dangerous outlaws." Travis heard the stool he'd sat the boy on hit the floor as Duck must have jumped off it. He ran to Travis's side, telling all that anywhere the tall man went, he went as well.

When Mike pulled the door open and stepped aside, Travis and Duck walked into the cell. "Bring us some coffee, would you, Mike?" Travis asked. "And make a fresh pot. I have a feeling it may take more than one cup to straighten this out."

"I prefer tea," Rainey added.

"Wine for me." The widow giggled. "I think there are a few bottles on the desk."

"Coffee," Travis corrected. "Just coffee all around."

Mike disappeared. At last he'd been asked to do something that made sense.

With both women staring at him, Travis walked across the cell and sat down on the bunk, stretching his leg straight to ease the discomfort. Duck stayed right with him. The boy didn't look like he liked the idea of being in a cage, even a big one, but as long as Travis was with him, he'd survive.

Duck sat as close as he could beside Travis and wrapped his thin arm around Travis's elbow.

The widow bent in front of Duck. "What's your name, son?" Her smile softened years off her face, and Travis didn't miss the laugh lines around her eyes. She might be in mourning now, but she'd known happier times. She had a kindness in her eyes that would have taken a master actor to fake.

Duck moved his head behind Travis's arm.

"He doesn't talk, ma'am," Travis answered for the boy, "but we call him Duck."

She peeked at Duck and in a kind voice said, "Well, hello, Duck, my names start with Ds too. I'm Dottie Davis."

Then the widow straightened and stared at Travis. "You'll have to give that boy a proper name. It's your duty as his father. He can't grow into a man with a name like Duck."

Travis started to explain that he wasn't the father, but he figured he was about as close to it as Duck had. He changed the subject. "You used to be a teacher, Mrs. Davis?"

She nodded slightly. "I used to be a lot of things, but right now it appears I'm a criminal."

"I'm sure this is all just a misunderstanding." Travis glanced over at Rainey hoping she knew his words were for her as well. "Sometimes situations look like one thing and in reality they are quite another. I've had a few months to study the law lately, and maybe I can straighten all this out for you two ladies."

The widow took a deep breath but didn't look like she held much hope in his prediction. "Thank you. Are you a lawyer or a Ranger?"

"I'm taking the bar to be a lawyer tomorrow, but right now I'm a Ranger. Travis McMurray at your service."

"Well, Mr. McMurray, how do we go about getting out of this place. You're not going to believe how horrible we've been mistreated. No water to wash, and we had to sleep in our clothes last night. And this morning we awoke to find a strange man standing by the door staring at us." The widow looked about ready to cry. "I'll never get the smell of this place out of my clothes."

Travis glanced at Rainey again. She'd turned toward the window and didn't even look like she paid attention to the conversation. She was the one who stood him up for lunch, who got herself in jail, but she acted as if he should be the one apologizing.

Maybe in kissing her last night he'd gone too far, but it felt so right. She'd seemed fine until he started talking and made a fool of himself asking her to marry him. If he even had another moment alone with her, he swore he'd forget talking all together.

"First lets get the facts right," Travis began. "What were you doing at the time you ran into Ranger Dillon?"

Mrs. Davis straightened as if she were under oath. "Stealing two bottles of wine."

Rainey laughed. "Tell the truth, Dottie. You were only stealing one bottle. I had the other one in my hand."

"Yes, that is right, dear, but you were only holding it until I
climbed out of the cellar. So, Mr. McMurray, you need to explain to your friends that they should let Rainey go immediately."

Travis frowned. This wasn't going to be as easy as he
thought. He leaned back against the bars. Duck crawled up in
his lap and put his head on Travis's shoulder. The tiny boy fell
asleep with Travis patting his back.

"Do you want me to hold him?" Dottie asked.

Travis passed the boy slowly to the widow. She cradled him
and begin to hum making Travis wonder how women instinc-
tively knew how to do that. She seemed to have forgotten all her
problems as she rocked the boy in her arms.

Travis stood and joined Rainey by the window. He raised
his hand to the bars a few inches from her head, but made no
attempt to touch her. "Were you planning to meet me before
this happened?" Travis had no idea why it was important for
him to know.

"Yes," she answered. "I needed to tell you that I think Snort
and Whiny were only talking. For some reason planning a
man's death seems to be their favorite break conversation. I've
listened several more nights since I wrote the letter to you and
they haven't progressed in their plot."

He relaxed, moving closer so that their conversation became private. "When I saw them last night, I almost laughed out
loud. They were exactly as you described them."

Rainey turned from the window and looked up at him. "I've
never really seen them clearly. Mostly they're just shadows below. What do they look like?"

He shrugged. "Snort isn't that old, maybe thirty, but her
face is lined and tired. The one you call Whiny is thin, bony really, with breasts that look like puppy dog ears."

Rainey's eyes narrowed. "And how do you know that?"

Smiling, he admitted, "We had a few drinks and the strap on
her dress slipped. I saw more than I wish I had." He laughed.
"Believe me."

To his surprise, Rainey blushed. She held her head high as
she asked, "And do you see quite a lot of women's chests in
your line of work?"

Brushing his finger over her warm cheek, he whispered, "I don't think we should be talking about this. I shouldn't have said anything." In fact, if anyone would have asked him if he'd ever talk to a young woman and use the word *breast,* he would have denied it. But, in a funny way, he and Rainey were close friends. Two currents ran between them. One of attraction he'd felt from that first night at the barn dance, and one of friendship that had grown in the letters and in conversations he'd had with her in his mind. He had the feeling she'd known the same kind of conversations.

He wondered what she would say if he told her that he'd never forget the way her breasts felt, firm and round. Just the right size to fill his hand. He brushed his fingers across her hand.

She moved away from his touch. "Can you help us get out of here, Travis? Dottie took the wine for a good cause, and it truly did belong to her late husband."

"If I get you out of here, will you have dinner with me?"

Her green eyes stared directly at him. Poker eyes, he thought, for he couldn't read them at all. "Will you help us no matter what my answer?"

He nodded. How could he refuse?

"Then I will have dinner with you if I'm free tonight, but you have to stop telling people you plan to marry me. I can't marry you. I made a promise to myself when I left home. I want to know what it's like to be free, truly free of a controlling parent or a husband." He caught a glimpse of unshed tears before she lowered her gaze. "We can be friends, Mr. McMurray. That's the most I can promise."

He fought the urge to hold her. Suddenly he was back to being Mister. "Friends is a good start." Travis offered his hand. "I'll see what I can do to get you both out. It's not exactly like you're a criminal and have stolen before." He frowned and ignored his own words.

After checking that Duck was sound asleep, he slipped from the cell and disappeared. There was only one place to turn on a Sunday afternoon for justice.

Ten minutes later he was back with a stocky little man in a wrinkled suit by his side.

When Mike let them both in the cell, Travis introduced the man as Judge Gates.

The judge sat down beside the widow and said in a calm

voice. "Now tell me all your story, madam. If Ranger McMurray thinks this problem is important enough to disturb my Sunday nap, I plan to give it my full attention."

Travis listened as the widow told her sad story of helping her husband as he built a restaurant in one half the building while his partner built the saloon in the other half. "He sent all the way to New Orleans for the best wine, but when he died, the partner claimed all the liquor belonged to the saloon."

Dottie Davis looked quite beautiful, Travis thought, as she wiped her tears on the judge's handkerchief. "I have no way of proving it, Judge, but anyone who knows wine would know that the bottles packed in straw in the cellar are not meant to be served in a saloon."

Travis wasn't surprised when the judge ordered the women released and asked that they appear in his office Monday to solve the problem. He patted the widow's hand and told her that he felt sure this had all been a misunderstanding and her husband's former partner would see it that way once in the judge's office.

They drank coffee and visited until Dillon returned. Travis watched Rainey, who had very little to say. In fact most of the time she stared out the window as if wishing she were a million miles away.

When Dillon signed their release papers, the judge offered Dottie a ride home in his carriage.

Travis reminded Rainey of their dinner as they stepped outside in the cool afternoon air.

She said her goodbye to the widow and declined the judge's offer for a ride home. The older couple drove off.

Travis shifted Duck to his other shoulder so he could use his cane while they walked back to the same café he felt like he'd eaten half his meals at while in Austin. Most of the tables were empty, too late for lunch, too early for dinner, he thought. Duck stretched out on the bench by the window and slept while Rainey and he ordered and ate.

They'd ordered coffee and dessert when the boy woke and crawled up into Travis's lap. As always, he hugged Duck tightly, letting him know he was safe.

"You do that so well," Rainey commented.

"What?"

"Hug him."

Travis shrugged. "When our folks died my sister was a

baby. Seems like for the first five years of her life she wanted to go everywhere with us. Martha used to complain that Sage would never learn to walk because one of us was always carrying her. I guess I got used to a little one on my shoulder."

Rainey smiled. "What I meant was that you give him a real, honest hug. I see it in the way he relaxes. You make him feel secure. It's the kind of hug every child needs now and then."

"The kind you miss now you're here without your parents?" He saw an opportunity to learn more about her. He doubted the story Mrs. Vivian had told him, about Rainey's parents being dead, was true.

"No," she answered. "I never had that kind of hug, so it wouldn't matter if my parents were here or not. In truth, I never remember either of them ever touching me except to discipline me." Her smile was somehow sad. "I guess they weren't the hugging kind."

He watched her. She hadn't told him where her parents were, or how long she'd been separated from them, or even why, but Rainey had just told him a great deal about herself.

They walked home with him telling her about the capital and where Sage and he stayed. He kept hoping she'd share something about herself, but she remind quiet.

"I've heard of the Bailey residence. Someone said that she doesn't see her guests as boarders, but as family. Family that pay, of course."

Travis laughed. "That's about right. The other day I was working late, and she tapped on my door and offered me milk and cookies."

When she didn't comment, he added, "When I'm in Austin, I sometimes bunk in the cell you stayed in for the night, but with Sage on her first trip, I wanted it to be something special."

"She's never been to Austin?"

He shook his head. "Teagen and Tobin would keep her on the ranch forever if they could. While she was going to school at Mrs. Dickerson's, she seemed happy, but the brothers say she's been restless since last year, when she graduated from all eleven grades. A woman with that much education can't be kept on the property for long. Lucky I had to be in Austin or she might have come on her own."

"One of you wouldn't have stopped her?"

He shook his head. "We'd have tried to talk her out of it, but she's a woman with her own mind."

Rainey nodded slowly and they walked in silence for a while. Finally she asked casually, "Why did you come to Austin? And don't say to find me. I know that can't be the truth."

He wanted to say that finding her had been the exact reason, but he figured that would probably frighten her, so he said the reason he'd told everyone. "I came to take a test I've wanted to take for several years. Judge Gates has been giving me law books to read. I've packed them in my bags for hundreds of miles, and finally a few of the facts have begun to sink in. I think I'd like to try my hand at being a lawyer."

"And give up being a Ranger?"

"I don't think I've thought that far ahead. Passing the bar seems like enough of a dream right now. But I see folks robbed on paper now and then as sure as if someone held a gun to their back. It's frustrating when the law can't help them. Judge Gates and I have been friends for years. He says the courts could use a fighter like me." He lifted his cane and frowned. "Maybe he's right."

They strolled in silence for a while, each lost in their own thoughts. Duck reached out for dried leaves as they passed a tree growing near the walk. He laughed when they fell on Travis's head.

Rainey laughed as Travis complained and pulled dead leaves from his hair.

Halfway to her boardinghouse, Rainey tucked her hand beneath his elbow. He wasn't sure she wanted to be close, or if she was simply making sure he didn't fall.

At the front steps she thanked him and said goodbye as if they were no more than polite strangers.

He walked home in a dark mood. Maybe that was all they were, he thought. Polite strangers. He's spent so much time away from people or hunting down outlaws that, if he ever thought he knew anything about women, he'd forgotten where the lines should be drawn.

They'd been friends enough to eat together today, and they'd certainly been friendly last night, but she didn't seem to want more. He on the other hand would like to be much better friends, and daylight or dark didn't matter to him.

The day had worn on his leg. By the time he made it back to the Bailey home, pain throbbed with every heartbeat. Sage lifted Duck from his arm and put the boy to sleep. She didn't ask why they'd been out so late; she was far more interested in telling him about all the important and interesting people she'd met at the church lunch.

Travis sat by the fire and stretched his leg out. By the time Sage wound down and went to bed, his muscles had eased enough for him to bend his leg without feeling a shooting pain.

He knew he should look over notes before the questioning tomorrow, but he watched the fire and thought of Rainey. They'd talked easily at dinner. She'd admitted she made the pies and told him how she found a way to support herself. She talked of a woman named Pearl and her husband Owen, but she never mentioned her past. When he'd asked if her mother taught her to cook, she'd simply said, "No."

He leaned back in his chair and decided that if they were destined to be just friends, so be it. It appeared neither of them wanted what most people seem to want and need. Maybe marriage and a family weren't for the likes of them.

When he moved to his desk by the window, he thought of her laugh and smiled. He liked the way she laughed. In truth he liked everything about her. He even liked the way her fingers held tightly to his arm as they walked.

Closing his eyes, he realized the need for her was strong. A hunger just to be near her ached inside him, and somewhere, some time, he knew it would have to be satisfied. He also knew, deep inside on a level where there are no words, that she felt the same. And somehow that feeling, that need, had nothing to do with being just friends.

CHAPTER 22

❧

Rainey curled beneath her covers and smiled. She'd enjoyed the evening. Travis wasn't a man who talked much, but he seemed to have made an effort at dinner, telling about his plans for the future. Now and then his questions had been too direct about her past and she ignored them, but he didn't seem to mind.

He told her about the time when he'd been a boy and his brothers had ridden the ranch borders firing at anyone who rode onto their land. He'd laughed saying that he'd been such a poor shot then that it would have been a miracle if he'd hit anything, but those trying to invade their property didn't know. He said they'd only been twelve, ten, and six, but the three had formed a bond that year. They had become men.

He'd also told her why he thought the barmaids might be in trouble. If Seth Norman came in to visit his girl, Whiny just might be caught in the crossfire. There was enough money on the Norman brothers' heads to make some men foolish enough to try and collect the bounty.

In her tiny bedroom she closed her eyes, almost still hearing Travis's rich voice. No matter what they were talking about, she caught herself staring at his mouth and wondering what it would be like to kiss him once more.

She wished she'd come from a family like his, strong and honest. Her father never fought for anything except for more money. In fact, he'd given her, his only child, away just because he didn't want to bother with her anymore. Most of her life she'd felt as if she hadn't been important enough for him to even talk to. If he wanted her to do something, he'd say to her mother, "Tell the girl to do this," and if she didn't act fast enough, he blamed his wife by yelling something like, "Your daughter's as slow as she is plain!"

But Rainey would show him. She'd make her own way in the world. She'd grown up hearing her father remind her mother that she'd be starving on the streets without him. Now he must think the same of his daughter. But she wasn't starving. She had a business and she was making it just fine without him.

Voices drifted up from the alley. The drunk who stumbled out of one of the saloons every night to relieve himself swore against heaven because angels must have come down and moved the privy again.

A man sleeping a few doors down yelled for him to be quiet.

The drunk threatened to kill the man if he would only show himself.

Rainey laughed.

Then Snort's voice sounded from almost directly below Rainey's window demanding that they both be quiet.

Rainey leaned closer and waited, for if Snort were on the back porch it wouldn't be long before Whiny showed up also.

Sure enough, the younger woman's drawl drifted up to the window. "There ain't enough men in tonight to keep me in smokes, much less beer."

"It's the weather, getting colder, makes folks want to huddle down in their own beds and sleep till spring." Whiny mumbled her agreement and Snort continued. "I'm thinking of turning in early. I already got my bed bricks warming by the fire in the kitchen." She laughed. "I could use a little beauty sleep."

"Haskell won't let you leave early. I heard him say he's expecting somebody important to come by in the next few evenings. Says some fellow is going to get him a great deal of money."

Snort sounded interested. "We'll keep our eyes open. When Haskell gets the money, that's when we should make our move. I've been thinking about it. We got to hit him before he puts it in the safe 'cause we'll never get that thing open."

"But we'll be caught. I just know we will," Whiny whimpered. "How are we going to look invisible in that little office of Haskell's? If he even thinks we're planning something, he'll beat us to death, then throw us out with the trash."

"All we got to do is get our hands on the money. Look at it

this way, we works for Haskell. Any money he gets belongs to us, too. We just got to be brave for once and take it."

"There ain't no way."

"Yes, there is. I'm working on something he'll never see coming. By the time they find his body we'll be long gone, and we'll have enough to live in style for the rest of our lives. If Haskell says big money is coming in, this may be our one chance. All we got to do is kill one man. That ain't much, 'cause he ain't much of a man."

The women talked on and Rainey listened for details, but they changed the subject.

Whiny said, "Wish that big fellow would come in again tonight. He bought us a whole bottle of whiskey and didn't ask for nothing in return."

"He's got Indian blood in him, I'll bet." Snort sounded as if she were drinking during her break. "That dark hair and brown eyes marks him as breed."

"I don't care as long as he's got money. Half the folks in Texas are mixed blood," Whiny answered. "Long as he don't try to scalp me, he can warm my bed."

"You scared him off," Snort scolded. "With men like him you got to act like a lady. Didn't you notice how polite he was? His clothes were clean, too. A man like that has to be handled differently than most. He thinks you're a tramp and he's going to toss you aside."

"I didn't do nothin'!"

Snort continued. "You showed him too much of the merchandise."

Rainey giggled, guessing who they were talking about. Travis had already told her he'd met them. Now she knew he also bought them a bottle of whiskey.

"I did not," Whiny answered. "He said he was out of money. That's why he left."

"He weren't out of money. Didn't you get a look at those boots he had on? Those are handmade of prime leather down in San Antonio just for him. I've seen a few pair of them before. They say the cobbler makes one boot for each foot, not both just alike the way most boots come. I've heard ranchers say they don't have to wear a boot six months to break it in when it's made like that. Any man who can afford them kind of boots don't run out of money."

"You mean he paid for someone to make a pair just for him?" Whiny obviously didn't believe Snort.

"Yeah, and you can bet they slide up his leg almost to his knee and got his name on the inside. If he ever comes in again, we got to ask Haskell to send over some of the special whiskey. Two drinks of it and he'll be acting like he's had a bottle."

"But Haskell charges us for that stuff."

"It'll be worth ten times what we have to pay. When the big man wakes up in your bed, he'll never remember what a great time he had, but he'll pay up all the same."

Whiny giggled. "I wouldn't mind having a peep at what that one looks like without his clothes."

"He's fine, I bet, but I'm guessing he's also picky about his women, not like some. He probably selects his women with twice the care he picked those boots."

Someone yelled from inside and the women shuffled back to work. Rainey lay awake thinking of everything they'd said. She now knew that they planned to kill Haskell, but what bothered her more was that they planned to trick Travis.

She sat up in bed trying to think. They could have been talking about someone else. But Travis had been in there last night. He was a big man and probably had plenty of money. It all seemed to fit Travis, except for the boots. She'd never thought to look at what kind of boot he wore. He must have had something on his feet, but most of the time they talked they were sitting at a table, or walking in the dark.

It was almost midnight and she remained wide awake. She'd never be able to sleep, worrying about Travis. Tomorrow was Monday and she had to go to Judge Gates's office the first thing. Travis had left her without making any plans to see her tomorrow, so she might have no way of passing on what she'd heard. Haskell must be expecting Seth Norman to show up. That had to be where his sudden fall of money was coming from.

Travis had commented that he would be sitting before a panel of lawyers to answer questions.

She couldn't go to the saloon and head him off tomorrow night. She might be too late, and that street was definitely not safe for a woman alone at night. She couldn't just stand around waiting for him to come by.

Rainey crawled out of bed and began to pace. She could write him a note. When they'd walked earlier, he'd told her that he and Sage were staying at the home of the Baileys, who lived just across the street from the capital. He'd even pointed in the general direction. She could find the house and deliver a note tonight, then he'd be prepared and know about both Haskell's plan to collect the reward on Seth Norman and the barmaids' plot to drug him. If he knew he was walking into a trap the next time he went to the saloon, they'd never be able to trick him.

Rainey pulled the ragged old clothes she'd worn when she'd ridden into Austin from the bottom of her tiny chest. The capital was only three blocks away. She could run to it, walk about the square, and find the home of the Baileys. If they rented out rooms, it must be a big house, and most of the big houses in this town had the family name on the door.

She'd find the place, slip a note to Travis under the door, and be back in her bed in minutes. As she pulled her hair up under her floppy old hat, she thought of the distance between the laundry room window and the street. She'd never made the journey alone.

This time she'd have to make it not only alone, but invisible. The only way she'd be safe was to pass through the streets unnoticed. She'd done it the first time running away from a marriage and a life she didn't want. She'd do it this time to save a friend.

She glanced in the mirror. In the weeks she'd been in Austin, she'd gained a little weight. She didn't look as much like a boy as she had when she'd been starving most of the time. But it was a moonless night and she would pass. Who would be on the streets to see her?

Only criminals and outlaws and murderers, she answered her own question. But she had to help Travis if she could. She'd never forgive herself if Whiny and Snort tricked him and she could have stopped them. Plus, if they thought he had money, they might decide killing him could be their ticket out of town. Travis had said Sage came to shop, so he might be carrying more money than usual.

Rainey scribbled the note to Travis, shoved it deep into her shirt pocket, and tiptoed down the back stairs. Even Mamie, who always worked late, had gone to bed. Rainey opened the laundry room window and slipped out, then put a stick at the frame so the window wouldn't close completely. She was out into the alley before she remembered that without the stool she wouldn't be able to crawl back inside.

Slipping into the night, she decided to worry about that later. The odds were good that she'd never make it back alive, so she didn't want to worry about something needlessly.

The air hung cold and still. Rainey moved slowly, keeping to the blackness close to the buildings. She'd looked down the alley several times from her window, and, when the moon was full, she'd noticed where the drunks slept. She only hoped they were in the same places and she didn't step on one.

Inch by inch she tiptoed along the alley until finally she reached the street. From there she turned north and crossed to the boardwalk. Here there were street lamps, but no one around. She could hear the faint sounds from the bars a few blocks over, but on these streets lined with shops and offices, nothing moved.

She crossed one intersection, and then another. The lanterns from the new capital building came into view. Rainey moved toward them.

A wagon rattled down the street and she slipped into the shadows until it passed. The driver looked like he was asleep on the bench and letting the horses lead him home.

She hurried on until she reached the fine houses. The expensive women's boardinghouse was on the corner of the first block. She saw a candle shining from one of the upstairs windows. One of the women might still be awake, but the rest of the house was dark.

A few homes later she found a red stone house with the name Bailey on a plaque by the front door. As she passed, she noticed light still shining from one wing of the structure. Curiosity got the better of her, and she slipped into a tiny garden area only wide enough for a path leading to the back of the house.

Rainey walked slowly, thinking that, though only a few feet from the street, this would be a beautiful private space in the summer.

A light from the window flickered across the path. Rainey leaned to look in, hoping for a glimpse of what the home might look like inside.

To her shock, Travis sat not three feet from the window. His head was down, but the light still shone on the book he'd been reading. He must have fallen asleep.

She stepped closer and realized the window was open.

The thought that she could slip into his room and leave the

note on his book almost made her laugh out loud. Before she had time to reconsider, she tugged the window opening wide enough to slide through. Warmth greeted her and the smell of tea drifted in the air. A fire in the hearth made the room dance in light and shadow off fine furniture and rugs. She tiptoed to the polished desk littered with papers.

Just as she laid the note in the center of his book, Travis said in the low voice of a man very much awake, "Good evening, my little thief. Looking for wine, or just breaking into homes tonight?"

Rainey jumped and would have screamed, but his hand brushed her mouth. "Not a sound, the boy is sleeping."

She fought down the cry that was already halfway up her throat.

He stood, careful not to make a sound, placed his arm about her waist, and pulled her across the room. His strong grip no longer frightened her.

She noticed Duck sleeping on a huge buffalo hide by the fire in what looked more like a drawing room than a bedroom. A bunk had been shoved along the other wall that had windows. The covers on the bed were messed. She guessed that must be where Travis slept, when he slept. From that spot he could watch the boy and still have the fresh air blow across him.

She also noticed papers and books everywhere. He obviously had been studying hard for something, and here she was waking him. No, she corrected, she definitely hadn't awakened him. He'd probably heard her from the time she left the street. He'd only been pretending to sleep, probably trying to figure out just how close she'd come.

They stepped out into a hallway but Travis didn't close the door all the way. He was so close she thought she could hear his heartbeat. "What are you doing here, Rainey?"

Shoving her hat back a few inches, she looked up at him. "I came to warn you. Snort and Whiny are plotting against you. They plan to drug you and take all your money."

His low laughter seemed to rattle from his whole body. "You're worried about two barmaids taking advantage of me? I don't know whether to be flattered that you care enough to risk your life to warn me, or insulted that you think I can't defend myself against those two."

She leaned closer. "Don't you want to know what they've planned?"

"I can guess." He leaned down as he whispered. His warm breath brushed her cheek.

"I wrote it all down."

He made no effort to take the letter as he tugged off her hat. "How could anyone ever think that you're a boy. He'd have to be blind or simple. Dear God, you even smell like a woman."

She straightened. "I didn't fool Martha, but she didn't seem to care. I did, however, fool your whole family. You know, the blind, simple folks you call kin."

He laughed at her insult as he touched her hair. "It's amazing how your hair tangles in curls. When you're not around I can't sleep for thinking about touching it."

She backed away, bumping into the wall. "I didn't come here to have you play with my hair, and I don't think I want to know what you want to touch. I came as a friend to warn you, and I'll be leaving as I entered, since you don't seem to need or want my help."

He plowed his fingers into her hair, gently pulling her head back.

She closed her eyes and tried to remember why she'd came. "If the barmaids get you and have their way with you, I'll not hold myself responsible."

He leaned closer, pressing the length of his body against her as he lowered his mouth to hers. This time his kiss wasn't gentle or newborn, but hungry with need as if he'd been thinking of kissing her for hours.

She meant to let out a protest, but when she opened her mouth, his tongue pushed between her lips and the kiss turned liquid with passion.

Rainey didn't move. She didn't reach for him, or fight to get away. She just let the feel of him wash over her. His body warmed her, as his kiss took full measure, letting her know how hungry he'd been for the taste of her.

Finally he slowed, allowing her to kiss him. He leaned away so that she could breathe, but with each deep breath, she rubbed against his chest. His mouth moved to her throat. Rainey moaned softly as he kissed the hollow of her neck.

"I have to go," she whispered, feeling as though she might faint with pure pleasure. "It's very late."

He leaned away and straightened as if surprised at how quickly he'd lost control.

He brushed her shoulder as he lowered his hand from her

hair. "I'll get my boots and coat and walk you back to your place."

Lowering close to her ear, he whispered, "I didn't hurt you, did I?"

She couldn't help but smile. He had lost control, maybe for the first time in his life. "No, Travis, you didn't hurt me."

He hesitated, as if wanting to touch her, but knowing he should follow her wishes. Despite his passion, he was not the kind of man to force a woman into anything.

"There may be little chance of my being tricked by Snort or Whiny, but there is a good chance of you getting into trouble before you reach home."

"I can take care of myself. I don't need . . ." She started to argue further, then remembered the high laundry window. Nodding once, she followed him into the drawing room. He sat on the corner of the cot and pulled on boots that came almost to his knee.

She whispered at his side, "Doesn't this place have a bedroom?"

He pointed with a nod. "Sage is in there. There's another one through that door, but Duck likes to sleep by the fire. I think he must have been cold for a long time, because he loves being close to it. I don't want him to wake and be alone, so I had a cot moved in here. All the things Sage bought almost take up the spare bedroom anyway. Once she gets the dresses from the three sisters who live at your place, I'll be lucky to get it all home in one wagon."

Rainey leaned against him as he pulled on his boot, hardly aware that she was touching him. "Are those specially made boots?"

"You bet. Teagen and I both have a pair a year made by a man who can get them to fit like gloves. Tobin prefers moccasins, but I've grown used to the boots."

She leaned closer to his ear. "The girls were talking about your boots. They think you must be rich to have them."

Travis laughed. "No, just comfortable."

He straightened and she almost fell into his lap. His arm circled her waist, catching her and pulling her close. For a moment he stared at her as if surprised she was in his arms so easily.

She panicked, not intending to be so close to him again. "I . . ."

Awkwardly he pulled her against him, holding her.

She shoved at his chest.

"It's all right, Rainey, you're safe."

She realized he was saying the same words he'd said to the boy. "I don't need your . . ." She stopped hearing her own lie.

He didn't turn loose of her, but she no longer struggled and he held her tight. For long minutes he just held her, giving her the hug she'd said she never had.

Rainey let one tear fall and drop onto his shirt. Her breathing slowed and she felt surrounded by his warmth. It had been so long since she'd felt safe, truly safe. He offered what her father never had, but it was too late, she decided. She'd been cold too long for any fire to warm her.

After a while he whispered, "You all right?"

She pulled an inch away. "I'm fine, but I'm not a child. You don't have to protect me, Travis. Or give me hugs."

He smiled down at her. "It wasn't you," he said. "It was me. I've wanted to hold you all day long. For some reason I find it very hard to keep from touching you." He watched her as if expecting her to say something.

Rainey stood and was thankful he didn't try to keep her from doing so. "You can walk me back, Travis, but only as a friend. I'm not ready for more. I'm not sure I will ever be." She felt she had to admit more. "It's not you. I think you are a wonderful man. It's me." She didn't turn around to see his eyes. She didn't want to know how her words probably hurt him. How could she begin to tell him that she had to believe in herself before she could believe in anyone else?

"Because of your criminal past?" he asked from behind her.

"No," she answered. She couldn't tell him that she'd run away to prove something not only to her father, but to herself. She had to know that she could stand on her own. Rainey wasn't sure she could ever be happy living and depending on a man. She'd seen her mother too unhappy. She'd seen her waste away believing herself worthless. Rainey never wanted to feel that way again. "We need to say goodbye." She waited a moment and added, "I'm not the right kind of woman a man like you should have."

"If that is the way you want it, I'll not argue tonight." He tugged on his coat, picked up his cane. He seemed angry, as if he heard more in her words than she'd said. "There is a door off the hall that will take us to the garden." His voice was cold, totally in control. "I'll open Sage's door in case Duck wakes."

They walked side by side, not touching into the cold night air. Though he used his cane, his steps were faster than before, making her almost run to catch up. They were back to the alley entrance in minutes. He took her hand as they moved through the alley, but there was only purpose in his touch, no gentleness.

When they stood at the open window, he reached to help her in, but she stepped back. She didn't want it to end like this, with him cold to her. He had a right to know that she was stepping out of his life because of her needs, not her feelings toward him.

"What is it?" he asked, as if in a hurry to leave.

"I don't want it to end like this between us."

"Right. You just want it to end." He almost mumbled the last words. "I'm not your kind."

She could see his outline. He looked as granite hard as he had that first night they met and the cowhands confronted him about being a stranger. There was so much she wanted to say, she feared that if she started talking she'd never stop. He probably didn't want to know how dull her life had been or how unloved she'd been. Or, worse, how willing she'd been to accept it all until the very last.

She moved back in place and felt his hands circle her waist, ready to lift her up.

"One last thing, Rainey, if that even is your name," he whispered against her ear. "Why'd you come to warn me if you're not attracted to me? Why'd you kiss me back on the capital steps and again in the hallway tonight? Were you just playing me like the barmaids plan to?"

She turned, but couldn't see his face. "I am attracted to you. How dare you think of me as a liar."

He laughed, hard and unbelieving. "I should have known you'd play it to the end. You'd think I'd learn."

Rainey had no idea what he was talking about, but she didn't like the idea that he thought she'd somehow used him and lied to him. "I didn't kiss you for any reason than because I wanted to, you idiot. In truth, I had no idea how wonderful a kiss could be until you, and I thank you for that memory."

"Stop lying to me," he hissed.

Before Rainey thought, she raised her hand and slapped him hard across the face.

For a moment, the sound echoed off the walls of the alley,

then the silence smothered every sound except that of her breathing.

She didn't know what to say. She had too much pride to apologize and too little bravery to tell him the full story. Straightening, she prepared for him to hit her. Her father would have hit her mother—she'd seen it a hundred times when she was growing up. Her mother would make the wrong move, say the wrong thing. Her father would glance around to make sure no one from the school saw, then he'd double up his fist and with one blow knock her to the floor. He'd learned over the years never to hit his wife in the face, but when he'd finish, he'd step over her and mumble, "Silly woman," as he left.

Rainey waited. There was nowhere to run. She had to stand her ground even knowing that one blow from this man, a foot taller than her father, might kill her.

He didn't raise his hand to his face, or to her. He just stood very still. Finally he said. "What are you waiting for? Go."

She fought to keep her voice from shaking. "I'm waiting for you to hit me. I'll not cower or say I'm sorry."

His hand moved and she braced for the blow, but he only rubbed his cheek. "I guess I deserved that slap. You can't help the way you feel. Lots of folks are afraid of my Apache blood. But, no matter what you say, I have no intention of ever hitting you or any woman.

"I should probably even be the one saying I'm sorry. I guessed, since we'd never talked about it, that my blood didn't matter to you. After all, you were at our ranch. You must have seen my father's tartan and my mother's wedding beads in the great room. You knew they came from two worlds." He laughed. "Which pretty much makes me belong in neither."

Suddenly Rainey understood why he'd called her a liar. He truly thought she wasn't attracted to him. "I've never given one thought to your blood, Travis. Of course I knew the story of your parents. The only thing I've ever thought about was that you were the only one lucky enough to get your mother's brown eyes."

She wished she could see him. It all seemed clear now, his awkwardness around her. He was afraid she'd reject him. And she had rejected him, but it had nothing to do with him.

"The reason I have to say goodbye to you is mine, not yours," she tried. "But believe me, I'll always remember your kiss."

"So, the attraction was there." He sounded doubtful. "I didn't imagine it."

"It was there," she whispered. "It still is."

"Then there is only one way for us to say goodbye."

He leaned forward and lifted her off her feet. For a moment, he held her up, then lowered her mouth slowly to his lips. She knew this was the way they had to say goodbye. The only way that would be right. She wrapped her arms around him and pressed against him.

At first he offered a gentle kiss that warmed her insides. Then, as she kissed him back, he shifted his stance and leaned her against the wall, pressing his body like a warm blanket over her. The kiss deepened.

She felt like she was melting in his embrace. He wasn't demanding but offering her a pleasure she never knew existed. The gentleness surprised her, and like a slow moving current, she floated with it.

She could feel his heart pounding against her as his chest pressed her breasts. With each breath he seemed to be caressing them with his slight movement. She heard herself moan, and then his tongue slid into her mouth, exploring, tasting.

When she broke the kiss to breathe, she held on to him not wanting him to move. But he did. He kissed her throat. While his body pressed against her, his hand tugged at her tattered shirt, pulling several buttons free. Now her throat and neck were open to him all the way down to where her camisole rose with the swell of her breasts.

He leaned back for a moment. "I wish I could see you," he whispered. He touched the tiny bag tied to a string around her throat. "I wish I knew what treasure you keep in this."

Before she could think to answer, his mouth lowered to her again, this time hungry and demanding. Her mind circled from the flood of senses. She could feel the roughness of his cheek against hers, the desire in the depth of his kiss, the need in both their bodies to be closer.

His hands moved over her, branding her with his touch as he memorized the feel of her body. The kiss deepened suddenly with a hunger that rocked her senses, and to her surprise, she answered back in kind.

When he broke the kiss again, his hands circled her waist and lifted her quickly into the window. "Go," he said. "And don't come to my room again unless you plan to spend some time in my bed."

She wanted to cry, to hold him back, to make him say something gentle and not sharp to her before he left.

But he was gone, vanishing into the night with one step. She stood at the window for a long while letting the night air blow against her open shirt. She didn't feel the cold. All she felt was a longing for a man she knew she had to see again.

Part of her was splitting in two. Her need to be free. Her need for him.

This time he'd been the one who ran, not her.

CHAPTER 23

TRAVIS WALKED SLOWLY BACK TOWARD HIS ROOMS AT THE BAILEYS'. He needed time to cool down. He'd never felt such a need for a woman—no, not a woman—Rainey. If he'd stayed any longer, he would have made love to her right there in the alley.

He laughed. Maybe he had it backward. Maybe she would have taken him, for she was definitely doing her part. What they did couldn't be called a good-night kiss. What he'd felt was a mating. A mating that would leave a hunger in him for the rest of his life.

He knew now for a fact what he'd sensed from the first. She belonged to him, just as he belonged to her. It didn't matter if they were together or not, she was and would always be his match.

Judging by what she said, she'd made it plain she didn't want to see him again. But that last kiss had made all her talk a lie. She wanted him, needed him the same way he needed her, but she didn't want to love him. She didn't want marriage and forever, and he knew he'd never settle for something less with her.

He looked around. The saloons were closed, the cafés hadn't opened yet. It was sometime after two. The only place he knew of where people would be awake was the Ranger office. If any bad guys slept in jail tonight, some Ranger would be keeping an eye on them, and there he'd find company.

Ten minutes later when he opened the door, Mike looked up at him from the desk and smiled.

"Come in," Mike almost shouted. "It's so quite around here

I was starting to get spooked. All we got are drunks tonight, and they're no fun when they start to sober up."

"You here again?" Travis raised an eyebrow. "Don't they let you go home anymore, kid?"

Mike shrugged. "I played poker with Roy yesterday and he won the night off. Come to think of it, every time I play cards with Roy, I end up pulling his night duty."

Travis laughed. "He has to win, kid. He's got two wives to keep happy."

Mike leaned closer as Travis took the seat across the desk. "You really think that's true? About the two wives and all those children."

"I know it's true. I'm met them both."

Mike shook his head. "Why do you think a man would do that, saddle himself with two women? I'm not even sure I could handle one."

Travis poured a cup of coffee, then stared at it. "Maybe it's true love. If it can happen once, maybe it can happen twice." He sloshed his coffee around in the cup. "How many days has this pot been warming on the stove?"

"Not long. I just forgot to dump out the grounds from the last pot. It's all right if you drink it through your teeth."

Travis frowned before he realized Mike was kidding.

A prisoner from just beyond the open door leading to the cells yelled for them to call it a night. "I need my beauty sleep before my hanging tomorrow." The man sounded like he'd had far too much to drink.

Travis pointed toward the cell and lowered his voice. "We got a hanging tomorrow?"

Mike shook his head. "No, I just told him that if he threw up in that cell, I'd see him hang." The kid shrugged. "I may have gone a little overboard with the threats, since he believed me, but I sure do hate cleaning that place up after Dillon lets the drunks go come morning."

Travis laughed, remembering his early years when he'd been the lowest-ranked Ranger and had to do the jobs no one else wanted. "What you got planned for your life after you've served your time as a Ranger?" He leaned back in his chair, knowing the one question would help pass the night.

Mike stood and made a new pot of coffee as he talked. "I've never given it much thought. I guess I always figured I'd die in the line of duty. My family's all gone. There'll be no one crying over my grave." He smiled. "I guess if I had one wish, it'd be to have some pretty girl miss me when I'm dead, but that ain't likely. Roy has time to find two wives, and I don't even know an unmarried girl that don't charge by the hour."

"You're better off," Travis answered, thinking of Rainey. "The more I'm around them, the more I think I'll never understand them. Take my sister, she's got this crazy idea that one day she'll just bump into a man and fall in love."

"Is that how it works?"

"Hell if I know. The last one I bumped into stole my horse."

Both men laughed. The drunk yelled again. They lowered their voices and decided to play cards for who would buy breakfast. The night passed with good company and bad coffee.

At dawn Travis silently slipped back into the drawing room. Duck was still sound asleep by the fire. He sat down on his bunk and pulled one boot off when the door to Sage's room opened.

"Oh, good," she whispered. "You're up."

He slowly put the one boot back on and stood, trying to look like he'd just woke. "I couldn't sleep," he answered honestly.

"Me, either. I'm picking up my new dresses from the sisters this morning."

Travis thought if such a thing ever kept him awake, he'd shoot himself, but he tried to focus as he gave up the hope he'd had of sleeping a few minutes before he had to meet Mike and buy breakfast.

Sage tidied up the room, something she always did when she couldn't sit still. Her long braid swished back and forth as she circled. "Mrs. Bailey won't be up for another hour to cook breakfast. I feel trapped in here. If we were home we'd all be having coffee by now. What is it about these people in town who start their day by the clock and not the sun?"

Duck sat up and rubbed his eyes. He looked so tiny in his big white nightshirt. Thank goodness he no longer woke frightened and crying.

Sage tossed Travis the boy's clothes. "Your turn."

Duck saw the clothes and came fully awake and ready to run.

Travis laughed. "I'll buy you a cup of coffee at the bakery if you'll help me catch him."

Sage nodded and circled behind the boy. Together they fought their way through dressing him in no time. When they finished, Travis brushed down Duck's hair with his hand.

Duck smiled up at him and Travis wondered if all this battle over clothes wasn't a game to the boy. He offered his hand. "Want to go have a cookie?"

Duck climbed into Travis's arms.

"He can't have a cookie."

"I'm sure the bakery has one," Travis answered. "We can't feed him breakfast or Mrs. Bailey will get mad at us."

"You spoil him."

Travis laughed as he opened the private exit from their wing of the house. "And you don't? You're the one who taught him that his pockets were for carrying cookies. Half the time when I pick up his clothes at night, crumbs tumble out."

Sage followed. "I'm not the one who bought him a knife. A knife, Travis, for a three-year-old."

"It'll be another year before he's got the grip to open it."

She lifted her skirts an inch as they walked through the tiny garden with its beds covered in straw. "Oh, then he'll be four and I guess it will be fine."

Travis didn't understand her problem about the knife. It was better than a rifle. "We all had knives by the time we were his age, and none of us cut off our fingers."

Sage didn't look relieved. She pulled the fur-lined hood to her new velvet blue coat high and smiled up at the gray sky. "Do you think it will warm up enough today for me to go riding?"

He knew his sister missed riding every day, but he couldn't let her go alone, and he didn't think his leg was strong enough yet. He'd thought of trying it, but wasn't sure he wouldn't make a fool of himself. He'd wait until he got back to the ranch and then test his leg. "I tell you what, you find someone who can keep up with you on a horse, and I'll keep Duck while you ride."

"It's a deal. But what about your test at nine?"

He felt safe. "I'll take him with me if you find a riding partner on this cold morning." Dr. or Mrs. Bailey didn't look like they could even climb up on a horse, and the only other people Sage met were dressmakers.

The wind hit them as they reached the street, and Sage pulled deep into her coat as they hurried to the tiny bakery that opened at dawn. Travis held Duck close. He fought the wind, trying to keep up with Sage, but she was several steps in front of him when she turned the corner.

A moment later when he looked up, his sister was bundled

into the arms of a man. They were both circling in the wind almost as if they were figures whirling atop a music box.

Before he could reach her, Sage laughed. "I'm sorry, sir. I wasn't watching where I was going."

The man still held her at the waist. "That's all right, miss. You can run into me anytime."

Travis was about to step in and end this conversation when the man removed his hat.

Travis frowned. "Saddler."

Mike had the nerve to smile. "Sorry, sir, I hope I didn't keep you waiting."

Travis took one step closer. "If you'll let go of her"—he frowned at Mike—"I'd like to introduce you to my little sister."

Mike kept smiling.

An hour later Travis decided that he and Duck might as well be fence posts for all they added to the conversation. Sage and the young Ranger were identical idiots. They never stopped smiling or talking. Sage asked Mike questions she already knew the answer to. Mike complimented her on just about everything she had on including her gloves, which, Travis noticed, were just plain old gloves, nothing special.

While Travis paid and bought Duck an extra cookie, he heard Sage explain to Mike that she'd love to go riding, but her brother said she had to find someone who could keep up with her.

"I'm a fair horseman," Mike offered. "I'd be honored to give it a try."

They made plans while Travis choked down his comments. He had promised Sage, and Mike was not only fair, but one of the best men on horseback he'd ever seen. The boy must have been riding by the time he walked, and he'd need all his skill if he planned to keep up with Sage.

He followed the couple out. Mike took Sage's hand in both his and asked if she'd be too cold riding in this weather.

Travis wondered what other weather there was, but didn't say anything.

His sister said she'd be ready in an hour.

Mike finally gave her hand back and saluted. "I'll have two horses outside ready and waiting in one hour, Miss McMurray."

Sage suddenly looked shy, something Travis had never seen in his sister before. She took Duck's hand and turned toward home.

Travis stopped Mike from leaving with a stare. "Aren't you tired?"

"No," the young Ranger answered. "Not at all. Thanks for the breakfast."

"You're welcome and—"

Mike raised a hand. "I know. You'll kill me if I hurt her."

"You got that right," Travis answered, smiling for the first time since he'd suggested the idea of breakfast. "And I should also warn you that I've got two brothers who aren't as friendly as I am. After I kill you, they'll ride down from Whispering Mountain, dig you up, and kill you again."

Mike laughed. "Maybe I should think about going riding with girls who don't have any brothers."

"It wouldn't be a bad idea," Travis suggested.

Mike waved. "See you in an hour."

Travis walked in the opposite direction. When he turned the corner, Sage was waiting.

"Did you threaten him?" she asked as they walked.

"Yes." Travis saw no need to lie.

"Is he still coming to pick me up?"

"Yes."

"Good."

She didn't say another word. An hour later she kissed Travis on the cheek and wished him good luck with the questions he'd be answering in front of a panel of lawyers. "I'll be back in two hours and wait for you here. When you return, we can go pick up my new dress. I can hardly wait to see what Mike thinks of it."

"I don't know how long the questions will take."

"Not long, I hope."

Travis mumbled. "I'll be back as soon as I can." As he left with Duck, he noticed Mike riding up to the house. Somewhere he'd found a sidesaddle. Travis laughed. Sage had never ridden sidesaddle in her life. It would almost be worth being late for his testing to watch her face when she saw the saddle.

He walked across the street to the courthouse and slowly climbed to the second floor. A secretary told him that Judge Gates was finishing up with a case and would be with him as soon as possible. She pointed down the hallway. "You can wait down by the courtrooms, but make sure that boy doesn't make any noise."

He thanked her, then wondered why. If Duck would say something, Travis wouldn't care if he yelled it to the roof of this fine building.

As he walked down the hall, Travis figured it might be Dottie Davis's claim on the wine that held the judge up, but decided that would have been over at least an hour ago. To his surprise, Rainey was sitting on the bench outside the judge's chambers when he got there.

"Mind if I sit down?" Travis wasn't sure where he stood with Rainey. But then, why should today be any different than others? He never knew where he stood with her.

She looked up, but didn't smile. "No. I don't mind." She moved halfway down the bench, giving him more room than he and Duck would need.

The boy sat between them and to Travis's surprise patted her hand.

"Problem with the court, or just unhappy to see me?" Travis asked as he removed his and Duck's coats.

He dug in his pocket for the top string and two other balls of yarn Duck insisted on bringing along. One of the strings was caught on a half a cookie Duck must have crammed in his pocket along with a leaf he'd picked up somewhere along the way. "I swear," Travis mumbled as he tried to straighten the mess out. "I need a pack mule to take the kid anywhere."

Rainey smiled as she watched but made no effort to help.

Travis unloaded his other pocket on the bench next to Duck. "He collects everything. Not just food and string, but leaves and nails. I gave him one of the boxes Sage brought home to keep all he collects. He sleeps next to it like he's guarding his treasures every night."

Rainey laughed. "I know how he feels. When you don't have anything, one box seems like a lot. And, in answer to your question, my problem is with the court, not you. The judge is talking to Dottie now. It seems the partner may have a right to the wine. If so, we may be charged. He asked me to wait out here."

"If I get a license to practice, you may be my first client." Travis frowned. He wanted to see her again, but not as a criminal he defended.

"I thought you were being tested to be a lawyer this morning," Rainey said. "I may be running out of time. I may be sentenced and in jail before you finish the testing."

He shrugged. "Maybe. There's been a delay."

They sat in silence for a few minutes. No one passing would ever guess that they had shared several passionate kisses the night before. In truth they looked like two strangers waiting.

Finally Rainey broke the silence. "Good luck with the panel."

"Thanks," he answered. "Would you mind if I talked to you about something?"

She looked like she might bolt.

"I could use some advice. It's about my sister," he quickly added.

Rainey met his eyes for the first time. "All right. If you think I can help."

While Duck played with his string, Travis explained everything that had happened that morning at the bakery. Rainey relaxed at his side, asking questions, offering comments. By the time he'd finished his account, she was laughing at his threats.

"She's just eighteen," Travis ended. "I don't think she knows what she's doing."

"I'm twenty-three," Rainey said. "And I'm not sure I know what I'm doing most of the time."

Travis almost forgot about his sister's problem. Rainey had just told him something personal about herself.

"What do you think I should do?" he asked.

She smiled. "I think you should back away. Trust her."

He didn't like her advice, but he didn't argue. "Thanks," he said.

"You're welcome," she answered. "You love your little sister very much."

"True. When she was a kid it was like she had three fathers. It's hard now thinking of her grown. You have any siblings?"

He waited, expecting her to change the subject, or lie, but she said simply, "No."

The chamber door opened and Dottie Davis hurried out. There was no more time to talk. Travis heard the judge promise he'd solve their problems with the partner.

The judge's secretary hurried down the hall and told Travis he could go into the courtroom. She took the time to frown at Duck, then hurried back to her desk.

He leaned close to Rainey for a moment and whispered, "I need to see you tonight."

She met his gaze. Though her head shook slightly, he didn't miss a sparkle of passion in her eyes.

Travis stood. When he collected their coats, he lightly brushed Rainey's arm as if the need to touch her just once was too strong to resist.

Her lips made a circle and he groaned under his breath. The thought crossed his mind that if she didn't plan to see him tonight, she might as well kill him now.

The doors to the courtroom opened and lawyers were already lining up behind a table to question him. He glanced back and saw Rainey start down the steps. She looked over her shoulder and whispered, "Good luck."

Travis turned and headed in, feeling less prepared than if he'd been an unarmed man in a shootout. But this is what he'd told everyone he came to Austin to do, and now all he had to do was see it through.

By the time the introductions were over and the questions began, Duck had crawled up on top of Travis's coat and was sound asleep in the pew behind Travis.

Two hours later when Duck awoke, the lawyers were still asking questions.

CHAPTER 24

Rainey walked home with Dottie. The widow talked all the way about how the judge promised to do his best to help her, but her dead husband's partner seemed to have the advantage. No matter how you looked at it, wine was considered liquor, and he did own the half that was a saloon.

"What did he do with the other half after your husband died?"

Dottie frowned. "It's sitting empty. I've tried to sell it, but nobody wants half a place. Jeffrey, my husband's partner, doesn't make it any too easy, either. The few people who have looked at it didn't like the idea of sharing the building with him after they met him. He's meaner than a snake."

They hurried up the steps of the Askew House. Dottie held the door against the wind. "I may have to move over there and live. The judge said if Jeffrey presses charges, and he will if I know him, I'll have to hire a lawyer."

Rainey hung her old navy cape on one of the hooks by the front door wondering where she'd find the money for her lawyer if it came down to a trial. If she didn't have one, she'd probably go to jail. Maybe she should ask Pearl and Owen if she could work one more day. The extra pies would sell and she could sock back the money just in case. But she felt she was already intruding on their privacy enough by working three days.

The widow turned from putting up her coat. "It's lunchtime. I've got tea and biscuits in my room."

Rainey smiled. "Texas biscuits or English biscuits."

Dottie winked. "English of course."

One of the sisters stepped from the drawing room and frowned at them. When Rainey looked puzzled, the sister smiled. "I'm sorry. I'm glad to see you two in from this bitter cold, but we are expecting a young lady for her final fitting this morning, and it doesn't look like she's going to show up."

"Sage McMurray?" Rainey asked.

Grace nodded.

"I saw her brother at the courthouse. It appeared he had urgent business, and if so, she may have to wait until he can escort her." Rainey didn't want to tell the spinster that the girl stood her up to go riding with a handsome young man. They'd never understand.

"Oh." Grace looked relieved. "I see. That's quite understandable. A young lady of her breeding and wealth should never go anywhere alone."

Rainey smiled, knowing that if Grace knew what a wild bunch the McMurrays were, she would never have made such a foolish statement.

Dottie whispered that she'd bring the tea and biscuits up to Rainey's room and then hurried up the stairs. She enjoyed the three sisters' conversations, but found them lengthy.

Rainey did her duty and stopped in to say hello to the other two sisters. The German mother and daughter had left two days ago for their farm near Fredricksburg. The house seemed quiet and empty.

Mrs. Vivian was picking up her stationery from the writing table by the window. If there was to be no guest, she had her shopping to do. She didn't bother to say goodbye to the boarders, but they all heard her yell for Mamie to bring the buggy around. Mrs. Vivian might only be going a few blocks, but she planned to go in style.

By the time Rainey made it up to her room, Dottie was already there with the tea. They pulled off their shoes and ate on the tiny bed, laughing at how improper Mrs. Vivian would think they were if she found them.

After several minutes the conversation turned to the mess they were in. "We were only trying to help Mamie get free, and now we may both be locked up," the widow mumbled with a biscuit in her mouth.

"Do you really think so?"

The widow smiled a wicked smile and shook her head.

"That's why I asked to speak to the judge alone. I flirted with him outrageously and he never caught on. If trouble comes, I can promise you he'll be on our side. The only problem is he's an honest man, and they are always harder to deal with."

"You're telling me," Rainey agreed.

They laughed and talked. Eventually the conversation turned to what Rainey had heard the night before. "Snort and Whiny are still planning to kill their boss, who claims he's coming into money soon. I talked it over with Travis, and he thinks Haskell plans to collect on the reward money for an escaped outlaw named Seth Norman who is sweet on Whiny."

Dottie wiggled her eyebrows. "I'll bet they make a cute couple."

Rainey laughed. Somehow the widow always managed to make things funny. Rainey opened the window in case they could overhear more. But all they heard was Mamie singing as she threw out the wash water.

Rainey leaned back, not minding the open window, for Mamie's voice sounded so sweet. "She always sings when Mrs. Vivian is out of the house."

The widow nodded. "Too bad it's cold. Our landlord likes to visit on warm days, but when it's cold she hurries back to take her afternoon nap." Dottie smiled her sweetest and added, "Which, by the way, you look like you might need a nap as well. Late night?"

She leaned close to Dottie and whispered what had happened last night when Travis had insisted on walking her back to the laundry room window.

The widow giggled like a girl. "He's got it bad for you."

"I know. I feel the same. But he's the marrying kind, and I think that's what he wants."

Dottie raised an eyebrow. "Then marry him."

"I can't. I promised I wouldn't tie myself down like my mother did. My father made her believe she would starve without him. Her days were miserable, but she wouldn't leave, not even when he hit her."

Rainey took a deep breath and told her what she'd never told another soul. "When I was six, my father's father died. We traveled all day to his farmhouse. My parents expected an inheritance. But it seems my father's education was all the old man planned to give his son. My father discovered he inherited nothing, not even his mother's jewels."

She closed her eyes as she repeated a memory she'd tried for a dozen years to forget. "My father had too much to drink. He drove far too fast on a rutted road. The carriage rocked and pitched. My mother fell against the side and was bruised badly. I remember how he yelled at her to stop whimpering. When we got home, her skirts were bloody. She'd lost a child and the doctor said she'd never have another."

"Oh, no," Dottie whispered.

"My father blamed my mother. For a long time I could hear them arguing at night. The next morning the bruising on my mother always seemed fresh. Until finally the life just went out of her and she became a walking ghost."

Dottie closed her hand over Rainey's. "She must have loved you. She must have."

"I wish I could believe that. All I know is I never want to be in that situation where I have no way out, where someone has control over my life. I love being near Travis. I love the way he touches me. If I could know for sure that I could walk away, I think I'd stay with him forever." Rainey shook her head. "It makes no sense."

"But marriage can be grand."

Rainey looked up. "Then why didn't you remarry, Dottie? You must have had many offers."

The widow took a long drink of her tea. "I'd never have a love like that again, and I'm too old to settle for less. I think I'll wear black until the day I die."

Something rattled in the alley, drawing both their attention. Three men were tying horses to the saloon porch.

"That's strange," Dottie whispered. "No one but delivery men bring horses to the back."

Rainey touched her finger to her lips and leaned closer. "This is a magic window. I can hear anything said below."

One man, a short barrel-chested fellow, mumbled, "You sure she came alone? I don't want the Ranger to surprise us."

"Yeah, she's alone, but we'd better act fast. That brother of hers could show up at any minute."

A large man dressed in black leaned over the saddle of his horse and ordered, "Kill him if he does. And kill that kid with him if you have to. I don't want nothing messing this up. I don't think I could stand another day of you planning to get even. We'll go in the back and out again before anyone thinks to stop us. By the time anyone outside the house figures out what's going on, we'll be miles away."

A voice that sounded like Haskell yelled from inside the saloon, "What can I do for you boys?"

The man in black stepped on the saloon's back porch and mumbled something.

Rainey leaned closer, trying to figure out what was going on. She could see all three men below, the one in black at the back door, the stout one between two of the horses, and another of average size and build. He walked across the alley and leaned against the boardinghouse steps.

Haskell didn't appear, but his voice sounded nervous when, a moment later, he yelled for Mamie.

The slave appeared on the back porch of the boardinghouse. "Yes," she answered.

"I need you over at the saloon, Mamie. There's four bits in it if you'll clean all the tables in the bar."

Rainey thought it strange Haskell didn't step out, but the man in black still framed the doorway to the saloon as if he were guarding it.

"I have to wait and check with Miz Vivian when she gets back from picking up supplies!" Mamie yelled. "She don't like me leaving the kitchen when she's not here."

"I already talked to her," Haskell snapped. "She told me to tell you when the saloon was empty and you could work." He hesitated a moment, then added, "I'll make it a dollar if you do a fast job. The extra money can be just between the two of us."

Mamie nodded. "I'll get my stuff and be right there."

The three riders moved to the center of the alley. "Once she's out of the way," the man in black said almost casually, "go straight in and pick up the girl. Even if some of the boarders are home, they won't be armed. Just knock them out of the way and get McMurray's sister." He nodded once toward the stout man. "Trust me, Seth, this will hurt that Ranger far more than killing him."

Rainey jumped back from the window. "They're kidnapping Sage! She must have come alone to her appointment."

Her mind raced. The outlaws Travis had told her about were just below her window. They planned to get even with Travis by taking Sage.

Dottie was already on her feet. "I'll get my gun."

"I'll alert them." Rainey followed, a step behind the widow.

They'd reached the second-floor landing when Rainey heard the sound of men storming through the kitchen. The faint rattle of laughter came from behind the closed door of the drawing room. The others would have no warning if she didn't hurry.

Dottie ran to her room.

Rainey dashed down the stairs, thinking she could get to the other women, but by the time she reached the foyer, she realized there was no time. She could hear the men moving across the dining room. They'd be in the foyer in seconds, and from there the drawing room was only steps away. Even if the women knew they were coming, there would be no time to escape.

She had to do something. She'd seen how the brothers loved Sage. They'd all be heartsick if something happened to her.

Rainey's gaze fell on a fur-lined blue coat hanging on the peg by the front door. It hadn't been there when she'd placed her cape by the door. It had to be Sage's.

In a run she grabbed the coat and whirled it around her, pulling the hood up just as the men stormed the foyer.

"There she is!" one yelled. "Grab her before she gets back outside."

Rainey didn't see which man seized her. She was afraid to show any part of her face. She didn't see him, but she felt his crushing grip as he lifted her off the ground and threw her over his shoulder.

Cocooned in the folds of Sage's coat, Rainey heard the drawing room door open and then screams. The man carrying her ran through the house, bumping her against furniture as he moved.

"Stop!" Dottie's voice yelled. "Stop or I'll shoot."

"Keep going!" one of the men yelled. "Get her out of here! I'll cover you."

A shot sounded. Then another.

Rainey cried out in pain as the man carrying her bounded down the stairs with her bumping against his shoulder. She heard horses and shouts but couldn't make out words.

Someone shoved something over the hood of her coat and she felt it slide down, blocking out the little light that could seep through the coat. Then she was thrown roughly over a horse. A moment later a man's knees slammed, one against her cheek, one at her thigh. Whoever had climbed behind her on the saddle didn't care that he was hurting her.

"Get her out of town fast!" someone shouted. "If she struggles, hit her upside the head a few times. Nobody will hear her crying through that sack, and if she has any sense, she'll stop yelling."

"Where's Frank?" the man holding Rainey yelled.

"He'll be along. Go. I'm right behind you."

Then the horse moved beneath her and they were off.

She didn't struggle. Her arms and hands were trapped inside the coat.

The horse turned at what she guessed was the end of the alley. She had no idea where she was going, or why. All she knew was that she'd just been kidnapped.

These evil men had planned to take Sage, not for money, but to hurt Travis. What would they do when they discovered they had the wrong woman?

What would Travis do?

CHAPTER 25

TRAVIS RETURNED FROM THE COURTHOUSE WITH DUCK. HE FELT LIKE his brain might explode any minute. He'd never been asked so many questions. The lawyers were polite, but gave no hint if he'd answered their questions correctly. They'd simply told him that they would be in touch.

Frustrated and hungry, he decided nothing about this trip was going as planned . . . except, of course, Sage's shopping. He'd found Rainey, but she didn't seem to want more than a friendship from him most of the time. His leg grew stronger each day from all the walking he did, but he knew he was weeks away from climbing back on a horse. Dr. Bailey had examined him and seemed hopeful that he'd heal, but cautioned him that it would take time and care. The doctor had also gotten close enough to Duck, thanks to a toy train set in his study, to determine that the boy would recover, at least physically, from his ordeal.

Travis walked into the Baileys' home and found Mike Saddler pacing the sitting room. He sat Duck down and faced the young Ranger. "Waiting for Sage?" Travis asked, deciding to take Rainey's advice and stay out of his sister's life.

"No, sir." Mike crushed the brim of his hat in his hands. "I was hoping Sage was with you. I came with news about the Norman brothers. They've been spotted in town."

Travis had to give Duck his attention for a moment. The boy was hungry and tried to pull him toward the kitchen.

"Just a minute, son." Travis stood his ground. "And?" he said to Mike, guessing there must be more the young Ranger needed to say. If he'd come to warn Travis to arm, it was unnecessary.

Mike swallowed. "And we think the target may be your sister."

"What?"

"We all thought it would be you, or maybe the judge, but a man fitting Seth Norman's description was seen following Sage." Mike looked sick. "I had the feeling we were being followed this morning when we were riding. I kept my gun ready but never saw even a man who looked like one of the Norman brothers."

His knuckles whitened around his hat. "After I left here, I circled by the office and heard the report myself. I came straight back here."

Travis couldn't breathe. "Where is Sage now?"

"Dr. Bailey said he took her over to the Askew House about half an hour ago. She told him she couldn't wait any longer to see what the three sisters were working on. The doc said she told him she'd wait for you to pick her up there."

Travis headed out the door with Duck right behind him.

Mike followed. "She said she'd be at least two hours, so we know she's safe."

"We know no such thing." Travis swore. "Did the doc see her in?"

"Of course."

Travis slowed, telling himself he was overreacting. Mike and Dr. Bailey had done all he would have done. At the time they didn't know Sage was a target. If she was a target. He was the one the Norman brothers wanted, not Sage. "Are you sure about this, Saddler?"

Mike nodded. "Dillon rushed in at the office to tell everyone and then left to go look for you. I just stopped by to tell the Baileys and then planned to stand guard at Askew House until Sage finished. We can't let her on the streets alone until this threat is over."

"We'll both stand guard."

Mike took a deep breath as his long strides matched Travis's. People moved out of their path as the stormed toward the Askew House.

Travis stopped and lifted Duck. The tiny boy had been running to keep up. "It's all right, Duck," he said. "We're going to get Sage."

As he hugged the boy to him, he said to Mike, "If this is true, I'll kill all of them for even thinking about bothering my sister."

Mike nodded. "I'll help you."

They walked on at as fast a pace as Travis could handle.

They turned the corner where the Askew House stood just as Sage ran out, her braid flying. "Travis!" she yelled. "You're here!"

Travis felt his heart slow to normal as she ran down the steps toward them. She looked upset. He could deal with that. He could deal with anything as long as she was all right.

But before he could shift Duck in his arms, Sage ran into Mike's embrace. The young Ranger hugged her wildly, lifting her off the ground.

"Thank God you're safe," Travis said. "We were worried someone might try to kidnap you."

To his surprise, when Sage turned to him, her eyes were filled with tears. "Not me, someone else!" she cried. "They stormed the house from the back to take her. We were all scared to death. One of the boarders shot one of the men."

Travis hurried up the steps knowing Mike would get Sage in safely. The young Ranger hadn't turned loose of her since the hug.

Stepping into the foyer, Travis heard women crying a moment before he saw a man dressed in black lying in a pool of his own blood. Travis glanced back and nodded once to Mike before stepping farther inside.

The foyer seemed so dark after coming in for the sunlight that it took him a few seconds to see the widow.

Dottie Davis sat on the third step of the wide stairs, both her hands around an old gun. "I had to load it," she cried. "It took only seconds, but I was too late."

Mike moved to the body and knelt over the man. He lifted one shoulder, revealing a leaking chest wound at heart level. Meeting Travis's gaze, Mike shook his head. "Dead" was all he said.

Travis sat Duck a few steps above the widow so he'd be out of view of the body. He leaned down to see the widow's face. "You got him, Mrs. Davis. You weren't too late. The intruder is dead." He touched the widow's arm with one hand as he pried the gun from her fingers. The black lacy sleeve of her dress was soaked in blood. "You're wounded, Mrs. Davis. You've been shot. We'll get you taken care of right away."

"It doesn't matter." Dottie shook her head. "I missed."

"No." Travis never knew what to do with women after a gunfight. He wasn't sure reminding her that the man she'd shot was dead would help. "You missed who?" he finally said.

Dottie looked up at him with so much sorrow in her eyes, Travis swore he felt a chill. "I missed the man who took Rainey. She must have put on Sage's coat trying to fool them. She made it to the door before one grabbed her."

"No." Sage moved to the stairs, her face pale with confusion and fear. "Why would someone pretend to be me? Why would the men be after me?"

The widow leaned back. "We heard them planning it from the window in Rainey's room. We couldn't get down both flights of stairs fast enough. I didn't find the gun in time to stop them. Maybe Rainey thought if she grabbed your coat and ran out the front door, she'd be safe and she'd get them out of the house. I don't know. It all happened so fast."

Travis straightened. His heart felt like it might break through his ribs.

"Oh, Travis!" the widow cried. "I'm so sorry. I know how much she means to you."

"How much who means to you?" Sage watched her brother as if she'd never seen him before. "Travis, did you know the woman they kidnapped? Why did they do it?"

Mike answered from just behind Sage. "They thought Rainey was you."

Sage glanced from Travis to Mike. "You knew the kidnapped woman, too."

Mike nodded.

"No!" Sage yelled. "No!" She stomped her foot as if she could banish all the pain before her away. "I don't even know a woman named Rainey. How could she know about me? How could she risk her life for me?"

"Because," Travis said almost calmly. "I told her all about you."

The three sisters were huddled in a corner by the drawing room door. They were crying and holding on to one another.

Mike moved toward the door. "I'll round up a few of the men and be back ready to ride. They can't have gone far."

Sage shoved her tears away with the palm of her hand as she gained a bit of control. "Bring an extra horse, Mike, I'm going with you. If some woman is willing to risk her life for me, I can return the favor."

Both men answered, "No."

Mike didn't take time to argue further; he disappeared.

Travis stood and put an arm around his sister. "I need you to stay here. I have to have someone I can trust." His sister was shaking, but she wasn't falling apart. She would have made a good Ranger, he thought.

Sage shook her head. "But she's kidnapped because of me."

"Not because of you. You're not to blame for those men. I'll find her, I swear, but I need you here to watch over Duck and the Baileys. I'd give anything if I could be two places, but I can't. When the men find out they have the wrong woman, they may come back for you and if Duck or the Baileys are in the way, they'll be killed."

Sage nodded. "If they return, I'll be waiting and armed."

Travis saw it then, the McMurray spirit in her. All her life he'd worried about her, protected her, and now he knew that she would take care of herself.

"You'll have Mike to help. He's young, but he's the best."

Sage straightened and reached for Duck.

Mrs. Vivian rattled up in her carriage. While she was screaming and demanding to know what was going on, Travis loaded the widow and Sage, with Duck in her arms, in Mrs. Vivian's carriage and headed toward the Baileys.

While Travis changed into his leather trousers and his winter coat, Dr. Bailey bandaged the widow's arm and Sage unpacked the guns.

When Travis stormed toward the door, he noticed Sage had strapped a double gun belt around her waist. "Dottie's agreed to stay with me until you get back to help with the boy."

Travis nodded. The widow would be good with Duck, and the doctor would see that her wound was treated properly.

"Be careful," Sage whispered as she followed him to the door.

"I will," he answered as he kissed her head. "Make sure everyone is safe. Don't leave the house, and keep a gun within reach."

Duck blocked the door. Travis knelt on his good knee and pulled the boy to him. "I have to go," he whispered, "but I swear

I'll be back." He had no idea how much the boy understood of what he said. But Duck had seen the blood and heard the screams. He knew what Travis had to do. "I have to go save Rainey. She's been kidnapped."

Duck nodded and stepped back as though he understood. Tears silently ran from his blue eyes. Sage moved behind him and held his shoulder as Travis left.

A few minutes later he pulled the buggy up to the boarding-house just as the Rangers rode in. Seven men, all ready to ride for as long as it took.

Dillon was already ordering the men to spread out and enter the alley from either side.

Mike jumped down from his mount. "We'll bring her back."

Travis moved close to the young ranger. "I need a favor," he asked.

Mike might have argued with an order, but a favor was an-other story. "Name it," he said.

"I need to borrow your horse and I need you to stay with Sage until I get back."

"But—"

"Rainey's mine. I have to go after her." Travis's words reg-istered against his heart. Rainey was his; she'd been his fairy woman since the moment they met. He added, "And I have to know Sage is safe."

Mike understood. He handed over the reins. "We'll be wait-ing when you bring her back. I'll guard her with my life."

Travis smiled. "I had a feeling you would."

Without another word, Travis hurried into the boarding-house. Nothing had changed since he'd left. The sisters were still crying, Mrs. Vivian was still yelling, and the man in black was still dead.

Travis and the Rangers went through the house, following the same path the kidnappers had used for their escape. Travis missed nothing. Several dining room chairs had been over-turned. The back door had been left open.

A young black woman sat on the porch steps crying.

Travis motioned for the others to look around while he knelt. "Mamie," he said, remembering the name Rainey had called her. "Did you see anything?"

Mamie kept crying. "No, I was cleaning across in the sa-loon," she whispered. "But I heard the shots and I ran to see what was happening. Just before I reached the back door, Mr.

Haskell slapped me so hard across the face I hit the floor. He told me to stay clear or we'd all be dead. Mr. Haskell sounded like he'd seen the devil. I ain't never seen a man look so scared. "When I finally got to my feet, he didn't even notice me leaving."

"McMurray!" Dillon yelled from halfway down the alley. "They went this way. Two horses traveling fast." Dillon looked directly at Travis. "You riding lead?"

"I am."

Dillon nodded and followed Travis to the horses. "I've left men assigned to clean up. I'm riding with you."

"Thanks," Travis answered, knowing there were none better than Dillon.

He checked the saddle and shoved his cane in with the rifle. The hardest part would be swinging into the saddle, he told himself. From then on, there would be no stopping.

Dillon stood close, one hand on the reins, ready to help if needed.

Travis bit his bottom lip and forced his body up. His muscles responded to the years of climbing into a saddle and he swung up in one fluid motion, not feeling the pain until he landed.

"Ready to ride?" Dillon asked.

"Ready," Travis answered as the other Rangers circled around him.

They shot out of town at full gallop following the trail easily.

He hadn't been on a horse in months and his leg ached all the way to the bone, but he didn't stop, couldn't stop, because his heart hurt twice as much.

CHAPTER 26

AT THE RIVER, THE RANGERS SPLIT UP. DILLON TOOK TWO MEN AND moved downstream. Travis, leading an extra horse, rode with Roy Dumont heading upstream. The kidnappers were obviously trying to hide their tracks, but they'd leave a trail coming out of the stream long before a Ranger would give up looking.

"I'll fire a round if we see where they exit," Dillon said. "You do the same."

Travis knew there was a good chance they'd be too far apart to hear one another's shots, but he also knew outlaws were often not the brightest men around. Last year he'd worked a stage robbery where the bandit shot his own horse in a display of gunfire meant to frighten the passengers. Riding in the stream might be a good way to hide their trail, but it was also more dangerous and slower.

Roy Dumont didn't say a word as he took the left bank of the stream and began to look for sign. With the man in black dead, only two men stood between them and Rainey. Travis would worry about who else might have been in on the plot to get even with him later.

He planned as he rode. Now was not the time to hope; he had to use all his skill and look at the facts. He had to get to her fast. Once the men discovered she wasn't Sage, they might kill her—or worse. Surely they knew the Rangers would be after them. The Rangers would have been even if someone kin to a Ranger hadn't been the target. How dare the outlaws think they could commit such a crime within blocks of the Ranger headquarters? The Normans were either stupid or very sure of themselves.

Seth and Eldon would probably ride until their horses gave out, which would be long before any Ranger's horse stopped.

If their horses made it until dark, there would be lots of places they could hide in this country. With only a sliver of a moon to see by, tracking could be difficult. If the Normans had any sense, they wouldn't light a fire. In the dark they might not know they had the wrong woman until morning. If they did set up camp, even in the firelight they'd see that Rainey wasn't Sage.

Travis pushed harder. He had to reach Rainey before dark. Her abductors might have decided they had gotten away with the crime if no one caught up with them by sunset. They'd build a fire and have their first good look at Rainey. With her blond hair she couldn't fool them into believing she was Sage for a moment.

He closed his eyes, thinking how frightened she must be. And she had a right to be. Seth and Eldon planned to make Travis suffer. They probably saw it as only fair to kill his sister since Travis had killed their brother in a gunfight.

Travis forced his mind away from thinking about how they'd kill her.

"Here!" Roy yelled as his horse climbed up the left bank. "Two sets of fresh tracks."

Roy slipped from his mount and knelt. He read the sign easily. "One is riding heavy—that's the horse with the girl and the stout man you said the widow described. It has to be Seth. The other mount stumbled coming out of the water. He won't last long if they keep riding him so hard."

Slipping back on his horse, Roy raised his rifle and fired once.

"You think Dillon heard?" Travis asked. They'd only split up thirty minutes ago, but Dillon and his party would be moving faster traveling downstream.

Roy shook his head. "Looks like we're going this one alone."

To Travis's surprise, Roy winked and added with a smile, "More fun that way." He must have seen the worry in Travis's eyes because he added, "Don't worry, we'll get her back."

They rode on for an hour across rolling countryside before Roy stopped again to study the ground. Travis wanted to look, but he knew if he got off, he might not be able to climb back in the saddle. His leg had finally stopped throbbing and was numb. He'd be no help to Rainey on foot.

While Roy read the trail, Travis cut one of the leather straps off the back of Mike's saddle and laced it around the top of his leg, tying himself to the saddle.

He took a drink from his canteen, realizing he hadn't eaten since yesterday. He wasn't sure he could eat anything until he found Rainey. He thought of how frightened of the dark she'd been. She wouldn't go into the alley alone, and now she was miles from anything she knew. She must be mad with panic. She had no way of even knowing he was looking for her.

"I'll find you," he mumbled to himself. "No matter how far they take you, I swear, I'll find you."

"The horse that stumbled coming out of the water is near finished." Roy removed his hat and wiped his brow. "The man riding single, probably Eldon, turned off here. If he doesn't stop, he'll have to put the horse down."

Travis saw a stand of thick oak maybe half a mile away. "He's planning to hold up in there. My guess is he's already found him a safe place to hide where he can see if anyone's coming."

Roy nodded. "He won't see me. I'll go get him." He covered his eyes and looked up at Travis. "Can you handle the other outlaw alone? I could ride with you and let this rabbit go."

Travis shook his head. "No. I want them all caught, but if you finish, leave him tied up somewhere if he's alive and ride to join me."

Roy smiled. "I'll do that. Maybe once I save this young lady, I'll have me three wives." His eyebrows danced up and down. "Women can't resist a hero."

Travis frowned and Roy changed the subject. "You know that burned-out mission due south of here?"

"I know it," Travis answered. "I was thinking the same thing. Our last kidnapper will feel safe in there with rock at his back. It would be the place I'd head to if I planned to hold up for the night, and if he's riding double, he'll have to stop soon."

Roy saluted and kicked his horse. "I'll catch up to you."

Travis put the cap back on his canteen and headed due south toward the remains of a mission. The ground was damp, making the tracks easy to follow. His left leg had started to swell. His boot felt tight, but there was no time to stop.

He reached the remains of a mission just before the sun set.

Jagged white rocks lined the perimeter of the grounds like broken teeth no longer useful. He circled, keeping the sun at his back, and rode between the walls that had once held trouble at bay. Anyone at the mission would have to be staring at the setting sun to see him.

On the east side, where the walls were almost ten feet high, he found a horse tied to the last pole standing in what once had been a corral. Travis knew he'd found them. He pulled his knife and cut the leather holding his leg still, then slid slowly from the saddle. He wasn't surprised when his left leg wouldn't hold his weight. He pulled his cane and walked across the rocky ground knowing that if he stumbled and fell, he'd never be able to get to his feet. The ride had undone weeks of healing, but it couldn't be helped. He had to find Rainey.

First, he unsaddled the outlaw's animal, consuming valuable time, but delaying the outlaw's escape if he returned to the horse. Then he walked his horse and the extra mount he'd brought several feet away and tied them out of sight. His gun belt held two weapons, but he pulled the rifle from the sheath tied to his saddle. What he lacked in mobility, he might need to make up for in firepower.

He limped his way slowly through the maze of rocks as the sky blackened. Time was running out for Rainey. He needed to find her fast.

With each step he tested his weight against his left leg. He felt like he was counting down until he took one final step and the leg would no longer take any of his weight. He held to the wall when he could and moved as silently as the rocks would allow. He knew even if he fell and had to crawl, he'd find Rainey.

She was near. He could feel it.

Every few steps he'd stop and listen, hoping to hear voices, afraid he'd hear her scream.

Half an hour passed and the night blackened. Travis felt like he was lost in a maze made of stones.

He crossed between two rock walls. His boot struck against something that wasn't rock hard . . . something that gave when he shoved slightly. Travis almost tumbled as he tried to move forward again. Placing his rifle on a crumbled wall, he carefully felt his way in the darkness.

Travis brushed something furry and velvet bundled at his feet. Sage's coat? He'd held it for her a dozen times. Now there was no doubt Rainey was near. Also no doubt that Seth Norman knew he had the wrong woman.

Reaching again, Travis heard the sound of his own heart pounding. Something lay beside the coat. He spread his fingers wide and moved across it.

Blood, warm and sticky, wet his hand as the smell of it filled his lungs.

He lay his hand flat, feeling flesh, but no life beneath it. With careful circles, he tried to find the wound. Beneath the jacket, the body was too hard, too thick to be a woman's. Travis took a deep breath of relief and continued searching.

In the center of a man's chest he found a small knife planted as deep as the blade would go. Judging from the small hole and the great amount of blood the man had been bleeding for some time before he died.

Travis leaned back away from the body. Come morning he'd take a good look at the body and make sure it was Seth Norman, but right now, in the blackness of the mission, he knew two things. The man was dead and Rainey had to be the one who killed him.

The only question remaining: Where was Rainey? The possibility crossed his mind that someone might have been waiting here for the outlaws. Maybe crazy Old Man Norman, or someone else who'd escaped with the brothers and had offered to help in their revenge. If someone had been waiting at the mission, Rainey may not have bought her freedom with the killing.

He struggled to stand and resume his search.

"Rainey?" he said in a low voice that carried several feet. He didn't want to frighten her even more in the dark, but if she was hiding, he might not find her until morning if she didn't make a sound. "Rainey, it's me, Travis."

He'd moved about twenty feet when he heard someone crying softly. He hurried toward the sound.

"Rainey," he whispered when he saw the outline of her tiny form balled up in a corner near the opening. "Rainey?"

He knelt beside her but didn't touch her. "Rainey?"

She stopped crying and for a long moment remained as still as the rocks around her. Then she raised her head and whispered back, "Travis, I knew you'd come find me."

He sat beside her and wrapped her in his arms. She cried on his shoulder as he moved his hands slowly along her body, making sure she wasn't hurt. He didn't tell her to stop crying, or ask any questions, he just held her.

Finally she grew quiet and he felt her body relax next to him. After a while she whispered as if someone might hear them. "Travis, I killed a man today."

"I know," he answered. "Now go to sleep, Sunshine. We'll talk about it tomorrow. You're safe now." He didn't want to add that he doubted he could get to his feet if he tried. He needed time to rest and so did she.

She pressed against him as he covered them with his coat. He pulled both his guns from their holsters and placed them on either side, then he wrapped his arms around her. He wanted to tell her how he felt . . . like a part of him had been ripped away when he'd learned of the kidnapping . . . but he wasn't sure she'd understand. She thought they were friends. Deep down, he'd realized that she was his. Whether they ever married, or admitted it, didn't matter. She was his and he was hers.

Her breathing slowed and he knew she was asleep, but he stayed awake, listening to the sounds of the night just beyond the mission. Nothing would hurt her, now that he'd found her.

She moved in the night, shifting against him. He'd whisper that she was safe and she'd return to sleep.

She didn't seem to notice as he moved her fingers through her hair, loving the way it felt.

Finally he relaxed and closed his eyes.

Just after dawn, her wiggling woke him. He opened one eye to find green eyes watching him.

"Morning," he mumbled.

"Morning," she answered, as if she'd responded that way a thousand times. "You awake?"

"I am now." He stretched his back, but didn't remove the arm that had grown numb from being around her. "How are you this morning?"

"I think I'm all right."

He held her at arm's length and studied her. "There's a bruise on your cheek."

She nodded.

"Anywhere else?"

She lifted her chin. "There's probably one on my backside, but I'm not going to show it to you. My ribs are sore, my feet are freezing, and I'm hungry."

He looked down and saw her stocking feet tucked against his calf. "Where are your shoes?"

"Upstairs in my bedroom, I think. When I left yesterday to warn the others, I didn't have time to put them on. I had no plan of leaving the house at the time."

Travis touched her cheek gently. "Why'd you put Sage's coat on? You must have known they were storming the house to kidnap her."

"It was the first thing I thought of to help. I couldn't let them take her. She's your sister. You love her." She pushed away from him and stood suddenly. "Are you arresting me for killing that disgusting man?"

"No. If you hadn't done it, I probably would have. Want to tell me what happened?"

Rainey ran her fingers through her hair and brushed the dust from her dress. "We made it to this place before dark. He pulled off a bag they'd tied over my head and arms. When the hood fell back, he knew I wasn't Sage. That fact made him furious. He hit me hard, knocking me down and swearing in two languages at me like it was all my fault. When I fell, I stayed down. He must have thought he knocked me out, but I reached for my knife tucked away in my pocket. He grabbed the coat in one hand and tried to pull me to my feet with the other. I knew I would only have one chance to fight and I had to hit his heart. If I missed, he'd kill me." She took a breath, shaking at her own words. "He was screaming about different ways he planned to kill me when he was finished with me. He said the sight of how he planned to cut up my body would give you nightmares the rest of your life."

Travis stretched his leg and slowly rose from the ground using only his right leg for support. The swelling in his left leg had gone down some.

"I took a step back and held the knife with both hands. When he came at me, I fell toward him using my whole body to propel the knife." She covered her face. "I couldn't look. He stumbled backward and fell first to his knees, then forward without saying another word. I think I must have cut open his heart."

Travis tugged her hands away from her face. "You did what you had to do. Don't ever think of it again, it's over."

"How did you find me so fast?"

"I followed your trail. The guy you killed left tracks Duck could probably keep up with. I must have got to the house within minutes after you left. Sage had bolted the doors and was watching for help to arrive. She ran out as we neared."

He couldn't stop touching Rainey. He pulled her to him as he continued. "The men who stormed the boardinghouse were brothers. They've had a hatred for me that goes way back." He kissed her head, needing to reassure himself it was all over even as he recounted every fact. "The widow shot one of the brothers. She took a bullet in her arm, but she's in good hands."

"No." Rainey stopped him by brushing her fingers over his lips. "How did you get here?" she repeated.

"I rode."

"You're not well enough to ride." She looked at his leg that he had been rubbing since he stood. "Oh, no . . ."

He watched her pale and had to smile through his pain. She cared. "Now, don't worry. I'm all right. To tell you the truth, I was so worried about you I hardly noticed the pain."

She moved to him. "I'm sorry."

He hugged her close. "It would have hurt far more to find you dead in this graveyard of rocks."

He kissed her then, long and hard. She circled her arms around his waist and held on tight. Though their embrace warmed him with need, it was not passion that demanded he hold her so tight, but caring. A caring that ran so deep he knew he'd never know peace if she were in danger.

Without a word he leaned on her, and together they walked out of the ruins. When they were in the morning sun, it didn't seem so cold. He insisted she wear his coat. She made him rest on a rock while she brought the horses around to him. After she brought them, saddled and ready, he rummaged through the saddlebags and found jerky for breakfast. They were both tired and healing so neither talked, but they touched.

He moved his big hand along her back as she sat next to him. She patted his arm in thank-you when he passed her the canteen. They didn't talk of the fear they'd both felt or the worry. They didn't need to.

By the time the sun began to warm the day, Roy rode up from the north. He was alone.

When Roy was inside the border of the mission, he swung down from his horse and ran to Rainey, grabbing her in a bear hug. "Glad you're alive!" he shouted. He whirled her around and then sat her back on her feet and apologized for being so forward.

When Rainey looked pale, he apologized again, and Travis thought he saw a hint of the charm that must have won him two wives. He asked about her bruise and said he'd gladly kill the man again for putting such a mark on a pretty girl like her. He worried over her lack of shoes as Travis had never thought to do and offered her his good socks to wear.

Travis finally told Roy to stop being a mother hen. They needed to get her back to Austin as soon as possible.

"Where's the man you went into the trees after?" Travis asked as they collected supplies.

"He gave me a grand chase, but I lost him." Roy didn't like admitting he'd failed.

"We'll get him," Travis said. "What matters is we found Rainey."

Roy nodded. "Yeah, but I got a feeling he's going to show up before long to pester us again. Seth might have been the meanest brother, but Eldon is sneaky. We both better be watching our backs until he's behind bars again."

Travis agreed.

Roy loaded Seth's bloody body on his horse. As they packed up, Roy wanted to hear the whole story of how such a little lady killed a man he could barely lift.

Rainey told him, then asked if he'd help Travis mount his horse. She said that Travis had reinjured his leg.

Travis protested, but Rainey continued to beg Roy. Travis claimed he could mount the horse alone, but if it made her happy, he'd take the help.

Roy mumbled as he helped Travis, "If you were married, you would know that sometimes it's just better to go along than to try and reason with a woman."

Once Travis was on his horse, he glanced at Rainey, silently thanking her for making such a fuss. If she hadn't begged, he wouldn't have made a show of giving in, even though, in truth, he wasn't sure he could have climbed on his horse alone.

Once they started back, Roy asked one question after another. The rough, fighting Ranger turned into a gentleman worrying about Rainey. Travis noticed she barely knew how to ride a horse, but Roy kept saying she was doing grand.

Halfway back Roy insisted they stop and let Rainey rest. He built a fire and made coffee from his pack and then said he had to go down by the river and rest for an hour before he could go any farther. "I didn't get a wink of sleep last night," Roy complained.

Rainey retrieved a blanket from the saddle and spread it by a tree, insisting that Travis sit down. When he did, she rolled his coat and placed it under his left knee, relieving a little of the pressure he felt.

"How'd you know that would help?" Travis asked as he leaned back against the tree trunk.

"I was hurt once in an ice-skating accident." She spread the extra blanket over Travis.

"I'm not an invalid," he mumbled.

"I didn't say you were. The blanket is for me."

Travis watched Roy disappear in the cottonwoods down by the creek. "He's giving us time alone. He doesn't need a nap."

"I know, he's sweet."

"Sweet," Travis grumbled. "If he were here alone with you, he'd have you with child before the hour was up."

Rainey laughed. "I doubt it. You see, I'm not the least attracted to him."

"How about me?" Travis thought he already knew the answer.

"You I can't keep my hands off of." She laughed. "But, I'll try."

"Roy is right about one thing. We do need to talk."

Rainey sat next to him on the blanket padded with the dried grass beneath a tree. "About what?"

"When we get back, there will be no time for us. The Rangers, the newspaper, everyone will ask what happened. In most places you'd have to tell the story once or twice, but in Austin everything turns into a sideshow."

She cuddled closer to him, pulling the blanket over her shoulder. "What do I say?"

"The truth of course. Tell them all about why you put on Sage's coat. How the Norman brothers kidnapped you. How you killed Seth. All they'll have to see is that bruise on your cheek to believe every word you say."

She laid her head on his shoulder and spread her fingers over his heart. "Well, if all I have to do is tell the truth, I guess our talk is over. Mind if I take a nap? I dreamed last night I was sleeping in a cave with a hibernating bear. He was delightfully warm, but noisy."

He put his arm around her and tugged her closer to him. How could a woman feel so right? "That's not all. There is one thing I want you to lie about."

Rainey raised her head and looked at him. "What?"

"I want you to tell people that I found you huddled in the ruins at dawn."

"But you found me last night."

"I know I did and you know I did, but no one else has to know."

"But nothing happened last night."

"I think I know that, too. I'm just thinking of your reputation."

Rainey laughed. "I don't have a reputation, good or bad." She smiled at him. "So I guess I shouldn't mention to the paper that I came to your room late the night before."

He didn't answer.

"Or that we kissed in the alley long after the boardinghouse was locked up. We kissed and you opened my shirt."

His arm tightened slightly, but she didn't stop.

"Or maybe I should leave out all together about how we met and how you accused me of stealing your horse."

"You did steal my horse. Twice."

She slid her hand to his collar and touched his hair. "I have a little trouble with what to leave out of my life when you tell me to be totally honest. I figure on a good day the best you'll get is about fifty-fifty." Her fingers moved into his hair, closed into a fist, and tugged.

Travis cracked and pulled her to him. He kissed her hard on the mouth. "You're going to drive me to drink, Rainey."

She smiled and felt her body relax in his arms. "Kiss me again, but don't ask for honesty. Kiss me hard like you did before dawn. Kiss me like you'd die if you didn't get to kiss me."

He turned her until she faced him and kissed her gently. "I don't want to hurt you here." He brushed her cheek. "Or here." He slid his hand over her backside. "You're nice and rounded here."

She smiled up at him, guessing that it was his turn to tease her. "It doesn't hurt and I don't mind if you touch me. After all, I touched you plenty while we slept together."

He raised an eyebrow. "You didn't." He studied her green eyes and had no idea if she was lying or telling the truth.

"You'll never know, but I promise you, you'll wonder."

His hand moved along her waist as he kissed her again. He would have kept the kiss soft, but she would have none of it. This time she wanted passion and would settle for nothing less.

When his hand slid to her hip, he pressed gently, then slowly, moved up until his fingers covered her breast. If she said he could touch her, he planned to call her bluff.

But she didn't move away. In fact, she shifted slightly, filling his hand with her ample breast. Through the few layers of clothes, he could even feel the point of it brushing his palm. She felt like heaven hidden beneath a few layers of cotton.

Suddenly he was very glad she'd placed the blanket over them. He'd thought her small, slim, but she was very much rounded in all the right places. Breaking the kiss, he stared down at her eyes as his fingers unbuttoned a few buttons on her blouse. When he slipped his hand beneath the dress, he saw surprise in her green eyes, but she didn't move away or tell him to stop. When his touch moved over the thin camisole and once more closed around her breast, he saw fire flicker in her eyes.

Then, to his surprise, she arched her back slightly, closed her eyes, and let him enjoy exploring the softest flesh he'd ever touched. He wished he could pull the blanket down and see her, but for now it was enough to watch her smile and feel her flesh grow warm beneath his hand.

He kissed her gently and whispered against her lips, "I could get used to the feel of you."

She moaned and stretched like a cat as he continued.

He told himself that maybe she just needed to feel alive, or maybe she wanted to know what the touch of a man felt like. It didn't matter that she'd allow no promises of the future. For right now, it was enough to hold her.

He gripped one breast tightly and smothered her surprise with a kiss. While his tongue tasted her, he held her breast boldly.

When he released her mouth, he expected her to pull away. He knew he'd been too forward.

But she only whispered, "Again, please. I like the way you hold me."

He laughed, deciding he was her slave. He had no choice but to grant her request.

But when he started to kiss her, she leaned away, smiling shyly as she unbuttoned the rest of her blouse so his hand could move freely between her breasts.

He kissed her as he explored, then whispered against her ear, "I'd love to taste all of you."

Her cheek warmed against his, and he knew he'd shocked her, but she didn't pull away. He kissed her tenderly then, trying to remember that all this was new to her. He wanted nothing more then to tell her that she was his and would be all their lives, but he knew he'd only frighten her. So he kissed her gently and touched her as if she were a treasure.

By the time Roy came whistling into camp, she looked like she had a fever and she definitely knew she'd been both kissed and touched. He buttoned her blouse beneath the blanket and sat her beside him before Roy had walked close enough to notice what they'd been doing.

"We'll continue this discussion later," he whispered.

She smiled and nodded slowly as if she'd already decided to do that very thing.

CHAPTER 27

⚭

Rainey rode toward Austin feeling as if her mind were weighted with lead. In the past twenty-four hours she'd been kidnapped, attacked, forced to murder an outlaw, rescued, and almost made love to by a man she'd told never to ask her to marry him again.

She felt like her life was galloping along at breakneck speed and any moment she'd slam into a wall and it would be over. Refusing to look back at Travis, who rode several feet behind her, wouldn't erase him from her thoughts. She couldn't decide if he'd taken advantage of her condition, or if it were the other way around. Only hours before she'd been too frightened to move. He'd comforted her, held her through the night. Then, with only a little encouragement, he'd made her feel more alive than she thought possible.

The heat of his fingers sliding across the camisole still warmed her. The way his hand had gripped her breast as he'd kissed her deep made her ache for more. Maybe she was exhausted, but she felt as if lightning had struck her beneath that tree. With his touch she'd discovered why a woman would both want and need a man.

If she were honest with herself, she did need him. She could very quickly become addicted to his kiss, his touch. But she didn't want him. She had not fought her way to freedom only to marry the first man who kissed her. No matter how fair he seemed, the fact remained that once she married she would belong to a man. She'd be like her mother, trapped.

Maybe she'd been too straightforward with him. Maybe she

should have told him she didn't like his kisses. That would have put a stop to everything. How could she tell Travis that she was attracted to him but she wanted time to be on her own for once in her life? She wasn't ready for love.

It occurred to her that maybe he wasn't interested, either. He'd never said a word about love.

Rainey closed her eyes. She was too tired to even think straight.

When they crossed the creek, the other Rangers joined them. All of them seemed as happy to see her as Roy had been, and if she hadn't been on horseback, she feared they all would have hugged her. Like palace guards, they surrounded her and rode toward town.

Once on the streets of Austin, Rainey noticed people stopping to watch them ride by, and as they neared the Ranger headquarters, several shouted praise.

In front of the office Roy jumped from his horse and helped her to the ground. Travis stayed on his mount. She wanted to help him, knowing that the ride must have been hard on him, but she was surrounded by Rangers. They all hurried her into the office with Dillon shouting orders for one man to take Seth's body to the undertaker.

Once inside, Rainey tried to see over the men to find Travis, but he was nowhere in the room. They offered her coffee and Dillon asked if she needed to see a doctor before she gave her statement.

"No," Rainey whispered, overwhelmed.

Dillon was all business, but Roy stepped in at her side. He wrapped a blanket over her knees, hiding the fact that she had no shoes, then winked at her as if telling her he'd keep her secret.

Roy then stepped back all formal and said, "Miss Adams, we just need a short statement. I think I can fill in the report of how you killed Seth Norman from what you told me." He lowered his voice as if he could somehow make his statement less frightening. "Three men went into the boardinghouse after Sage McMurray. Frank Norman was shot during the attack. You killed Seth. Eldon got away. To your knowledge was there anyone else involved?"

Rainey shook her head.

Suddenly everyone started talking and asking questions at once. It appeared Governor Peace had gotten involved. For a town fighting to remain the capital of Texas, this could only look bad. The residents of Houston had been fighting for years to have the state papers and offices moved. This kind of thing would only give them ammunition. The governor wanted Rainey's kidnapping solved as fast as possible.

Roy bounced with excitement. Though it had been Travis who reached her, he seemed to be the one taking the lead. He related the details of the rescue in rapid fire, slowing only as he ended with "Travis found her this morning at the ruins south of here. She'd killed Seth with a small knife she had in her pocket after he roughed her up a bit. We brought the body in."

Rainey stared at her hands. She needed Travis, but he was nowhere in sight.

"Is there anything you need, Miss Adams?" Dillon interrupted. The older Ranger looked like he'd been petrified by the sun and wind, but his eyes were not unkind.

"I want to see Dottie," she whispered. She'd worried about her friend ever since Travis told her the widow had been shot.

"We'll take you to her in a few minutes." Dillon would have had to be blind not to notice how tired she was. "Now, tell us about the kidnapping, starting with what you and Mrs. Davis overheard from your window."

The room grew silent as she described first what she'd heard, then running down the stairs. She told of how she realized there was no time to warn the others and thought if she could reach the coat, they might mistake her for Sage.

"You were willing to risk your life for a woman you never met?" Dillon asked, his bushy eyebrows almost reaching his hairline.

Rainey nodded, thinking it best not to mention that she had met Sage at the McMurray ranch when she was dressed as a boy. If she revealed any part of that story, there would be questions asked having nothing to do with the kidnapping. "I've met Travis McMurray, and I know how much he cares for his little sister."

Dillon opened his mouth to ask another question, but Roy interrupted him. "Tell us about the three men. Every detail you remember or anything they might have said."

Rainey explained that she couldn't see anything. She heard one say that they'd paid Haskell in the saloon to get Mrs. Vivian's slave out of the way. They were afraid she'd scream and warn everyone.

Rainey explained that when they were loading her on the horse, the one who held her kept saying that Frank would follow. They couldn't have known that he was dead.

Several of the rangers mumbled. One asked if the brothers mentioned their father.

Rainey shook her head. "Can I go now?"

The old ranger held up one finger. "One more thing." He looked pained when he asked. "When you stopped at the ruins, was anyone there to meet you?"

She shook her head again, too tired to answer.

He continued. "What did Seth say? Did he give any hint that he planned to meet someone?"

Rainey gripped her hands tightly in her lap. "He said he wanted me to take off my clothes. When I refused, he slugged me and started telling how he planned to cut me up in little pieces just like he would have Sage. When he came at me again, I had the knife in my hand."

The room was silent. She stared at Dillon. "I'm very tired. May I go?"

Dillon looked like he wanted to ask her more questions, but Roy stepped before her and offered his hand. "Of course," he said. "Someone take her to where the widow is recovering." He looked sad. "I'd take you myself, but I must file a report."

"I understand." Rainey felt like a sand doll with a hole in her toe. All the sand in her was draining out fast and she needed to get somewhere where she could rest. "You've been very kind, Ranger Dumont. If you weren't already married a few times, I'd set my bonnet for you."

The other Rangers laughed and Roy looked proud of himself.

Dillon stood between her and the door. "You understand, Miss Adams, that your life is still in danger."

She nodded, wanting to ask when it hadn't been. Since she walked out of the dorm months ago, she felt like she'd been looking over her shoulder for trouble. At the time her greatest fear had been that her father would catch her. All she'd thought of was disappearing. Now she knew there were men far worse than her father.

Dillon moved aside, letting one of the others escort her to the door.

By the time Rainey got to the porch, a buggy waited for her.

The Rangers helped her in, and a young man drove her straight to the Baileys' home.

"Are you sure Dottie Davis is here?" Rainey said as she climbed out.

"Yes, ma'am. She's recovering under Dr. Bailey's care. Miss McMurray insisted on it." He walked her to the door, knocked, then handed her over to Mike Saddler.

She smiled, remembering the young Ranger and thinking that he must be Sage's riding partner that Travis had been so worried about.

Ranger Saddler looked overjoyed to see her and, like Roy, hugged her as if she were kin. He directed her inside, and within minutes, Rainey was sitting in the Baileys' huge formal dining room. Dottie, wrapped in a quilt that covered most of her bandaged arm and shoulder, sat across from her while the housekeeper served them the first meal Rainey had had in two days.

Mike disappeared, saying he'd be back in a few minutes.

The two friends both talked at once, telling each other what had happened while they were apart.

"We're heroes." Dottie laughed. "Everyone in town knows about us. We're all the talk."

Rainey found that hard to believe.

Dottie shoved around food on her plate, trying to catch it using the fork in her left hand. "It's true. Everyone has stopped by to check on Sage and to tell me how brave I was having a shoot-out with the Norman boys. Even Judge Gates stopped by twice. He sat by me on the couch and patted my hand." She giggled. "I don't know if he likes me, or if he figures he was next on their list."

Rainey found it all too much to take in. "Where are the Mc-Murrays?" She thought Sage at least would have greeted her. In fact, now that she noticed it, the entire house seemed empty.

"Travis came in half an hour ago. He told us he got you safely to the Ranger station, then said he wanted to see the doctor right away." Tears bubbled in the widow's eyes. "He collapsed a foot inside the door and Ranger Saddler had to carry him to his room with a little help from Sage and the Baileys. They're all in there now, I think. He's hurting bad."

Dottie gripped Rainey's hand. "I was so excited to see you, I forgot about him. I'm sure he'll be fine. When Mike came through to answer the knock, he nodded and said, 'Travis is in good hands. Dr. Bailey is the best in Texas.'"

"But he never complained, not once." Rainey lost her appetite. "I knew he was hurting, but I didn't know . . ."

The widow stopped her rant. "Now, don't you worry, dear. Men can be all brave and silent for just so long. As soon as they get home, they let a wall down and stop pretending they're invincible. He had a job to do, and he did it." She smiled. "And I'm guessing he didn't want you to see how badly he was hurting. You should have seen the look on his face when he discovered you'd been kidnapped. I almost felt sorry for the outlaws."

Rainey watched the door as she nibbled at her food. She wanted to run and find Travis, but maybe Dottie was right. Maybe he didn't want her to see him as less than her man-of-oak.

After dinner Rainey curled into the chair feeling warm and safe. For a while, they didn't talk, they just relaxed. Then the housekeeper came in to tell Rainey that her room was ready.

"But I have to go back to the boardinghouse."

"It's been closed," Dottie whispered. "The three sisters refused to stay there after the kidnapping. They moved into their half-finished living quarters over their shop. The last I heard they were helping with the hammering."

"What about Mrs. Vivian?"

"She refuses to leave her home. The sisters said she was bolting all the doors and windows as they were leaving." Dottie shook her head. "She thinks her husband is coming back to that house and nothing short of a fire will get her out of there."

"But I can't afford to live here." Rainey looked around her at the fine furnishings.

"There is no charge," the housekeeper said. "Dr. and Mrs. Bailey would like you and Mrs. Davis to stay here as their guests."

"Really?"

"I have the room next to Mrs. Davis made up for you and a bath is waiting." The housekeeper smiled a true welcome that Mrs. Vivian would have never given away.

Rainey almost said she would sleep here in the chair, but a bath sounded wonderful. She followed the housekeeper up a flight of stairs and into a bedroom four times larger than her little place at the Askew House. It had curtains over the windows and a rug that almost touched the walls on all sides of the room.

A big bed with a nightgown folded atop the covers stood to the left, a tub in front of the fire to the right. A teapot warmed on the bricks and crisp white bath sheets waited in a chair next to the tub.

"Will there be anything else?" the housekeeper asked.

Rainey turned to thank the housekeeper. "Would someone let me know how Ranger McMurray is when they know something?"

"Of course," the housekeeper said as she pulled the door closed behind her.

Rainey slowly removed her clothes, feeling every sore muscle and bruised place on her body. She looked in the mirror, seeing a dark spot along her ribs and an almost black circle on her hip. Her cheek had turned several different colors of skin and her left eye had a mark so black it looked like she'd spread a finger-width of coal across it.

Slipping into the tub, she let the warm water wash across her tired body, soothing all the aches. She washed her hair and scrubbed the dirt from her hands with a soap that smelled like a flower garden. Her feet were finally warm. She leaned back in the tub and closed her eyes.

She was almost asleep when she heard a knock at her door.

Rainey jumped, surprised that the water had grown cold. Splashing out, she wrapped in a towel, then crossed the room and slipped into a nightgown that someone had laid out for her. "Yes?" she said, finally answering the door.

"It's me, Sage McMurray."

Rainey opened the door, and the strange thing that had happened to her very few times in her life before today happened again. Sage rushed toward her and hugged her.

"Thank God you're safe," Sage said when she stepped back. "I was so worried about you."

When Rainey only stared, Sage's eyes widened. "You are Rainey Adams, aren't you? Don't tell me I got the wrong room."

Rainey smiled. "I am."

Sage relaxed. "I can't believe you were so brave. I'm so glad Travis found you. I wanted to come along, but he wouldn't let me. You could have been hurt or killed."

"I'm fine," Rainey answered. "How is Travis?"

Sage put her arm around Rainey as if they were old friends. They moved to the fire. "He's sleeping. The doctor gave him something to help him rest. We'll know tomorrow if he did any damage to the muscles, but Dr. Bailey is having his leg wrapped in hot towels every two hours to increase the blood circulation. After seeing him hurt months ago, I should have been prepared, but I swear I feel his pain." Sage rambled on. "He's my big brother and I can't stand it when any of them are hurt."

"He shouldn't have come after me," Rainey whispered.

"No one could have stopped him," Sage answered, her eyes wide with surprise that Rainey didn't seem to understand. "He said you were his." She said the words slowly, watching Rainey's reaction.

"I am his friend," Rainey managed to say.

"Would you mind if I stay for a while?" Sage tilted her head. "You look familiar."

Rainey pulled a lap quilt around her shoulders and pointed to the two chairs by the fire. She was glad for Sage's company, but she needed time to figure out how to tell Sage that their paths had crossed once before. "Please, sit down. We have lots to talk about." She didn't meet the girl's gaze. "I think the housekeeper left tea in that pot. Why don't we have a cup?"

Sage looked nervous but got right to the point. "You mean a great deal to my brother. Have you known him long?"

"No." Rainey wasn't surprised by Sage's directness, and she had no idea how to answer the girl.

"You don't have to tell me anything, you know." Sage laughed. "We're going to be best friends either way."

Rainey handed her a cup of tea.

Sage smiled. "Mrs. Bailey does love her tea. Travis hates the stuff, you know."

"I know," Rainey answered before she thought and caught Sage's blink of a smile at her words.

As they drank Sage talked about all that had happened after Rainey had been kidnapped. Finally she noticed Rainey fighting to keep her eyes open.

"We'll talk tomorrow. Or maybe I'll listen tomorrow because tonight I seem to be the one doing all the talking." Sage stood.

Rainey nodded and walked her to the door. She said good night and climbed into bed without turning off the light. Before her body warmed the covers, she fell asleep.

Deep in the night Rainey woke with a start. For a moment she couldn't remember where she was. All she knew or felt was a deep need to make sure Travis was all right. As sleep left her brain she feared someone looking for her might have gotten into the house. What if the Norman brother who got away had returned to kill Travis or her?

With a lamp she slipped from her room and climbed down the stairs to the left wing, telling herself she'd check on Travis and be back in her room before anyone knew.

CHAPTER 28

⤬

Travis didn't bother to open his eyes. He'd heard the mantel clock chime three and knew it would be at least another hour before anyone checked on him. Dr. Bailey had insisted on tying him down, claiming he didn't want Travis rolling over in his sleep. Travis felt like a prisoner. His left leg had been wrapped and soaked in an oil the doctor swore would take the swelling out. The doctor had also put something in the tea Sage had forced down him, but it wasn't working. He remained wide awake.

The doc had probably been right about tying him down. He would have been up checking to make sure Rainey was all right if he could have gotten out of bed. He'd caught a glance of her just before she disappeared into the Ranger station office. She'd looked frightened, her green eyes darting around searching for him. His pride wouldn't allow him to ask for help to get off the horse. Instead, like a fool, he'd let her go in alone. He told himself Dillon would go easy on her. Roy would watch over her.

So he'd ridden over to the Baileys' knowing he had to see the doc. He'd all but fallen off his mount and stumbled up to the door like a drunk. He hadn't made it more than three feet inside the house before the pain peaked and he blacked out. He had no idea how they got him to bed, but when he woke up, everyone was crowded around following the doc's orders and treating him like some kind of puppet they all wanted to handle. He fought them worse than Duck usually did when they removed his clothes for a bath. But between trying to stay dressed and trying to hold his leg still, he lost the battle with clothes.

The whole experience had been painful and humiliating. The only thing that would have made it unbearable would have been if Rainey had been there.

Travis heard Michael Saddler snoring in the seating room beyond his bedroom door and knew the young Ranger was there not only as guard, but to keep Duck happy. The boy had dragged his bedding into Travis's bedroom three times before Mike showed him that the door between the rooms would stay open, the fire would be left burning, and Mike would be near.

"I plan to beat a few years' life out of Saddler when I get on my feet," Travis mumbled. The young Ranger had held him down while the doc dug into his leg. Just before Travis passed out, he heard the doc say he knew there must be lead left in the leg, but he couldn't seem to find it. Saddler smiled and said, "Keep digging." Then he'd slammed all two hundred pounds of himself onto Travis's chest to hold him down.

When Travis came to again, the doc had quit digging into his flesh and was busy wrapping his leg so tightly he could feel it throbbing. The bandages were warm and soaking wet. As they cooled Travis felt warm spots where his blood soaked through. As if the whole operation hadn't been humiliating enough, Dr. Bailey ordered the bandages changed every two hours. He'd heard of Indian torture ceremonies with less pain.

And through it all, the boy watched, shaking with fear. Duck didn't like sleeping a room away from Travis, but he finally curled down in his covers making sure he could see Travis through the open door.

Travis hoped that in an hour when they came to change the bandages, they'd be quiet enough that they didn't wake the boy. He promised himself he wouldn't swear, no matter how much it hurt.

When Sage had last checked on him, Travis had heard Mike gently tell her to get some rest, there would be plenty to do in the morning. He'd said that Travis had been drugged and would sleep for a few hours.

Only I'm not asleep! Travis wanted to yell. *I'm awake and bored.* While he'd been out the second time, someone had tied him down at the waist with a sheet and bound his good leg into the covers so that he couldn't move it. His arms and shoulders

were free, but they might as well have been bound as well for all
the good he could do.

Travis felt like his mind was sloshing through a fog. He
was surprised his body didn't hurt. The last few miles to town
he'd had to struggle to keep from screaming. If he hadn't been
so worried about Rainey, he would have demanded they stop.
But with Eldon Norman still loose, they needed to get her to
safety before the outlaw figured out that she'd killed his last
brother.

Closing his eyes, he remembered how Rainey had melted
into his arms so easily when they'd stopped to rest. She'd acted
as if she would have stayed on that blanket beneath the tree for
the rest of the afternoon and he wouldn't have minded at all.
He'd forgotten about the throbbing in his leg when he'd touched
her. She'd been the only medicine that he needed.

Rainey had no idea of the danger she was in. All the Normans were hate-filled men, even the old man. The Rangers had
never been able to pin anything on the father, but the sons were
reckless. They'd all been in and out of jails by the time they
could shave. Every time they went on trial, Old Man Norman
would ride into town and be in court every day. When his boys
were sentenced, he'd wait outside to cuss every Ranger and
judge involved.

Travis turned his head slightly. He sensed someone in the
room. A movement in the air that hadn't been there before. A
shifting of shadows.

He reached for his gun that he'd insisted Mike leave near
the side of the bed and slowly opened his eyes a fraction.

Rainey stood before him in a nightgown that covered her
from throat to toes. She leaned over him, looking very much
like an angel come to call.

He returned the gun to its hiding place. "Looking for something?" he whispered.

She jumped, then like a child looking at a snake, leaned a
bit closer. "You scared me to death," she scolded. "I was just
making sure you were breathing."

He studied her closely in the light coming from the door. If
she knew just how much the firelight revealed what lay beneath
her nightgown, she would have been horrified. He decided,
purely to save her feelings, he wouldn't tell her. "I'm breathing.
Come closer, I don't want to wake the others."

Rainey glanced at the open door. Duck was curled into a

ball by the fire. Mike's snoring kept time with the ticking of the clock.

She moved closer. "How are you?"

"Thanks to the doc," Travis lied, "I feel much better, but for some reason, I'm wide awake."

She sat on the edge of the bed. "Me, too."

"Think you could keep me company for a while?"

"Of course, but I have to be gone before anyone wakes. I think this is most improper to be in your bedchamber."

Travis smiled. "I know it is." He slid his hand over hers. "Tell me how it went at the station. Dillon wasn't too hard on you, was he?"

Rainey curled atop the covers on his right side and pulled her feet beneath her gown. "No. I think he might have been, but your friend Roy wouldn't let him."

Travis didn't look happy. "Any word about the last brother?"

"Not that I know of." Her voice shook slightly.

"Rainey," Travis whispered. "Are you cold?"

"A little," she admitted.

"Curl up beside me like you did last night. We could talk and pass the time."

She hesitated. His arms and chest were bare tonight. She could see the strength of his muscles and the dark tan of his skin. She wasn't surprised to find his chest looked like it had been carved of oak.

"Are you afraid of me?" He had to ask.

"No," she answered without thought.

He waited.

Slowly, so that she didn't touch him, she moved beside him. He could feel her warmth an inch away. For a few minutes she shivered, then finally relaxed.

"You smell good," he whispered a few inches from her ear. Moving his cheek against her hair, he breathed deep. "I love your hair."

"We should talk of something else."

He nodded, touching her curls with his face once more. "All right. How about you tell me a little about you?"

Rainey didn't say a word.

"I don't even know where you're from."

"Up north," she said.

"And your parents didn't die on the trip over like you told

Mrs. Vivian. If I were guessing, I'd say they are very much alive."

"My mother died a few years ago. My father was alive when I left."

"So, why'd you run, Rainey, and keep running until you got all the way to Texas?"

She was silent so long he decided she didn't plan to answer, then came a whisper, "My father tried to make me marry."

Travis laughed. "Oh, and we both know how dead-set against that you are."

She turned to him, an inch away from his nose, and whispered, "No one, nowhere on this earth, will ever make me marry. I'll not be treated that worthless."

He laid his hand gently over hers. "Not all wives think of themselves as worthless."

"But they are. The minute they marry, everything they have becomes their husband's. He can treat them any way he likes and there is nothing they can do about it."

He watched her closely, loving the fire he saw in her eyes but hating the anger that put it there. He could read her parents' marriage in those green eyes without asking another question.

She propped her head up and said, "Now, it's my turn."

"All right, fair enough."

"Why'd you come to Austin?"

He didn't even try to think of a lie. "To find you."

"Why?"

"Because I thought you might be in trouble."

She waited, staring at him.

He almost got lost in those green depths, but he knew he had to say more, had to be honest with her. "And because I had to see you again. That night at the dance we had so few words together, but you stayed in my mind. I had to see you again."

"I know what you mean. I read a poem once about how the moments in your life change you, not the big crashing crisis or grand award, but the small times when you gently shift within your skin and become a slightly different person."

He opened his arm and this time she rolled against his side. "If you'd have told me that before we danced, I would have never believed it, but now, I think I understand."

Neither of them said another word. He could feel her breathing against his side. When the breaths grew further apart, he knew she was asleep. She seemed so soft and helpless beside him, but she'd run away from home alone, and somehow survived for months. No doubt in his mind existed. He'd always thought of himself as strong, but in truth, the tiny lady at his side was a giant beside him.

She spread her hand out across his chest. He fought the urge to pull her closer. Then he realized just having her near was enough for now.

He listened to the clock ticking and her breathing as an hour passed. When he heard the first footsteps in the hall, he kissed her head and whispered, "Rainey, move to the chair."

She barely had time to slip from the bed to the rocking chair before someone opened the door.

The doctor came in and didn't try to hide his surprise when he noticed her. "Miss Adams, you shouldn't be in here."

"I had to check on him," Rainey answered. "The Ranger saved my life."

Dr. Bailey nodded. "I see, but you'd best get up to your room before my wife wakes. I can take care of this hero of yours until morning."

Rainey looked like she debated leaving, but finally slipped from the room. Her last glance back told him all he needed to know. She didn't want to leave.

Travis let the doctor poke on him awhile, then took the medicine the old man gave him without complaint. By the time the doctor was finished wrapping his leg and hip in oily towels to keep the swelling down, it was dawn.

"Glad to see you've got your senses back, son," the old doc said as he finished. "We all figured you'd shoot us for sure if you got the chance a few hours ago. That's why the young Ranger took the bullets out of your gun before he gave it to you."

Travis nodded. He hadn't grown any calmer; he'd simply realized he'd have to endure this quietly until he talked someone into letting him out of this bed. As soon as he was free, he planned to continue the discussion he'd had with Rainey under the tree. The discussion they'd shared without words.

Travis heard Mike and Duck stirring in the sitting room and a moment later, Duck hit the foot of his bed. The boy scrambled up, sat cross-legged with his elbows on his knees and his fists on his chin. He stared at Travis as if he planned to stay put for the day.

"Help the boy into his clothes," Travis said casually.

"Glad to," Mike answered from the door. The young Ranger picked up the clothes, and a moment later the race was on.

CHAPTER 29

With Duck finally dressed and sitting at the foot of the bed watching, the doctor showed Travis the tiny piece of lead he'd taken out of the bone in his leg just below his hip.

"It might have stayed there for the rest of your life pestering you occasionally, but that ride you took caused an infection and made it imperative that I remove it." The old man scratched his head. "I took a risk cutting into you like that, but I decided you weren't a man who'd settle for riding in a buggy the rest of his life."

Travis had to admit that he felt better. The dull ache that he'd known for months was gone even though his skin was sore where Dr. Bailey had made small cuts. "Thanks, Doc," he managed to say. "I'm glad I didn't shoot you last night." He reached under the pillow and produced a handful of bullets.

"But how . . ." Mike looked up from several feet away where he was trying to get a coffee stain off his shirt, thanks to Duck.

"A Ranger always checks his weapons." Travis shrugged. "I'd never be too out of my head to forget that. When you handed me the gun, I knew it was light. I had no problem borrowing a few of your bullets."

Mike fingered the empty loops on his gun belt.

Dr. Bailey laughed. "I'm not surprised. I've been patching up Rangers since the battle at San Jacinto. They're like dealing with frozen rattlers. If you bring them inside and take care of them at some point you come to expect them to be ornery."

Sage entered with a tray of breakfast rolls and fresh coffee. "Top of the morning to you." She bowed to all, but smiled at

Mike. "What could be so funny so early?" She patted her brother's shoulder as she handed him his second cup of coffee. "Good to see you back with us, Travis."

"I never left," he mumbled, not wanting to admit how close he'd come to the edge of sanity when the pain gripped him. "I was just a little tired yesterday."

"Then you'll rest today," the doc insisted as he covered Travis's left leg with the sheet.

Travis nodded, silently agreeing, then turned his attention back to Sage. As he explained about the bullets, he noticed that she moved close enough to Mike for him to tug on her braid. Travis thought of reloading. No one but her brothers had a right to touch his sister's hair. Then he remembered what Rainey had told him and forced a smile. It was almost as frustrating to admit that Sage didn't seem to mind Mike's teasing as it was to watch a man flirt with his baby sister.

It crossed his mind that Sage should have started with a boy, not a man. Saddler was young, maybe twenty or twenty-one, but he was a man. The Ranger might not be satisfied with innocent kisses.

Frowning, Travis realized he wasn't satisfied with just kissing Rainey. He wanted more. A lot more. He'd go slow . . . as slow as she wanted . . . as long as they were moving. He stared at the young couple, wondering if they felt even a fraction of what he felt for Rainey.

Mike didn't notice he was being watched. He seemed to have Sage blindness whenever she was in the room.

"How is he today?" Sage asked the doctor as she pretended to pay no mind to the young Ranger.

"Much better. The cold wrappings brought the swelling down, and except for the cuts I had to make on his leg, he's much recovered. He's even stopped bleeding around the stitches I made."

"Then someone untie me," Travis demanded.

"Tomorrow. I want another day of the oil on that leg." The doctor packed up his supplies and left the room as if he didn't hear Travis yelling.

The rest of the day drifted by in hell. Everyone dropped by to check on him and to ask how he felt. No one untied him. He spent an hour trying to reach the knots himself, but with no luck. Finally he downed the bitter tea Sage insisted he drink, then slept the rest of the day away.

When he awoke, the room was dark with only the light of the fire from the sitting room slicing across his bed. Travis remained still for a while, letting his mind clear. He felt no pain.

He tried to move.

He was still tied, but the bandage around his leg was no longer slippery with oil.

The clock chimed eleven times and he heard someone in the shadows move.

"Who is it?" he said calmly.

"It's me," Rainey whispered. "I just wanted to check on you one last time before I turned in. The doc said he planned to check your bandages at midnight."

"Where is everyone else?" Travis didn't move. He just waited for her to come closer.

"They're all asleep. I checked on you twice today, and both times you were out from the medicine doc put in your tea."

"I thought it tasted funny," he mumbled, silently swearing he'd never drink a drop of tea again. "I'm thirsty now. Got anything but tea?"

"I'll be right back."

He almost yelled for her to stop. He didn't want her to go, but in truth he felt like he hadn't had a drink in days.

Rainey was back in minutes with a large glass of milk, a plate of cheese, and bread. "Mrs. Bailey had this left out for you. I heard her tell Mike that if you woke before morning, he was to feed it to you."

Travis listened. He could hear Mike snoring in the other room. "Great nurse you all left me with."

Rainey sat the tray between them and cut him bread and cheese while he drank the milk and ate all she handed him. They didn't talk. Neither seemed to want to take the risk of waking others.

When he finished the food, she removed the tray and reached for the napkin she'd spread across his bare chest. His fingers closed gently around her arm and pulled her forward.

She made no protest as he opened the covers and drew her down next to him. When she was cuddled close, he whispered near her ear. "I've wanted you against me all day. Stay with me, if only for a while."

Her body shook slightly.

"It's all right, Rainey. I'm not going to hurt you. I'm never going to hurt you." Travis pulled at the bindings that kept him in place. The need to touch her was stronger than any hunger he'd ever known. Without a word, he threaded his fingers into her hair.

Rainey lay beside him, not moving as his hand traveled down her throat and began unbuttoning her gown.

There seemed so much he had to say to her. He wanted her to know how he'd felt when he'd thought she might be in danger. How his heart had almost shattered when he'd learned she'd been kidnapped. How he'd been drunk with relief when he'd found her.

But he didn't say anything. He just unbuttoned her gown.

When the cotton lay open past her waist, he slid his hand inside and felt the flat plain of her stomach. Then, slowly so his touch had time to take in the feel of her, he moved up, passing over her breasts with great tenderness.

He stared down at her face. Her eyes were closed, but he could see the slight smile on her lips.

Moving down her body once more, he learned the curves of her. His hands seemed rough against her soft skin, but she didn't complain.

When he passed her waist, he let his fingers go lower until she shifted slightly and moaned softly. Only then, with his hand resting over her most private part, did he lean closer and cover her mouth with his.

The kiss was soft and intimate. He pressed the palm of his hand against her and felt her body respond in surprise. There was no need for words now. He knew she wanted his touch. Their kisses grew long and warm with need as she began to shift slightly as his hands caressed her.

The clock began to chime the midnight hour. A door opened somewhere in the main house. Travis raised his head to listen, but before he could speak, she was gone. Sliding from the bed and into the shadows of the room before he could stop her.

A moment later when the doctor opened the door from the hallway, Travis knew she was gone. He closed his eyes, fighting the need to roar against the void her vanishing had left.

"You awake?" the doc asked.

Travis couldn't answer.

The doc sat in the chair by his bed, stretched his feet out on a stool, and relaxed. Within a few minutes his breathing deepened and Travis knew he was asleep.

He also knew Rainey would not return tonight.

At dawn, when the doc examined him, the first question Travis asked was if he could be untied.

Dr. Bailey pointed a finger at him. "Only if you swear to be careful. I don't want those stitches to break open. You can move around from bed to a chair for a few hours a day, but no more than that for at least a week."

"I'll try," Travis grumbled, thinking two days in bed was enough. "But no more of that bitter tea."

Bailey laughed. "It was the only way I could get you to rest. But no more and I'll untie you. I guess you've suffered bedrest long enough."

As Dr. Bailey pulled the sheets free from the bedding, he mumbled, "I'll ask Miss Adams and the widow to come in to keep you company. I know Sage will need the Ranger's help giving Duck a bath this morning."

The boy was up and across the room before the doc could turn in his direction. He climbed as far as he could into the bay window.

Sage looked puzzled. "He doesn't need a bath again today."

The old doc smiled. "I know. I also know that he understands what we're saying. I thought he must when Travis said his goodbyes, but I know it for a fact now."

Sage stomped her foot and yelled, "That wasn't fair to scare him like that. I'm going to go bake him cookies to make up for it."

Duck reached her side before she made it to the door. She smiled down at him. "You're a grand boy, Duck McMurray. Fast as lightning and silent as a spring thaw." She took his hand and disappeared out of the room.

The doc looked at Travis. "You going to claim him?"

"The only clue about his folks we may have found was a two-year-old report a neighbor made up near Fort Worth. A young couple was killed and their farm burned. The neighbor said he thought they had a blond boy just learning to walk. I'm having the report mailed here, but it doesn't look good. No kin requested the few belongings the couple had left or their bodies. The county records had no next of kin listed for either of them on file when they married."

"So you'll keep him?" Bailey raised an eyebrow. "There's an orphanage here in Austin for kids like him."

Travis shook his head. "I think it's more that Duck claimed

me, but he's not going anywhere if his parents are dead. We've already talked about it. If he has no name, he'll be a McMurray and his home will become Whispering Mountain."

Mike helped Travis stand as the housekeeper came in to put fresh sheets on the bed. Travis was surprised how little his leg hurt when he shifted a slight amount of weight on it. Dr. Bailey knew what he was doing. Travis had been lucky to make it to his door.

With Mike's help, Travis managed to get dressed just as Dottie Davis tapped on his door. He insisted on moving to the little drawing room between the bedrooms. It didn't seem right talking to the widow in his bedchamber.

After Mike got them settled and the housekeeper brought more coffee, the young Ranger left, saying he had to check in at headquarters.

As soon as Travis was alone with Dottie, he began to ask questions about all she'd seen and heard the day of the kidnapping. He couldn't help but smile as her part in the raid grew with the telling.

Dottie was more than happy to talk between bites of rolls, but her conversation galloped from one topic to another without pausing long enough for Travis to ask more questions. She was a woman who liked to take her time with both eating and telling a story.

About the time Travis thought he might need a gag for the little widow, she stumbled into the topic of Rainey.

"Sweet girl," Dottie said. "Loving and giving as I've ever seen." She frowned and stared at Travis. "But if you don't mind me saying so, Ranger, you're about as bright as rained-on ashes. Even considering the fact that you're a good-looking man, I can't see why she even cares for you."

Travis frowned. He'd thought he measured a little higher in the widow's opinion. After all, he had brought Rainey back after she'd been kidnapped. He'd made sure the widow got to the doctor after she'd been shot. He'd even had the widows' things moved to the Baileys' so she'd feel more comfortable.

He knew he'd regret it, but he had to ask, "And why is that, Mrs. Davis?"

Dottie leaned back, her smile saying she knew she had his attention. "A man shouldn't propose after the first kiss. You scared that poor child to death. She told me she'd spent her life at a girls' school and you were the first man to even try to kiss her." The widow shook her head in disgust. "And what do you do, you ask her right off to marry you."

"She told you?" He wasn't surprised. What little he knew of women, they seemed creatures who shared everything. He'd often thought the need for newspapers would be lost if Western towns had more women to spread the word.

Dottie wiggled in the chair as if fluffing herself, took another roll, and continued. "I shouldn't be saying anything, Rainey being my friend and all, but the judge and I were talking and we agreed you could benefit from a little motherly advice."

Great, Travis thought. The judge was involved in this.

"Women like Rainey need a bit of a challenge. She's a survivor, a fighter. Did you ever think that maybe she should have to fight a little for you? Fish that hop up on the bank ain't near as fun to catch."

Travis stared at the little lady, having no idea what to say to her. She was right about him having little experience with women, but it seemed to him a woman would much rather have an offer on the table and then make up her mind than be wondering how a man felt about her.

"Would you like some more coffee?" was all he could think of to say.

Dottie seemed to understand. "No, I think I'll go to the kitchen and have a cup of tea. Will you be needing anything? I could have someone bring it to you."

Travis shook his head.

Ten minutes later he was still staring at the fire when Rainey walked in.

"Morning," she said. "Dottie said you wanted another cup of coffee."

"Thanks." He didn't look up as she handed him the cup. One good thing about this place, he'd never finish all the coffee.

Rainey stood in front of him as if waiting for him to do or say something. Her hand was so close he could have reached out and held it, but he didn't. He wasn't sure how she felt about what they'd done last night. He thought she enjoyed it, but he wished she'd had time to say something before she vanished.

"How are you feeling?" She finally broke the silence as she leaned toward him.

"I'm feeling tired of people worrying about the way I feel," he answered, his words sounding colder than he'd intended.

Rainey took a step backward.

Travis swore he could feel the coldness between them. She sure wasn't acting like she wanted him to play hard to get. He glanced up and saw her green eyes staring at him. She looked like she wanted to be kissed, he thought. Or maybe that was just what he wished she was hoping for.

"I was just about to leave to go bake today. I have orders for pies that are late. No one seems to need me around here." She waited as if expecting him to say something. "I'd also like to go back and get my shoes. Sage loaned me a pair of hers, but I keep walking out of them."

He wanted to tell her to forget about work, he needed her. But Dottie's comments lingered in his thoughts. He didn't want to say anything that got repeated to Dottie, who'd repeat it to the judge. Hell, he thought, I might as well just shout everything I say so that everyone can hear the first account.

"Travis?" She stepped back in front of him.

He thought he knew what she wanted. They were alone. She was close. In one step she could be in his arms. But he didn't reach for her.

To his surprise, she leaned forward and kissed his cheek. "I'll be back before dark."

He watched her go.

If black moods could darken, his did. He sat, staring at the fire trying to figure out where he stood with his fairy. He'd told Mike she was his, but he wasn't so sure. She'd slept beside him part of the last three nights, but he hadn't touched her until last night. She'd swore she'd never marry him, but she worried about him worse than both Roy's wives put together worried about Roy. Every time he mentioned marriage she said she never wanted to see him again and every time she thought he was in trouble she risked her life to let him know.

He leaned his head back against the leather of the wingback chair. The worn leather conformed and he closed his eyes, drifting back into the dream he'd had on Whispering Mountain.

He heard Mike's boots stomping in from the side door. The Ranger ran through the hall as if on full alert pulling Travis from his dream.

Travis glanced up just as Mike Saddler rounded the corner, his face red from the cold. "McMurray!" Mike took a quick breath. "Where's Miss Adams and Widow Davis?"

"Rainey left to go make pies. I think the widow said something about going with her, but I could be wrong. I don't know women all that well." Travis straightened, sensing something was wrong. "What is it, Saddler?"

Mike's tanned face paled. "Eldon Norman has been spotted in town. We've got men looking for him everywhere. The undertaker said he came by to pay his respects to his brother and left swearing that he'd pay back the witch who stabbed Seth."

Travis braced himself on the arms of his chair and slowly stood. "Is he in custody?"

Mike shook his head.

Travis reached for his cane. Carefully, so he didn't pull stitches, he made it to his guns. "Get the wagon from the barn out back and pull around to the side door. I'll inform Sage and meet you out there. We're going after Rainey."

Mike nodded. "You're thinking the same thing I am. I heard Dillon tell two men to go check on the three old maids just in case Rainey or the widow goes there, and a pair of Rangers were knocking on the front door when I came around back. They'll be here with Sage until we find Rainey and make it back."

Travis strapped his guns on and reached for his coat. His left leg took the weight when he shifted with only a bit of pain. He was healing; now it was time to concentrate on keeping Rainey alive.

By the time they made it to the Langland Mercantile, Rainey already had pies in the oven and refused to leave until they were done.

Pearl kept calling Travis "Rainey's Ranger," which left no doubt that he'd been discussed, as she showed him to the extra chair.

The widow had taken up residence at the kitchen table, her arm resting beside two freshly made pies. Mike stood near the back door, looking very much like he was on guard. Travis pulled his chair to the opening into the store after he gave up trying to get Rainey to abandon her baking. He might not be able to tell Rainey what to do, but he didn't plan to leave her alone.

Rainey's fear shifted quickly to bother that she had to work around so many people in such a small space. She kept having to swing Mike out of the way as if he were a door to her supply cabinet. When she stepped around Travis and into the store, he heard her say she was sorry about the bother. He smiled when Pearl answered back that she thought this was all so exciting.

"Oh," Pearl added just before Rainey passed through the curtain and back into the kitchen. "I think your paper Ranger is handsome. His frown is a little frightening, though. Aren't you scared?"

Rainey laughed. "Not in the least."

The others heard their comments through the thin curtain. Travis's frown deepened, realizing Rainey had told Pearl about their letters.

Widow Davis must have decided she was queen of the hive, for she divided her time between talking to Mike, telling Rainey how to cook, and bothering Travis with questions about what the Rangers were doing to keep her safe. He was glad when Pearl let her son join them, for Dottie took up a game of teaching the boy, who could only babble his ABCs.

By the time Rainey put another set of pies in, Judge Gates showed up with Roy Dumont at his side. Pearl pulled the stools in from the store, and they all consumed one of the pies.

Almost growling aloud Travis decided that if anyone else wanted to come into the small room, they'd have to get on the waiting list. Pearl came in several times to pick up pies. "Folks are coming to the store wanting them. I'm selling them as fast as you can make them."

Travis watched Rainey as she worked silently. The warmth of the stove had made her cheeks glow. The room was full of people and all he saw was her.

After eating, Judge asked Dottie if she'd like to join him for dinner that night at one of the restaurants in town. Roy mentioned it might be better not to make her a target. The judge suggested his house and waved his arm to include everyone in the invitation.

"A dinner party—how wonderful." The widow lifted her bandaged arm. "If I could, I'd love to cook for it."

The judge smiled looking younger than he had in years. "If you'll tell me what to do, I'll be your hands, madam. I have a housekeeper who'll clean up the mess, so you won't have to do a thing but talk."

Travis almost lost his battle not to laugh.

Dottie giggled. "I'll tell you how. You cook and we'll have a great meal." She glanced from Roy to Ranger Saddler. "Would it be all right to send the young Ranger to ask Miss McMurray and the Baileys if they'd like to come, also?"

"Of course, I haven't had a proper party since my wife died." Judge Gates stood and offered his arm. "Shall we go shopping for what we need?"

They moved into the mercantile. From the sound of it, the Langland would be stocking tonight after they got home from the dinner party, of course, for the judge insisted they come as well.

Travis looked at Mike. "Sounds like you'll need the wagon to get all the supplies to the judge's. If Roy stays with the widow, see if you can't talk Sage and Duck into coming over to help. I'm sure the judge can use the help." He met the young Ranger's eyes. "Stay beside Sage all evening."

Mike nodded once. "I promise. Anyone getting to her will have to go through me first."

Travis knew Mike meant every word.

CHAPTER 30

WHEN EVERYONE BUT RAINEY AND TRAVIS FINALLY LEFT THE LANG-lands' home, the one-room apartment seemed roomy. She'd been surprised when he hadn't argued about her insisting on making more pies before leaving. In fact, he'd simply nodded and resumed his place on guard after the others left.

Surrounded in the aroma of apple pies, the silence weighed heavy between them. Even Pearl raised an eyebrow in question when she'd passed Rainey to put little Jason down for a nap. But Rainey didn't say anything. She didn't know what to say. Travis didn't seem angry, or bothered. If anything, he seemed bored.

She felt like they'd been on a runaway train since the kidnapping. He'd risked his life to save her. All the other Rangers thought she was his, but he'd never once mentioned love, or even liking her. In fact, except when she visited him late at night, he barely acted as if he noticed her around.

"Want a piece of pie?" Rainey tried to shatter the ice between them.

He shook his head.

"Want some soup?"

He didn't answer. He simply folded his arms and leaned back in the chair.

"Want me?" she whispered as she turned back to work. They'd been alone for an hour, and he'd made no move to touch her, or even talk to her. She frowned, thinking of how quickly she'd become addicted to his touch and wondered if he'd mind if she curled into his bed every night to sleep. Somehow the rhythm of his breathing matched her heart's beat. When he held her at the ruins of the mission, it had been the first time she hadn't feared the night.

Rainey considered if feeling safe could equal love. She decided it didn't. Maybe she should look at the reasons why he'd asked her that first night to marry him. He could just want a wife to come home to, but she'd be the last one he'd pick for that. He'd have to find her every time. Maybe he felt sorry for her. After all *she* was the pitifulest person she knew even if that wasn't a real word. She could see lots of reasons why any woman, but her, would want to marry Travis, but she couldn't find one reason why he'd want her.

Rainey continued to work until the table was filled with pies cooling, but Travis never made any attempt to talk to her. Once, when he'd stood and walked to the water bucket, he'd been careful to get a dipper of water without touching her. He'd hung the dipper back on its nail a few inches from her head and hadn't touched her hair.

She wanted to ask how he was feeling, but didn't dare. He'd rubbed his left leg several times, but she didn't miss that he'd left his cane by his chair when he'd walked across the room to get a drink.

When she finished the dishes and pulled off her apron, he stood . . . waiting.

Pearl crossed through from the store and glanced at both of them. "Owen just pulled up. He says he'll make your deliveries today."

"Thanks." Rainey didn't try to protest. She looked at Travis. "I'd like to go by the boardinghouse and change into my other dress."

Travis nodded once as if she were no more than an assignment he'd been given to keep up with. "I'll put the wagon around back. Don't come out until I'm at the porch."

She slipped into Sage's too-big shoes and watched him go.

When he'd disappeared, Pearl moved to her side and put her arm around Rainey's shoulders.

Rainey blinked back tears. "I don't know what's wrong. It's like I don't know him at all. He held me last night, but we had little chance to talk. Now we have nothing to say."

"What do you want him to say?"

Shaking her head, Rainey whispered, "I don't know. I wish he'd talk to me like he did in his letters. I liked hearing about what he was thinking and feeling and worrying about."

Pearl shrugged. "I don't know what to tell you except your paper Ranger is there somewhere in that hard man. All you've got to do is look for him."

A few moments later they heard the wagon. Rainey ran out. Travis made no effort to get down and help her up so she climbed in beside him. When she accidentally brushed his arm, he moved a few inches away.

They rode in silence to Askew House. The roads were muddy and each time the wagon rocked, she'd touch him, and each time he moved away.

When they reached the steps of Askew House, Rainey jumped out as soon as he slowed the horses. "I'll only be a minute."

He shoved the brake stick forward, tied the reins around it, and said without looking at her, "I'm going with you."

The front door was unlocked. Their steps echoed in the foyer across air as still as a tomb. Rainey called for Mrs. Vivian and then Mamie, but no one answered. All the weeks she'd lived there she could never remember the house being silent. There had always been the sounds of someone talking, or Mrs. Vivian yelling at Mamie from the kitchen, or Dottie singing in her room.

The blood that had been spilled in the foyer had been cleaned up, but the stain still darkened the wood. Rainey carefully walked around it. She took the first few steps up the stairs and turned back. "I'll change and be back down."

Travis followed her. "I said I'm going with you."

"All the way to my room?" She took the next step. "It's not allowed."

Using only his right leg to climb, he moved up the stairs. "I'm going with you," he repeated more slowly as if he thought she'd missed a word.

By this point she was so frustrated she wanted to kick his good leg. The man was taking his guard duty to the extreme. She lifted her head and walked up the stairs not even glancing back to see if he followed.

When she reached her door, she was surprised to find him only a few steps behind.

"Turn around," she said, blushing.

"What?" He moved closer.

"Turn around. I have to get my key."

He raised an eyebrow. "Afraid I'll see where you hid it?" He glanced around, as if he could guess.

"No, I'm afraid you'll see what I hide it in."

Travis didn't move.

"Suit yourself," she finally said as she lifted her skirt and pulled the key from deep inside her petticoat pocket.

When she looked up, he seemed totally surprised and embarrassed. "I'm sorry. I didn't know ladies' underwear had pockets."

She rolled her eyes. "Did you McMurray men split one brain evenly among yourselves, or did you get short-changed?"

He grinned. "Maybe the widow's right. Maybe I don't know much about women. Sage usually wears trousers and when she does wear a dress, she has no use for a place to put a key."

Rainey unlocked the door and he pushed it open, brushing her shoulder as he walked in ahead of her. "Lots of room," he mumbled as he took one step and bumped into the bed.

"It's plenty of room for me." She gathered up a change of clothes. "I can go downstairs to change."

"I'll turn around." He shifted until he was looking out the window. "I don't want you that far away in case there's trouble." He tested the bed. "Mind if I sit down?"

Rainey bit her lip. She wanted to say that nothing had happened all day, surely she'd be all right in the bathroom. The hip tub and washstand wouldn't harm her. "Suit yourself," she finally answered.

She unbuttoned the buttons at her throat and hesitated. "I don't think I can do this," she whispered. "Not with you so near."

He looked back at her. "Don't you trust me?"

"I do. But this isn't proper."

"And sleeping with me in your nightgown is?" he questioned, then turned back to the window. "Forget I said that. Just get changed."

She unbuttoned her blouse as he opened the window. He hadn't shown any interest in her all day; why should she think he'd change suddenly?

"What was the first sign you saw or heard that told you trouble was near the other morning?"

She slipped out of her skirt. "We heard the four horses in the alley."

"Four?" He glanced back at her, then raised one hand as if to say he was sorry and returned to stare out the window. "I thought there were three men."

Folding her skirt and blouse, Rainey tried to remember. "Three men came into the house. One was killed in the foyer, two rode away with me. But . . . I remember looking down and seeing four horses."

Excited, she leaned one knee on the bed beside him and gripped his shoulders, turning him to face her. "Travis. Why would they bring four horses?"

Travis frowned. "Maybe they planned for Sage to ride one? No," he answered his own question. "You said they put a bag over you. They would have had to take the time to tie you up if you were riding alone."

"Maybe there was another man out front."

"Maybe, but why didn't he ride off with them?"

"I don't know. I don't remember them saying anything about anyone but Haskell and Frank, the brother in black whom Dottie shot." Rainey moved closer and asked, "What happened to Haskell?"

Travis turned to look at her. "They brought him in to question. He said he planned to hold Seth at gunpoint and get the reward, but when he saw them all at once he chickened out. All the money he got was the double eagle they offered him for calling the slave over."

He looked past her toward the door. "You'd better get dressed. The extra horse could be nothing, but it's a clue. We probably need to tell Dillon. If there was someone with them, who knows what extremes he'll go to keep quiet."

She looked down, realizing she wore only her undergarments. Travis wasn't even looking at her. She had a feeling if she stripped down to her skin, he'd probably jump out the window to get away from her.

She stood, walking right into his range of vision.

He looked back toward the window.

"How long until we need to be at the judge's?" she asked.

"It's another hour until dark. The judge likes to dine late in southern style. We've probably got a few hours if you want to go by the station first."

Rainey studied his profile. Her man of oak. How could he have held her so tenderly last night and not look at her now? She guessed it would be a waste of time to ask him what was wrong. He'd never tell her.

She touched his shoulder. When he turned to see what she wanted, she moved between his knees and wrapped her arms around his neck. If he was no longer attracted to her, he was about to have to prove it.

For a moment he didn't move.

She leaned into him, letting her body make contact with his as her cheek pressed against his hair.

When he looked up at her, she held his face in her hands. She could think of nothing funny or smart to say. She voiced the only thing on her mind. "Don't you want me anymore?"

He snapped. His arms circled her waist and he crushed her to him. He buried his face against her throat and breathed deeply. "Want you," he finally said in an angry rumble. "I haven't been able to breathe with the need for you all day."

Twisting, he lay her on the tiny bed and pressed her to the mattress. When they came face-to-face, he kissed her hard with a hunger that shocked her.

She shook with the sudden flood of feelings volting through her body.

Travis pulled an inch away, breathing heavy against her ear. "I didn't mean to frighten you, Rainey. I think I've answered your question; now answer mine. Do you welcome my advance?"

Trying her best to stop shaking, she whispered, "Yes."

He kissed her gently then, as he had the first time. Slowly he lowered his body over her, allowing her time to welcome him.

She lay her hands back on the pillow above her head and invited his advance. When he finished kissing her lips, he moved to her throat as if he were dying of thirst and she was his only drink. She could feel his breathing as his chest pressed against her breasts, and his warm breath tickled the flesh he'd left damp with kisses. Any doubt that he wanted her was erased as his hands moved over the cotton of her underthings, feeling, exploring.

"You feel so good," he whispered. "So soft. I've been starving for the need to touch you since the minute you left my bed last night. If I could have, I would have climbed the stairs to you."

She let out a small cry of pleasure when he covered the camisole over her breast with his hand.

"And this," he added against her ear, "feels better than anything I've ever held in my hand."

She turned her head away, trying to remember to breathe. When she looked back, she saw only worry in his dark eyes. "Are you all right? I didn't hurt you?" His hand still lay on her breast, but he was no longer branding her with his touch.

She smiled. "No, you didn't hurt me." She wanted to ask him why he'd been so cold all day. Why he hadn't touched her or even kissed her when they were alone. But his actions now told her all she needed to know.

She tugged his hand away. He watched in silence as she untied her camisole and let the cotton fall open. Then, she put his hand back on her breast with no material between them.

"Continue," she whispered against his ear.

He laughed. "I always follow orders."

A few moments later she cried again in pleasure as his kisses moved down her throat and found the breast he'd already warmed with his hand.

She rocked gently in paradise as he explored her body, kissing and tasting. The gentle warrior she'd seen before returned as he touched her in places no man had ever seen. It crossed her mind, as his fingers molded into the flesh at the back of her leg, that maybe she should be shy, or even hesitant, but Rainey could never pull off such a lie.

He took his time showing her that he thought she was beautiful, and with each touch, each kiss, she wanted more.

As the room darkened into shadows, her underthings fell one by one to the floor of her tiny room and she was wrapped in his warmth. He took great care in moving his hands from her hair down along the center of her back to her hips, then he'd turn her to face him and kiss her until she felt she was floating. While she drifted, he explored, gently pulling her legs apart until she felt a fire of need build deep in her belly.

When she stretched like a cat across him, he whispered, "I want you, Rainey. I want to watch the graceful way you move all day and hold you like this every night. I want to move inside you so deep that we won't even know where I end and you begin. Marry me."

"No," she answered, no longer angry at him because he asked. "I can't."

He pulled her close. "And I have to have you." He spread his hand wide across the inside of her thigh and gripped her flesh. Covering her mouth with his, he caught her sigh of pleasure and tasted deeply as she pressed her body gently against him in wave after wave of sensations.

She wanted to feel his flesh against hers, but when she began unbuttoning his shirt, he stopped her.

"I have about one ounce of self-control left, my fairy, so

don't push this further. I have to think of your safety and be ready to act without having to look for my clothes first."

She laughed. "But it's not fair. I have nothing on."

He kissed her hand. "I agree it's not fair, and believe me I'm fully aware you have nothing on." He ran his hand along the curves of her side stopping to grip one hip.

Fisting his other hand into the curls of her hair, he pulled her head back. "You have no idea how perfect you are." He kissed his way down to her breasts. "I'll never again look at you clothed without seeing you like this."

Rainey hardly noticed the room slip into darkness as she drifted on wave after wave of pleasure. She knew there was more to lovemaking, much more, but she felt she might go mad if he went further. She'd simply float off the edge of passion and shatter into a million tiny drops of paradise.

They lay together for a long while. His hands slowly circled over her body, exploring, getting to know every curve, learning how she liked to be touched. She wanted to tell him that he could have her if he wanted. Hadn't she already made it plain that she wanted him? But she didn't talk, for she knew if they did, they'd only argue. For now maybe it was enough for both of them to hold each other. She'd start believing in marriage when he started believing in love.

The opening of a door sounded from floors below.

Travis brushed his fingers across her mouth and pointed at her clothes. She stood, fumbling in the shadows, and dressed. He shifted and lit a candle without making a sound. She could still see passion in his eyes, and when his gaze moved down her dress, she knew what he was thinking.

Silently she packed her few things and followed him down the stairs.

Mrs. Vivian sat on the last step of the stairs in the foyer when they reached the bottom. Rainey expected the woman to yell at her for having a man upstairs, but she stared at them with glazed eyes.

Travis touched her shoulder. "Are you all right, ma'am?"

She looked up. "I'm finished. I'm bankrupt. No one will ever rent from me again."

"Folks have short memories," Travis said. "They'll forget in time."

Rainey wasn't so sure. They were still talking about the French girl from years ago. "The women will come back." She tried to sound hopeful. "You can cover the outlaw's bloodstain with a rug and his death will become part of the legend of this place."

Mrs. Vivian shook her heard. "I tried to keep it going. I tried everything. But now I'm finished. When my husband comes back, he'll blame me for not keeping the house."

Travis shrugged at Rainey, but tried again. "Rainey's right, a rug would cover it up."

Mrs. Vivian looked at them with vacant eyes. "And who will cover the woman's body on my back porch," she asked as if they had the answer. "Who will wash up her blood?"

CHAPTER 31

T RAVIS HELPED RAINEY GET MRS. VIVIAN INTO HER ROOM. THE SCARE-crow of a woman seemed nervous that they were in her private quarters. Travis figured it was because she had enough furniture for five rooms crammed into the space. She'd even suspended drapes in places where there were no windows to give the look of tiny rooms within the area. He felt like if he breathed he'd knock something over. He stopped about three feet inside and watched the landlord crumble into a chair by the window.

"Lock the door when I leave," Travis whispered to Rainey. "Will you be all right in here?"

"I'll be fine." Rainey didn't look too sure.

He turned at the door and took one last glance at the woman he knew very well by touch. Rainey looked so beautiful when she was trying to be brave, he thought.

"I'll not open the door until I hear your voice on the other side," she whispered, and he fought the urge to return for just one last kiss before the world stepped between them.

Travis looked over at Mrs. Vivian and decided he had the easier job of going to look for a body. Rainey had to deal with her.

He stepped to the front porch and yelled at the first rider passing to go to the Ranger station and tell anyone there that McMurray needed assistance at Askew House. The young kid of about fifteen galloped away, excited to help.

Then, Travis walked through the kitchen to the back door forcing his mind to not allow his body to react to whatever he might find. Something had frightened Mrs. Vivian into hysteria and she didn't seem the type to rattle easily.

The kitchen was a mess with laundry and dishes piled around.

He stood in the shadows by the back door for a few minutes waiting to see if anyone or anything moved in the alley. But all was still. He lit one of the kitchen lamps and placed it in the window so that he could see the porch more clearly. Mrs. Vivian had been correct. Looking like a rag doll, the body of a woman sat in the corner of the porch, her eyes staring sightlessly at him. Her arms were at her sides, a knife in one. Deep cuts ran across her wrists. Blood pooled around her.

It took him only a moment to recognize the woman who'd ended her own life. Rainey had called her Whiny, the thin barmaid. The one the Rangers thought was sweet on Seth Norman.

"McMurray!" a man yelled from inside the house. "Travis, it's Dumont and Price. What's the problem?"

"Ask the boy who delivered the message to wait on the front porch!" Travis yelled back. "I have something important I need him to do." The last thing Travis wanted was for the young man to witness this suicide. It wasn't one that would wash out of anyone's mind easily.

Two Rangers had followed his voice and stood at the kitchen door.

"Oh, my God," Roy whispered as he lowered his gun. "What happened?"

"Looks like she killed herself," Travis answered. "Bring the other lantern and we'll have a closer look." Travis was glad Roy Dumont had answered the call.

As Roy lit the lantern, Travis heard him say to the other, younger, Ranger, "Stand guard at the front, Philip. We don't want anyone showing up just to sightsee."

The Ranger seemed happy to accept the new assignment. Travis had no doubt he could smell the blood from the kitchen and probably see the outline of the body through the kitchen window.

Reluctantly Roy joined him on the porch. He'd pulled a sheet from the laundry piled by the door and covered the dead woman almost tenderly. Blood soaked through immediately.

Roy squatted and took his time looking at details. The man was hard as they come at being a Ranger, but he had a soft spot for women.

"I was directly upstairs." Travis also began to study the

area. "I didn't hear a sound. How could a woman slit her wrist without making a sound?"

Roy tugged at the rope holding one of the dead woman's hands. "She must have really wanted to die."

Travis nodded and lifted the sheet. "She's got bruises all over her. My guess is life finally got to be too much for her."

Roy moved the lantern. "She works at the saloon across the alley."

Travis took a closer look. "She looks younger here than she did the other night when I talked to her." He headed back inside ordering, "Stay with the body."

Roy nodded.

Travis stopped long enough to tell the kid at the door to find Judge Gates's home on Eight Street and tell a man named Dillon to come fast.

"There's been another murder?" the kid asked.

Travis shook his head. "Suicide." He offered the kid a coin.

The boy waved his hand. "I'm happy to help. One of these days I'm going to be a Ranger."

Travis watched the youth run for his horse. Then he crossed to Mrs. Vivian's room one door down from the drawing room. When he knocked, Rainey answered too fast to have been anywhere but beside the door waiting.

She moved out into the hallway and silently closed the door. She didn't say a word, just waited.

He wanted to touch her, to hold her, but now was not the time or place.

"It's bad." Travis didn't have time to break it easy. "The woman you called Whiny took her own life."

Rainey's eyes filled with tears, but she stood straight and still. "She kept saying she'd find a way out."

He caught her as she began to crumple and held her tight. She felt so good against him. He wished he could take the sadness away.

"I should have broken that a little easier, Rainey. I'm sorry." He kissed the top of her head.

"No, there was no easy way." She took a deep breath. "I'm fine. I just felt a little light-headed. Mrs. Vivian's been crying and mumbling about how this has all been her fault. Somehow she blames herself. She keeps saying that no one would have been killed if she'd been here when the kidnappers came."

Travis brushed her hair away from her face with his hand. "As soon as Dillon arrives, I'm getting you out of here."

His fairy looked up at him with her huge green eyes. "You still think I'm in danger?"

"I'm not taking any chances. If Eldon is out there, he'll want both of us dead. And if there was a forth man the day of the kidnapping, he might be helping Eldon find us."

Rainey shivered as if the hallway had suddenly grown cold. "You have to send someone to check on Snort."

Travis wanted to tell her he couldn't worry about every woman in the world. He had his hands full with her. "I'll tell Roy to check on her."

"What about Mrs. Vivian?"

Travis didn't want to talk about the details. He had a feeling Mrs. Vivian was up to her neck in trouble. The fact that she'd been gone when it happened had nagged at the back of his mind for days.

He held Rainey close and asked, "Where's Mamie? I saw laundry piled up in the kitchen and you told me she did it every night."

A single tear rolled slowly down her face. "Mrs. Vivian said she's disappeared. Oh, Travis, you don't think someone took her?"

He wished he could lie to her, but he only said, "I hope not." Mamie had seen the Norman brothers in the alley.

The blast of a gun rattled through the hallway. Travis pushed Rainey against the wall and covered her with his body as he pulled his gun.

Before the echo died in the air, he heard Philip running from the porch and Roy stomping through the dining room. Both were shouting his name.

"Stay here," Travis ordered as he pushed her into the dark corner. "Don't move unless I call you."

Rainey nodded.

He joined the other Rangers at Mrs. Vivian's door. "It came from in here!" he shouted as he tried the knob.

The door was locked.

"Ready?" Travis said as all three men raised their guns. A moment later Travis's shoulder slammed against the door, shattering the lock.

They all rushed into the cluttered room. Dressers and chests, tables loaded down with keepsakes, chairs stacked on top of other chairs, all made a jungle for them to stumble through.

Roy mumbled an oath as he knocked over a chair. "What a mess."

By the window sat a small table with one chair. On the rug beside the chair lay a body curled up like an infant asleep.

Roy reached her first. He knelt and grabbed her shoulder. With little effort he rolled the thin woman onto her back. "Mrs. Vivian," he whispered as they all stared at a gaping hole that now marked the center of her chest. Her eyes were open, but there was no sign of life left. The gun rested a few feet from her.

"She killed herself!" Philip's voice squeaked with youth. "She had to have killed herself," he mumbled, trying to make sense of the death he saw. "She was locked in here alone."

Roy's gaze met Travis, and Travis knew they were thinking the same thing. Women take pills or cut their wrists; they don't shoot themselves.

Travis was out the door and back into the hallway. He didn't breathe until he had Rainey in his arms.

She was shaking as if near frozen. "I saw . . . I saw . . ."

He moved her into the light coming from Mrs. Vivian's room.

"I thought I saw a shadow move out the door right after the three of you went in," Rainey whispered. "I'm not even sure it was a person. Just a shadow. It must have been in Vivian's room."

Travis didn't want to tell her any more bad news, but he couldn't protect her unless she knew the danger. "Mrs. Vivian is dead," he said as calmly as he could. "It was made to look like a suicide."

She wrapped her arms around him and held on as tightly as she could. He hugged her, wondering if his arms were enough to protect her.

"I'll get you out of here as soon as it's safe."

She cried softly against his chest.

The silence ended with the arrival of Dillon, Mike Saddler, and Sage along with what seemed to be half the Rangers stationed in Austin. Suddenly their shouting and questions were coming from every direction.

Travis handed Rainey over to his sister and moved directly to Mike. "Why'd you bring Sage here?" Travis fought to keep his fists balled at his sides.

Mike looked miserable. "You ever try to stop her when she gets something in her head? I'd sooner milk a bull."

Travis almost felt sorry for Mike. "I understand," he mumbled without smiling.

Dillon organized the men, then asked to see Mike and Travis in the dining room. Neither man wanted to leave the women in the hallway unprotected, so they asked Sage and Rainey to join them. When the door was closed, Dillon stated the obvious. "I think this might have been Eldon's work. Maybe he thinks if he gets rid of everyone who might have seen him kidnap Rainey, we'll have nothing on him."

"So the barmaid might not have killed herself?"

"It's just a theory."

Dillon paced as he talked. "I sent a man over to the three dressmakers' apartment. They'll be sleeping below in the shop tonight to make sure no one gets to them. Dottie says she has a safe place. Other than them"—he looked at Rainey and Sage—"you are the only two alive who saw the kidnapping. We need to get you somewhere safe fast. Somewhere no one will think to look for you."

Sage met her brother's glance. "I'm going home," she said simply.

"But . . ." Mike started to argue.

Travis understood. For a McMurray there was no safe haven but Whispering Mountain. "Let her go," he said, knowing that whoever was killing the witnesses would be after Rainey next, not the old maids or Sage. "Mike, get her the best horse you can and ride with her. Even if you two are followed, there's not an outlaw in Texas who can keep up."

Mike smiled. "I'm not sure *I* can even keep up with her. Once she switched saddles the other day, I saw what riding-like-the-wind truly looks like."

Dillon stopped pacing. "I can send guards out with them the first day."

Travis shook his head. "They'd be safer leaving town unnoticed"—he looked back at his sister—"and well armed."

Sage nodded slightly. "I'll be ready to leave in an hour. We'll be well away from Austin before dawn. The roads are good for miles. We'll make good time."

Travis looked at Sage. "You'll be home in less than half the time it took to get to Austin. I'll hire someone to follow in a few days with the wagon."

"What about Duck? He won't go with me without you along. I left him with Dottie, but he won't stay for long. She said if you can get Rainey to her, she'll take her into hiding."

"I'll take care of Duck and Rainey," Travis said. "You worry about getting home safely." He wished he could send Rainey and Duck to Whispering Mountain, too, but Rainey couldn't ride well enough to keep up, and if they slowed they'd be sitting ducks on the road.

Sage hugged her brother.

"I wish I could ride with you," he whispered, hating that he wasn't the one taking her to safety, but his leg, even now that it felt like it was healing, would only slow Sage and Mike down.

"I know," she answered. "But you're needed here."

Dillon interrupted. "Right, McMurray. And the first thing we have to do is get Rainey out of here without anyone seeing her. I'd bet a month's pay that someone is watching the house right now just waiting to see where she goes."

Sage hugged Rainey and left the room, but Travis stopped Mike Saddler before the young Ranger could follow.

"I'll get her home safely," Mike promised.

Travis didn't let go of his arm.

Mike smiled. "And you don't have to say it. I know, you'll kill me if I touch her."

Travis smiled. "She's not the kid I thought she was. *She'll* kill you if you touch her. I'm just telling you to take care of her."

"I will."

He disappeared and Travis turned back to Dillon to plan how they would get Rainey out of the house safely.

A tap on the dining room door disturbed them a few minutes later. "Sorry to bother you," Roy said. "Your sister left here riding lightning fast. Anyone following her would have to have wings."

"Good." Travis smiled. He knew Mike would circle until he knew no one followed before he took her back to the Baileys' place so she could change.

Roy handed over a coat lined in fur. "Only problem is she picked up the wrong coat. I could have sworn she wore this in." He turned to Rainey. "I think she must have taken yours."

CHAPTER 32

Rainey slipped from the laundry room window into Travis's arms. She felt numb with worry and fear. She'd let Dillon and Travis discuss protecting her as if she were not responsible for herself, but deep down she knew that the longer she stayed around Travis, the more danger she put him in. When she got the chance, she needed to disappear.

But tonight didn't seem the time. A fog had settled over the town earlier, and now a slow rain hung in the air. The weather would make her escape easier, but it left a feeling that the whole world was crying.

Travis held her hand as they moved in the darkness down the alley to where Roy had the wagon waiting. When he reached the wagon, he turned and lifted her into the back between boxes and bundles of what looked like supplies, then swung in beside her. In an instant they vanished beneath blankets.

Travis opened his arm and pulled her against him as Roy set the horses into motion. He moved slowly, as if he were in no hurry. To all that might glance in their direction, Roy looked much like Owen did when he made deliveries.

"You all right?" Travis whispered. They were so close she felt his breath on her cheek.

"Yes."

They remained silent for a few minutes, and then he whispered close to her ear. "I wish we were back in your room on the third floor."

"Me, too," she answered, remembering how she'd lain beside him without her clothes and without embarrassment.

"Rainey?" he mumbled.

"Yes."

"I love touching you."

She stilled. It was the first time she'd heard him use the word *love*. He hadn't said he loved her, just touching her. The wagon rattled along. Rainey closed her eyes and remembered how it had been for a few short hours. No one would ever guess that the hard man beside her could be so tender. He'd made her feel beautiful, if only for a few hours. The memory of the way he'd kissed her warmed her still.

After a while the wagon came to a stop and Travis slipped from beside her. "I'll be back in a minute. Don't move."

Rainey poked her head out enough to see the outline of the judge holding Duck at the back door. The boy began to fight and kick the moment he recognized Travis coming toward them. The judge let him go. Duck flew down the path to Travis.

As always, Travis engulfed the boy in his hug. Watching, Rainey saw how much the child meant to him.

"Thanks," she heard Travis say as he moved closer to the judge. She couldn't hear more. Roy climbed from the wagon and loaded more supplies.

Travis finally stepped away from the judge and said, "We'll be in touch."

When he put Duck in the wagon, Travis told him to lie down in a voice Rainey thought sounded harsh. Duck didn't seem to mind. He smiled back at Travis and cuddled down next to Rainey. Travis lay on the other side of the boy and covered them all with a buffalo hide as Roy started moving again.

Rainey reached her hand above the boy and touched Travis's shoulder. "Where are we going?"

"You know that cellar where Dottie collected the wine you stole?" Travis whispered.

"No," she said. "I'm not going there." She couldn't bring herself to even think of climbing back in that cellar. She'd face the kidnappers again before she'd hide in the darkness of that place.

His hand gently brushed her cheek. "Dottie's waiting there with a lantern. The saloon is long closed. We'll only have to pass through to her part where her husband's restaurant used to be. It was the only place we could come up with where no one would look and you both would still be close."

Rainey tried to slow her breathing as the wagon rattled. The boarded-up restaurant would be the perfect place to hide. It was right in the middle of town so the Rangers would have no trouble watching over them, and no one probably even remembered Dottie's husband once ran the place.

When they got to the alley, she pointed to the cellar door. Roy opened it and Travis moved down first with Duck on his arm. The boy didn't like the idea of going into darkness any more than Rainey did. He hid his face in the collar of Travis's coat.

Rainey followed once she saw the warm glow of a lantern lighting the way.

The cellar didn't look nearly so frightening in the light. Bottles and barrels were scattered around, but after a few feet there was a clear path to the back stairs. Halfway up the stairs divided, one set to the saloon, the other to the restaurant.

"My husband's partner closes when the last customer leaves, and doesn't open up until noon or after. We'll be settled in by then."

Rainey followed Dottie into the small restaurant kitchen. Two huge ovens stood in one corner with a low fire burning in one. Pots and pans hung from an iron circle above a worktable. Except for the dust the place looked as if the cook had just walked out.

Dottie spread her hands in welcome. "Roy and I thought no one would notice smoke in this fog, so we braved a fire. I've been dusting off everything while I waited for you to get here, but I'm afraid the place still has a layer of dirt on it."

Travis sat Duck by the lantern and crossed to the far door. "I'll check out the front. Duck, you stay with Rainey."

To Rainey's surprise, Duck nodded.

Dottie set another lantern on the counter. "My husband loved this place. He'd cook every night, but we didn't make any money until he started having a private card game in the restaurant after nine." She sighed as she ran her hand along the wood as if saying hello. "Life was so sweet. We'd work here, then go home to a little house he'd built for me. When he died, I tried, but I couldn't sell this place. Finally I had so much debt I had to sell my house. I thought of trying to make this into a home, but who wants to try and sleep when the other half of the building is a saloon."

"I love the kitchen," Rainey whispered. "Your husband really knew what he was doing when he set it up. It's a baker's dream."

Dottie looked around. "It's cozy, isn't it? The judge said I could stay with him and the Baileys' were nice enough to offer me a place until my arm heals, but somehow, I wanted to come here. It's like I'm scared and I need my Henry to protect me." She smiled. "Maybe a little part of him is still here."

Roy bumped his way into the kitchen carrying blankets and supplies. "Where do you want these?" he said. "The judge sent over food enough for an army."

"Here, on the counter," Dottie said. "The front is full of the furniture I couldn't sell."

Travis returned. "Roy give me a hand and we'll move something against the front door. Then the only way in and out of here will be through the cellar. There's a streetlight right outside the windows. It shines through the boards, so we'll have no trouble seeing in there."

Roy dropped the supplies and followed Travis.

Dottie pointed with her free arm as Rainey began to organize the blankets. "The judge insisted on sending twice what we'll need." She grins. "He worries about me as much as my Henry would have. Do you think it's a sign that his name is Henry, also?" She smiled. "If I married him, I wouldn't have to go about learning a new name."

"I see your point. It wouldn't do to call your second husband by your first husband's name."

Dottie nodded. "I think it's a sign."

Rainey carried another load to the corner. "We can make beds over here. We'll put Duck's closest to the stove so he'll be warm."

"He might get burned."

Rainey shook her head. "He's careful and I think it makes him feel safe."

A half hour later Duck was sound asleep and Dottie lay beside him, her injured arm propped on pillows. Her soft snoring blended with the crackling of the fire. Roy sat on the chair by the stairs to the cellar half asleep. In many ways he reminded her of Travis. Neither man ever seemed to go off alert. Being a Ranger was far more than a job she realized; it was a way of life.

Rainey poured out a cup of coffee from the pot left warming on the stove and passed through the door to the front room. Travis sat watching the street from a small opening in the boards covering the windows.

"You awake?" she whispered, knowing he would be.

He turned in her direction. "Coffee would help."

She moved slowly toward him. "I've got a cup."

He was no more than a shadow, but she watched him lower his rifle as she neared.

"I know you don't like me to ask, but how is your leg?"

Thin beams of light slashed through the boards, and she could see his face clearly for a moment before he moved. He looked tired and worried.

"It aches a little. If I could I'd check to make sure none of the stitches are bleeding. Much as I hate to admit it, the doc's wraps did the trick. Between that and taking out that tiny piece of metal, my leg's stopped swelling. But the doc told me to keep an eye out for any bleeding."

Rainey handed him the cup and turned back to the kitchen without a word. Five minutes later she returned with a small pot of warm water and a stack of bandages.

"What's that?"

"Water," she whispered. "Now, keep quiet of you'll wake the others." She couldn't see his face, but she guessed he'd raised an eyebrow like he always did when he thought she might be crazy.

"Stand up," Rainey whispered.

"Why?" he asked as he did what she asked.

"I want to check for bleeding on those stitches. I don't want you getting infected."

He didn't move. "Where'd you find bandages?"

"I ripped a few strips off of one of the sheets the judge sent over." She moved closer. "Now remove your trousers."

"I don't think so. You couldn't see if I'm bleeding in this darkness, and we can't turn a lantern up for fear that someone passing might see in."

Rainey tugged at his belt. "I don't have to see the stitches. I only have to feel them. If I feel blood, or even dried blood, I've got water to wash it off and clean rags to wrap the wound." She put her hands on her hips. "Now, are you going to take those trousers off, or am I?"

He laughed. "All right, Rainey, I'm too tired to argue." He unbuckled his gun belt and lay it beside him on a table.

"Don't worry, Ranger, it's so dark in here I won't see a thing."

He didn't laugh as he shoved down his pants. "The cut is on the back of my left leg, just below my hip," he instructed. He pulled up his shirttail and turned so that one of the beams crossed his leg.

She would have bet she'd embarrassed him, but she didn't stop. They both knew the wound needed tending. Rainey was thankful for the dark. She'd never seen a man's leg exposed, and this wasn't just any man's leg. This was Travis's.

Her hand touched his hip, and she felt the muscles tighten beneath her fingers. Her fingers moved down to the bandage at the top of his leg. Several spots of caked-in dried blood stained the soft cotton. She pulled a chair up and sat as he turned the wound toward her and waited. Her hand shook as she wet a rag in the warm water. She dripped water over the bandage and slowly soaked the cotton away from the wound. No wonder he hadn't been comfortable with the bandage of dried blood tied to his leg. She brushed her fingers over the unharmed skin as if in comfort.

He took a breath when she tossed the bandage aside, but didn't look at her.

Again she slid her hand down his hip slowly until she brushed over the stitches that had poked into his flesh on either side of a two-inch cut.

He sucked in air.

"I'm sorry," she whispered.

He didn't answer, but the muscles in his leg were so tight she thought he really could be made of oak. Carefully, with feather touches, she washed the wound, then let it dry. Her hand moved up to his waist.

"I've no more cuts," he said almost harshly.

"I know. I just wanted to touch you. In the times we've been alone and you've touched me, you've never let me touch you."

"It's not something a woman wants to do to a man."

Rainey spread her hand over his warm skin. "How do you know? Have you been with many women who told you that, or are you just guessing?"

"Just check the wound." His words could not have been colder, but his skin remained warm to her touch.

She brushed her fingers over the stitches and found the skin dry. "No more bleeding."

When she started to wrap the leg, he took the bandage away from her and did it himself, then he pulled up his trousers.

"I thought men wore long johns all winter."

"Rainey, we shouldn't be having this conversation and yes,

they do. Mine, however, seemed to have disappeared when I collapsed at the Baileys'."

"Oh," she whispered. "Wonder who took them off." She couldn't help but giggle at the possibility of the round little housekeeper doing it.

He buckled on his gun belt. "Good night, Rainey," he said as if they'd never been more than strangers. He obviously didn't see any humor in their conversation.

"Good night." She was almost to the kitchen door when she stopped, turned around, and went back. "Are you angry, or just being you? Sometimes, I swear, I can't tell."

"I have no idea how to answer that question," he snapped. "I'd find it hard to be anything but me."

She tried again. "All right, answer me this. Would you like to kiss me good night, or do you prefer to just snap at me in the hope that I'll run away?"

He lowered his voice, his words meant for just her ears. "I wouldn't mind a kiss, if you're offering. But this is hardly the time or place. You've been through a lot tonight. You probably need rest."

Before he could continue with his list of reasons not to kiss her, she rose on her tiptoes and kissed him. He didn't respond. She might as well have been kissing a statue. So she leaned closer and tried again. If he planned to remain cold, she wasn't going to make it easy on him. Her fingers dug into his hair and pulled him down a few inches. "We've both been through a great deal tonight," she whispered, her lips brushing his. "But I need to know how it is between us."

When her lips pressed against his, he snapped inside. Like a dam breaking, he pulled her against him and kissed her soundly. The hunger she tasted in his assault no longer frightened her.

When she pulled away, she whispered, "Travis, you remind me of a river. There's a strong current of feelings flowing in you, but I swear I have to crack the ice every time I want to get to you."

"Are you complaining, or bragging that you can do, so easily, what no woman's ever been able to do?"

"What's that," she whispered as she rubbed her cheek against his shoulder.

"Make me feel," he whispered. "Make me care."

He lowered into the chair and pulled her on his right leg.

Then he kissed her again the way he swore he'd wanted to all night.

Rainey returned his kisses, but as he drank his fill of her, she moved her hands over his shirt. She wanted to know this man. She wanted to know his body as well as he knew hers.

When she unbuttoned the first few buttons of his shirt, his hand closed around hers, stopping her progress.

Rainey straightened, pulling away from him. "You're not stopping me from touching you, Travis McMurray, so there is no use in fighting."

He laughed and pulled her hand to his lips. After kissing her palm lightly, he whispered, "I've no desire to stop you, but now is not the time or place. I promise one day I'll spread out for you on a real bed and let you touch me wherever you like."

She pulled her hand away and unbuttoned another button. "Then, tonight, I'll be satisfied by feeling your heartbeat."

He didn't stop her and she moved her fingers beneath his shirt and slid across the wall of muscles to cover his heart.

She smiled as she pressed her palm over the beating. "I feel the center of you. I feel your heart."

"No," he whispered as he kissed her ear. "You are my heart."

They held each other until dawn. She'd drift into sleep and awaken to the feel of him moving his face against her hair, or sliding his hand gently down her body. When she stirred, he'd rock her gently against him and kiss her softly. She'd slide her hand over his heart and fall back asleep with the pounding of it against her palm.

When sunlight woke them both, he straightened and set her away from him. "Go back to the kitchen. You'll be safer there."

His words didn't sound harsh, but they weren't loving, as she'd hoped for. He was ordering her again. Doing his job, nothing more.

Rainey picked up the cold coffee cup and moved toward the door. She wanted to turn around and run to him. She wished she could make the gentle man who held her in the night be the man who faced her in the day.

"What is it?" He stood behind her.

Rainey didn't turn around. "I wish . . . I wish . . ." How could she tell him? He'd had to be strong to survive. He needed to be strong for them all to be safe, but she needed to know how he felt. Just saying he loved the way she felt wasn't enough. Just telling Mike that she was his didn't matter. "I wish," she tried again. "I wish I could write to you about how I feel. I wish you could write to me. Somehow in your letters I saw you clearer. I felt closer to you all the time, not just at night when we touch."

"I've never had time for words," he answered.

"I know. I understand, but I still need them. Maybe because I never had them, either."

He grabbed her shoulder and turned her against a dusty table. Standing behind her he shoved with his body until the table pressed into her legs. Then, he leaned over her, bending her down until his hand touched the thick layer of dust.

Rainey fought down a cry. She knew he wouldn't hurt her, but she wanted gentleness, and, except for the shadows, Travis didn't seem to have any.

He slid his free hand around her waist and held her tightly against him as his fingers moved in the dust, printing boldly three words.

I love you.

When she didn't move, he wrote them again and again and again. His hold around her was tight, his body stiff behind her, but he wrote the words over and over.

Tears filled her eyes and dripped atop the dust.

She fought his grip and twisted in his embrace. "How many times are you going to write it?"

He stared down at her, his jaw set in granite, his body unyielding, his eyes filled with need. "Until you believe me."

CHAPTER 33

Travis knew if trouble found them, it would be before sunset. He'd talked with Roy and Dillon after breakfast. The three old maids seemed to think the Rangers protecting them were gentlemen callers. They were happy to be in protective custody.

Dillon said he had one Ranger follow behind Mike and Sage as they left Austin. After a few miles they were well ahead of him, so the shadow stopped and waited. No one else followed the couple. So Travis assumed Sage was safely on her way home.

Travis almost laughed. If Mike Saddler thought he had trouble with him, wait till her met her other two brothers.

Mrs. Vivian's slave was still missing, but at least they hadn't found a body. Travis considered that good news.

Dillon planned to bring Haskell in for more questioning, but he thought the saloon owner was probably only guilty of wanting to make some fast money.

That left Dottie and Rainey to watch over. Whoever was trying to wipe up the mess left from the kidnapping would want them the most. Dottie had shot one of the brothers, and Rainey had not only ruined their plan, she'd killed another brother. If Eldon wanted revenge on Travis before, he must be double mad at the women.

Travis leaned against the wall and tried to sleep. Anyone trying to enter the restaurant from the front would have to make some noise and he'd long ago trained himself to come fully awake at the slightest sound.

In a few hours the saloon would open next door and they'd

no longer be able to slip into the place through the cellar. It was only a matter of time before someone figured out where they were and came after Dottie and Rainey. He thought of taking them and running, but he didn't want either woman to spend her life looking over her shoulder.

He hoped they'd get this mess straightened out before anyone found Rainey or the widow. The Ranger station was half a block away. Close enough to hear a shot if Travis needed help.

Travis fell asleep and dreamed once more of the smell of tea around him. He was reading in a chair by a fire and all was right with the world. He shifted in his sleep and the dream shifted as well. Now he was standing before a man holding up a Bible. Travis looked down into the man's eyes and saw a question, even though he stood silently in front of Travis. As before in his dream, Travis knew the Bible held a gun.

The light touch of a little hand on his arm woke him.

Travis growled at Duck. "Morning, son."

Duck smiled and growled back. He climbed into Travis's lap and stared up at him.

Travis patted the boy's head. "I needed to talk to you," he began. "If trouble comes . . ." He hesitated, thinking of how to word what needed to be said. "If I pull my gun or anyone else does, I want you to disappear as quick as a rabbit jumping in a hole."

Travis looked at the boy. He knew there would be all kinds of trouble if he tried to make Duck leave him, but he didn't want to think about the boy being in harm's way. "Do you understand?"

Duck nodded and leaned against Travis.

Travis whispered, more to himself than the boy, "They'll be coming after Rainey, if they come. I'll need to be protecting her, so I have to know you're safe."

Duck pulled the knife Travis had given him from his pocket. It wasn't large, but it was still too big for him to open.

Travis smiled. "I guess we're about as ready as we can be."

Duck nodded and slipped his knife back into his pocket. He pulled out a string and began playing with it. Travis watched him for a while in the silent stillness of the morning.

Roy wandered in with a cup of coffee and sat down across from Travis. He watched Duck for a few minutes and said, "Beats me how kids and women take to you, McMurray. You're about as friendly as a rattler. I never see you say one nice thing to that pretty little Rainey Adams, and you growl at the kid like you're a bear fixing to eat him."

"Mind your own business," Travis said without looking away from the window.

"You see." Roy pointed at him. "That's what I mean. We've been riding together off and on for years, and I didn't even know you have a ranch north of here. Wouldn't know now if Rainey hadn't told me."

Travis changed the subject. "Do all women talk so much?"

Roy laughed and straightened. Now they were on a subject he considered himself an expert in. Women. He opened his mouth to start twice, then stopped. Finally he simply said, "Yes."

They sat in silence watching the street beyond the boarded window come to life.

Roy finally remembered his coffee. After he took a drink, he put his elbows on his knees and leaned forward. "They found some interesting things in Mrs. Vivian's room last night. It seems she was a bit of the thief. She not only stole from her boarders from time to time, but she lifted things from homes around her block when she knew her neighbors were away. Even furniture. She must have had some help because there was no way one woman could haul a dresser down the street."

Travis listened without being surprised.

Roy continued. "She'd been selling some stuff off. According to her accounts at stores around town, she was in deep debt, but the day of the kidnapping she paid for everything with cash."

Travis grew more interested. "You think someone paid her off to be gone during the kidnapping?"

Roy shook his head. "I think someone paid her to tip them off that Sage was coming that morning."

"But she knew I was a Ranger and always traveled with Sage."

Roy nodded. "I think she was planning on that. She took the money and tipped the Normans off thinking that you'd be in the foyer like always and you'd save the day. Then her house would be talked about in a good way. Sage would be safe. The Normans would be in jail or dead, and she could keep the money. I think the old crow thought she'd come out ahead."

Travis agreed. "And since she was gone at the time it happened, no one would look in her direction."

"Right. There was only one person close enough for her to pass the message to when Sage came."

"Haskell," Travis answered. "No matter which way we turn, his name keeps coming up."

Rainey stepped into the front room. "Morning," she said, aware that she had broken up their conversation. "Sorry to interrupt."

Roy stood and offered her a chair, claiming she'd always be a welcome interruption.

Travis studied her. Something had changed about her. She hadn't said a word all morning, but he could tell something was different. She moved with more confidence. There was a glow about her. He grinned, wondering if it could be something as simple as the fact that she knew she was loved.

"Rainey," Roy commented. "Are you sure there were four horses?"

Rainey frowned. "It all happened so fast. I could be wrong."

"The undertaker put Seth's out front of his store yesterday as soon as he got the box made. Several people walked by and identified him before they nailed the lid on." Roy glanced at Travis. "We kept a man watching. No sign of Eldon or Old Man Norman."

Rainey looked from one to the other. "You were hoping Seth's body would draw them out?"

"It was a chance. We'd like to get this wrapped up."

"It would be a bigger chance of him coming out if he knew where I was."

Travis wanted to call her a liar. But she was right. He also knew she was drawing a target on her back.

Rainey straightened her shoulders. "Tell Dillon I'm tired of hiding. Dottie and I have been talking about opening this place back up as a bakery someday. Tell Dillon someday is coming tomorrow."

Roy said he'd be back as soon as he could and left. When he was gone, Travis said as calmly as he could, "You shouldn't have done that." He'd considered yelling but knew it wouldn't change her mind. She'd run into trouble full speed since the night she'd met him and thought she was saving him from the cowhands. She'd done it again to save Sage.

She faced him. "I can't hide forever. I've been thinking about it. If Eldon knows where I'm at, he'll come after me. I've

got you and Roy to protect me. Mamie may be hiding somewhere with no one watching over her."

Travis read her mind. "You know where the slave is, don't
you?"

She raised her chin. "I have a good idea."

"This isn't a game, Rainey. Mamie may already be dead.
You're betting your life here."

"Then why didn't you stop me?" She moved closer.

He shrugged. "Because I'd have done the same thing. The
longer we wait, the less the threat seems real. In a few days, a
week, we'll get reckless, take chances we shouldn't. If trouble's
coming, I'd just as soon face it now."

He circled his arm around her. "And if trouble comes for
you, he'll have to step over me to get you."

CHAPTER 34

∞

Aᴛ ᴛᴡɪʟɪɢʜᴛ Rᴀɪɴᴇʏ ʟɪᴛ ᴛʜᴇ ʟᴀᴍᴘ ɪɴ ᴛʜᴇ ᴋɪᴛᴄʜᴇɴ ᴀɴᴅ ꜰᴇʟᴛ ᴀ sʜɪꜰᴛ in the air. A breeze, as if someone had opened a window in another part of the house. Only there were no windows in Dottie's kitchen.

She glanced at Travis and saw him lift his head ever so slightly. He'd felt it, also, but he made no sudden move.

The day had been exhausting but they were still both on full alert. First, when Roy returned just before noon, he brought two Rangers with him. He said that if she wanted to make pies, they'd go get her supplies from the Langland place and bring it over. He also said Dillon had told him to unblock the front door. The restaurant might not be open for business, but they were no longer hiding. The Rangers would bring her supplies in through the front.

When Rainey nodded, Roy winked and added, "We all think you are one brave lady, and we'll do our best to protect you."

"Thank you," she said, hoping the best would be enough.

An hour later Dottie's dead husband's partner showed up to demand they leave. He claimed the smell of pie was filtering through to his half of the building, and he was losing customers. Apparently the smell reminded the drunks that they needed to go home.

Dottie stood up to the man. She was surprised how fast he backed down and started acting respectful. She didn't see Roy standing behind her checking his gun. By midafternoon the little kitchen was as busy as a train station with Rainey making pies and Dottie visiting with people who stopped by to see what was going on.

The judge dropped in to tell Travis the group of lawyers had approved him to the bar. Judge Gates promised if he'd hang around for six months and intern, the judge would sign his state license to practice.

Rainey was surprised at how little the news seemed to matter to Travis, but she had a feeling the judge understood.

Pearl and Jason followed the Rangers carrying supplies over to make sure Rainey was all right, and she stayed to hear all the details.

Even the three sisters came over with their protectors in tow. Rainey had to admit that they all looked fine, dressed for their stroll.

By the time she finished baking, everyone in town knew where she'd be staying for the night. The place was finally quiet. Dottie, Rainey, and Travis ate the soup she'd made while Duck played on the floor. He'd eaten too many slices of pie to want supper.

"Roy will be back before it's late. He just went home to say hello to his wife," Travis volunteered to break the silence.

Rainey wasn't hungry, but she took another bite. She hadn't been alone with Travis all day and knew there would be no chance of it now. He'd want to stay with Duck and Dottie to make sure they were safe. Anything said between them would be heard by all.

"This is good soup," Travis added, as if he were making an effort to say something.

"Thank you." She smiled at him over her cup of tea. He hadn't mentioned marriage in a while, and she wondered if he even wanted to marry her any longer. She told herself that it wouldn't be a bad thing if they were friends, maybe even lovers. She'd see him whenever he came to town and they'd write.

It surprised her to realize how much more she wanted from Travis. She wanted to sleep with him. She wanted to wake up with him beside her. She would almost give up her freedom for the pleasures of being with him as man and wife. Almost.

She touched the tiny bag at her throat and remembered what her mother's life had been like. She also remembered the promise she'd made to herself the night she'd boarded the train. Never would she be worthless again.

Dottie cut another slice of the bread Pearl had brought them. "You going to take the judge up on his offer?" she asked Travis. "He told me he'd swear you in as a lawyer any day you wanted. The judge and I talked about it, and we thought we'd give you a party at his house after the ceremony."

Travis looked at Rainey. "I haven't decided yet. I'm not sure I have a reason to stay in Austin."

She didn't meet his eyes. She knew how much his love meant to her, but she couldn't return it. She couldn't give up the freedom she'd fought so hard to get.

Something rattled beyond the door and all were silent. It was probably only the bartender moving down the stairs for more beer, but still they listened and waited.

"I locked both the doors when the sisters left," Travis said.

Dottie nodded, but didn't look reassured. "Want to play some poker?"

Travis declined. "I've never won at that game. As far as I'm concerned, it's a waste of time to play."

Rainey agreed just to calm Dottie. Travis stood and paced around the room. He barely limped, but she noticed when he thought no one was looking he sometimes rubbed his leg as if to force the pain out.

"Roy will tap three times when he wants in." He told them the code they already knew. "Once he's here, we can settle down for the night."

Rainey tried not to look like she was watching him, but she knew Travis was on edge. Every now and then he touched the handle of his gun, and his gaze circled the room every time a log snapped in the fire. Somehow his gaze always ended on her as if watching her relaxed him.

Rainey took a deep breath and jumped at the sudden crack of wood. Duck dived beneath the table, disappearing completely in an instant. Dottie's cards flew across the table.

Travis pulled his gun and stepped in front of the women. "Get down!" he yelled.

Rainey hugged Dottie, and they joined Duck beneath the table, holding on to one another tightly.

She heard a thump. The door to the cellar crashed open and slapped against the floor.

Dottie screamed as a man tumbled with the door to the floor of her kitchen. He jerked once, twice, then collapsed. The back of his head was splattered with blood.

A moment later Roy appeared with a board in his hand. "Got him, Travis!" He laughed, and a wildness danced in his eyes. "Eldon came through the cellar just like you said he would."

Travis fired one signal shot that echoed off the walls like thunder. Then, as calmly as if nothing out of the ordinary had happened, he turned and held his hand out to Rainey. "Come on out. It's all over."

Rainey wasn't sure she wanted to, but she took his offered help and crawled out from beneath the table, pulling Dottie with her. The little widow jumped up like a jack-in-the-box asking questions in rapid fire.

Travis pointed with his gun. "Ladies, I'd like you to meet Eldon Norman, the last brother. We've been waiting for him all day."

Dottie took a few steps toward the man. "Is he dead?"

"No," Roy answered. "I kind of hope he wakes up so I can hit him again. He's sneaky. I never seen a man move so silently. He'd crossed the cellar and was halfway up the stairs before I even knew he'd come in from the alley."

Roy pulled Eldon to his feet as Rangers stormed both the front door and the back stairs. They'd obviously been near, also watching and waiting.

Rainey stood frozen. It was all over. The nightmare that began when she heard men talking of kidnapping Sage had finally ended. All the outlaws had been caught.

In all the confusion, Travis moved close to Rainey and asked quietly, "If you ladies have no objections, I'd like to have a few of the men take you back to the Baileys' house. They'll stay with you until I get there. I'd like to go with Eldon to jail and see what the man has to say for himself."

Rainey nodded. She was ready for a quiet room, a cup of tea, and a real bed. "What about Duck?"

"He can go with me." Travis pulled the boy from beneath the table, but when Duck climbed out, he took Rainey's hand.

Travis raised an eyebrow. "You want to go with her for a while, son? I should be back at the Baileys' house before you go to bed."

Duck nodded.

Travis touched the boy's head as he looked at Rainey. "You don't mind taking care of him?"

"Of course not. He can be my guard." She smiled down at

the boy, having a feeling that her pies did more to win him over than anything else.

They left by the front door for the first time. The air felt cool and fresh. Rainey couldn't remember how long it had been since she'd taken a deep breath.

"It's finally over," Dottie said. "I'm terribly sorry it happened, but it did get me off the rock I've been sitting on for a year and back into living. Nothing like worrying about getting killed to make you wanta live."

The Baileys treated them as family when they came in. Mrs. Bailey ordered them both a bath, and Dr. Bailey wanted to take a look at Dottie's arm as soon as possible. The housekeeper and Dottie kept Duck busy in the kitchen while Rainey took a quick bath and changed into a clean nightgown and robe.

When Rainey joined them in the kitchen, she heard Duck laugh and it warmed her heart. An hour later when she rocked him by the fire in the tiny sitting room between Travis's and Sage's rooms, she hummed softly. "You're too big to rock," she whispered, "but thanks for letting me. It's nice to relax."

He looked up and smiled, not at her, but at the man standing in the doorway watching.

Travis crossed the room without a word and took Duck from her. He knelt and laid the boy in his covers by the fire. "Sleep well," Travis said as he covered Duck. "You did a great job of doing just like I told you."

Duck closed his eyes and Rainey knew that he felt safe for the first time in days.

They moved away from the boy and into Travis's bedroom, but he didn't close the door. "What did you learn?" she whispered.

"Eldon confessed to killing the barmaid. She drove him to it, he claimed. Seems he'd always been jealous of Seth and her. He couldn't understand why she'd be upset about his brother's death when he was standing right in front of her alive." Travis shook his head. "He wasn't too bright. It took Dillon less then an hour to have him confessing everything. He told Dillon about jobs his brothers did that the Rangers hadn't even connected them to yet."

Travis leaned against the doorframe and pulled her gently against him. He played with her hair as he talked. "When I left he was claiming he didn't have anything to do with Mrs. Vivian's death."

"Do you think he's telling the truth? I could swear I saw a shadow, but I was so tired. Is it possible that Mrs. Vivian really did kill herself."

"Looks that way."

"And there was no rider for the fourth horse I thought I saw?" Travis rubbed his big hands over her shoulders. "Forget about it. Maybe they'd thought Sage would ride without fighting." He combed his fingers through her curls as if touching her were the most important thing he had to do in the world. "It's over. You're safe and we're finally alone."

Rainey glanced to where Duck was sleeping. "Almost alone."

Travis smiled. "Almost alone is about as good as it'll get for the next fifteen years or so."

She kissed him lightly on the cheek. "You'll be a great father for the boy."

He returned her kiss with long slow caresses as he molded against her, letting her know of his need for her.

She didn't pull away. The feel of him so near seemed right somehow. The warmth of him spread through her, making her feel alive. She felt wanted. For the first time in her life, she felt loved.

Leaning against him made her smile.

He kissed the corners of her mouth as his chest pressed lightly into her breasts. When she moaned softly against his ear, his hand moved over her until her breast filled his fingers and he made her moan again in pleasure.

She circled her arms about his neck and melted against him as he caught her next moan of pleasure in his mouth. His kiss was deep and tender, as his hands slowly moved over her body. The gown and robe did nothing to mask his touch as his hands warmed her and surprised her with their boldness.

He shifted and she felt his desire for her press against her abdomen. All the world slipped away as the need for him consumed her. Pulling his mouth down a few inches, she kissed him hard.

Finally he straightened as if fighting for control. His hands moved over her once more in need, then he shoved her gently away. "Good night, Rainey."

She saw it then, a sadness in his brown eyes. "But we're alone." She'd slept in his arms through all the danger and fear. Now, finally, when they could relax, he was turning her away.

Something in the back of her mind said she should be the
one walking away, but she couldn't. She wanted him, all of him.

"Good night," he said again and walked her to the door.

"But . . ." All the old fears came back. The panic that he
didn't care for her, that no one cared for her.

How could he kiss her like that, hold her so close, and then
turn her out of his room?

"I'll see you in the morning," he whispered as he held her
tight one last time in a hug that was little more than friendly,
then let her go.

Rainey didn't know what to say. She couldn't run back and
beg to sleep in his bed. It didn't seem fair to ask him to say he
loved her when she knew she wouldn't be saying it back. They
might not marry, but he could still hold her, touch her, make
love to her.

She wanted to bang on his door and make a bargain. She'd
sleep with him. She'd be his lover.

She'd settle for that, she realized. But, deep down, she knew
he wouldn't.

She climbed the stairs to her room next to Dottie's and cried
herself to sleep.

The next morning her eyes were puffy and red when she
came down late to breakfast. Dottie and the judge were having
coffee. When she asked, they told her they'd had breakfast with
Travis and Duck before they left.

Rainey knew she should be happy. Her life would get back
to normal now. The Baileys had told her she and Dottie could
stay at their home until they found other lodging. Pearl would
be waiting to visit tomorrow when Rainey went back to making
pies. And Travis . . . where would Travis be in her life? He'd
made it plain he didn't want to be just a lover last night.

Dottie broke into her thoughts. "The judge and I are going
over to the restaurant to collect all the things we left there.
Would you like to ride along with us in a few hours?
Henry"—she said his name slowly as if using it for the first
time—"said he'll take us out to eat lunch then we might go
shopping for something new to wear at Travis's swearing-in
tonight."

Rainey looked up. "Travis is accepting the internship?"

"He told the judge he'd do it for three months, not six, because that's how long he needs to let his leg completely heal.
Travis said after that, he'll decide between the law and being a

Ranger. Henry agreed. Travis will become a lawyer tonight, but the judge won't sign the license until he's served his time in court."

She had the feeling that Travis was moving on with his life. He'd done his job. He'd kept her safe and now he planned to step out of her life. She knew little about men. Maybe he only said that he loved her to calm her when they were in danger. Maybe he hadn't wanted her last night no matter how much it seemed like he had.

Two hours later she sat beside Dottie as they rode in the judge's buggy toward the restaurant. Rainey didn't really have anything she cared about collecting from the place, but she wanted to see if any part of the words Travis had written in the dust still remained. They would be proof that somehow, if only for a moment, his love had been real.

When they pulled up to Dottie's place, Rainey noticed someone had pulled the boards from the windows.

"Oh," Dottie patted Rainey's hand. "I forgot to tell you. I lost this place in a poker game last night."

Rainey remembered hearing Dottie go downstairs late last night, but because she was crying, Rainey didn't join her for one of their midnight meetings.

Dottie shook her head. "The winner played a grand game, but when he won the place, he asked that I deed the restaurant over to you."

"What?"

"You need some place to make your pies and this will work perfect. You can even close off most of the front room for a little apartment if you wish."

"But I can't afford—"

"There is no afford to it. It's all yours, paid and clear. The judge as my witness, I swear I always pay off on a bet, and I lost the place fair and square."

Before Rainey could believe all Dottie was saying, she saw Mamie step out with a broom in her hand and begin sweeping the entry.

Rainey was out of the buggy and hugging Mamie a moment later.

Mrs. Vivian's slave backed away, hiding her smile. "I ain't no slave anymore. I'm a free woman. A married woman. And if you need me I'll work for a fair wage for you, but come supper-time, I'm going home to my man."

Rainey laughed. "But how?"

Mamie smiled. "Mrs. Dottie knew I'd run to my man when the trouble started. She got the judge to marry us and to set my price so low from Mrs. Vivian's estate that I bought my own freedom. That way I'm not beholden to anyone. Then she found me before dawn and told me what a cleaning this place would need if you was going to take over today."

The idea of her own place was starting to settle into Rainey's brain. "I'd love to have you help me make pies, and maybe we can make some of your wonderful bread and sell it as well. Wait till you see the size of the ovens."

"I already cleaned them first thing. Mr. Travis said he wanted them ready for a shipment of wood and coal that'll be here directly."

Travis. Rainey should have known he'd be at the bottom of this. She turned to Dottie. "Just out of curiosity, who'd you lose this place to last night?"

Dottie laughed. "Your Ranger. I found him in the kitchen when I went down for my midnight snack. You know, for a man who claims he doesn't like to play cards, he sure had some great hands last night."

Travis walked out of the restaurant. His sleeves were rolled up and his shirt spotted with sawdust. "I thought I'd have everything ready by the time you got here, but Duck decided to help me."

He reached in his pocket and handed her a set of keys. "This is yours, Rainey. All yours. The judge and I made sure that it will stay in your name even if you marry, and all the profits will be yours alone to do with as you please."

Before she could say more, he reached for a box Duck carried out and pulled out a shiny new gun. "This is yours, also. If you don't know how to shoot, I'll teach you." He brushed her cheek with his thumb and whispered, "No one will every make you feel helpless or in danger again."

Rainey stared at him, not believing what she was hearing.

"And one more thing, I found that horse you borrowed. I really don't want him back. He's become a town horse, you know, and they don't mix well with the ranch horses. So, after seeing how you ride, I figured I'd save the horse some confusion and have him hitched to a buggy. Now you can make your deliveries, and if you decide to run, you'll have a good horse and room to pack everything you value."

"What are you doing, Travis?" She could hardly believe all he'd given her.

"I'm making it where, if I ever decide to ask you to marry me again, you won't say no for all the wrong reasons. You'll never have to worry about being worthless or losing all you have to a husband. You'll be able to take care of yourself, protect yourself. You'll even be able to run if you decide to."

He lowered his voice, but he knew everyone was still listening. "The next time I ask you to marry me, say no only if you don't love me."

"Fair enough," she answered. "But I'll pay you back for the horse. A dollar a month."

"Fair enough," he answered.

Dottie had been quiet long enough. "I'd like to see what changes you plan for my old place."

They toured the small restaurant as if they hadn't spent two days in it. Mamie had spent the morning cleaning and had several ideas for where things should go.

When Rainey finally got Dottie off by herself, she whispered. "How could you do this, Dottie? What about the ghost of Henry being here?"

Dottie laughed. "He's the one who told me to get rid of it. I'd never do anything with the place and you will." She waved at the judge. "I've got other plans."

Rainey thanked everyone, even Duck, who'd sawed one of the legs off a table in his attempt to help. Dottie asked her to go to lunch, but she refused. She wanted to stay and work with Travis and Mamie.

They spent the afternoon getting everything ready to begin baking the following morning. Owen delivered supplies and helped Travis stack them on shelves he'd built across the door leading to the cellar. The saloon could have the cellar; Rainey would have her safety knowing that there was only one way to come into her store.

The last thing she did was watch Travis hold Duck high as he hung a huge bell over the front door.

As she locked up, she handed Mamie the spare key. "I'll meet you here at eight tomorrow, but you'll need this in case you make it here first."

Mamie stared at the key. "What do I do if I'm first?"

Rainey shrugged. "Let yourself in and make the coffee."

"But you don't drink coffee."

"I know, it'd be for you. Unless, you'd rather have tea."

Mamie slipped the key into her apron pocket. "I'll make me a pot of coffee if I'm here before you. Then I'll have me a seat and think about what needs doing until you get here."

Rainey nodded. "That sounds good. If I'm first, I'll do the same."

Mamie turned toward the blacksmith's shop and walked away with her head high.

Rainey took Duck's hand and walked to where her horse and little buggy were tied. When she glanced back, she noticed Travis standing watching her. "Would you like a ride, Mr. Mc-Murray? We've not much time to get ready for your ceremony tonight."

Travis hurried toward her. "I forgot about it." He laughed. "And I'd love a ride. You *can* drive this cart?"

She said yes, but he gave her instructions all the way home anyway.

CHAPTER 35

Rainey watched with pride as Travis took the oath to practice law. He looked like a fine gentleman in his black coat. The lawyers sat on the first row behind him as if backing him up. All their friends were watching—the Rangers, the Langlands, the Baileys. Even Roy had brought his wife and six children.

Duck sat beside her on the second row, looking around and wiggling. He seemed to enjoy watching the candles along the walls and the way the dark blue drapes shifted gently in the breeze from the open windows.

She'd tried to understand all Travis had done for her today. He still hadn't said he loved her out loud, but he'd proved it. He'd given Rainey her dream of freedom. He'd known her well enough to understand her. He'd shown his love without asking for anything in return.

Rainey closed her eyes and realized she loved him so much her insides hurt. She must love him now the way he'd loved her from the first, and he'd been right, just sleeping together would never have been enough.

The bailiff stood and held out a Bible for Travis to swear on.

Travis glanced at her. He looked as nervous as if he'd been asked to dance.

Duck suddenly darted beneath the bench, disappearing just as Travis was about to be sworn in.

Rainey reached for him, but couldn't find him without getting to her knees and she didn't want to make a scene.

When she looked back at Travis, he also began to move. In

one fluid movement, he shifted his stance, grabbed the Bible, opened it and pulled out a gun.

Everyone in the courtroom seemed to suck in air at the same time he held the weapon with both hands and fired directly over their heads.

A second later the Bible hit the polished wood floor of the courtroom.

Dottie screamed as a wiry old man tumbled from the curtain near where she sat. His hand held a gun.

Suddenly the courtroom was chaos. The Rangers moved to cover the doors. The doctor rushed to the man who'd been shot. Mothers hurried their children together.

Rainey looked back at Travis. He stood frozen, the gun still in his hand. One of the Rangers yelled that the shooter was Old Man Norman.

She ran toward Travis, knowing that if he hadn't fired, he would be the one dead on the floor now. The Rangers had told her the old man hated them all, but no one thought he'd do more than cuss them out.

The bailiff mumbled, "How'd you know I keep a gun there, son? I've never told anyone, not even the judge."

"I dreamed it," Travis said. Then he knelt, lifted the Bible, and handed it and the gun back to the bailiff. "Thanks for keeping it there."

Travis turned back to Rainey and opened his arms. "Don't cry, fairy. Everything's all right."

She hadn't even been aware she was crying. Wrapping her arms around him, she held on as tight as she could, thinking of how she'd almost lost the only man she'd ever love.

As he held her, the tears wouldn't stop.

He kissed her cheek and smiled. "It's all right, Rainey. It's all over."

She shook her head, feeling like a fool. "No. It's not all right. You almost died before I told you I love you."

He grinned. "About time you realized it. I've known it since we danced." He kissed her on the mouth in front of everyone.

"Travis McMurray," the judge interrupted finally. "Travis, if you had a ring I'd be marrying you two for acting like that in my court."

Rainey pulled away and reached for the bag around her

throat. "I have a ring," she whispered as she pulled out her grandmother's only valuable. "But he'll have to ask me first."

Everyone in the room grew silent waiting, and Travis knew he'd have to do the asking in front of them all.

"Will you marry me?" he said without a smile.

"I will," she answered and was surprised he kissed her full on the mouth again.

Everyone shouted, except the judge, who hammered his desk and demanded they get on with the swearing in of Travis. "Soon as that's done, we got a wedding to have," he said and everyone broke into another round of shouts.

After several minutes the judge finished, and Travis signed the papers while Roy pulled the body of Norman from the courtroom.

After all the hugs and handshakes, Judge Gates called for a ten-minute recess to give time for Rainey to walk from the back of the courtroom and Duck to stand beside Travis.

The judge married them with simple words, but Rainey wasn't listening. All she could hear was the pounding of her own heart as Travis slipped the symbol of her freedom on her finger.

CHAPTER 36

After several toasts, hugs from everyone, and advice from Roy about marriage, Travis, Rainey, and Duck made it back to the Baileys'. The old couple had left a note saying they'd already gone to bed but would serve breakfast in the morning in the private drawing room.

Travis carried a sleeping Duck to his covers by the fire. "He saved my life tonight," Travis whispered. "He remembered what I told him about if anyone pulled a gun he needed to disappear. The moment I saw him vanish, I glanced around and saw the barrel of a gun pointing directly at me from the curtains."

Rainey pulled the ribbon from her hair and moved toward Travis's room. "Now tell me about the dream again."

He followed. "I'll tell you about it tomorrow. Right now I'd like to help you get undressed."

She laughed, moving out of the light. "I can manage quite well on my own."

He crossed to her. They were lost in shadows now, but very much aware of the other being near.

He moved up behind her and circled his arms around, taking over the unbuttoning. "Let me do it," he whispered. "I've practiced a hundred times in my mind."

His fingers tickled her, warmed her as he slowly removed her clothes. His hands moved over the material first, then gently pulled the layers away. Before the cool air chilled her, his fingers slid over her skin, caressing each inch as he undressed her. When he reached her stockings, he knelt and felt his way to the top of each before sliding them down. Once she was free of one, he lifted her foot to his knee and let his fingers brush along her flesh.

She closed her eyes, feeling a fire building deep inside her. Part of her wanted to hurry him, to beg him to satisfy the ache within her, but another part of her wanted him to continue torturing her with his gentle touch. She dug her fingers into his hair and tried to stand perfectly still as he continued to explore every part of her.

When she stood before him with nothing on, he stared for a long while. His hands spread down her body, molding her shadowy form. When his fingers closed around her full breasts, she swayed with the pure pleasure he brought her. His hands moved behind her, holding her hips as he pulled her close and kissed her. When she cried softly in need, he lifted her gently and carried her to bed.

Pulling the covers to her throat, he leaned over, kissing her cheeks. "Before I found you, I don't think I was alive. You make me believe in magic." He brushed her hair away from her face. "I doubt I'd get enough of you if we both lived ten lifetimes."

Rainey couldn't answer. He was saying the words to her she thought she'd never hear.

The room was dark, light drifting only from the fire beyond the door, but Rainey wasn't afraid. She'd never be afraid of the dark again.

He crossed to the other side and slipped into bed.

They were both still for a moment, then he whispered, "Come closer, Rainey."

She rolled toward his open arms.

When she touched him, she froze. There was nothing, not one stitch of clothing between them.

"I promised"—she could feel him grinning as he kissed her gently—"that you'd have your turn."

She laughed and spread her hand across his chest, knowing she'd learn every part of her Ranger before the night was over. "I love you," she said as she tasted the warm skin of his chest.

"And I love you," he answered.